# At The Edge Of The Stairs

Phil Stephens

Edited by BooksGoSocial.

My dearest darling, Abe,
Please fear not the road I went down.
Understand I've never once left you
It's my loving embrace that still surrounds.

I could never have taken this journey
Without your love's embrace.
Do not mourn for me
I want no tears on your face.

The hour will come
When we will be together again.
You will know the place.
The present, plus twenty-two,
Will be when.

So, stay free for me, my love,
And take comfort in knowing
That, once such time passes,
My presence will be shown.

# Contents

# Chapter One:
# Crystal Mikalya Arabella

It was the most beautiful day of her life when she gave birth to her precious Crystal Mikalya Arabella. Shelly Arabella, Mikalya's mother, had debated long and hard whether to have her.

The unplanned pregnancy would be difficult. While she did love the man who had gotten her pregnant, Clifton Throckmorton, it was way too early for this.

She tried hard to make him fall in love with her. They had fun together, and he knew how to show a girl a good time in more ways than one. She was nineteen and horrified when she found out. She remembered just sitting down on the toilet, crying. *But isn't this the way all hillbilly women who barely get past high school wind up?*

Shelly was an only child whose life hadn't been easy. Her mother had left them when she was only six years old, and her father only talked about her when he was drunk. He did his best to raise her alone, and she loved him deeply for sticking by her the way that he had. He worked at a local factory during the second shift, which meant that he would come home late at night after she was already asleep. She could always tell when he came in and kissed her goodnight; she felt comforted afterward.

Being alone half the time caused Shelly to grow up quickly. It also taught her how to take care of herself.

Her father saw her graduate high school, then died in a freak accident at the factory a few months later. Devastated, Shelly managed to handle the funeral and claim the proceeds from a small life insurance policy. She decided to stay in the mobile home where they lived and make a go of it. She did well with the cards she was dealt.

Clifton stopped communicating with her after she told him that she was pregnant. However, after a couple of months, it began to sink in, and he sought to re-establish communication with her. Reluctantly, she took him back.

She remembered the day she broke the news as if it was yesterday. Clifton came over to her dingy trailer to pick her up so they could attend a football party at the home of one of his friends. She was nervous as he walked in the door. She didn't know which was making her sicker: the pregnancy or the anxiety she felt in telling him.

"Hey, Cliff, how's it going?" she asked. He'd already told her about his rough week, so she knew the answer to the question even before she asked it.

"Just more of the same. If Ed says one more thing to me about how I run that cutting machine, I'm going to throw *him* on it. That'll shut his ass up," he replied.

Shelly rolled her eyes. There would be no good day, time of day, or way to tell him, so she decided just to blurt it out while they were both still sober.

"Um… Cliff… there's something we have to talk about, honey," she stammered.

His demeanor immediately changed as he detected the seriousness in her tone. He stared at her with anticipated surprise.

"I'm pregnant. I'm sorry to have to tell you this just before we go to your friend's house, but the sooner you know, the better. I thought long and hard about it, but it's my first child, and I've decided I don't want to have an abortion. I mean, I don't think it's fair to do that. I am so sorry, and we certainly don't have to get married if you don't want to. But I thought that if… and I know it's a big if, if you want to somehow go forward together on this, I would love it!"

Cliff just stood and stared, his expression unchanged. He looked at everything in the room but her.

"Please, please tell me what you're feeling right now," Shelly pleaded, her eyes welling up with tears.

Then he looked at her, and Shelly stared back. The longer he remained silent, the more the look on Shelly's face turned to despair.

Turning his face downward, Cliff blew out a loud sigh, turned, and walked right out the door.

Shelly stood there, an immense feeling of loneliness surrounding her. Sobbing quietly, she took a seat, staring up at the ceiling. *No football party today, or tomorrow, for that matter.*

After sitting for several minutes, she called her best friend, Jenny, to see if she was up for drinks. With no answer from Jenny, she wanted to call Latisha but decided against it as she was on vacation.

Jenny and Shelly had become close friends in high school. The two-year age difference between them seemed to draw them closer. They met at a dance one Saturday night when Shelly's date had stood her up. Jenny noticed Shelly alone, huddled in a corner with a bummed look on her face.

"Hey, my name's Jenny. What's your name, and what are you doing over here alone? Don't you have a date for tonight?"

Shelly was stunned by all the questions being fired at her all at once from a stranger. "My name's Shelly," she replied.

Jenny saw the sad look in Shelly's eyes and immediately decided to take her under her wings as a friend and social mentor.

"Well, whoever the jerk is, he's a certified jackass to not show up for you tonight. You can come and hang with Bill and me for a few hours. Would you like that?"

Shelly didn't know Jenny from a hole in the wall, but she got nothing except good vibes from her. She didn't know what she would do at the dance by herself, so she accepted the offer and followed Jenny over to the table where they were sitting.

"Thanks. Just to let you know, my dad is picking me up at ten. I can stay with you until then if that's OK," Shelly said.

"Yeah, sure," Jenny replied, with Bill nodding his head beside her.

For the next few hours, the three had a great time. Shelly had made a new best friend.

When Jenny and Bill departed for the dance floor, Shelly's thoughts wandered back to her memories of Cliff.

She'd see him on Fridays when he and the other quarrymen would come in to pick up their paychecks. He had a confident, rugged sureness about him that turned her on. And he made good money, too, which was equally as appealing. Working in the office, she knew what he made, when he made it, and how he made it. He was one of the stonecutters who earned more money than the straight laborers did.

Shelly guessed him to be in his early to midtwenties. She recalled the first time she saw him when they shared a brief exchange about where he had to go to pick up his paycheck. He was a dreamboat in her eyes. All of 6′2″, she guessed him to be about 200 pounds, but it was 200 pounds of pure muscle. He was the perfect height because she stood 5 feet 8 inches tall. Shelly hated her height because she adhered to a self-imposed rule that she would never date men shorter than her. *That* was a no-no!

A few years back, she had run into one of her old high school classmates who had married a man five inches shorter than her. Shelly thought they looked awkward together. She found nothing attractive about a woman towering over a man. By her rule, men always needed to be taller than the women they dated, so any man she dated had to be 5′9″ or taller.

Clifton Throckmorton paraded right past her desk on Friday afternoons to pick up his paycheck at the cash window. She watched him out of the corner of her eye when he strutted past with that cool walk, making most of the girls, including her, swoon.

He never really had much to say to her, not even small talk. He'd just nod and give her that *howdy, ma'am* expression. One day, she decided she would go ahead and make the first move.

"Hey, there, Mr. Throckmorton! What are you going to do with all that money?" she asked with a grin. His puzzled expression quickly made her realize that he found her comment inappropriate. Although she'd meant it to be cute, he didn't see it that way.

"Excuse me, ma'am. What did you say?" Clifton asked.

"Oh, um, I was just asking where you bank because I'm getting tired of waiting in the long lines at First National," she said, trying to think of a good comeback to get her out of the hot water she'd landed in. She knew immediately he'd smell BS, but good or bad, she ran with it, looked him right in the eye and smiled. They broke into laughter.

"Well, I heard you the first time, but I just wanted to see how intently you were reading my mind," he said.

"I think I read it a little too well," Shelly replied, blushing.

"So, let's see, you're sick of waiting in line at First National. Wow, you must go there a lot! And, if you go there a lot, you surely meet with the executive officers there instead of the tellers like I do," he said.

"Only when I need a loan," she retorted.

"Is that a lot?" he asked.

She felt her face growing hot, imagining it turning white to red, then red to white and back again, like flashing lights on the hood of a fast-moving police car. With an awkward smile, she stared up at the ceiling. Her attempts at being clever were getting her nowhere. She hoped and prayed that he would steer the conversation in a more productive direction.

"What's your definition of a lot?" she asked.

"Do you borrow money frequently?" Clifton replied.

"No, of course not. Well, sometimes… in the past, I have. But I always pay it back."

Clifton smiled. "Well, Shelly, that is your name, isn't it? Shelly Arabella?"

*How in the hell does he know my name?* "Yes, and you're Clifton Throckmorton," she said.

"Yeah. We talked a little bit a couple of months ago when I first started here. I think I asked you to direct me to the place I'd need to pick my pay up from."

Shelly was thankful the conversation had taken on a more intelligent tone. As intelligent as she could handle, anyway. *Flirting is such BS, but it's so much fun.*

The slam of a car door interrupted her thoughts. Thirty minutes after she had left Jenny a voice mail, she pulled up to Shelly's trailer. That was a record for Jenny, who was notoriously late for everything except for work.

Before Jenny was halfway up the walk, Shelly opened the door, tears running down her cheeks.

"Hey, honey, what's wrong? What happened? Did Cliff say something?" Jenny asked.

"It's what he didn't say," Shelly replied.

Jenny looked confused. "Do we need a drink for this?" she asked.

Shelly nodded as she turned and headed to the refrigerator for a couple of beers. She popped them open and sat them in front of Jenny.

"OK, lay it on me, girl," Jenny coaxed. They had been confiding in each other for years, and today would be no exception.

Shelly loved beer. She swished the Bud Lite around in her mouth like it was expensive champagne, then gave Jenny a sorrowful look before she let it out.

"I just found out a few days ago I'm pregnant; before you ask, there's no doubt."

Jenny's mouth fell wide open. "Does Cliff know?"

"I just told him an hour ago in this exact spot."

Jenny took another big gulp. "Sweet Cream Jesus! You're pregnant?"

Shelly put her face in her hands. "Yep. With cherries all around and one big nut on top."

Jenny let out a loud laugh. "Do you have any idea how far along you are?"

"I'm not one hundred percent sure, but I think maybe a month or so. I was feeling weird a few weeks ago. The feeling wouldn't go away, so I thought it was possible that I could be pregnant. And guess what? I am. I've got an appointment with the doctor on Wednesday to confirm it and find out for sure just how far along I am. I've decided I don't want to abort it. As bad as the timing is, it feels right for some reason."

"OK, I have to ask. You said you told Cliff, and I am guessing by your red eyes that he didn't take it well," Jenny said.

Shelly got up and grabbed two more beers. "We were supposed to watch the Bears vs. Packers game at his friend's house, and I decided to tell him beforehand. I knew he had to know right away and didn't want to tell him when he, or I, for that matter, was drunk and around other people.

"I told him we didn't have to get married, but I was hoping we would go through this together. He just stared at the ceiling and the floor and looked around the room… everywhere except at me. Then he walked out, and that's when I called you," Shelly said, bursting into tears.

Jenny rushed over to hug her friend.

"Let it out, honey, it's OK," her friend soothed.

Breaking away from Jenny's comforting arms, Shelly grabbed a Kleenex and wiped her eyes. When she blew her nose, it sounded like a foghorn and made Jenny laugh. Shelly smiled, too.

"So, he just walks out the door, and I'm sitting thinking I'm going to go through this alone. You know, Mom and Dad are gone, and all I have is you and Latisha. And speaking of Latisha, I think she gets back from her vacation next week. I didn't want to call and bother her while she was enjoying herself," Shelly sniffled.

"Yeah, honey, you have the both of us. We'll be there for you every step of the way. Do you want me to go to the doctor with you next week? I have Wednesday off," Jenny offered.

Shelly nodded and hugged her. "The appointment is at ten. Can you come here around nine-thirty, and we'll go?"

"Sure, I'll drive. We'll grab lunch after that… on me, sweetie. We'll go to that one place with the good chili dogs. You know which one I'm talking about?" Jenny asked.

"I do. It's close to the doctor's office. That sounds great, Jenny. What would I do without you?"

"You'd frickin' die, girl!" Jenny replied with a smile.

"Want another beer? Are you able to stick around and party?" Shelly had called Jenny at the last minute and had yet to determine if her friend had other plans for the rest of the day.

"Well, yes, I do, and yes, I am. I was just going to go shopping later. I have to be at work by eight, but that doesn't matter. I've gone in hungover before. Can I crash here?" she asked.

Shelly let out a huge smile, almost leaping into her friend's arms.

"You know, we *do* have to go shopping," she said.

"For what?" Jenny asked.

"More beer. Let's make a run. I've only got two more Frosties left. If it's going to be my last night of drinking for a while, might as well make the most of it."

"Sounds good to me. We'll hit the store and grab some ingredients for some lasagna and garlic bread, too," Jenny replied.

Snagging the last two beers, they headed out the door. Jenny put the windows down.

Shelly put her right arm out and let the strong wind catch it. "God, that feels good. Do you remember how much we used to do this in high school?"

"Yeah, we'd go by that one little grocery store, the Food Mart there on Tunnel Street, and walk out with a couple of six-packs of Little Kings Creme Ale. It was filthy, but the only place we could get beer. That one guy in there had the hots for you. I think his name was Harry. And we'd have to go in when he was there. The only reason he didn't card us is because he knew we'd keep coming back for more," Jenny said.

Shelly rolled her eyes and smiled. "God, I remember. And if I wasn't flirting with him, you were. We double-teamed the poor guy, but it worked. You think it was me he liked the most?"

"No question about it. I could see it. He was nice enough, but he was about six inches shorter than you. And he had one of the biggest butts I'd ever seen on a guy." Jenny laughed.

Shelly took another sip of beer. "You're right. Men aren't supposed to have butts like that. That's a privilege that should only be bestowed upon women. Hey, do you want to head over there now? It's not that far. We can see if Harry's still there."

"That should be fun! We can be there in about ten minutes. First, though, there's a liquor store to grab a cold one for the ride," Jenny pointed. "I'll run in and get us restocked, then we'll head to the Food Mart. We may be able to get everything we need there, anyway. I can't believe we're doing this!"

As they approached the Food Mart, Jenny and Shelly got very quiet.

Jenny made sure to park a little farther away so as to avoid being seen by anyone inside.

"How long has it been since we were here?" Shelly asked.

Jenny turned the car off and stared out the window in thought.

"Well, I know we haven't been in there since I turned twenty-one. It's out of the way. So maybe it's been a year? Who knows! You know, the last time I was here, I don't recall seeing Harry," Jenny said, staring at the front door.

"Well, what are we going to do? Do we go in separately or together?" Shelly asked.

Jenny shrugged. "We should have picked up a couple of wigs first."

Approaching the front door with caution, they entered slowly, scanning the premises. With every step, they looked front, back, and sideways.

"If he's here, I haven't seen him yet," Jenny whispered, half giggling.

"Let's just get what we need and get out of here. I'm getting creeped out already," Shelly replied.

They hurried down the aisle, gathering what they needed for the lasagna, stuffing everything in their arms because a cart would have slowed them down. Still no sign of Harry.

"OK, I think we've got everything. Let's get the hell out of here… now," Jenny whispered.

As they rounded the last corner to the checkout counter, a large figure popped out in front, startling them.

"Hello, ladies… may I help you? Do you need a cart?" a booming voice asked.

The women dropped half of the items in their arms. They both looked up in utter shock, right into the face of Harry or what resembled what they remembered of Harry.

"Here, let me help you," he said, grabbing a nearby cart and carefully picking their items up off the floor.

Shelly and Jenny were stupefied to see a much more muscular and trimmed-down Harry. A slimmer, firmer version had replaced the fat butt. He had lost a significant amount of weight and was now quite handsome and well-built.

"I think I remember you girls. Remember me? I was the guy who always sold you beer without checking your ID," he said.

Jenny attempted a response. "Yeah… you're… Harry, right?"

"Yes, but not the one you remember," he replied, with a strong air of confidence that he lacked back then.

"Well, not exactly. How are you?" Jenny asked.

"Just fine. Let me get you checked out, and you can be on your way."

All Shelly could do was nod. "Hello."

Harry knew exactly what was going on and refused to play the charade. He checked them out quickly and thanked them for shopping at Food Mart.

Shelly and Jenny slowly pushed the cart out the door, looking at each other in shock. With groceries safely inside the car, they rushed to open more beer.

"Did you just see that? Was that really him?" Jenny asked.

Shelly nodded in disbelief.

"Let's get back to my place before you get hammered over the legal limit. We need a few more beers on this one," she replied. "I'm going to shut up and let you concentrate on the road."

"Not a bad idea. When we get there, we can swing from the chandeliers." Jenny chuckled.

"What do you mean? There isn't one chandelier in the place. You think I own a double-wide?" Shelly blurted out.

They laughed hysterically.

"Shut up, girl!" Jenny yelled.

Back at Shelly's, they made one of the best Italian dinners they ever had and drank beer until they couldn't see straight. After she had downed a few, Shelly was able to get Cliff off her chest.

"If he's going to act like that, I'm just going to let him stew. He didn't have any problem with sex. I don't need his money, and I certainly don't need his penis. I'll figure it out. I always do."

"*We'll* figure it out. *We* always do," Jenny replied.

Shelly's ringing phone broke the melancholy mood. It was Latisha.

"Hey, girl, I'm sorry I haven't called sooner. Everything OK?" Latisha asked.

"Well, as a matter of fact, no!" Shelly screamed into the phone.

Shelly put her phone on speaker so that Jenny could chime in the conversation, which turned into a thirty-minute gripe session, ending with plans to get together the following weekend.

Later, Jenny and Shelly toasted their last beer and decided to call it an evening. Although it was one of Shelly's worst days, it turned out to be one of her best nights.

****

The following Wednesday, Shelly received confirmation—she was six weeks pregnant. But still no Clifton.

Latisha worked with Shelly at Roberts & Sons Limestone. They didn't talk much initially, but she had admired Latisha's style from afar. One day in the lunchroom, Latisha walked in late, and there were no seats available. Shelly noticed her grab her food tray and then wander around, looking for a place to sit. She was almost done eating herself, so she flagged Latisha over.

"Hey, come on over here, girl. You're Latisha, right?" Shelly asked.

"Yeah, and you're Shelly, right?"

"Unfortunately, yes, but don't tell anyone," she joked.

Shelly got up from her seat.

"Shelly, you're not even done yet. I don't want to take your seat."

"It's OK. I'm ready to leave anyway. I've always wanted to meet you, though, and I thought now would be a good chance," Shelly said. "Maybe, one of these days, we can go out for a drink. I have a good friend, Jenny, and I think you'd like her."

"I'd love to. Here is my phone number. Call me when you get a chance." Latisha smiled, passing the piece of paper before Shelly went on her way.

****

Almost seven months to the day since she had told Clifton about the pregnancy, Shelly and Jenny went to Latisha's house for drinks and card games. Shelly knew that she shouldn't be drinking and had been good since that night out with Jenny. But she had been having a little pain and figured that a few drinks were in order.

Jenny and Latisha put up a weak argument that she shouldn't be drinking, but they eventually laughed it off.

As the evening wore on and the drinks flowed, Jenny and Latisha could tell Shelly was feeling down that Clifton still had not contacted her.

"That bastard still hasn't called. Hell, that was months ago—the night we went to see Harry at the store," Jenny said.

"I have a mind to call that jackass myself. I know he ignores you at work, too," Latisha added.

"Of course he does," Shelly nodded.

Latisha rolled her eyes and looked up at the ceiling. "I try not to say anything to him, but it's hard. Surely he's noticed your stomach! How can he just ignore that? How?" she grumbled.

"It's a good thing I don't work there, and that's all I'll say," Jenny added.

Shelly's friends knew that she wasn't OK. The situation was bad enough, but she and Clifton worked together, which made things even worse. She put on a brave face as best she could.

"Listen, I have to go potty again. Be right back," Shelly said.

"Well, who's up for another beer while I'm right here by the fridge?" Jenny asked when Shelly returned.

Both girls raised their hands.

Jenny came back into the living room and sat the beers in front of her friends, acting like a server in a five-star restaurant.

"For you, madam, and you, mademoiselle," she said in a drunken French accent.

"That's pretty fancy, Jenny. Do we have to tip you, too?" Latisha asked with a giggle.

Shelly burst into laughter.

"Well, no, mademoiselle, but it would be pretty cheap of you if you didn't, now, wouldn't it?" Jenny asked, still in character.

"I'll give you a tip, but I'm going to stick it in your snood," Latisha said.

"What in the world is a snood? Some sort of private part?" Jenny asked.

Latisha and Jenny were laughing so much that they didn't notice that Shelly's laughter had turned exclusively to coughing.

They finally settled down and noticed their friend's distress. "Hey, it wasn't that funny," Latisha said.

Shelly's coughing finally subsided but was replaced by moaning. She clutched at her stomach.

"Shelly, honey, what's wrong? Are you alright?" Jenny asked.

Shelly continued to moan. "Something's not right. I'm getting cramps, I think."

Jenny and Latisha exchanged glances and then moved closer together.

"Is she going into labor now?" Latisha asked.

"I don't know, but we can't take any chances. I think we should call 9-1-1," Jenny said.

Inebriated but still with the presence of mind to know something wasn't right, Latisha scrambled for the phone, knocking Jenny's beer over in the process. It splattered all over Shelly.

"Goddammit!" Latisha yelled.

Jenny gently coaxed Shelly down on the floor and put a pillow under her head, then ran into the kitchen for a wet towel.

"It's going to be OK, honey," she soothed as she wiped Shelly down.

Shelly rolled her eyes. "God, help me," she said, a faint smile crossing her lips as Jenny continued to clean her up.

"Hello, 9-1-1, what is your emergency?" the dispatcher answered.

"Hi, my name is Latisha Foreman, and I live at 1413 E. 17th Street. I think my friend is going into labor. We probably need an ambulance here right away."

"Probably?" Jenny yelled over to her friend.

Latisha looked over and shushed her.

"OK, ma'am, we're dispatching an ambulance. What is the woman's name who is in labor?"

"Shelly Arabella," Latisha replied.

"What is she doing right now?" the dispatcher asked. "She's moaning and breathing heavily."

"Do you know how far along the pregnancy is?"

"I'm pretty sure she's about eight months." In her drunken state, Latisha was trying hard to keep it together and focus and not slur her words.

"Make her as comfortable as you can. Get a pillow under her head. Help is in the general vicinity and should be there in a few minutes. For now, stay on the line with me, and let me know if her condition changes," the dispatcher directed.

"OK, I need to leave the phone. Be back in just a couple of minutes," Latisha responded frantically, looking over at Jenny, motioning for her to come quick.

"Shit, let me clear these beer cans up, then I have got to take a piss!" Latisha said, throwing her hands up in frustration. It took her only a couple of minutes to clear the mess, make a bathroom run, and return to the phone as though nothing had happened.

"OK, I'm back, ma'am," she said calmly.

"How is Shelly now?" the dispatcher asked.

"I think she's OK but still breathing heavily and moaning," Latisha replied.

"Can she talk at all?"

With Shelly all cleaned up, Jenny kneeled beside her, holding her hand.

"Shelly, honey, can you talk?" she asked.

Her moans and the taut expression on her face spoke for her.

"Not very well," Latisha spoke into the phone.

"OK. I've gotten word the ambulance is close. Just keep her comfortable."

"I think I hear a siren. Do you hear it, Latisha?" Jenny asked.

Latisha nodded and knelt next to Shelly and Jenny.

"Shelly, honey, the ambulance is almost here," Jenny said. Shelly rolled her eyes, squeezing both her friends' hands. "Thank you so much. I know this is a lot," she said in barely a whisper.

Jenny laughed.

"Honey, no, not at all. We're here to take care of you," she said.

The sound of the ambulance grew closer until, finally, it was right outside Latisha's house.

Jenny exhaled a sigh of relief. "Thank God!"

"I know. If she'd gone into labor, I don't know what we would have done," Latisha said, ushering the paramedics into the room.

"OK, what do we have here?" asked the first paramedic, rushing through the door.

"About twenty minutes ago, she started coughing and moaning, then holding her stomach. She's eight months pregnant, so we just weren't sure what was going on, and that's why we called 9-1-1," Latisha replied.

With Latisha's speech slurring, the paramedics sensed they were tipsy.

"Has Shelly ingested any alcohol to your knowledge?"

Jenny and Latisha looked at each other.

"Yes… she has," Jenny replied hesitantly.

"Do you know how much?" one of the paramedics asked.

"About five beers," Jenny said.

"OK, we'll take it from here," the other one replied, as he relayed the information into a radio device clipped to his shirt pocket.

Jenny and Latisha nervously looked from one to the other.

"Her contractions are very close together. We may have to deliver this baby here. Hope you don't have a problem with that," one of the paramedics said.

"No, of course not," Latisha responded, with a look of sheer terror on her face.

"Good, because her water just broke," the paramedic said as the other one rushed out to bring more supplies from the ambulance in preparation for the delivery.

All Latisha and Jenny could do was watch.

"God, now's when I need another beer. This could be a mess," Latisha whispered to Jenny, with Shelly's contractions becoming more intense.

"Where is the bathroom?" a paramedic asked.

Latisha motioned to the end of the kitchen.

"If you two want to leave us for a bit while we deliver her baby, you can. We'll let you know when all is done, or you can come back when you hear the baby's cry."

Jenny and Latisha quietly grabbed the rest of the beer from the fridge and slipped out the back door onto the deck.

"Well, we might as well kick back and let them do their thing. We can't help her anymore," Latisha said.

"We'd just muck it up. We're lucky she didn't go into labor sooner, and there was still time for the ambulance to get here," Jenny replied, plopping into a chair.

"I hope the beer and all that laughing didn't screw her up." Worry was all over Latisha's face.

"No, I don't think *that* was what did it, but it sure messed us up," Jenny said with a chuckle.

Latisha got up and peeked inside from the patio door.

"This could go on for a while. You can't drive home. Just stay here. After they get the baby out, they'll probably take her to the hospital. What do you think it will be, boy or girl?"

"I don't know, but thanks for offering to let me crash here, Latisha. I think I will. Cheers, girlfriend!" Jenny said, raising her can.

The girls sat on the deck and nervously finished off the last of the beers while the paramedics helped Shelly inside. After thirty minutes had gone by, one of the paramedics came out and got them.

"OK, we're done, and everything's fine. It's a girl. We're taking the mother and baby to the hospital now for observation. We didn't make too much of a mess of your living room floor. We always have supplies for situations like this. Anyway, she'll be at Saint Francis tonight," the paramedic concluded.

"Can we come in now and say goodbye to her?" Latisha asked.

"Sure," he said.

The girls followed the paramedic inside, where Shelly was already arranged on a gurney.

They each took one of her hands.

"Hey, way to go. We're gonna be a family now! Are you OK?" Jenny asked her friend, trying to peek further into the ambulance where the baby was being positioned for safe transport.

"Yeah, could you hear me grunting from outside?"

"We thought that noise was the furnace kicking in," Latisha answered.

"Have you thought of a name for your baby girl?" Jenny asked.

"I like Mikalya; I don't know why, but I like it. Been thinking about it for a while if it turned out to be a girl."

Latisha leaned down to kiss her friend goodbye. "We like it, too, sweetie. No, we love it, and we'll love her. We'll check in on you tomorrow. Go to the hospital and get some rest. Love you."

With the ambulance's siren fading into the night, the drunk pair looked around and assessed the damage to Latisha's living room.

"Hell, it's not that bad. All we have to do is move some furniture back and wipe down a little. I'll get the sofa sleeper ready for you. Dang it! I still have spaghetti on the stove. It's excellent if I say so myself. Let me heat it up. You hungry?" Latisha asked.

"That sounds great. And yes, I'm starving. Latisha, thank you again!"

"Oh, you're welcome. You can use my makeup in the morning. We're about the same size, so I have plenty of clothes for you to select from tomorrow. It'll be easy for you to head into work right from here," Latisha offered.

"You know, I'm going to call in tomorrow. Can you?" Jenny asked.

Latisha thought for a moment. "Yeah, why not? Nothing is going on tomorrow, and I've got a lot of time saved up. My supervisor is on vacation so they won't care."

"Pretty much the same here. Let's go for it," Jenny added.

****

The next morning, Latisha and Jenny both called in sick. Still a little hungover, they drank a pot of coffee, grabbed breakfast, and then jumped in the car to head to the hospital. Shelly was in room 426. Before they could even knock on the door, they heard a baby crying.

"Come on in," Shelly called. "Hey, you look great. How are ya?"

"Well, Miss Shelly, the question is, how are you?" Latisha asked.

"I haven't slept all night, but it was well worth it. Girls, I give you Crystal Mikalya Arabella." Shelly held out the baby as Jenny reached to carefully pick her up.

"God, Shelly, she's a doll. I guess everything went OK last night. We were just too drunk to follow the ambulance over," Jenny said.

"Well, I'd had a few myself, and I was just praying Mikalya didn't come out drunk."

"She looks like a Mikalya, doesn't she?" Latisha asked.

"Yeah, she does," Shelly agreed.

Shelly noticed the intensity of how Mikalya looked up at her. She had never felt such a rush in her life as when the paramedic put the baby in her arms right after birth. She would never again meet a man she would want to have a baby with.

"Well, honey, we'll stick it out with you until they let you go home. Latisha and I took the day off."

Shelly loved her friends. They had been loyal to her since the day she had met them.

****

Three months later, Clifton approached Shelly at work. She had just returned from maternity leave and, for obvious reasons, completely ignored him. She didn't even want child support. If Clifton wanted her or Mikalya in his life, he would have to make the first move, and she wasn't even sure she wanted him to. Her feelings had changed, but for the baby's sake, she was willing to rebuild if a hint of something was still there.

"Hey, Shelly, how are you doing? I heard about the baby and everything. You named her Crystal Mikalya?" he asked, approaching her desk.

Shelly looked up in complete shock and just stared at him. She had thought long and hard about this moment, should it ever arise. Should her response be polite or hostile? She continued to stare at him a bit longer before responding.

"Yeah, her name is Crystal Mikalya. Any other questions? I'm busy," she said.

Shelly could sense that he was taken aback by her response, but what had he expected?

"I just want to say I'm sorry for the way I acted and for not being around. It was selfish. If there's any way that I can make it up to you, I'd like to try," he said.

Trying to formulate a response, Shelly stared down at her computer. "Well, I'm shocked as hell, Clifton. Why the 180?" she asked coldly.

"I realized what a jackass I was. Let me know if you want to talk away from here sometime."

"OK, I'll tell you what... come over to the house this weekend, and you can meet your daughter. We'll talk then."

Clifton nodded, then turned and walked in the other direction.

Shelly wondered if she had done the right thing by inviting him into their lives, but she felt that Mikalya should know her father.

****

The weekend came quickly. Clifton was expected to visit on Saturday evening, so Shelly prepared a modest dinner. Their visit began as soon as he arrived at the front door.

"Well, it's been... let's see, about a year since you stormed out of here, leaving me pregnant, alone, and in tears," she greeted.

Without being invited, Clifton stepped inside. "Yeah, it's been about that long. But how many times do I have to say I'm sorry? Can we drop it for now?" he asked.

"For now. Come in here, and I'll introduce you to your daughter," she replied, leading him into her bedroom, where she had fixed up a nursery in a corner of the room.

Clifton peered into the crib, seemingly hypnotized.

Shelly bent over the crib, picking up Mikalya. "Here, you need to hold her," she said, gently handing the baby over to him. "It's not so bad," she said.

As she watched Clifton hold his daughter, she noticed the way he looked at her. She felt the old feelings for him surge but knew she had to be cautious. She would not be hurt again.

Clifton rocked Mikalya slowly. "God, she's so beautiful. Look at her eyes. She's got your eyes," he said with a smile, never looking away from his daughter.

"Yeah, I suppose she does. Here, let's put her back down, and hopefully, she'll go to sleep. I've got some dinner ready. I hope you're hungry."

"Starving. What did you make?"

"Lasagna, which, as I remember, was your favorite."

"Yeah, it was. Yours was always better than the stuff I used to fix," he said.

When they sat down to dinner, all was civil. The wine and conversation flowed freely. But as Shelly sipped more and more of it, Clifton noticed her demeanor begin to change. He had anticipated this. She had set this up to get some things off her chest. He tried to head her off at the pass, but it didn't work.

"Shelly, Mikalya is beautiful. She's got most of your features and none of mine, thank God," he said cautiously.

Shelly swished her sip of wine while she took in Clifton's comment. "Yeah, well, the features I hope to hell she doesn't have are your lack of responsibility and commitment," she blurted.

Clifton took another sip of wine and stiffened. "Shelly, listen…" he began.

"No, Clifton, you listen," she interrupted sharply. "That day you stormed out of here after I told you I was pregnant with your child, it felt like my world was crashing down! If it hadn't been for Jenny coming that night, I don't know what I would have done. As time went on, I decided I didn't need you, and I would raise my baby on my own. I've been doing that. I'm going to raise her to be independent, to take care of herself, and not have to be accountable to anyone! But there were times I needed you, wanted you, and you were AWOL, buddy. Do you hear me? Do you?" she yelled.

All Clifton could do was listen. He knew that he deserved all that was coming at him.

"For the past year, you made me feel like shit. You knew I didn't have any parents and only a couple of good friends. If you didn't want to get married or stay with me, I could understand that. You didn't have any problem with sex. Or did that suck, too? Was I just a hole to you? Huh? How many other women were you screwing? Or do you even remember?" Shelly continued, wiping away the tears flowing down her cheeks.

"Shelly, I…" he started again.

"I what? What? We both know what happened. Yeah, I admit I should have been more careful, but I did not expect you to do what you did. I couldn't have been more stupid!"

Emotionally drained, Shelly stopped talking and stared into space. She had gotten everything that had built up inside of her since the day he walked away, out into the open. He finally knew exactly how she felt.

Clifton had no idea that he had hurt her as much as he had. At that moment, overwhelmed with a strong sense of caring and love for the mother of his child, he walked over and gently put his arms around her without even thinking. She put her hand on his arm, and he pulled her into an embrace.

Clifton spoke softly. "Honey, I am so, so sorry. You have no idea, but I am here for you now. I am. Please believe that. Please."

Although Shelly did not respond, Clifton could feel her tighten her hands on his arms. He took that as a positive sign and sighed in relief.

Embracing for several minutes more, Shelly broke the silence.

"Clifton, I'm sorry, too. I just had to get it all out. Thank you for listening," she said, a smile forming on her lips. "Now, after putting up with my shitty rant, would you like another glass of wine?"

"I'd love one."

Shelly poured them both another glass, then went to check on Mikalya, who was sound asleep. Before long, they had moved to the sofa, talking well into the night about what the next steps would be in their relationship and raising Mikalya together.

****

Clifton had never loved Shelly before, but he was sure that he did now, and Mikalya owned his heart. His ready-made family needed him just as much as he needed them.

Over the next two years, Clifton was as good a mate to Shelly and father to Mikalya as a man could be. He left Roberts & Sons Limestone and got his CDL. He made good money driving semi-trailers and handed over every dime to Shelly.

Shelly had never been happier than she was during those two years. Even Jenny and Latisha had forgiven Clifton when they saw how he had made things right. But, like everyone else in her life that she loved, it was not to last long.

Clifton had left a couple of days earlier to run a load of machinery several states away. He was only supposed to be gone for a few days. But late one night, around 11 p.m., there was a knock at the door. Shelly assumed it was Clifton, but she wondered why he hadn't called to say he was returning early. She turned on the light, then peeked out the door window. There stood two men in police uniforms. Shelly opened the door slowly.

"Yes?" she asked.

"Good evening, Ms. Arabella. I'm Sergeant Bill Evans of the State Police, and this is Trooper Dale Johnson. May we come in and speak with you for a bit, ma'am?"

Shelly stood there for a few seconds, wondering what the visit was about.

"*Uhhh*, yes, please come in," she stuttered, ushering them through the door. "Please, have a seat."

Both men entered slowly, but neither sat down.

"Can I get you a cup of coffee or some water?" she asked, her voice trembling.

"No, ma'am, we're here for a specific purpose. Your live-in partner is Clifton Throckmorton?" Sergeant Evans asked.

Shelly nodded her head, still unsure of what to make of this visit.

"Ms. Arabella, I'm afraid we have some bad news. Clifton was fatally injured in an accident on Interstate 55, about an hour south of Sikeston, Missouri. The papers he had in his wallet led us to you. He did not suffer, and we also believe that he was not at fault. It appears that he was sideswiped by another semi, which was driving recklessly. We're sorry to have to deliver this bad news, ma'am."

Shelly's gaze turned toward Mikalya's bedroom, then back to the policemen.

"Where is he now?" she asked, almost in a whisper.

"Ma'am, here's the phone number of the morgue he's at in Sikeston. All the information they'll need is on this paper. They can arrange to have him transferred anywhere you want. You'll be getting a copy of the accident report in a few days. Again, ma'am, we're sorry. Is there anything we can do for you?" Sergeant Evans asked.

"*Uhhh*, no, I don't think so right now. Thank you," Shelly said, looking frantically around the room, not knowing what to do.

"Here's my card. If you need anything, please call. You take care, and our prayers are with you," he said as they moved toward the door.

When the door shut behind the officers, Shelly stood in shock. Too numb to cry, she walked into Mikalya's room, where the toddler was still sleeping. She picked her up and held her while she paced back and forth.

"Crystal Mikalya, honey, something's happened to Daddy," she whispered. "He had to go to heaven a little early. But we'll see him again soon. I know we will." She lay Crystal Mikalya back down. It was practice for her. She knew that she would have to repeat those exact same words in the morning when the child woke up.

Shelly walked into the bathroom, took three sleeping pills, and lay down on the floor. As she lay there crying, she thought back to a couple of days earlier. As Clifton was leaving, he told her he loved her, blew her a kiss, and got into his truck. Shelly smiled and blew him a kiss back, then waved him off. She cried until she fell asleep.

****

The next morning, Shelly made the necessary phone calls and arrangements. She got into Clifton's files and found that he had left behind a rather substantial life insurance policy for two hundred and fifty thousand dollars, naming her as the sole beneficiary. That would pay off their modest house and the funeral costs and leave some money in savings. She would also give some to his parents, who had been a big help through it all.

After the burial, she purchased three additional cemetery plots at Mount Olive—one for her, one for Crystal Mikalya, and one for whomever her daughter would eventually marry, or even possibly a grandchild.

****

As the years flew by, Crystal Mikalya grew up quickly. Shelly based her parenting skills on her own experiences of growing up fast and determined that Crystal Mikalya would come up the same way. She was a stubborn child, never admitting to Shelly's face that she was listening to her but quietly absorbing her wisdom behind her back. She also insisted on being called Mikalya—not Crystal Mikalya.

Mikalya was stubborn and didn't like her mom telling her what to do. Shelly always explained that she was giving instructions to teach and not to harm her. She made sure that Mikalya fully understood the *why* of every directive.

Shelly knew that she was giving Mikalya too much responsibility too early. However, Mikalya picked it up without hesitation and embraced her independent nature. She didn't stay in precious, cute little girl mode for long. After her first period, she could be a monster at times.

"Mikalya, honey, I'm headed to the grocery store to pick up some things. Can you finish the dishes and put the clothes in the dryer? Then, when they're dry, bring them back upstairs, and I'll help you fold them when I get back. Can you do that for me? I won't be gone long," Shelly said.

Mikalya immediately put a wall up before Shelly could get out the door. "Why am I the only one to do this? You get out of the house and go shopping, but I'm stuck here. I have a math test the day after tomorrow, and I haven't even started studying. Or do you not care about my grades?" she blurted out.

Shelly laid her keys down on the counter and looked at Mikalya. Mikalya lowered her eyes, immediately regretting what she had said and how she had said it.

"Do you want to repeat that, young lady? Go ahead. I'm all ears," Shelly dared.

Mikalya could tell that she had stepped too far out of line, and her mother was upset, so her demeanor softened before she replied.

"I can't remember it all."

"It's a good thing you can't, girlie," Shelly said sternly, walking over to get in Mikalya's face, staring her in her eyes.

Although terrified of her mother standing so threateningly close, Mikalya didn't back down and stared back intently.

Impressed by her daughter's fearlessness, Shelly softened. "Honey, listen, I know that what I just asked you to do seems like a lot. But I need you more than you know. I couldn't begin to get everything done around here without you. I cannot imagine my life here or anywhere without you. I won't be gone long. There aren't that many dishes… maybe ten minutes' worth. I like to get them over and done with so there's no water sitting in the sink. That attracts cockroaches. They're gross and filthy."

Mikalya made a sour face.

"By the time you finish the dishes, the laundry will be done. Just throw the clothes in the dryer, and by the time I get back, they'll be finished, and we can fold them together. That will take about ten minutes, too. Then I can help you study for your math test if you want," Shelly offered.

Embarrassment swept across Mikalya's face.

"Would you really help me with my math test?" she asked with a faint smile.

"Well, what kind of math is it?"

"Algebra," Mikalya replied, immediately sensing that her mom knew nothing about algebra by the frown on her face.

"Mom, it's OK. By the way, I'm sorry I didn't tell you this sooner, but Karen's coming over to help me. She's smart. You've met her before. That's why I got a little miffed at the dishes/laundry thing. But it's OK. Really, it is. I'll get everything done. Like you said, it won't take long."

Shelly had met Karen. But there had been times when Karen had come over reeking of marijuana. Shelly didn't think Mikalya was smoking, though; she would have seen evidence of it. Karen was polite and well-spoken, and she treated Mikalya like a true friend. She was also a straight-A student, and Shelly hoped some of her smarts would rub off on Mikalya, who was more of a B and C student.

They gave each other a hug. *Another teen crisis avoided*, Shelly thought. *This time, I'm thankful that Karen is coming over.*

Shelly had a way of climbing over the walls Mikalya threw up—and always in a constructive manner. The way she communicated with her daughter would strengthen their connection forever.

****

One beautiful spring afternoon, fourteen-year-old Mikalya was walking home from school when she noticed a colorful object about ten feet into the wooded area near her home. As she stepped closer to look at it, it appeared to be a cool little wooden storage chest, which she instantly fell in love with.

Deciding to go after it, she laid her books down and carefully navigated the low-hanging tree branches, sticker bushes, and weeds. She finally reached the box and opened it, but there was nothing in it. She found it odd that someone would throw such a beautiful thing away.

*Perhaps they had to get rid of it fast*, she thought.

As she looked around, she decided to find a way out of the wooded area with less resistance. She thought she'd found one a few feet away, but as she started back toward the sidewalk, pushing bush branches out of the way, she heard a loud buzzing noise.

Scores of bees, coming out of nowhere, buzzed dangerously close to her. They appeared to be yellow jackets, but it didn't matter; she couldn't shake them off. Unbeknownst to her, she had stepped on a bee's nest on the ground.

"Darn, where did they come from? Get off me, you little shits! Get OFF!" she screamed. She couldn't run fast, as she was still several feet from the edge of the woods, still in heavy brush.

Mikalya tried to move faster, but the bees increased their attack and found their chance as she got stuck at the sticker bush. The stickers caught on the billowy sleeves of her top and her exposed skin. They were penetrating her blouse and jeans as well. She could feel herself being stung in several places simultaneously as her arms, face, and neck were all exposed. Knowing that she was immobile, the bees attacked even more forcefully.

"STOP IT, STOP IT!" she screamed.

Her last scream attracted a couple taking a stroll back home. Ryan Kincade and his wife, Roberta, had been at a neighborhood bar for several hours celebrating Roberta's work promotion. The two were quite smashed and in a more fearless mood than they normally would have been.

"Honey, I think that sound came from over there. Sounds like a girl. Did you hear it?" Roberta asked, pointing across the road.

Ryan looked over. "Shit, what is she screaming about? Is she in trouble?"

They ran across the street—right up to the wooded area where Mikalya was.

"Oh, God, I think she's trapped in there! Do you hear that buzzing? Those are bees! We have to move NOW!" Ryan shouted.

"Honey, stay right there… we're going to get you out!" Roberta yelled.

"Roberta, where in the hell is she gonna go?" Ryan yelled back.

"Oh, God! Can you please hurry?" Mikalya cried out.

When they got closer, the couple noticed that she already had several bee stings all over her body.

Ryan quickly pulled his blazer off and wrapped it over his hands, bulldozing his way into the mess Mikalya was in.

Roberta came in from a different angle, shooing the bees away as best she could.

"God, there are bees all over!" she shouted.

Ryan quickly moved the stickers out of the way to get to Mikalya. He brushed as many bees off her as fast as he could.

Mikalya clung to him like a drowning victim clinging to a lifeguard.

He carried her out of the woods to the safety of the sidewalk, laying her gently on the grass. There were no bees on her, but the couple noticed considerable bee stings on her arms and upper chest. There were a few on her face, as well, along with some scratches from the stickers of the bushes.

"Do you live close by here? I think you're going to be OK just as long as you aren't allergic to bees," Roberta said.

In a bit of shock but still able to talk, Mikalya tried to lift herself onto her buttocks. "Thank you both so much. No, I'm not allergic. I live just three blocks over. My mom should be home by now. Let me call her," she said, looking around for her phone.

Roberta handed Mikalya her phone that had fallen from her pocket when Ryan picked her up. Her hands shook as she attempted to press the keys on the phone.

"Mom, it's me. I had a little accident. I…" Mikalya began. Mikalya had developed a habit of being accident-prone.

When she was thirteen, she had cut herself with a kitchen knife, which required several stitches. She had also sprained her ankle in a fall, burned her fingers on a hot pan, and dropped a large pot of spaghetti sauce on her feet. But Mikalya survived it all. Shelly was thankful for the good insurance she had through her work.

"Another one? Where are you? What happened? Are you OK?" Shelly asked in rapid succession.

"Yeah, I'm OK. This nice couple helped me out. They are bringing me home right now. I may have to go to the clinic, though," Mikalya said.

Shelly and Mikalya thanked Roberta and Ryan repeatedly. Shelly even invited them over for a future dinner. The couple politely accepted.

On their way to the clinic, Shelly reflected upon Mikalya's accident-filled history. *A cat has nine lives. I sure hope this kid has the same!*

****

Mikalya grew into a beautiful young woman with a strong personality that intimidated boys her age. She wasn't going to let Shelly control her, and be damned if any guy tried to, either. She was a tomboy, and although some mothers might, Shelly didn't see this as a bad thing. She assumed it would serve her well later in life. Mikalya dated a little here and there but never really got serious with anyone.

****

A few months after turning eighteen, Mikalya graduated from high school. Shelly was so proud of her, and she knew that Clifton was watching from the other side and was equally proud.

After the graduation ceremony, Mikalya took pictures with her best friend, Karen, and a few other kids. Jenny and Latisha showed up to support Shelly. They remembered well the night Mikalya was born.

"Mom, come on. You get in here, too!" Mikalya called, reaching out her hand to pull Shelly into a picture.

Shelly smiled, reluctantly joining in the photo op. She was grateful for Mikalya's friendship with Karen. Despite her bad ways, Shelly was sure that it was Karen who had helped Mikalya get the above-average grades that she received throughout high school. They studied together constantly. All of Karen's good study habits had rubbed off on Mikalya, and their friendship seemed genuine and strong.

Shelly had learned long ago that if a person had only one or two genuine friends in the world, they were ahead of the game. Acquaintances, coworkers, drinking buddies, casual friends, family, neighbors, wives, and husbands could never replace the rarest of treasures in one's life—a true friend who would stand by you no matter what. Shelly was thankful that Mikalya had that.

After the photo op, Mikalya pulled Shelly off to the side. "Mom, is it OK if Karen and I go to one of the graduation parties? I won't be late, and it's not that far from our house."

"Whose house is it? Do I know them?" Shelly asked.

"Yeah, it's Dan Haskell's house. I went out with him a few times last year. Remember?"

"He wasn't a bad-looking guy. I never understood what happened between you two," Shelly said.

Mikalya shook her head. "Well, let's just say I wouldn't play ball with him the way he wanted, and we'll leave it at that."

Shelly gave her daughter a big squeeze.

"That's my girl! You be careful. If you need me, call. You're old enough now, so I'm not going to tell you what time to be home. The light will be on. You go and have fun."

Shelly watched as Mikalya rode off with Karen and a few of the other girls. She watched until the car disappeared from her view.

Five hours later, Shelly heard a loud noise outside the front door. It was almost 2 a.m., and she hadn't been able to fall asleep. When she peered out the door window, Mikalya was kneeling, trying to pick up the pieces of the planter she'd knocked over.

"Honey, what are you doing? It's OK, I'll get that in the morning," she said.

Mikalya didn't look up.

Shelly knelt and could see that Mikalya was crying.

As she wrapped her arms around her daughter, Mikalya stopped picking up the broken pottery pieces and hugged her mom tightly.

"Baby, are you OK? Did something happen at the party? What's wrong?" Shelly asked.

Mikalya looked up at her. "I'm fine, Mom. Well, no, I'm not," she said.

Shelly remained quiet, allowing her child to speak.

"The party was fun, for a while, anyway. I mostly just sat and drank wine with Karen and a few others. And, yes, we smoked a joint. A lot of people were bragging about where they were going to college and all, or where they were going to travel to, or how they just wanted to get the hell out of here. I didn't have a lot to contribute to that conversation. I didn't want to. I didn't understand it all until tonight. I didn't know until now. Mom, I now understand all that you've done for me."

It was obvious to Shelly that Mikalya was completely out of it, but now was not the time to lecture her.

"I was having fun for a while, but then my mood changed. I started thinking about you and me and us and our lives up to this point. I know I didn't know my father, but I always felt I did through you," Mikalya said through sniffles.

Shelly had only spoken well of Clifton to Mikalya. She had never told her about his running away in the beginning. It didn't matter.

The tears continued streaming down Mikalya's face.

"I know if he was here, we'd be a good family, and I know he's still with us in some way. I can feel him a lot. He comes back to me in dreams sometimes, Mom. I try to remember what he's trying to tell me, but it's all so complicated. I can't understand them all the time. He shows me things that he wants me to know," Mikalya continued.

"Honey, he comes back to me now and again, too. He talks about you. And, when he's done, I go to hug him, and he's gone. I want to feel his touch so badly. In those dreams, he lies with me in the middle of the night. I can feel him embracing me. It's so intense that… sometimes, it wakes me up."

Mikalya looked at her mom.

"I know. He was talking to me in one of my dreams, but I couldn't make out his words clearly. But when I woke up, I had such a strong love for you. It's like he was telling me to take care of you, Mom! I think that's what he was trying to tell me… you know?"

Shelly held her and said nothing.

Mikalya pushed herself from her mom's arms. "Mom, I know I've been a pain in the ass sometimes, fighting you here and being a bitch there. I never mean it the way it comes out. I don't know what I would ever do without you. I'll make you proud of me. I promise. I promise!"

Shelly stroked her daughter's hair. "Sweetie, you make me proud every time you get up in the morning and muddle into the kitchen with your hair all messed up, going after that first cup of coffee. You make me proud when you come home from school with another excellent report card. You make me proud when you help me keep the house clean. Mikalya, you make me proud by just existing.

"I don't know where I'd be without you, either, and I never intend to find out. I have no idea when a child is born, if the mother subconsciously chooses the child, or if the child chooses the mother. Is there some sort of divine celestial process to it all? I don't know. I think some people are being tested with the children they have. I think other parents are punished with the children they have, a sort of karma. And I think some people are gifted with the children they have. I, honey, was gifted with you. There is no doubt in my mind about that," Shelly said, looking off into space.

"My God, Mom, I… I'm going to put out some applications here soon. I know nothing is open at Roberts & Sons, and that's OK. Maybe I could go to beauty school and learn to be a stylist? I'll live with you and help out with all the bills, the lawn, the housecleaning, and—"

Shelly put her fingers over her daughter's mouth. "Honey, you can be anything you want. I'll support you, no matter what, and you can stay here as long as you want. This is your home, and nothing will ever change that. Even if another man comes into my life, if you don't like him, or the other way around, he can't stay here. And that's that!" she said.

Mikalya looked at her mom again through teary eyes.

"I'll never have any more children, Mikalya, because no one could top you… ever."

Shelly sat on the step for what seemed like an eternity, comforting her daughter. She knew that Mikalya had probably partied a little more than she should have, but it was good that she had gotten those emotions out of her system. She held her until her breathing calmed.

"Sweetie, are you hungry? I can fix you a great hamburger right now," Shelly offered.

Mikalya looked up at her mom and nodded.

Shelly smiled back at her daughter, then slowly helped her to her feet, leading her inside the house to care for her.

****

Mikalya found a job at a local car dealership as the receptionist. Outside of the salesmen occasionally hitting on her, she found the job easy and the money decent. She continued living with Shelly, and although she dated here and there, she didn't find any man she wanted to have a serious relationship with.

# Chapter Two: Abraham Gallagher

Beth and James met while participating in a sit-in at the University of California Berkeley, protesting the Vietnam War. The year was 1968, and it was one year after the infamous Summer of Love, although the love had worn off and everyone was pissed. The year began with the Pope's plea for peace, but that was not to be. Violent protests in the streets were commonplace, and Robert F. Kennedy and Dr. Martin Luther King Jr. had both been assassinated. The Democratic National Convention (DNC) was marred by intense violence and property damage, and the Vietnam War was in full swing.

It was far from a romantic period, but Beth and James had met and fallen in love on their way to jail. The refusal to move their protest from a public spot by order of Berkeley police resulted in many being arrested, but the protesters wore their incarceration as a badge of honor. Beth and James sat close to each other during the protest, then wound up sitting next to each other in the back of a paddy wagon on the way to jail.

"Well, we didn't have a lot of chances to talk back there. What is your name?" James asked Beth.

"Beth Howard. I'm a sophomore here at Berkeley. How about you?" she replied with a smile.

"I'm James Gallagher. I'm a senior. I noticed you during the protest. You look like one of my cousins… and that is a compliment I'll have you know."

Beth looked at him, trying to decide if he was feeding her a line of bull. Though even if he was, she was going to let him continue. There was something about him that intrigued her. She figured he was OK because very few people would have the presence of mind to try to hit on someone handcuffed in the back of a police van.

Beth had been watching him closely during the sit-in. He was extremely confident and unafraid. She noticed, too, that people listened to him. And he was good-looking.

"What are you majoring in?" she asked.

They both laughed as James raised cuffed hands.

James had always been attracted to sassy dames, and this one certainly met his standard. She reeked of independence, strength, and smarts. She wasn't drop-dead gorgeous, but she was close enough. James always thought beautiful women were too stuck on themselves, but Beth didn't give him that vibe; she exuded self-confidence. And the fact that she seemed interested in him was a plus, as well.

"Well, I'm majoring in Electrical Engineering, but now it looks like I'll be standing on the back of a garbage truck. What about you?" he asked.

Beth laughed, then stared at him for a moment, contemplating a response as cute as his.

"I'm majoring in Political Science, but it appears now I'll be standing next to you on the back of that truck," she said.

"OK by me!" James replied.

The man sitting next to them chimed in.

"Hey, guys, don't be so pessimistic. I've known a lot of people to get arrested for these things. They handcuff you and throw you in the back of their transport vehicle, then they haul you downtown and throw you in the slammer until they feel you've cooled off. So, you see, those people I referred to weren't really under arrest, per se. The same may happen to us. They just want to rattle us a bit and give out a few citations. But, if we're caught a second time, it could be a different story," the man said.

"That's good to hear. What's your name?" Beth asked.

"Tim Maloney. I go to Berkley, as well… a Political Science major. I already heard what you guys are going after."

"Hey, is it true Johnson may not run for a second term?" James asked out of the blue. "Have you guys heard anything? There's a rumor he's not. All that bastard did was ramp up the war for the corporations! He was the one who pushed the Gulf of Tonkin resolution! If they hadn't murdered Kennedy, none of this would have happened."

"You're one hundred percent right! I know a couple of people in the Democratic Party at Berkeley. The rumor, and it's just speculation at this point, is that he may not. The war's taken a toll on the asshole. I hope he burns in hell for it. They're saying there may be some sort of announcement on TV in the next month or so," Tim said.

"No, shit?" James replied.

"Yeah. Listen, once we get to the police station, we won't be able to talk much. I wait tables part-time at Luca Cucina's on San Pablo Avenue in Berkeley, mostly on weekends. Come by and see me in the next couple of Saturdays, and we'll have a few drinks when I get off," Tim said.

"Oh, I love Italian food! I've always wanted to try that place. Is it pretty good?" Beth asked.

James's antennae went up. This was his *in* with Beth for a first date. He immediately took the reins before Tim could respond.

"Wait a minute. I know some people who have eaten there. They say it's fantastic," he said, although it was a lie. "And, yeah, I know where it is there in San Pablo. Beth, you want to go, assuming we're out of jail by then? I can come and get you," James said.

Tim looked over at Beth, waiting for an answer, too.

"Yeah, that sounds great. Do you know where the Hour House is on Walnut Street?" she asked.

"I've been there a million times," James answered.

"Can you meet me there this Friday, around seven? We can have a drink and talk this whole thing out," Beth replied.

"See you there at seven, then."

"Guys, I get off at 10 p.m. If you want to come and grab a glass of Chianti, then two glasses of Ornellaia Bolgheri Superiore are on me. It's excellent," Tim said.

"I don't know what the hell you just said, but that sounds wonderful! We'll see you then, Tim. Glad we met you," Beth replied as she felt the police wagon slowing down.

"OK, I'm sure we're probably here. You know the plan. See you both Saturday," Tim said.

James nodded and looked over at Beth.

"And I'll see you Friday at seven at the Hour House." Beth nodded back.

The back doors of the police vehicle swung open, and the police motioned for everyone to come out. A policewoman was there to escort the females.

Once separated, they were herded into a processing area and asked for their driver's licenses. After about five hours, they were issued citations and released one at a time. Fortunately, the university didn't want to prosecute first-time offenders.

****

Friday rolled around, and James was looking forward to meeting Beth at the Hour House. He was nervous, as he wondered if she would show. He had no idea where she lived or anything else about her. All he knew was what she had shared with him on their drive down to the station, and that was enough to make him fall hard in that short period of time. He was hoping that she had felt something, too.

He pulled into the Hour House parking lot about twenty minutes before 7 p.m., walked in and ordered a Strohs on draft, then waited. He chose a table within view of the front door, but one also not easily visible to everyone who came through it.

Taking his first gulp of beer, he looked at his watch. It was ten minutes 'til seven. Looking around, he was happy to see that there were very few people in the place. It wouldn't be noisy. He took another gulp of beer at five minutes to. He was so nervous… he couldn't even taste the beer. It was now four minutes 'til.

Then, at precisely three minutes to seven, Beth walked through the door, looking around.

James saw her immediately but chose to stare at her for a few moments. She looked fantastic in her pink top, tight jeans, and a cute little purse over her shoulder. She wore an intense expression.

Based on his stealth table location, she could not locate him.

He finally decided to stand and motion her over.

"Beth, over here," he said, waving his hand in the air.

As she wandered toward him, he noticed how nicely she moved and carried herself.

"Hey, you. How long have you been here?" she asked.

"Oh, not long. I just got here a few minutes ago," he lied.

Beth put her purse on the floor and sat down.

"I'm going to get a beer. Do you want anything?" James asked.

"Uh, a glass of Merlot sounds good," she said.

James ordered, and while they were waiting for the drinks, the conversation began.

"Let's see, the last time I saw you, we were in handcuffs," Beth joked. "I'm glad you remembered our plans to meet tonight."

"Well, I did. So, what happened to you after they separated the boys from thc girls?"

"It's not every day I get arrested, so this is an easy recall. After they let us go to the powder room, we were herded into this holding area, where they processed us and took our things. We were there for a few hours, I think. God, it was depressing. They had one toilet for like one hundred people, and, good Lord, it stank. Then, they called us one at a time and did some more processing. We weren't really under arrest. I got a citation, which I think is a slap on the wrist.

"Then, I was told if I did this again, they would arrest me. I got my things back, and they let me go. I was in for about four hours total. When I got out, I looked around for you, but no James. I was just hoping you'd remember our date," Beth finished.

"Yeah, I did, and I'm glad you did, too. My experience was similar, but I think I got out sooner than you did. I looked around for you and that Tim guy. Remember him?" James asked.

"I do. Did you see him later?"

"Yeah, we kind of got out at the same time. He still wants us to come to Luca Cucina; if not tomorrow, then maybe next Saturday. I think it'll be fun. Still game for it?"

“I’d love to, but I can’t tomorrow. I have work. How about next Saturday?” Beth asked, taking a sip of her wine.

“I’ll make sure I am available. I can pick you up, say, around 6 p.m.?”

“It’s a date, Mr. Gallagher,” she replied with a smile.

They raised their glasses in a toast and chatted about their pasts, their futures, and their dreams. As the conversation progressed, so did their connection.

The more she talked about her life, the more James felt a strong desire for her to rise in him. It was a tasty cocktail of emotional and spiritual desires. In past situations like this, his only thought was how he would sleekly railroad his date into the sack, but not this time.

The more wine Beth consumed, the more she talked. She would lace her stories with light humor, tangents, and animations that fascinated him. Combined with her cool and goofy facial expressions, he couldn’t stop laughing. She talked non-stop for almost forty-five minutes. When she took a breath, he could tell she was winding down. Her mouth probably needed a rest.

“And then, he finally said, ‘Well, Miss Howard, can you please wipe that nutty smile off your face and remove that balloon off of my ear?' And he was serious!" Beth finished with a sexy, controlled laugh.

He loved the way she put her hand over her mouth. James sat there mesmerized. She had dominated the evening with her stories, and he had enjoyed it all.

"So, Mr. James Gallagher, tell me a funny story or two about your grade school years," she said, putting the wineglass up to her lips and taking a slow sip, her eyes never leaving his as she awaited his response.

"Uh… well… OK, I have to think," he said. James knew that he had nothing to share that would top anything she had said, but he gave it a try.

"It's embarrassing, but here's my story and it involves being at Mass when I was a schoolboy," he said.

"Where'd you go to grade school?" she asked.

"Saint Michael's," James replied.

"So, you were an altar boy. How cute. Did you wear those black and white robes? I'm not Catholic, so I don't know a lot about it. I've been to Catholic Mass a few times with friends, and I know a little about what goes on, but that's the extent of my Catholic knowledge. OK, I'm shutting up now," Beth said.

James looked at her. "Well, this time, it wasn't so cute. It was after Communion, and I was following the priest back up to the altar. There were three other altar boys also assisting, but just two of us were helping the priests. I was the main altar boy at this Mass. As I followed him up, I tripped on my robe and lurched forward. Something like this is an altar boy's worst nightmare," he said, cracking a smile as he remembered how funny the story was.

Beth smiled, too. "So, you tripped… on the altar… in that robe and, like, teetered for a little bit? In front of everyone?" she asked, unable to contain her laughter.

"In front of everyone? Heck, it was the eight o'clock Mass, and the whole school was there. My classmates, the principal, all the nuns, and teachers. The maintenance guys were even standing in the back," James said, laughing harder.

Beth giggled louder. "That's a riot. Please go on!"

"Well, after I tripped, I caught myself but then got my robe caught on the end of the wine table, and it took me a few seconds to get loose. And I looked back at Tom Whitmoyer, the altar boy next to me. He had his hands folded over his mouth, trying to keep from laughing. I thought, *Oh, no! If he saw it, so did everyone else. God save me*."

"I finally got my robe free and knelt back down next to Tom. His face was red. Then, I looked across the altar to the other two guys, Randy Johnson and Kevin Thompson, and they were doing the same."

Beth composed herself for a few seconds. "You still remember their names?" she asked.

"How in the hell do you forget someone's name in a situation like that?" he replied.

"You're right," Beth agreed.

"So, this is where it gets worse," James continued.

Beth interrupted. "It gets worse?"

"Oh, much worse! Anyway, I could hear Tom snickering and see the guys across from me. I knew if I started to, I wouldn't be able to control myself. I prayed to Saint Anthony to make them stop, but they didn't. So, I tried another Saint, and that didn't work, either."

Beth was in hysterics. "Did you try Saint James?" she asked, wiping tears from her eyes.

James stopped and looked up. "No, I didn't, but that is a hell of an idea; ten freaking years too late, though. But that would have made it worse!" he said.

"Anyway, all hell broke loose. I started to laugh, too, but had to keep it in. I folded my hands in prayer like the others and held my mouth shut. It worked for a little bit, but then my bladder started to… well, not cooperate. I had to pee even before Mass started but didn't have time because I got there late. So, anyway, here I am trying like hell not to laugh while at the same time keeping from pissing in my pants or keep from pissing in my cassock!"

Beth reached for a napkin to wipe her eyes.

"Then, another one of an altar boy's nightmares unfolded in front of me, or should I say under me. The pressure in my bladder exploded. It happened so fast that I didn't know what hit me. First, I felt this warm squirt engulf my crotch. Then I snickered again, and that forced a second stronger burst. Thank God I had that robe on because it hid the water spot," James said.

Beth's laughter was now out of control.

"What's so funny? Just kidding. I'm sorry. You're not going to pee in your pants, are you?" he asked.

Beth shook her head slowly.

"So, anyway, I'm kneeling there on the altar, pissing in my robe big time. And while urine is streaming down my legs, I'm looking off toward the statue of Saint Joseph and shaking my head, thinking, *Why me, God?*

"Well, anyway, Father Ron finished up the closing prayers, and we had to stand up, and wouldn't you know it, all the pee that dripped to my knees had trickled down into my shoes! I could feel it! As we walked back into the sacristy, my shoes were squishing from all the pee in them. Oh, God!" James said.

Beth was howling with laughter as James looked around the room.

"Listen, I better stop. Everyone's looking at us now," he said.

"Oh, hell, I can't imagine why. Can you? Stop making me laugh! My stomach hurts!" Beth said.

"I'll finish the story later. I can't think anymore." James smiled, happy that he could make her laugh.

Beth excused herself to the ladies' room to regain her composure.

"That was one of the funniest stories I've ever heard in my life, and you didn't even finish it," she said upon her return.

"Oh, well, madam, another time."

They sat at the same table until midnight, consuming beer after beer and several glasses of wine. James wanted to control himself, so he decided to take a premature, gentlemanly, and chivalrous approach to end the evening. He didn't want to get any drunker in front of her and risk making a fool of himself.

When Beth yawned under her breath, he knew that was the right time. He told her he had to go because he needed to get his car into the shop early in the morning for repairs.

"I agree. All this must end for now. Let's get going. If I have another drink, I won't be able to function tomorrow. What's wrong with your car?" she asked.

The question caught James off guard, so his response was slow. He wasn't as sharp as he normally would have been had he not had so many drinks.

"Uh, I think one of the pistons is acting up, but I'm not sure," he replied, hoping she didn't know a lot about cars.

"Well, that doesn't sound good. Listen, are we going to go to Luca Cucina's and meet Tim for sure next Saturday? Please say yes. I've had a great time with you tonight… and I mean that."

"Yeah, I thought we would. He seems like a pretty OK guy. Besides, I would like to talk with him about how to counter all the crap that's going on in Washington without getting arrested. There's got to be better ways. Then, of course… and this is the most important thing; I want to see you again, Beth. This was one of the coolest nights of my life."

Beth reached over the table and gave James a little peck on the cheek. "Same here. Here's my address. I don't live terribly far from campus. If you want to pick me up, that would be great."

James took the slip of paper, then hurried off to pay the tab, with Beth following close behind.

Still a bit tipsy, he walked her out into the breezy night to her car, careful to not act like a drunken, horny jerk, although that's what he was feeling.

"Hey, Beth, I had a really nice time. I'm looking forward to next Saturday. See you at your place at… say, 6 p.m.?" he said, trying not to slur his words.

"That sounds great. I can't wait."

Placing his hand on her face, he leaned in and gave her a slow kiss on the lips, then quickly withdrew.

"Goodnight, Beth. Until Saturday."

"Bye, James."

As they parted, they touched each other's hands. Driving home, James knew she was the one; heading in the opposite direction, Beth felt the same.

****

The following Saturday, James drove over to pick up Beth in his beat-up 1964 Volkswagen Beetle. It was black with a stick shift, and it got him where he needed to go. It was also cheap to maintain. He wasn't sure how Beth was going to perceive him in it, but she seemed like the kind of woman who didn't care about material things.

Although he was clean-shaven and well-groomed, he was dressed casually in a pair of beat-up old jeans and a blue work shirt with the sleeves rolled up.

Beth saw him from the window and came out to meet him. She wore a classic hippie dress, the top flowery and billowy. Her long hair blew in the warm evening breeze, her makeup was perfect, and her turquoise necklace shone beautifully. She wore Chanel No. 5, although she had no idea it was James's favorite.

"My God, Beth, you look absolutely gorgeous!"

Beth looked at him and put her hand on his cheek. "Thank you, sir. You look nice, too."

James opened the car door for her, and as she slid across the seat, her dress lifted just enough to expose her legs. They were perfect. As he waited for her to settle in, he got a strong whiff of her perfume and smiled.

"Ready?" James asked, starting the car.

"I hope Tim's there. If he's not, I'm in the mood for a glass of wine," Beth said, rolling down the window and letting her arm hang over the side.

"Same here. It's been a rough week of classes. Engineering is a little harder than I thought, but I'll get through it. How'd your week go?"

"Not too bad. I had a couple of exams and essays, but I got through them OK. I'm done stressing for now. Let's just kick back."

"I agree. Like I said, I do want to talk to Tim about other, less dangerous ways to protest this war going on in Vietnam."

"We'll see what he has to say."

James pulled up in front of Luca Cucina's and got out first to open Beth's door, hoping his chivalrous side would impress her. Following behind as she led the way into the restaurant, he noticed how stunning her butt looked, even in her loose-fitting dress.

Tim noticed them walk through the door. "Hey, guys, you made it! Have a seat over here, and I'll get you taken care of. I've arranged to get off in an hour. Are you two in the mood for a glass of the best wine you've ever had in your life?" he asked.

"Yes, yes, yes!" Beth blurted with enthusiasm. James nodded his head in agreement.

"I've had this waiting for you," Tim said, reaching under the counter and pulling out a bottle of Ornellaia Bolgheri Superiore, one of Italy's leading Bordeaux-style red wines.

"Have you had this before?" he asked. They both shook their heads.

"Hell, I can't even pronounce it," James said.

Tim placed two wine glasses in front of them, then opened the bottle with military precision.

"I could never do that like you just did," Beth said.

"Lots of practice," Tim replied. Like a professional, he poured a bit in James's glass first and urged him to taste.

James did so, sending an expression of sheer delight in Beth's direction.

"You're going to like this a lot," he said as Tim began filling both their glasses.

At that moment, Merrillee Rush's "Angel of the Morning" filtered the air from the jukebox in the corner.

"Oh, wait… I love that song!" Beth exclaimed, swiveling in her chair in the direction of the music.

"Then, let's toast to the angel of the morning," James said, holding up his glass.

Beth looked at him, caught completely off guard.

Tim could see what was developing between the two and discreetly backed away.

"Do you realize you said just the right thing at just the right time in just the right place and about just the right song? Do you?" Beth asked with a giggle.

James stared into her eyes.

"Yes," he said softly, leaning over and kissing her lips, then stroking her face. Every time he looked at her, he couldn't help but smile.

As if in a trance, they stared at each other for a few moments until a woman walking past lost her footing and bumped into Beth.

"Oh, I'm so sorry. I think my heel broke. Forgive me," the woman said, composing herself and moving along. Luckily, none of the wine spilled.

"Let's have that sip while my song is still playing, James!" Beth said.

Tim made his way back over to their table, anxious to know their thoughts on his wine choice.

"This really is the best wine I've ever had!" Beth said excitedly, swaying to the music.

"What is this called again?" James asked.

"Ornellaia Bolgheri Superiore. I knew you'd like it. How 'bout I get you guys another bottle while I finish up? Then we can talk."

Tim hurried off again while Beth and James continued to enjoy their wine. When he finally finished and was off the clock, he joined them.

"You guys seem to be having a good time. Let me get a third bottle of that. Work has made me thirsty."

The wine and politics flowed with intensity.

"I'll raise a toast. It's nice to be out of jail, isn't it?" Tim said.

"Yes, it is. So, are we doing any more protesting or calling it quits for now? I can't afford a police record when I'm going to be looking for a job after graduation," said Beth.

James nodded in agreement. He was one year older than Beth and would graduate a year ahead of her.

"I hear you. I still hate what's going on, but I, or we, probably need to keep a low profile. I graduate next year, and the job market's good for engineers, so I can't mess it up. And besides, there are better ways to fight all that corrupt stuff that's going down. We can still go to protests and keep a low profile by just marching. There's strength in numbers, ya know?

"Also, I'm going to start researching candidates more before I vote for any of them. Don't get me wrong… Johnson and McNamara have lied through their asses to us. They've lied to the press. Communism, my ass. Who knows what the hell we're over there for? But we have to keep cool heads because if we get hauled off one more time, we're going straight to jail to stay," James said.

"I understand… believe me, I do. I graduate in a year, too, and I plan on going to grad school. Maybe we should move more into the political end of it. Why don't I get some information on local party affiliations here, and we can check them out?" Tim chimed in.

"Sounds good," James replied.

"Does this mean we have to stop being hippies? I mean, I like the lifestyle," Beth chimed in.

James winked at Beth. "And if Beth likes it, so do I!"

"Well, I say we certainly live it until we are the hell out of here," Tim offered.

As the wine continued to flow, the trio talked about politics, music, movies, books and what they wanted for their lives after graduation. By the time the night was over, they had become good friends.

"Well, Miss Howard, I've had quite a bit to drink. Do you want to stop for a cup of coffee?" James asked as he drove toward Beth's home.

When she didn't answer right away, he looked over to see if she had fallen asleep. Her eyes were still open.

"Hey, are you OK?" he nudged, wondering if he'd said something wrong.

Beth looked over at him. "More than OK. Listen, we don't need coffee. When we get to my place, I want you to come in."

James nodded his excitement.

When they pulled up to the house and went inside, Beth kicked off her shoes and pulled James close to her. With no music, their hips moved in unison to the invisible sound of a love song. Soon, the dance turned into a kiss.

"You don't have to get your pistons fixed in the morning again, do you?" she asked.

"No, I think my pistons are working just fine," James replied.

With a smile, she took his hand and led him into her bedroom.

****

The following year, James graduated with a degree in Engineering and landed a great job a couple of hours away from home. He patiently waited for Beth to graduate the year after him, which she did with a double major in Political Science and Education. She went on to snag a position at the local high school teaching Political Science.

James had fallen for Beth hard and wanted to spend the rest of his life with her. She was the only woman he wanted to mother his children, so soon after she graduated, they were married.

Two years later, she gave birth to their first child, Abraham Charles Gallagher, or Abe, as he preferred to be called. Beth had decided long ago that should she ever have a son, that would be his name, as she associated it with strength.

James and Beth knew early on that their son was different from most other kids. He was a quiet boy who chose to spend his time studying, playing football, and helping around the house. He was a good student who excelled in his sport, and although not very social, he was a leader on the field and very competitive. Abe liked the concept of team spirit and synchronicity.

When he was a junior in high school, Beth and James attended one of his home games. Abe sensed more tension in the air than usual that day, but he couldn't put his finger on it. It was excessively hot out, which didn't help matters. They were playing their biggest rival from across town, and this win would decide which team would go on to the playoffs. That, alone, added more electricity to the air.

His position was right guard on the offensive line. His mentor on the field was Jeff Atwood. Jeff was a big guy, about 6′5″ and all of 249 pounds. He was a nice, quiet boy, and no one messed with him. Abraham was lucky to have him as a friend.

There was one play at the beginning of the fourth quarter that horrified Beth and even caused James to flinch. The score was tied 7-7, and Abe's team had the ball. They were on the rival team's twenty-seven-yard line and needed to force the lead. It was third down with five yards to go, and they had only one more chance for a first down.

Mark Forsythe, their quarterback, set the play up and started to call the signals. Mark was a good quarterback and had led the team into a winning season. Abraham was nervous, as the team could not afford to make any mistakes.

"We're going to kick their asses. We've run this play a hundred times," Atwood said to Abraham.

The signals were called, and the ball was snapped into Mark's hands. Mark, who rarely made any mistakes on the field, dropped the football once it was handed to him, and chaos ensued.

The ball fell out of Mark's hands and rapidly rolled over, across the line of scrimmage into the opposing team's territory. This was not good.

Sitting on the sidelines intently watching everything unfold, Beth had no idea what was happening, but with all the screaming and yelling about it, she quickly deduced it wasn't good. Things were moving so fast that James didn't have time to explain it to her, barely taking it in himself.

"Shit, the goddamn ball!" Forsythe yelled. The ball had rolled forward right under Abe's legs, but because of his position, there was no way he could have seen it until it rolled past him. That was when Atwood spotted it.

"Fuck, he lost the ball. Follow me!" Atwood yelled to Abe, cutting in front of him and knocking one of the defensive linemen to the ground. Atwood then steamrolled into another opposing player, knocking him off his feet, as well.

Several of the other players converged on the rolling ball, with Atwood being closest to it and Abe right behind him. The second player that Jeff Atwood had knocked over suddenly fell directly in front of Abraham, causing him to trip.

Abe fell hard on his knees. As he was trying to recover and get back up, another player was heading toward him backward at a high rate of speed.

The player had been hit by someone else and was now cartoonishly careening into Abe, who was just starting to regain his coordination. The player hit Abe so hard that he did a full backward somersault.

Witnessing the impact of the hit on her son, Beth screamed at the top of her lungs.

After the Olympic-quality acrobatic move he'd made, Abe found himself on all fours. The force with which he had been hit tore his chinstrap off. With his helmet halfway over his head, he sat with a confused, goofy look on his face. The entire ordeal was over in seconds; Abe didn't know it, but the play had ended.

Looking around, dazed, he tried to focus on two figures running toward him. It was Jeff and Coach Robinson, but still unable to communicate yet, Abe just stared up at them.

"Honey, can you run down there and see if he's OK? Please!" Beth pleaded.

James jumped out of the bleachers and was by his son's side in seconds.

Beth noticed the couple sitting in front of them turn around, look at her, then turn back to face the field. Her temper flared when she overheard them talking.

"How many high school football games do you think they've been to?" the man cracked with a snicker.

"It sounds like it's her first one; she'll get used to it," the woman responded with a laugh.

"Hey, Abe, are you OK? We got the ball back, man! We got it back!" Jeff screamed.

Coach Robinson stepped in. "We did get the ball back, Abe, but I need to know you're alright," he said.

"Son, are you OK?" James asked, kneeling at his son's side.

Abe moved to a full sitting position. Everyone around him waited for a coherent response.

"Sorry, I had to get out of that position. It didn't feel right," Abe said slowly.

Jeff and Coach Robinson laughed.

James looked up in the stands toward Beth, her hands still over her mouth in horror. With a thumbs up, he motioned to her that their son was OK.

"Son, you just sit there for a bit. We're gonna have Doc Kennard come out here and take a quick look at you," Coach Robinson said.

The doctor examined Abe briefly, and after a few basic tests and questions, he patted him on the back.

"He appears to be fine, a little shaken up, but fine. I'd leave him out for the remainder of the game, though," the doctor said.

"Coach, just leave me out for the next play, and that's it. I want to finish the game," Abe said, hearing the doctor's recommendation.

Jeff nodded. The coach looked over at the doctor, who also nodded.

"Son, maybe you should…" James began.

"No, Dad, just the one play. I can do it," Abe replied, getting up on his own, with all the men following him back to the bench. The crowd cheered as he walked back.

"Dad, you can go back and sit with Mom. She needs you. Tell her I'm OK and am going to finish the game."

"Oh, thank God he's not going back in," Beth said to James upon his return, sighing deeply as she noticed her son taking a seat on the bench.

"Uh… well… no, he's not. I mean, he's out for just this next play, then he wants back in," James stuttered.

"What? Tell me you're kidding. He what?" Beth demanded.

"The coach couldn't even tell him to stop him. He's going back in after this play," James said.

"I can't watch this anymore," Beth mumbled under her breath.

As she got up to leave, James grabbed her arm and gently pulled her back. "He'll know you've left. Do you want to do that to him? I think you should stay," he said.

Beth looked at his hand on her arm, then sat back down.

Coach Robinson signaled to end the time out. The fumble worked to their advantage. After one play, Abe went back into the game.

Beth and James were impressed with their son's determination to see the game through.

His team scored another touchdown and eventually won the game.

James learned a lot about Abe that day, and Abe learned a lot about himself.

****

Abe graduated high school with above-average grades, and although his football career was just as impressive, he wasn't quite ready for college. What impressed James and Beth the most was how he never missed a practice, stuck every game out, and was a well-respected member of the team who all the other players looked up to.

"Well, are we finally all packed up?" James asked.

"Honey, yes, what more do we need to take? There's barely enough room for us in the car, let alone any more luggage," Beth said, rolling her eyes.

Beth, James, and Abe were on their way to Abe's cousin's wedding in Bowling Green, KY. It would take several hours to get there, but James and Beth wanted to see the countryside, so they decided to drive. They thought it would be a good chance for Abe to get some driving experience as well. He had driven on short trips around town, but he needed more interstate experience, and this was the perfect chance for him to get some.

With James behind the wheel, the family cruised at a comfortable sixty-five miles per hour speed down the interstate. Out of nowhere, a yellow Dodge Viper raced past them as Beth was sharing an old college story.

"Did you see that guy flying by? He's going too damn fast!" James yelled.

"Jesus, what a lunatic! He must be doing at least a hundred! What's the big hurry with people today?" Beth asked, stopping her story in mid-sentence.

Taking notice from the back seat, Abe sat erect as an intense sense of dread washed over him. James followed the Viper as it made its rapid ascent up the interstate.

In a matter of seconds, a pickup truck pulled out to pass the vehicle in front of it but did not see the rapidly approaching Viper as it continued to speed down the highway. Neither vehicle had time to react before the Viper slammed into the rear of the truck.

"Oh my God!" Beth screamed.

James started slowing down. All they could see up ahead was dust as the two vehicles spun off the interstate.

"Oh, my God!" Beth said again. "Oh, no! James, what are we going to do?"

"We have to stop! We have to! I'm going to pull up as close as I can get to them. Abe, call 9-1-1 and give them a good idea of where we're at! I do remember passing the Loren Road exit, and we are a few miles east of that, off-road!" James shouted to his son.

As they got closer, they could see flames pouring from the pickup truck. James pulled over and got out.

"Beth, you stay here. Abe, come with me!" James said. He could see the tears streaming down her face as he whispered, "I love you," before running toward the fiery chaos.

"Please, be careful!" Beth screamed out the window, starting to pray out loud.

As James and Abe got closer to the carnage, several other drivers were running along with them. The occupants of both vehicles were still inside. The fire that started in the back of the pickup truck was now spreading over the entire vehicle. James had to decide which vehicle to go to first.

Since the Viper had caused the accident, he motioned Abe to head over with him to the truck. He was impressed that his son showed no fear and stood with him.

They got as close to the truck as they could, with three other men standing with them, ready to help. James could hear people screaming from inside the truck. He could make out a man at the wheel and a woman on the passenger side; he also heard the faint cries of a child. Both the driver's side door and the passenger door had been hit hard and were smashed in. Abe could see the driver trying to kick the windshield out in desperation. The fire was quickly spreading toward the cab.

"How close can we get?" one man screamed.

"It's getting too hot! I don't know if this thing's gonna blow or not!" James said. Several more men were now circling the cab, looking for a way to get close enough to the doors. One man did manage to get to the driver's door handle and pulled.

"It's getting hotter! The door is stuck!" the man said, looking around at the desperation on the faces of the others.

Both adults in the cab were desperately motioning to the men outside to help them.

"Dad, hang on! Let me try!" Abe said, running up to the passenger side of the car and pounding on the window with a large stone he found on the ground. The glass smashed on impact.

Gasping for air, the woman stuck her head out the window.

"Oh, God! Oh, God! Please help us! Get us out of here! We can't breathe! Please!" she pleaded.

Abe pulled his shirt off and wrapped it around his hand. He grabbed the door handle and pulled as hard as he could, but it wouldn't budge. Another man ran up to the door and tried to help him but to no avail.

Wide-eyed, the woman continued kicking the door while still pleading for help.

"Can't you pull harder? Oh, God! Help us!" she screamed, kicking the door with even more force as smoke continued to pile into the cab.

Abe and the others began backing away from the vehicle as it became apparent it might explode.

"Can you climb out the window?" one of the men yelled.

"We can't get our seat belts off! They are jammed! Can't you do anything? Please help us!" she screamed.

A strong feeling of helplessness washed over Abe. No one there had the proper equipment to get the people out of the truck.

A lone police car and a fire truck arrived on the scene. The fire was now spreading rapidly through the cab. Just to stand by and watch helplessly made Abraham physically ill.

The woman motioned Abe to come as close to the truck as he could. “Come here! Come here!” she screamed, waving her hand.

Abe ran as close to the vehicle as he could. He could see that the woman was trying to force something through the broken window; it was a child.

“Take her! Take her! Get her out of here!” the woman screamed.

As Abe reached for the little girl, another man ran up to help him pull her from the woman’s arms. The look on the woman’s face would haunt him for the rest of his life. He would never find the words to describe it.

Both men quickly backed away as far as they could with the little girl. As the firemen approached the cab with a fire extinguisher, a small explosion could be heard underneath the truck. Smoke was pouring out of the broken window, and the hideous screams coming from inside the truck were deafening.

“Dad, do something!” Abe screamed.

The policemen ordered everyone to stand far back from the truck. The flames were so heavy, Abe could barely see the two people squirming and screaming inside the cab.

Suddenly, the truck exploded.

Abe stood and stared as fire engulfed the truck. He fell to his knees, crying and praying, while the sound of sirens filled the air. An ambulance and another fire engine had arrived. The fire engine pulled up to the burning vehicle, and several firefighters jumped off, setting up the main hose. They immediately began spraying down the burning truck.

Abe watched every move they made. Finally snapping out of his sorrowed mindset, he raced over to the firemen.

"How can I help? What can I do? Hey, I can help you!" he yelled.

"You got some balls, kid, but you need to stay back!" one of the firemen yelled back at him.

"Hey, buddy, you need to get back! Now!" the policeman yelled over the noise of the water.

Abe reluctantly stepped back from the carnage, wiping tears from his eyes.

The firemen managed to get the fire out quickly, but it was still too late. The accident had taken place too far off the road for effective help to find them and arrive in time. The truck was a charred mess, and the two people inside were now dead.

In shock, Abe just stood there, watching the smoke continue to pour from the cabin of the truck.

Watching from the background, James walked up and put his arm around his son's shoulders.

"Hey, there was nothing else you could do. There was nothing else any of us could do. It all happened so fast, and the intensity of the collision and all, we couldn't have…" James said.

Abe cut him off. "Dad, it doesn't matter now! Those two people didn't deserve that! No one deserves to die like that! I'll never forget the look on that woman's face when she handed her daughter out the window to me. I won't! I won't!"

James pulled Abe closer to him as his own tears threatened to roll down his cheeks.

All the others who had attempted to rescue the family from the truck stood in a daze, looking from the charred truck up to the sky as if searching for God and answers.

Abe rubbed the tears from his eyes. "*That* is never going to fucking happen again if I'm around! Never!" he vowed.

"I'm sorry, son. Let's go back to the car. We need to be with your mother. I know she's been watching all of this."

Starting behind his dad, Abe suddenly stopped. "Dad, wait. Look."

James looked back and immediately noticed what he was talking about. Lying in the back of the ambulance was the little girl Abe helped pull through the window. He headed toward her but was stopped by a policeman.

"Hey, where do you think you're going?" the policeman asked.

Abe looked at him firmly. "I'm one of the men who pulled her out of that truck. I'd just like to see her for a second."

The policeman quickly stood aside and let him pass.

The paramedics had overheard the conversation between Abe and the policeman and allowed him into the back of the ambulance without question. The little girl appeared to be around nine or ten. She had an oxygen mask over her face and abrasions on her arms and neck. She smelled heavily of smoke. The blank stare on her face let Abe know that she had no idea who he was.

He looked into her eyes for a few moments. No words were spoken, and he could not define what he was feeling. Reaching for her hand, he leaned over gently and kissed her forehead. When he pulled back, he noticed a slight change of expression in her eyes, as if they were trying to say, "Thank you." She did know who had saved her.

He stroked her hair slowly for a moment, then got up and walked away. As he stepped down from the ambulance, he turned back to look at her one last time. Her eyes were still watching him. Walking back to meet his father, Abe knew he would never see her again, and the thought made him even sadder.

"Dad, I'm going back to the car with Mom."

James nodded as his son walked past, and he continued giving his statement to the police.

Approaching the car, Abraham could see that his mom was in shock, with her hands still covering her mouth. Before he could reach her, she threw open the car door and raced toward him.

"Oh, my God, honey, are you OK? Are you hurt? Oh, God, did anyone survive that? It looked terrible from up here, just terrible!" Abraham could see that his mom was crying. Her eyes were red, and tears were streaking her face. She reached out her arms to hug him, but he did not have the energy to hug her back.

Beth understood the state he was in and continued holding him. When she released her arms, he finally began to talk.

"There were three people in the cab of that truck… a man, a woman, and a little girl. The cab started to catch fire, but they couldn't get out. I managed to bust out the passenger side window, enough for some of the smoke to clear. It wasn't enough, though. But it was enough for us to get the little girl through."

"So those two people were still in there when the truck exploded?" Beth asked, alarmed.

Abe looked at his mom. "Yeah."

"Oh, dear God!" she said, her hands covering her mouth again. "Honey, you did a brave thing by running down there with your father. Most of the other people here stayed in their cars and just watched. Do you know that? You and your dad were so brave. You did the best you could under the circumstances."

Without warning, Abe reached out and hugged his mother as tightly as he could.

"Oh, God, Mom!" he cried.

Beth held him. She had to allow her own tears to dry so that she could be strong for her son. They had all just glimpsed the hideous evil side of life.

With the weight of his emotions burdening him, James headed back to the car. He was having trouble processing what had just happened, so he couldn't imagine what Abe was going through. Although Beth had witnessed the explosion, she would not have seen much more than that, based on their car's distance from the chaos.

When Beth saw him coming, she told Abe to wait in the car so that she could speak to his father. As he got closer, she reached for him. He, too, fell into her arms, sobbing.

Beth looked up at the sky as they embraced. "Honey, what happened out there? I saw the explosion, but if you don't want to talk about it, I understand. Abe told me about some of it… how you all saved that little girl, but how awful that her parents didn't make it."

James remained silent for a couple of minutes until his sobs subsided. He wiped his eyes, then spoke.

"The couple was stuck inside because the impact on each of the doors broke the handles. It was a freaky thing as the truck and the car spun around against each other. Those poor people in the pickup couldn't get their seatbelts undone. Then, the gas tank had an apparent rupture. Fuel was everywhere. Once it caught fire, it spread quickly into the cab.

"Abe and another man got the girl out, but unfortunately, they couldn't save the man and the woman. Beth, I cannot describe what that scene was like. I won't be able to get it out of my mind for the rest of my life," he said.

Beth looked back in the direction of the carnage. She could see the fire still smoldering while the firemen milled about. She imagined they were pulling corpses from the wreckage. The thought forced her to look away.

"Who was in the other car?" she asked.

James shook his head. "I have no idea who that was or if they're still alive. I need to get out of here right now. I never want to travel down this highway again."

Beth put her arm in his and led him back to the car.

Before they got in, James took her in his arms one more time. He looked into her eyes. "I love you so much, Beth. You have no idea. Please, don't ever forget that? Promise me."

"Yes, baby. I promise. And I love you with all my heart, too. And don't you ever forget that."

When he settled back into the car, James turned around to Abe in the back seat, who was staring out the window.

"Abe, that was a very brave thing you did back there, knocking that window out. At least you got the girl out."

Abe turned and looked at his dad. "But it wasn't enough," he said again.

James carefully backed the car up and got back on the highway. From the rear-view mirror, he could still see the wreckage behind them.

Suddenly, Beth jumped as if she had been electrocuted.

"Did you feel that?" she asked, looking around the car and placing her hands over her chest. "God, it felt good!"

By the looks on their faces, James and Abe had felt it, too.

James looked over at Beth, his mouth wide. "What in the hell was that? What a rush!" he said. "You know, the last time you told me you had that experience was when your grandmother died. You said you felt it was her spirit, thanking you for taking care of her and her way of saying goodbye to you. Do you remember that?"

Beth closed her tear-filled eyes and laid her head back against the seat. "Yeah, I do remember that. James, do you think it was the mother of that little girl thanking you and Abe for trying to save her family… and for saving her little girl?"

"Dad?"

James stared straight ahead. He could see the expression on Abe's face from the rear-view mirror, knowing he was also awaiting a response. "Yeah. Yeah, I do. It was her thanking us—specifically you, Abe, for saving her daughter. We all felt it at once. I'm sure it was her."

Abe believed every word his father said.

There would be several more hours until they reached Bowling Green. The events of the day had left them physically and mentally exhausted. Although a long it was a long drive, the remainder of their trip was made in silence.

****

No matter how much time passed, that accident was never far from Abe's mind. He couldn't shake the feeling that he had not done enough to save those two lives.

After graduation, he decided to take some time off, as he wasn't sure if college was the right choice for him. He would take on a job for a year or so to think about what he really wanted to do with his life. He was glad that his parents weren't pushing him in any direction they wanted him to go in. He knew they respected his decisions and had confidence that he would find his way and eventually land on his feet. During this time, they allowed him to live at home to save up his money.

After long and careful consideration, Abe decided he wanted to become a firefighter. Somehow, this profession had found its way into his heart, and he could not imagine himself in any other career. He was passionate about the idea and wanted his parents to be just as excited as he was. He planned a family dinner at their favorite restaurant to spring the news on them.

"So, young man, what's the occasion? This is really nice of you," Beth said.

Although technically not of legal drinking age, Abe's dad managed to talk the waitress into getting him a beer. His parents had understood his need not to rush into college, but he wasn't sure that they would understand his wanting to become a firefighter. He needed this liquid courage to get him through what he was about to say.

Hesitating for a few moments, Abe took a big swig of the beer and then blurted it out. "Mom, Dad, I've thought about this long and hard. I love helping people. I love challenges, and I love danger. I feel if I confront danger, it helps me to be a braver and less fearful person. More importantly, if I help people through their dangerous moments, it makes my life more worthwhile."

He paused long enough to allow them to speak, but neither said a word.

"Well, with that said, I've decided to get a Fire Science degree from Vincennes University! I've already checked it out, and they offer a two-year associate degree. And I can get my paramedic certification, too. I'll always have a decent-paying job, but most importantly, and will love what I'll be doing," he said, taking another swig of beer, awaiting their responses.

James took a drink and spoke first.

"You can't get that car accident out of your mind, can you?" he asked.

"Can you?" Abe replied.

"Honey, you know what? We admire you for taking the initiative on this. Vincennes isn't that far away, maybe thirty minutes or so. When does the program start?" his mom asked.

"In a couple of months, on September 5th. I meet all the requirements. I've already applied, but I am still waiting to hear back. And you guys don't have to worry; I've already applied for student loans. For the entire two-year program, including the full EMT certification, the tuition is going to cost about $7,000. I think I can handle it on my own," he said.

James could feel Beth's stare on him, almost shouting, *"You better tell him we're going to help him."*

"Abe, listen, we like the idea, but the most important thing… it's what *you* want. This is huge, but it's a worthwhile undertaking. Your mother and I don't want you burdened with student loans when you get out of school. We know that the program will be intense, so we want you to focus all your energy in that direction… not worrying about how you're going to pay for college. We can handle the $7,000. In fact, we've been saving for your college tuition for some time now. And if you want, you can continue to live at home through all this. We know you'll have no problem getting a job after you graduate the program."

"Odds are I'll find something right here, close to home, when I graduate. But, Mom… Dad… are you sure about the $7,000? If you are, I'm going to pay you back. I promise," Abe said.

"Don't worry about that. Do you want to stay at home until you graduate? We can buy you a good used car," Beth said as she stared searchingly into his green eyes.

"That would be great! Guys, I appreciate all this. I've got the best parents in the world. I'll make you proud of me; I will," Abe said, getting up to hug them both.

"I want to toast the best parents in the world. May I make them proud of me, and may they get their $7,000 worth out of me!"

The rest of the evening was spent drinking and celebrating.

Beth was genuinely happy for her son, but deep down, she knew the dangers he would face. The one thought that gave her comfort was that if she were the one trapped in a burning house, it would be a man of her son's caliber who would be the first one to save her.

## Chapter Three:
## Fire House Water Witch 64

Abe walked into the first day of class for his Fire Sciences Technology degree. He sat down in the third row of the lecture hall and looked around at the other students, while running his fingers through his dark hair. He felt comfortable and was anxious to get started.

Living at home while commuting to school was working out well. When he wanted to hang out and party with his friends, he did so with no problem. True to their word, his parents took care of his tuition, and purchased him a car, as well. Their generosity took two huge burdens off his shoulders. Because James vowed that he would never drive a Volkswagen Beetle again, the car they purchased for Abe was an old Toyota sedan, though it was in excellent mechanical condition.

Abe could feel someone staring at him. When he looked over, a Hispanic man around his age sat a couple of seats away from him, sneaking quick glances at Abe as if he wanted to speak. Abe thought it odd but figured he must be shy. There were still a few minutes before class started, so Abe decided to speak first.

"Hi, my name is Abraham Gallagher, but you can call me Abe. Are you from around here?"

The man looked up, seemingly shocked.

"Well, not quite. I'm originally from Mexico City, but I came up for my firefighting degree. My name is Luis Vicario. It's good to meet you, Abe," Luis said, extending his hand.

"Wow, Mexico City. That's cool. So, I assume the rest of your family is down there?" Abe asked.

"My wife, Carla, is here with me. She works as a chef at the Hilton downtown," Luis replied.

"I assume she can fix good Mexican food. How about you?" Abe asked.

Luis sat a little straighter with a cocky look on his face. "Abe, my friend, you are talking to the enchilada king and the prince of the best homemade tacos north of the Rio Grande."

"Well, Luis, my friend, I hope to put your culinary skills to the test one day!"

"That would be my pleasure," Luis replied, nodding his head of dark hair.

Abe liked the way Luis shook his hand. Firm. He knew he'd made a new friend, and he also liked Luis's accent.

"OK, class, let's get started. Everyone find a seat," the professor began.

The ninety-minute class flew by. Abe and Luis caught up with each other after it was over.

"So, what do you think?" Luis asked Abe.

"I love it and just want to get the next couple of years over with and on to being a fireman," Abe said.

"Same here. Hey, whenever you feel the need for a study partner, I'm your guy," Luis said.

"You got it!"

"If you're not doing anything Saturday, how about coming over to our place for dinner so that I can back up what I said earlier about those enchiladas."

"That sounds great, and I can't wait to meet Carla."

****

The following Saturday, Abe headed to Luis's apartment, which wasn't far from where he lived. When he got to the door, one of the most beautiful women he'd ever seen opened it. It was Carla, Luis's wife. She was tall and slim and had brown curly hair cascading down her back. Her brown eyes twinkled in delight.

"Hi, I'm Abe. I'm in the EMT class with your husband."

"*Hola*, Abe. Luis said you were coming. It's so good to meet you. Please, come in," she said, opening the door wider for his entry.

"So, you must be Carla. *¿Como esta?*" Abe asked.

Carla raised her eyebrows in admiration. "My, I'm impressed. You know Spanish."

"Just a little bit from high school. I think Spanish and French are some of the most beautiful languages. *¿Estas de acuerdo?*" he said.

Carla's eyebrows rose higher. "*Yo ser impresionar con tu*," Carla replied.

"*Gracias*," said Abe.

"*Muy bien*," she said as her husband entered the room.

"So how the hell are ya, man?" Luis asked.

Abe and Carla looked at each other and burst into laughter. "Hey, what's so funny?" Luis asked.

"*Cielo*, our friend Abe and I were speaking politely in Spanish, and then you stormed in talking in drunk sailor English. It was just funny," Carla said.

Luis rolled his eyes. "Oh, well. I'll be more polite next time. Abe, would you like a beer before we eat?"

"I'd love one. What do you have?"

"It's a Mexican beer called Dos Equis. Have you heard of it?" Luis asked.

"No, I haven't, but I need a good counselor to get me off Miller Lite. It tastes like water now."

Luis held his beer up in the air. "Toast first. Here's to Friends Forever, Enemies Never!" he said.

*"¡El amigo para siempre, enemigo nunca!"* Abe replied.

Luis smiled and gave Abraham a huge hug. With a Spanish radio station playing, Abe turned his head as he heard a song he liked but didn't know the artist.

"Luis, who sings this song? I'm almost sure it came out in the early seventies."

Luis's ears perked up. "I think, but I could be wrong, that's 'Eres Tu' by a Spanish band called Mocedades. Came out in 1974, and I think it hit in the top ten on the charts here in the United States. It's cool, isn't it?"

"I really like that. I'll have to get the album." Abe said. "Guys, thanks for dinner. It sure as hell beat Taco Bell!"

****

Over the next couple of months, Luis and Abe became close friends, drinking beer and studying together. Their first semester flew by as they studied subjects like fire health and safety, building construction, fire behavior, and personal protection equipment, amongst others.

Christmas came and went, and then the spring semester started. Abe and Luis decided they would take as many classes together as they could. In addition to being great drinking buddies, they also became good study partners. Abe attributed getting an A in EMT class to studying with Luis.

One day, as they sat in their English Composition class, waiting for their professor to arrive, Abe turned to Luis.

"I still don't understand why we have to take this class."

Luis smiled. "*Señor*, I am the one that needs it more than you do," he said.

"Are you sure about that? Your English is better than most Americans," Abe said.

"Well, don't be mad if I'm the one who gets the A then, and you get the C." Luis chuckled.

"That's a good one. I'll remember that."

At that moment, a young man walked in and sat down next to Luis. "Dammit, I still don't understand why we have to take this class," he said.

Luis and Abe looked at each other and smiled.

"That's what my friend here just said!" Abe exclaimed.

"What's your name?" Luis asked.

"Dennis Hampton… yours?" the newcomer answered.

"I'm Luis Vicario, and this is my buddy, Abe Gallagher."

Dennis reached over and shook their hands. "I'm from Dawson. Where are you guys from?"

"I'm originally from Mexico City. My wife and I moved here a couple of years ago."

"I'm from right here. I live only thirty minutes away," Abe said.

"Don't tell me you're both English majors," Dennis said.

"No. We're both in the firefighting program," Abe said.

"No way! Cool! So am I! Is this your second semester?" Dennis asked.

Both nodded.

"Do you guys drink beer?"

In unison, they nodded again.

****

Now they were a threesome: Abe, Luis, and Dennis. Dennis was happy to learn that he had two more classes with his new buddies, and by their third semester, they had all the same classes. They had also taken on a fourth friend, Lamar Jackson, who joined their study group. When they weren't studying, they were drinking beer, and when they weren't drinking beer, they were hitting the books hard.

The final semester was ending, and graduation was right around the corner. Abe would soon have his associate degree in Fire Science. Once he graduated, the university would assist him in getting his certification.

Finally, the big day came. Beth and James had gotten to know Lamar, Dennis, and Luis quite well during the frequent study sessions Abe hosted in their home. As their son and his three friends walked across the stage, James and Beth beamed with pride.

"Abe, we're so proud of you," James said. "All of you guys did a great job getting through this program. I don't think I could have been as disciplined as you all were."

"Sure, you could have done it, Mr. Gallagher. Just quit your high-paying job, enroll for the fall semester, and show us. You'll see," Luis joked.

"Well, Luis, I'm certain I would not be as good a fireman as you four will be."

James and Beth planned a celebratory dinner after the ceremony. Dennis and Lamar's families had planned to join them, as well, though Luis had no family in the United States.

"Abe, do you know if Luis has any plans right now?" Beth asked.

"Well, all of his family is down in Mexico. It's just him and Carla here, and I don't believe they have any major plans. Why?" Abe asked.

"Would they like to join us? I noticed them just kind of standing over there, talking to that couple," Beth said.

Abe walked over and invited Luis and Carla to join them.

They enthusiastically accepted.

A few nights later, the friends met up for beer. Lamar suggested The Fat Angel, a local pub with a tiny dance floor, a ten-seat bar with a huge mirror behind it, and a few tables and chairs. To add to its charm, the floor was lined with green and black tile, and the ceiling with laminated album covers.

The food was good, but their specialty BBQ sandwich with homemade sauce was a must-have, along with their hand-cut french fries. The old-fashioned jukebox that stood in the corner belted out great toe-tapping tunes, and their beer selection was unrivaled.

"Lamar, how did you find this place?" Abe asked.

"Since the first time I heard that firefighters hang out here, I come in now and again," he replied, pointing to a table where they could all sit.

After the first two pitchers of Little Kings Creme Ale arrived at their table, Abe did the honors of the first pour, then got up and headed toward the jukebox.

"I hope you guys like The Doors," he said, sliding back into his seat. "I'd like to make a toast. Here's to the sorriest lot of bastards that I have ever had the good fortune to meet. May we never lose our friendship or our callings!"

"I second that," said Lamar.

"Hear, hear," said Dennis.

"*Gracias*, my good friends," Luis added.

"I would love to see an extremely sexy woman slow dancing alone on that floor right about now," Abe said.

"I can't disagree with you," Lamar replied.

"Luis, remind me again how you and Carla met; maybe we can get some pointers," Dennis asked.

"We met in high school down in Mexico. I couldn't take my eyes off her the first time I saw her. And, if you can believe this, I get along well with her folks. They are proud to have a firefighter in the family."

Abe raised his glass again and winked at Dennis.

"What first attracted you to her?" Lamar asked.

"I have to be honest. It was her ass. One look, and I was hypnotized. That ass was so intellectually and celestially complex I didn't understand it at first. I was confused and frightened. It was like… a UFO; all I could do was stare in fear and wonder. Then, as I became more familiar with it and less fearful, I simply treated it like a Sony PlayStation."

The table roared with laughter, almost falling off their seats. Luis sat stoic, wondering what he had said that was so funny.

"I concur with Luis," Abe interrupted. "We should all be so lucky to have a woman like Carla. And Luis, my friend, that was the best description of an ass that I had ever heard in my entire life. So, thank you!"

"Do you guys want kids?" Lamar asked through his chuckle.

"*Sí*, we want two," Luis replied.

"Hey, we're just glad you're staying here in America," Dennis said.

"It's a great opportunity to send money back to our families. They need our support."

"Well, boys, I propose another toast. Here's to Luis staying with us here in America and helping his loved ones out at the same time," Abe said.

"Lamar and Dennis, what are your plans now that we've graduated?" Abe asked.

"I'll probably just stick close to home. I'm going to visit a few firehouses to see if they might have any openings," Lamar said.

"Same here. I like it here… and it's close to family. I need to find a job soon so that I can start paying off my student loans," Dennis said.

"Hey, listen," he continued, "do you see those guys over there who just walked in? I think they're firemen. As they walked by, I heard them talking about some sort of run they went on."

All ears at the table perked up as they eavesdropped on the guys who had walked in and sat down across from them, and from what they could make out, indeed, the three of them were firemen.

Abe got up and walked over to introduce himself.

"Hi, my name's Abe Gallagher. My buddies and I just graduated with degrees in Fire Science from Vincennes. Are you guys, by chance, firemen?"

"You're kidding! Yes, we are firemen! Get the hell over here! We'll put a couple of tables together," one of them said, waving for Abe's friends to come over and join them.

Two of the men got up and moved an empty table next to theirs while Abe stood, waiting for his friends.

"My name's John Winston, like the cigarette. This is Bob Watson. And the funny-looking guy to my right is Wayne Robertson. We all work at Water Witch 64 firehouse here on the west side," he said.

"This guy to my right is Luis Vicario. This is Dennis Hampton, and that's Lamar Jackson," Abe said, pointing to each of his friends.

"Hey, bring us a few more pitchers," John said to the waitress walking by. "What are you guys drinking?"

"Little Kings on draft," Dennis replied.

"Little Kings it is," John said.

"So, you guys are fresh out of school. Are you all from around here? Any idea where you want to go?" Bob asked the group.

"Yeah, we just graduated a couple of days ago," Luis said.

"We're from the area, except for Luis. He's from Mexico City," Lamar responded.

"Well, have you got a lot to look forward to? What are your plans?" Bob asked.

"We're open to almost anything," Dennis said, speaking for the group. "We're going to visit the different firehouses and see if there are any openings."

"Listen, why don't you check our firehouse out? We have two openings already, and another couple of guys are retiring at the end of this month… and, well, there are four of you. Your timing couldn't be more perfect," Bob said.

The men sat and talked for hours as they kept the waitress busy with beer refills.

Abe excused himself to go to the bathroom, with Dennis right behind him. When they got back to the table, Lamar and Luis were in deep conversation about the firehouse positions.

"So, who do we talk to over there?" Abe asked.

"Just give us your names and phone numbers, and we'll tell Chief Randy Callahan about you. We'll put in a good word for you guys, don't worry. You don't want to go in there tomorrow because you'll be hungover. Just come by the station Friday and pick up applications," Bob said.

"What kind of good word will you put in?" Lamar asked with a grin.

"That you drink Little Kings Cream Ale," Bob said with a hearty laugh.

The party of seven broke up after 1 a.m. Bob and his friends were adamant that they take care of the check.

"Now, don't go dicking around and forget to swing by the station and pick up applications," Wayne said.

"Oh, don't worry. We won't," Abe said as they all headed out the door.

****

As predicted, the next morning, Abe woke up with a tremendous hangover. He had forgotten to take his customary five aspirin before he went to bed on the nights he drank. He didn't make it home until almost 2 a.m., and it was now nearly 10 a.m. He rolled over, trying to recall the details of the last evening, but with his head banging as hard as it was, it was almost impossible.

When he finally pushed himself from the bed, he walked into the kitchen to find a note from his mom on the counter.

*Honey,*

*There's leftover meatloaf and green beans in the fridge. I figured you would need lunch instead of breakfast. Dad and I are going out after work, so we won't see you till later tonight.*

*Love you, Mom*

Abe put the note down and dug through the refrigerator for the food. As he sat at the table, slowly eating, he started to make plans to get down to Water Witch 64 and get the application. Then, he remembered—it was only Tuesday, and the guys had suggested they come on Friday. Thankful for the extra time he would get to rest, he returned to bed to sleep away the remainder of his hangover.

When Friday rolled in, Abe was good as new. Excited about the possibility of a new job as a fireman, he sprang from his bed to get ready. As he stepped out of the shower, the phone rang. It was Lamar.

Lamar's voice came through the phone. "Hey, man, are you OK? I just walked out of the fire station with a blank application."

"I'm great. Got over that hangover the next day—and you're there already? Have you talked to Luis or Dennis?"

"Luis has already been here and left. I'm going to call Dennis right now. And, yes, I'm just leaving. I talked with the Fire Chief Callahan. I told him that we'd run into three of his men the other night and that they'd told us about the openings. The chief's pretty nice. Those guys were telling the truth.

"There are two positions open now and two more opening at the end of the month, and they're looking for good candidates to fill them. One of the guys had already told him about us. Listen, man, this thing just might happen. And I also told him you and Dennis were getting your asses down here right away."

"*Uhhhh*, OK, Lamar. Thanks a lot, man. I owe you one. I am on my way."

"Good! Talk later! Good luck. I'm calling Dennis now," Lamar said.

Abe ended the call, finished dressing, and headed to the station. It was only a thirty-minute drive. He pulled into the lot and looked at himself in the mirror. For some reason his eyes were really red that morning. *Thank God this isn't an interview,* he thought. He walked in and looked around—not knowing which direction to go.

"Can I help you?" an imposing man asked.

"Yes, sir! I was wondering where I could pick up an application."

"What's your name, son?"

"Abe Gallagher, sir. A few of your guys suggested my friends and I come down here today to look into some positions you have open."

The man held out his hand. "Hello, I'm Chief Callahan. Why don't you follow me to my office?"

Abe obliged, hoping this wouldn't turn into an interview. When they reached the office, Chief Callahan sat down and lit up a cigar.

"Have a seat, man. How are you doing? So, you were one of the guys who ran into my men at The Fat Angel a few nights ago, weren't you?" he asked.

"Yes, sir, I am."

"You think you could help carry a three-inch fifty-foot hose as fast as you could into a burning house?" the Chief asked, staring Abe dead in the eyes.

"*Uhhhh…* yes, sir, I could, but the only real way to prove that to you is for you to give me the opportunity by giving me a job."

Callahan smiled at Abe's response, sat back, and took a puff of his cigar. He had already made up his mind that he was going to bring Abe on board.

"Bob said you guys tied a good one on Monday night. They were impressed with how you and your friends presented yourselves and the knowledge you had from your education at Vincennes.

"Most of all, they were impressed by your passion. He said you four seemed to click well together, and they liked you… said they had a great time. One of the main criteria for success here is teamwork. That is at the top of the list for me. Anyway, I didn't mean for this to turn into an interview, so here's an application. When you get it filled out, call me, and we'll get you in for a formal interview. I think your buddies, Lamar and Luis, were here earlier, and we had this same conversation. But I haven't seen the other one yet. There are four of you, right?" the chief asked.

"Yes, sir, and I believe he's coming by today for sure. You'll like him, sir."

"Well, if he's anything like the rest of you, I'm sure I will. Abe, as I said, call me when the application's complete, and we'll talk more."

"Yes, sir, I'll be calling you tomorrow. And thanks so much!" Abe said excitedly, reaching for the man's outstretched hand. He hoped he'd made a good impression.

As Abe drove back home, he thought back on the impromptu talk he'd had with Chief Callahan. He felt good about it and wanted to share that with Lamar, so he dialed him up as he pulled away from the station.

"How'd it go?" Lamar asked.

"I thought it went OK. I think those guys from the other night really liked us and that Chief Callahan listens to them. We just may have been in the right place at the right time," Abe replied.

"That's the feeling I got, too. We talked for a few minutes, and then he said to get the application back to him. I don't know, man, but I've got good vibes about this. Wouldn't it be a trip if he took all four of us at the same time?"

"That'd be great. Hey, let me call Luis and see what happened on his end. I plan on getting this application done tonight, then calling him back in the morning."

"Same here. We'll talk tomorrow. Good luck," Lamar said.

When Abe called Luis, he picked up on the first ring. "Hey, Abe, did you go?" Luis asked.

"Yeah, man, I am driving home now, and I just got off the phone with Lamar."

"What did he have to say?" Luis asked.

"Callahan told him the same thing he told me—get the application filled out, and when I return it, call him for an interview."

"That makes three of us, then. Those guys really did put in a good word for us," Luis said.

"And it's all thanks to Lamar that we were even there," Abe said. "So, let's cross our fingers and hope for the best."

"Sounds good. Talk to you later, man," Luis said.

When Abe walked into the house, his parents were chatting in the kitchen.

"Hey, where've you been?" Beth asked.

"Want something to drink?" James followed.

Confused by the onslaught of questions, Abe's eyebrows squinched as he slid into his chair.

"You're not going to believe this, but the other night, I met up with Dennis, Luis, and Lamar at The Fat Angel."

Beth and James nodded, awaiting the rest of the story.

"I'm getting the feeling this story goes way beyond having a couple of beers with the guys," James said.

"Well, Dad, yeah, it kinda does, but in a good way. While we were there, we ran into these firemen from Water Witch 64. We had a few beers together, and to make a long story short, now we all might have jobs at their station."

"What in the hell is Water Witch 64, and where is it?" Beth asked.

"All the firehouses have their little nicknames. It's a fireman thing. But it's that one up on 43rd Street. It's only about thirty minutes from here. We've passed it a million times," Abe said.

"Oh, yeah. I've seen it on my way to work," James said. "So, anyway, keep going."

"We overheard them talking, so we went over and introduced ourselves and told them that we had just graduated from Vincennes and were looking for openings in the area. There were three of them, and we hit it off beautifully. We talked shop for hours. They told us there were positions opening at their firehouse, and they'd put in a good word for us with their chief. Then they invited us to come by the station today to get applications, so that's where I'm coming from. As luck would have it, while I was there, I ran into their chief, and he invited me to his office for a little chat. That went better than

I expected, so once I completed and returned the application, he told me to give him a call, and he'll get me in for a formal interview… the same for Luis, Dennis, and Lamar. What are the odds, right?"

"About a million to one. It sounds like those guys were sizing you up there at the bar. You must have drunk your beer just the way they liked. What were you drinking, by the way?" James asked.

"Little Kings Creme Ale."

"We're really happy for you, honey, and it sounds like this might work out for all of you. We'd love for you to be close to home. Now, why don't you sit down, and I'll get some dinner ready," Beth said.

"Yes, son, sit down and have a before-dinner drink with your old dad," James said with a sly look.

Abe looked down at his dad's beer and rolled his eyes. Although several days had passed, he was not in the mood for a marathon session.

"Dad, how about we go out after I get the position?" He grinned.

James laughed heartily. "I'm teasing you, son. Why don't you go and crash for a bit? Dinner will be down here when you're ready."

Abe nodded and hugged Beth on his way upstairs.

Lying on his bed, he thought about the events of the past few days and how everything was coming together. For a moment, he wondered why he was getting so lucky, but he could hear his mom saying, *'Never look a gift horse in the mouth.'* So, he closed his eyes and let all the doubt float away.

****

Three days later, Abe got a call from the firehouse. "Hello," Abe answered.

"This is Chief Callahan at Water Witch 64. How are you doing?" he asked.

Abe looked up toward the ceiling and said a silent THANK YOU.

"I am doing well, thank you."

"I take it you're feeling a lot better now than you were a few days ago," Callahan said. "Those eyes of yours looked painful."

"Well, sir, yes, as a matter of fact, I am feeling fine," he replied.

"Listen, you don't need to call me sir; Chief works fine. Can you come in for an interview tomorrow afternoon?"

"Yes, Chief. What time?"

"Let's say 13:00. Just so you'll know, we'll be talking to your friends, too. See you tomorrow."

"Sounds good. See you then."

Abe hung up the phone and immediately called his parents, who were ecstatic. Then he called his buddies to see if they had gotten their phone calls yet.

Dennis's interview was at 9 a.m., Lamar's was at 11 a.m., and Luis's was scheduled for 14:30. Since Dennis would be interviewed first, he was to call the others immediately after to let them know what to expect.

At precisely 10:15 a.m., Abe's phone rang. It was Dennis. "Well, how did it go? What'd they ask you?" Abe asked.

"Well, first of all, I got the fucking job!" Dennis said.

"That's great, man! One down and three to go. I guess Lamar is there right now."

"Yeah, he was there early, waiting. I filled him in as best I could before he went in. I think he'll be OK, though."

"Now, fill me in," Abe said.

"When you sit in that chair in front of Callahan, sit up straight and alert. Look into his eyes with intensity when you answer his questions. They told me he likes that in a firefighter. And then he was asking questions like, *'Why do you want to become a firefighter? Can you handle the weird shift hours? Can you think on your feet in potentially deadly situations?'* Stuff like that. I don't think we have to BS our way through this. Just give him sincere, intelligent, hard-hitting answers, and I think you'll be OK. Remember, our new buddies have already put in that good word for us."

"Got it! Thanks, Dennis. I'm going to get ready now. Talk to you later."

Abe arrived at the station just as Lamar was walking out the door.

"How'd it go?" he asked.

"He told me on the spot that I had the job! It's beer time again tonight, my friend!" Lamar replied.

Abe gave his friend a congratulatory hug before walking into the station. He waited nervously until Chief Callahan came out of his office to get him.

"Abe Gallagher, how are you, young man?" the chief asked. Abe sat up straight, hands on the table, making eye contact. "Fine, sir, and you?" he replied.

"Good. It's been a slow day so far, thank God. Let's get down to business. If I hired you, what's the first thing you'd do when you got here at the start of your shift?"

"Chief, the first thing we do is check out all of the equipment and make sure it's functioning properly," he responded, giving the chief a steady gaze.

Callahan shook his head in admiration. "Good answer, man. I looked over your resume, and I liked it. You had some solid education in fire technologies at Vincennes.

"Let me tell you a bit about our firehouse. I know you already know quite a bit from talking to Bob Watson and John Winston, but I just want to go over a few things. We cover a mostly suburban area. Several neighborhoods and a few small businesses fall within our coverage area. We strive for our response time to be four minutes or less, but that doesn't always happen.

"We're about to be short four people right now due to retirement and transfers to other stations. We have one engine and no ladder truck. I have three firemen directly under me, plus two lieutenants. There are three more firefighters under each of the lieutenants. Some of them are engineers. The shift is twenty-four on and forty-eight off. Shift times are 7:00 to 7:00. New hires have a one-year probationary period. During that time, you're considered a probie—it's a bit of a boot camp. Let me ask you a question: why in the hell did you want to become a firefighter?"

"Chief, when I was still in high school, I was on vacation with my parents when we came across an accident that had just happened off the highway. One car was speeding and caused an accident with a pickup truck. There were three people trapped inside the truck: two adults and one child.

"I don't want to go into detail, but we managed to get the child out. Then, due to the intensity of the fire, we had to stand there and watch the other two people burn. That affected me deeply. I vowed I would never let something like that happen again if I could help, and I won't."

Callahan stared at Abe for a few seconds, then shook his head in admiration.

"Yeah, that shit is rough. Do you consider yourself disciplined?"

"Yes, I do, Chief. I really don't have any hobbies, just a strong desire to be a firefighter. I fully realize it's a one hundred percent commitment all the way around. When you possess that kind of dedication, the discipline comes easy."

"If the alarm went off right now, do you think you could flow right into it?"

The granite-like self-confidence exuding from Abe impressed Callahan.

"Hell, yes," Abe responded.

"How do you handle stress, and how would you deal with a stressful situation?"

Abe took a few seconds before he replied. He knew that it probably wasn't a good idea to tell him that he handled stress with a few beers, although it was an accepted unwritten code.

"Chief, the way I see it, when you love what you do and when your hobby and career are the same thing, there is no stress involved. There's only love of what you do."

Callahan sat back and nodded his agreement. "I've never heard it put quite that way, but it makes sense to me. Look, I'm done with this line of questioning. You're hired. Welcome to Water Witch 64. When can you start?"

"How about right now?" Abe replied anxiously.

Callahan laughed. "Let's do this. Go home and rest up, Gallagher. You'll need it. Come in tomorrow at 7 a.m., and we'll get the paperwork squared away. Then, we'll show you around the station. Bob and John will be here to do that. I'm interviewing one more of your buddies after you, anyway. Welcome aboard, Abe. We're proud to have you!" he said, extending his hand to shake Abe's.

"You don't know how glad I am to be here, Chief! I won't let you down!" Abe knew there would be no beers that evening.

"I know you won't."

When Abe walked out of the chief's office, Luis was waiting his turn in the lobby. He knew that Callahan was walking out the door behind him, so he gave Luis a little wink. Luis understood and returned a smile before heading into his interview. Luis was the last interviewee of their group, and when he was finished, the four of them would convene to compare notes of their individual interviews.

****

The next morning, at 6:45, Abe, Luis, Lamar, and Dennis arrived almost simultaneously at the firehouse. Callahan, John, and Bob were already there on their second pot of coffee. Callahan was supervising the shift change and was anxious to get his probies started.

"OK, boys, you're all here early, that's great. We have a lot to cover. Bob and John are more than capable of squaring you all away on the station. For right now, I'll go over all your employee paperwork with you regarding your insurance, our policy manual, etc. Then I'll turn you over to the guys," Callahan said.

After that part was out of the way, Callahan sent them on their way into boot camp.

"Gentlemen, welcome to Water Witch 64 and into the Fifth Circle of Hell!" Bob said.

Everyone chuckled.

"It's part of our dark humor here, gentlemen. I'm exaggerating a little, but not much. Let's start with the tour. The first year in any firehouse for new recruits is rough. I hope you guys can cook; if you can't, you're going to learn fast. We like to eat well around here, and the probies do a lot of the cooking for the rest of us. Luis, what's your specialty?" John asked.

"Well, I inherited my recipes and my cooking skills from my Mexican mother and grandmother. If you haven't had good homemade Mexican food, you will. It's not like that Taco Bell shit."

"That sounds great. We just might get you at the stove first. Lamar, what about you?" John asked.

"I'll make the best fried chicken you ever had," Lamar replied.

"Dennis?" Bob asked.

"Well, I'm good with chili dogs, tenderloins, and things like that. I can get my hands on the best damn coney sauce you've ever tasted. It's drugstore quality!" Dennis said.

"That works, too," Bob said before turning to Abe.

"How about you?"

"Well, believe it or not, I'm pretty good at desserts. I make a damn good coconut cream pie and pecan pie; I can make good meatloaf and mac and cheese, and I have a couple of good baked chicken recipes, too."

"Well, I can see that you guys are going to fit right in here," John said. "For today, we're bringing in pizzas for lunch so we can get through orientation."

After they were given a thorough tour of the firehouse from top to bottom, including the equipment room and even the engine of the firetruck, they were schooled on general housekeeping duties, as well.

After the initial training and after consulting with his lieutenant, Adam Carlson, Chief Callahan decided to keep the four of them together. It wasn't that the other firefighters at the house weren't good, but these four seemed to have a unique synergy. They never requested to stay together, but he could sense that they wanted to. It was the right decision for the firehouse and for them as well. Abe, Luis, Dennis, and Lamar were already acting like multi-year veterans right out of the starting gate.

****

The first nine months were hell, and since they'd had very little time for anything other than work and sleep, Dennis decided to arrange a boy's night out. Once again, they settled on The Fat Angel.

They looked upon their get-togethers as mental and spiritual healing ceremonies. In a strange way, it was almost like going to church, which was also hard for them to attend because of their crazy work schedules.

They all arrived late afternoon and got a table close to the jukebox. The Fat Angel had a good draft beer selection, and one of the specials that night was Foster's lager on tap. They went for it with a vengeance.

"Well, gentlemen, this is fucking long overdue. Here's to landing positions at El Wild, Wild West, and nine months of hell so far. But I wouldn't trade it for the world!" Lamar said, raising his glass to toast.

"Damn, that beer is cold!" Abe said.

"I know; it makes all the difference. I haven't had a beer so far this year. God, I forgot how good it is," Dennis added.

"How good is the beer, Dennis?" Abe asked with a grin.

"Heavenly!" he replied.

"I've never heard beer described as heavenly. They ought to make a TV commercial out of that. Here, I've got it. You see Dennis sitting in a church at the end of the service, in the very back pew, of course. You hear the preacher wrap up his sermon as the church organ plays ever so piously," Lamar said, giving his friends a laugh.

"Then, Dennis turns around to the camera with this angelic, virtuous look on his face, gently smiles and says, *'Foster's lager, easy-drinking, full-bodied, great taste, and the only beer that doesn't leave you with a hangover during church services on Sunday mornings.'*"

Abe spit up his beer.

As the four friends roared with laughter while holding their stomachs, Dennis gave them the finger.

"Then, the pastor comes up to him and says, '*And don't ever wear that damn Packers hat during service again!*'" Luis chimed in.

Laughing even harder, Abe fell back in his chair. It took them all several minutes to regain their composure. Once they did, a more tempered conversation began about the firehouse.

"Jesus, don't bring up that shit again. Anyway, how do you think things are going so far? We haven't had a chance to talk about anything outside of the firehouse. It's been so goddamn nuts," Abe said.

"Well, I like everyone at the house. Callahan makes sure it's got a family atmosphere to it. Hell, everyone even helps when there's a personal issue, too. That blew me away. It's like a club," Luis said.

"Yeah, it is. And it doesn't matter what color you are. The place and the culture of it are color blind," Lamar added.

"And the food. I've never eaten so well in my entire life. They all cook their own little specialty, and it comes out great," Luis said.

"Luis, how is Carla taking it? I mean, with you working crazy hours and all?" Abe asked.

"She's pretty cool about it. She's really supportive."

"Carla's a cool chick, Luis. You got lucky with that one," Abe said, raising his glass.

*"Gracias!"*

"Well, guys, we all know whenever we decide to get serious with someone, they'll need to be OK with this life—the long hours and shit, and sometimes we bring that shit home. Let's face it, our job is our priority," Dennis said.

They all nodded in agreement.

"Well, we're off fucking probation in a few months, like that matters," Luis said.

"I think I'm going to get my certification to be an engineer. I'd like to do that," Dennis announced.

"You'd make a good one, Dennis. You would," Lamar added.

"I'll talk to Callahan at some point about it," Dennis said. "There's talk about the city putting a new firehouse on the north side."

"The past nine months have flown by. I have no clue where it went. I was surprised Callahan kept us together on the same shift. And he did that while we were still in our first training. I like Callahan, and I think he likes us. He's anal but fair if you just do your shit," Luis said.

"I had that conversation with him right after he did it. He flat-out told me he was watching our training and how we handled it together. Then, he was convinced after the first few runs. Although they weren't really serious runs, he was impressed by the way we worked together. So, he went for it. That was it. He told me it was a good move for the firehouse keeping us together, which blew me away," Abe said.

"Shit, he said that?" Dennis asked.

"Yep, sure did."

"I never knew that. What a vote of confidence. But I must say, we are pretty good together," Luis remarked.

"I have to agree; it was a good move. But, boys, we've been lucky so far. We've never been tested yet in a big-ass house fire with potential casualties. I mean, we've been on pussy runs. We've had garage fires, car fires, brush-type fires, minor house fires… shit like that. But nothing on a massive scale that involved severe injury or death," Abe said.

"Not yet, but our time is coming, and when it does, we'll be the first fucking engine on the scene," Lamar asserted.

Abe raised his glass in acknowledgment. "Damn fuckin' tootin' we will be. It'll go down just like that, and maybe sooner than we think. Even Callahan said the firehouse is overdue."

"Well, if it goes down that way, I know we can handle it," Dennis stated.

"Oh, it will go down. The question is when and where," Abe replied.

"Well, God forbid, but when that tragic situation arises, we'll be the first ones to the rescue," Lamar said.

# Chapter Four:
# The Fire

Shelly finished her errands around 1 p.m. and headed home. Because there were so many weirdos in the world, she didn't like leaving Mikalya alone for very long. Who knew when the wrong person would somehow know she *was* alone and take advantage of the situation? She didn't even like thinking about that. Although Mikalya was a confident twenty-year-old, she was still a bit naïve and trusting. Unable to shake the thought, just when she decided to phone home, her phone rang. It was Mikalya.

"Mom, I am so sorry! I am so sorry! Oh, God, I'm sorry!" Mikalya screamed.

Shelly was completely caught off guard by the urgency in her daughter's voice. She had just chatted with her an hour earlier, and she was fine.

"What the hell is going on?" Shelly asked firmly.

"Oh, God, I don't know what happened! But there's a fire downstairs, and I think it's blocking the back door! I just called 9-1-1! I can see smoke at the edge of the stairs! I'm afraid to go down!" she screamed into the phone.

Shelly started to speak to try to calm her down, but Mikalya wasn't listening. The panic in her voice was evident.

****

Holding the phone, Mikalya could hear her mom's voice, but she couldn't focus on what she was saying. Her mind was racing. She knew she had to find a way to get out of the house. She couldn't wait for the fire engine to arrive, as the fire would surely soon find its way up the stairs. Jumping from the window was not an option, as she might not survive the fall. As she peered down the stairs, she could see the smoke intensifying as it traveled closer to the stairs.

****

Shaking and just a few minutes from home, Shelly sped down the road. Although Mikalya had said she'd called 9-1-1, Shelly wanted to call again, so when she noticed a phone booth along the roadside, she pulled over. She couldn't risk hanging up Mikalya's call.

"9-1-1, may I help you?"

"There's a fire at 1411 West Crestbaum Street, and my daughter is trapped on the second floor! I just talked to her, and I don't think she can get out!" Shelly said frantically.

"Yes, ma'am, we're getting calls in on it right now. You are the third caller, and we can confirm there is a fire engine en route. We are requesting more as well. What is your name, ma'am?" the woman asked.

"My name is Shelly Arabella! That is my home, and that is my daughter inside! There are no firemen there yet?"

"Ma'am, they're on the way and should be there shortly. They are making every effort to get there as fast as they can. Your daughter has already called and let us know what area of the house she is in," the woman said.

Without saying goodbye, Shelly hung up the phone and jumped back into her car. She had only a few more blocks to go. Once she got to her house, she pulled right up into the yard, put her car in park, and without even turning off the engine, she leaped out of the car, leaving her phone behind. She had forgotten that Mikalya was still on the phone.

Huge, red flames were visible from all sides of the house. The fire was coming from both the front and the back doors. Shelly knew that escaping from the second floor was not an option unless Mikalya jumped, which could easily kill her. Her panic began to spread just as quickly as the fire was spreading. As she circled the outside parameters of the house, she couldn't imagine that Mikalya was safe anywhere, but one thing was for certain: *if* Mikalya was able to escape, she would have by now.

*She's trapped!* Shelly shuddered at the thought, shoving it from her mind.

Mikalya could see her mom from the upstairs window. She opened it and yelled down.

"Mom, I'm up here! It's hard to get out. I think the bottom of the stairs is on fire!" she screamed.

A strong electric shock shot through Shelly's body as all sense of logic and rationale left her. She wasn't just going to stand by and do nothing while her daughter was inside that house.

****

Mikalya knew that she had to move quickly and carefully to make her way downstairs to assess the quickest and safest way out.

As she began her descent, she heard a loud pop.

*"What was that?"* she muttered aloud as her panic grew, and she began racing down the stairs. As she ran, she tripped and fell down the last few steps, rolling into the stairway banister and banging her head. Dazed, she struggled to get up but couldn't; the fall had broken her leg. Mikalya could feel the heat on her face as things started to blur. It wasn't long before she passed out.

****

Shelly raced around the outside of the house. Her neighbors rushed over to help.

"Shelly, we've already called 9-1-1! Help is on the way," her neighbor, JoAnn, said.

"Mikalya is up there! I have to do something! I can't just stand here and watch this!" Shelly screamed.

"The firemen will be here soon!" another neighbor, Don, assured her.

"Bullshit! They're not coming fast enough!" Shelly yelled. "They should have been here by now!"

Ignoring her own welfare, Shelly's maternal instinct kicked into high gear, and she took off at a full sprint toward the back door. It was locked. With shaking hands, she managed to get the key into the lock.

Charging into the house and through the back laundry room, she rushed into the smoke-filled kitchen to get to the stairway but couldn't find it.

"Mikalya, it's Mom! I am coming for you, honey!" she shouted.

There was no response.

She continued blindly until she hit a wall, falling backward. Then she felt the pain. When she looked down, she realized her left arm was on fire and began flailing it about, but the fire was getting larger and spreading fast. Panicking, she ran in the direction she had come from, trying to get out to extinguish the fire. Back outside, Shelly had barely swiped away the flames when she turned and ran back toward the door.

This time, she didn't make it quite as far when she realized she had been unsuccessful in putting it out. Her arm was still on fire, causing her to stop and cry out loudly due to the increasing pain.

Two of the neighbors grabbed her and pulled her down to the ground, throwing dirt on the burning arm. But even after the fire had been extinguished, Shelly still wouldn't sit still.

"I have to go back in there!" she shouted.

"You can't! You can't! It's too damn dangerous in there now. And those burns on your body are serious! Let's hang on! I hear sirens now!" Don said.

But Shelly wasn't listening. "It's not your fucking daughter!" she yelled, jumping up and attempting another run for the door. It took two neighbors and a policeman to restrain her. With serious burns on her arm and upper chest area and what felt like a sprained ankle, Shelly was physically and emotionally exhausted. The neighbors were still restraining her, and her body was in intense pain. All she could do was wail loudly.

"Oh, dear God, no! Don't let this happen to my daughter! Please, please, dear God, no! Please, where is your love?" she screamed, looking up to the sky.

Her neighbors gathered around her and started praying out loud. Some of them held hands as they prayed.

She continued crying out. "Dear God, if you're too busy, can you please just send a Guardian Angel down to save my daughter? Please. Oh, please," she prayed. One would arrive soon.

****

That morning, Abe barely arrived on time for the opening shift, with a nasty hangover. He and Lamar had gone out for beers the night before, not intending to have more than one. They had invited Luis and Dennis, but both had other commitments.

They ran into each other in the parking lot at 6:59, with Abe almost sideswiping Lamar.

Lamar got out of his car first and walked over to Abe, who was sitting with his face buried into the steering wheel.

"Shit, man, can't you drive? You damn near hit me," Lamar laughed.

Abe lifted his head from the steering wheel and gave Lamar the finger before slowly opening his car door and lumbering out.

“You’re lucky you didn’t get picked up last night. I followed you for at least a couple of blocks, per your request, before I called off the mission. I thought I’d better save myself first,” Abe said.

“I’m glad I took those five aspirin before I went to bed, or I’d be ten times worse,” Lamar retorted.

The clock read 7 a.m. on the dot when they walked into the station. Both of their eyes were so bloodshot that they looked like they were stoned.

Dennis stood inside the front door as they walked in.

“Oh, damn, here come the Budweiser twins. What fucking time did the two of you get home?” he cackled. He’d hung out with them enough to know that they had tied one on.

Abe and Lamar walked right past Dennis without uttering a word. That was Dennis’s green light to torment them more.

Luis just stood there smiling, silently egging Dennis on.

“Let’s see; let me give a synopsis of your evening. Stop me if I’m wrong. You both decided to go for one beer, just one. Once at your barstool, you scoped the place out for any signs of a decent catch. Of course, on a Monday night, there was none. So, the first beer went down pretty well, unfortunately.

“Then you looked at each other and asked if you had time for one more. And, of course, you did. The waitress came back around again and asked if you were ready for a third, which you agreed to. When the third beer was gone, you both thought, 'Why stop now?' Right?

"Then, you got into a deep discussion about work here. You spent three to four hours developing and implementing the bar sound improvements and how those said improvements would be implemented if only we had the money. That conversation alone justified the bar tab. Now, am I on the right track here?" Dennis quipped.

"You know, Dennis, after our seventh beer, Abe and I were discussing you, and we decided the one thing we want to do for you is set you up with a nice-looking drag queen. We know you like redheads, right?" Lamar asked.

"Sorry, but I don't go out with my coworker's ex-girlfriends," Dennis shot back.

Abe shook his head and headed toward the restroom, with Dennis, Lamar, and Luis right behind him. He knew that Dennis was just jealous because he couldn't go out with them.

"Hey, man, wait a minute!" Abe said, looking right at Dennis. "The sign says *MEN* on that door. That means you can't go in."

Lamar and Luis laughed, ribbing each other. Dennis gave Abe the finger.

"OK, OK, enough everybody. Please shut up until the Aleve kicks in. I haven't even had a shit yet, and I have to listen to all this. Spare me, please," Abe said, staring at his eyes in the mirror. It amazed him how they got every time he was hung over. Abe went into the stall and slammed the door shut, letting the guys know he didn't want to be bothered. When he heard the door close behind them, he smiled, welcoming the peace and quiet.

"I'm going to put some more coffee on," Dennis said, stopping to put on some Richard Marx. He liked Richard Marx, but there was one song he liked in particular… "Right Here Waiting." He knew the other guys liked it, too. That type of music had a calming effect on the tense atmosphere of the firehouse. You had no idea what was going to happen from one second to the next. One minute, you'd be sitting, relaxing on the toilet. Then, in the next instant, the alarm would go off, and there was no way you could sit there and finish in any kind of dignified manner.

"Anyone up for some cards?" Dennis asked. Most all the other guys in the firehouse were out in the engine rooms, cleaning equipment. When they played cards, it was always just a simple version of Draw Poker. They couldn't get too intricate or complicated because you could lose it all at a moment's notice.

"What the hell? I need to try to get back the twenty bucks I lost from you last week," Luis said.

"Count me in, but let's wait for Abe. Maybe I ought to go back in the head and pound on the stall door. That would wake him up," Lamar said.

"Yeah, you do that. He'll probably throw a wad of shit at you like the baboons do at the zoo sometimes," Dennis said. "Did you ever see that one on TV? I can't remember what zoo it was at, but this girl was making fun of one baboon in a cage. It tried to walk away and ignore her, but she followed it along the outside cage line and kept it up. And her friends were right there, laughing at it all.

"I guess that fucking baboon finally got fed up. It made some loud, weird noise, bent over, scooped up a pile of shit off the ground, and flung it through the bars right at her. Hit her right square in the damn face. It happened so fast; if I would have blinked, I would have missed it. That was the funniest damn thing I ever saw in my life. I had no idea those animals could move that quickly. The way it turned around and flung that shit as precisely as it did would put the best major league pitcher to shame. I'm serious!

"Anyway, they show the girl crying with crap all over her face, and her friends were laughing so hard they were falling on the ground. And it looked like the baboons were laughing their asses off, too. They were all running around screaming and jumping up and down. Was the craziest thing I ever saw."

"That's funny," Luis replied as Abe exited the restroom.

"What was so damn funny? You fools were making so much noise out here that I couldn't concentrate. You were talking about baboons or something? Right?"

"Kinda," said Dennis.

"So, anyway, I'll get the table set up for a few rounds. Luis needs to get his money back from last week," Lamar said.

"I can't keep up with you three in poker. I'm not that good at it, and I'm not a betting man," Luis said.

"Luis, OK, listen… this time, we'll take the time and teach you how to play and what to look for. I felt bad about your twenty bucks last week. I know I fleeced you, but man, you were so easy, I couldn't help it," Dennis said.

"Luis, you sit next to me, and I'll guide you against Abe and Lamar. I'll have you kicking their asses in no time. You'll be the Latino poker king, and they won't want to play with you anymore," Dennis continued.

"You're full of shit," Luis laughed. "OK, it's a deal, but if I don't feel comfortable playing with you poker hyenas anymore after this, that's it."

Dennis liked the card games, and he enjoyed playing them with Luis, who was a riot when he got frustrated. Sometimes, he would bitch in Spanish, and they loved it. But this time, he was sincere. If Luis continued to get frustrated at them screwing him over in poker, then he'd stop playing.

"OK, I'll deal the first round. Luis, I am going to sit next to you and read your cards. Then, I'll whisper in your ear what to do. How does that sound?" Dennis offered.

"Sounds good, man. Let's go for it."

The guys played a few hands and joked all the way through them.

"OK, assholes, I really need to get this round dealt," Abe said. He had not finished dealing with that fourth round of cards when the first alarm went off.

They all looked up at each other with that *"Oh, shit,"* look on their faces.

Out of nowhere, shockwaves shot through Abe's body. A voice inside his head was trying to tell him something, but his thoughts were swirling. Something wasn't right. The alarm sounded different this time. As he rose from his chair, he discreetly made the sign of the cross. It was the last thing he wanted his fellow firefighters to see him do. They'd never let him live it down.

*Dammit, right when I have this shit hangover. Oh, it's probably the same old crap,* he thought.

"Here we go again. Let's place our bets on a trash can fire or some idiot spraying his hose on an out-of-control leaf pile," Lamar said.

As they hurried about, they continued their loud diatribes.

"What timing? I was up quite a bit, for God's sake. I was going to wipe yo' asses out! I was da poka man god! I was Mista stud poka! I was stickin' it to ya! I was bending y'all over one by one! Pullin' ya panties down! Gettin' ready to lay on the Phisohex! But it wasn't meant to be this time, fellas," Luis boasted, scooping up his winnings and shoving the cash into his pocket.

Dennis, Lamar, and Abe just looked up toward the heavens and laughed.

"You mean the hexachlorophene," Abe said.

"Yeah, the hexachlorophene. Then top it off with a generous glob of Vaseline right up the chute," Luis replied.

"You mean the *petroleum jelly*, right up the chute," Abe said. Luis flashed a big grin and nodded.

"One, two, three!" Lamar prompted.

As if rehearsed, Dennis, Abe, and Lamar gave Luis the finger in unison.

The frolicking was interrupted when the 9-1-1 dispatches started broadcasting the nature of the fire: a large house fire.

"OK, you assholes, I'm driving, and I'll let the three of you put out the fire. Luis... Abe and Lamar might need help steadying the hose, so don't let them handle it at the same time," Dennis quipped.

Luis laughed. "I'm way ahead of you on that!"

The crew quickly moved into the equipment room and began suiting up. Up until that moment, their calls had only dealt with relatively minor situations like abandoned car fires and a trash barrel fire that some kids lit up for a prank. The largest fire they had faced thus far was a two-car detached garage fire. They hadn't yet faced anything involving death or injuries of any sort. This time, however, would be different. They had barely gotten the engine started when yet another dispatch call came in.

Theirs would not be the only fire department involved but would be the first on the scene, as this fire was in their immediate coverage area. The firehouse radio was blaring brief descriptions of the nature of the fire from callers. None of them sounded good.

"Shit, dispatch just said that someone is fucking trapped inside! This ain't no garage fire!" Lamar yelled.

"OK, girls, let's get a fucking move on! We've got a young woman trapped inside of a burning house. The phoned-in location was the second floor, but at this point, she could be anywhere. Fucking move it! Four minutes!!" Abraham screamed.

That was the first time anyone heard Abe scream like that.

Within a few minutes, Dennis was steering the engine out onto the street, siren blaring.

"Does anyone know for sure if she's still in there?" Lamar asked.

"We must assume she is. No reports that she made it out," Abe said.

Luis began silently praying the Rosary.

"When did that first call come in again?" Lamar asked.

"Shit, I'm not sure," Abe replied, "but in terms of a potentially rapidly spreading house fire, it's like eons ago."

Their ETA would be four minutes. Since their firehouse didn't have a ladder, it would be coming from another station. They all prayed silently that it would be there waiting for them.

As they approached the area, they could see a huge plume of smoke blanketing the sky, spreading far beyond the impacted area.

It was only the four of them who manned their engine. Lamar was the designated Supply Hose Operator, Dennis was the driver and engineer, Luis operated the main hose, and Abe served as lieutenant, directing the operation and serving as the radio communicator.

There were reports of police already on the scene, but there was only so much they could do. Abe hoped that there wouldn't be much traffic in their way. That was always a concern on any run, but now it was critical.

They sped up the street to the house. Before Dennis could come to a full stop, Abe jumped off the truck, rushing to get as close as he could to the horrific carnage. Although it would take more than just their engine to fight the fire, they were the first to arrive at the scene.

Abe wasn't prepared for what lay before him. At a time when it was critical that they move swiftly, all he could do was just stare for a moment—unable to move. It felt as if everything, including the fire, was moving in slow motion. He couldn't put his finger on it, but he knew that this moment would be different from all others.

Suddenly, he was jolted from his trance by a voice inside of him. *Move!* He knew that any decisions he made would impact the life of the girl inside the house; whether she lived or died depended on them. Then, a voice came over the radio in his hand. The ladder they needed was on an engine that had just been involved in an accident. *What else could go wrong?* he wondered.

His team members were moving like lightning around him.

Luis bumped him as if to tell him to move it.

Dennis pulled the engine as close as he could to the house and began the prep work. Lamar had already located the fire hydrant as Luis moved in to hook up a high-powered hose.

Several people rushed toward Abraham, all yelling that there was a girl upstairs in the house who could not get out, and her mother was on the other side of the house, being held down by neighbors so she wouldn't try to run into the house again. They told him that was where the main entrance was and led him in that direction.

Once Abe and his team arrived at the front entrance, Abe radioed in, requesting medical assistance as fast as possible for the girl's mother. Although she was hurt, she screamed at them loudly, in a voice that didn't sound human.

"Oh, God, I hope you aren't too late. My baby's still in there. Oh, Jesus... You have to save her! That's my little girl! They won't let me go back in! These motherfuckers won't let me go! They won't let me go! That's my baby! She's all I've got! And I'm all she's got! I mean, you have to go in and get her, or she's going to burn up in there! My baby's going to burn up in there! Do you hear me? Save her! God, please save her?" she cried hysterically.

"Ma'am, please try to calm down and give me your best guess of where you think your daughter is in there. Think back to where she was when you last spoke to her," Abe said firmly.

The people restraining Shelly released their hold on her. With Abe's assistance, she hobbled up from the ground and grabbed his arm tightly. The look of sheer terror in her eyes unnerved him.

Shelly calmed herself so that she could instruct him clearly.

"Go in through that door right there," she said, pointing. "It's still open. *Uh, uh,* go straight through the first room, which is the kitchen, then around to the right is the dining area. Then, past that is the bottom of the stairs that goes up to the bedrooms. Go up the stairs first, and my baby's bedroom is the first door on the left. But I don't know if she's still there." Her sobs growing loud again.

"Tell me where the location of that bedroom window is from outside here!" Abe screamed above the chaos.

Shelly looked around to her left and pointed toward the second-story window.

"*Uh,* it's there. Do you see?" she asked, pointing up and to the right.

"Are you sure about that, ma'am?"

"God, yes, I'm sure!" she yelled.

"What is her name? Your daughter… what is her name?" Abe asked.

"Mikalya. My beautiful Crystal Mikalya," Shelly's voice trailed off as her shoulders slumped over.

Abe turned around and radioed Dennis.

"Dennis, I need water, fast!" Abe yelled into the radio.

"Lamar, see how far you can get into that front entrance! Try to clear as much crap as you can out of the way so we can get a hose in there! I'll be right back!" Abe said, motioning back toward Luis as he dragged the hose forward.

In the distance, Abe could hear sirens, but time was wasted.

*Shit, they won't get here in time,* he thought, deciding to go on in.

Cautiously but forcefully, Lamar entered through the burning doorway, pushing away everything in his path. Attempting to make it to the stairs the way Shelly described, he could barely get through the first room before he had to rush back out the door. *My God, if she's still alive in there, it won't be for long,* he thought.

"I got as much cleared as I could," he said, bending over to catch his breath. "You get about six or seven feet in there before it gets worse!"

Putting his oxygen mask back on, Lamar turned to reenter the house with Abe hot on his heels, motioning Luis to come in with the hose. Just in case Mikalya was conscious and could hear them, Abe started to yell.

"Mikalya, stay down! Stay down close to the floor and cover your eyes! Stay down on the floor and cover your eyes!" he repeated. *Dear God, I hope she heard me.*

A tremendous burst of water forcefully streamed forward, knocking down everything in its path.

Lamar looked over at Abe. Knowing his friend the way he did, he knew the internal battle he was being faced with. Should he wait for the engine to arrive with the ladder, or should he go ahead and try to save the girl?

"Lamar, are you with me?" Abe shouted.

"I am. Let's rock 'n' roll, sir!" Lamar shot back.

"I did pay you that twenty dollars I lost on the last game, right?" Abe joked.

"Yes, you did," Lamar answered.

"Luis, keep that water coming! Lamar and I are moving in deeper," Abe yelled. He yelled out to Mikalya again in hopes that she would hear him.

Luis managed to make headway past the first room and kept the water flowing as he entered the kitchen. Abe and Lamar followed him past the kitchen on into the dining room.

"Lamar, check that door right next to you. What the hell is that?" Abe yelled.

Lamar opened it up. "Looks like the basement."

"Go ahead and check around down there if you can!" Abe screamed.

Lamar peered down the stairs. Not much of the fire had found its way down there yet. He quickly made his way down and shone his light around the small area that housed a washer, dryer, and a sump pump in the room. Finding no one down there, he quickly came back up.

Luis and Abe were well into the living room, still attempting to make their way through the intense fire and smoke. As Lamar got to the top step, he lost his footing and fell to his knees, hard. He managed to regain his footing and slowly moved into the dining room behind his teammates. The pain from his knee would hinder his ability to move fast, but he would not abandon Abe and Luis.

They inched their way into the middle of the dining room. The fire was spreading to the far end of the house. With all the dry weather they'd had the past couple of months, the entire house would be engulfed soon and then would begin to collapse around them. At that point, they would be forced out, and the search for Mikalya would be aborted. She would die. *God damn, where are the other engines? We're not going to put this fucking fire out alone!* Abe's thoughts were spinning in his head.

"Dennis, are any other engines here yet? It's a shitstorm in here!" Abe yelled into the radio.

"Yeah, two more just showed up, and they're setting up now. Hell, half the responders in the city are on their way here!" Dennis shouted.

Suddenly, there was a loud, explosive pop.

"My God, what the fuck was that?" Lamar shouted.

"I don't know, but it sounded like a gas explosion! It came from the direction we're heading into! That area is getting worse! We're not going to have much time!" Abe shouted.

Lamar nodded in agreement. The pain in his leg was getting worse, and Abe could see that he was limping.

"Hey, man, are you OK?" he asked.

"Shit, I don't know. I think I banged my knee pretty good," Lamar replied.

"Listen, start to inch your way back out. I can't afford to have you as a fatality here. When this gets worse, you may not be able to make it out, and I don't think you can make it up the stairs now anyway. Get out there and help coordinate with whoever shows up. Go on! Get going!" Abe said.

Lamar turned around, limping away. Abe got on his radio again.

"Dennis, Lamar hurt his knee pretty bad. He's heading back out."

"Got it," Dennis radioed back.

"Luis, it's just you and me now," Abe said. Luis nodded.

Luis was doing a great job of blasting their way through the fire debris. The original plan was to get to the stairway and up to Mikalya's bedroom. If they did, indeed, make it that far, and she wasn't up there, they'd have to abort and get the hell out.

Then, they heard a second loud pop and a flash ahead of them.

Luis kept the hose pointed in the direction of the sounds, but it was getting more difficult to see.

Abe inched a little past Luis, hoping he could get a better look into the stairwell area. The look in the mother's eyes kept him going. Then, through all the haze, he thought he saw the outline of a body right in front of him.

"Luis, put water around that thing right there, but don't hit it! I'm going to see what it is!" he yelled.

Luis maneuvered the hose in a circular fashion, giving Abe enough clearance to investigate what, hopefully, could be Mikalya.

Ever so slowly, he inched forward, stepping over the smoking chunks of furniture and other debris. Standing about three feet from the object, Abe was relieved to find that it was a body.

"Luis, I found her! She's here at the edge of the stairs!" Abe yelled, pointing wildly.

"Thank God. Now, we need to get the hell out of here and fast!" Luis replied.

Abe did not have time to see if Mikalya was still alive, nor did he have time to assess the extent of her injuries if she was.

"I'm gonna scoop her up as fast as I can. Point the hose back out and lead us out of here!" Abe said. Although they had recovered the young woman inside the house, their focus now was on getting out alive.

As Luis turned the heavy fire hose back around, saturating the same way they had entered the house, Abe removed his coat and covered Mikalya as best he could. She was either dead or out cold from the fall down the stairs and probably had a broken bone or two. There was no way the falling debris had missed her as she lay on the floor face down, so she'd probably have some burns to her back, as well. He was hoping she hadn't broken her neck or back.

"Better hurry up; we don't have any more time!" Luis yelled. The entire downstairs was ablaze, and the ceiling was starting to come down in chunks.

"Where the fuck are you in there?" Dennis's voice came across the radio.

"We found her! We're on our way out!" Abe radioed back, trying not to let Mikalya slip from his arms.

"The paramedics are here waiting! You need to get the fuck out… now! If you could see what I see from outside, you'd shit! Two more engines just got pulled up and are moving in!"

"I have her, and we're on the way out!"

Luis was blasting everything in sight with the powerful hose. Abe moved cautiously, yet swiftly, behind him. They had only gone about thirty feet from the door they entered, but it seemed like a mile on their mission to get out.

They entered the kitchen area and were finally headed toward their exit when they heard a loud crash behind them. The walls were falling in. Luis motioned for Abe to get in front of him and out the door as he continued fighting the fire.

As Abe brushed past Luis, he had to sidestep a substantial amount of debris blocking his path. He continued to be as careful as he could with Mikalya, but getting out fast was key.

Inching his way out, he could see other firefighters going in. Abe was finally outside and safe, with Mikalya still in his arms. The police had put a barrier between the civilians and the burning house.

Shelly, still in shock from the situation and the burns to her arm, was waiting at the front of the barrier line, still frantic about her daughter's safety. The police kept her back from Abe until he could carefully set Mikalya down in front of the paramedics.

Once she finally saw Abe, she broke down. "Oh, my God, is she alive? Is she? Please, God! Let her live!" Shelly screamed.

Several firefighters were attacking the house from other angles as the fire continued to spread. The ending was clear—the house and all its contents would be lost. But the most important thing had been saved.

Abe stood over Mikalya, exhausted and dirty, with smoke still coming off his fire coat. He watched nervously as the paramedics began the process that would hopefully save her life. He did not want to walk away from her, but another paramedic pulled him away so that he could get checked. But with all the noise and chaos around him, he could only focus on her.

As she lay on the stretcher, the paramedics took her pulse and then placed an oxygen mask over her face.

Shelly's prayers had been answered when she saw the paramedics place the oxygen mask over Mikalya's face. That simple act reassured her that her daughter was still alive. A massive weight, the size of the sun, lifted from her heart. Her body shook as she prayed silently, thanking God for sparing her daughter's life.

The medics began cleaning Mikalya's burns, applying splints to her broken leg, and installing an IV. Their synchronicity was perfection in motion. If it all weren't done just right, she could still die.

Abe watched, and he prayed. Unsure of why, this was one of the few times in his life he was terrified. *God, please don't take her. Please don't.* Despite how grim her situation appeared, he vowed that one day he would hold her.

****

"Ma'am, are you related to that girl?" the paramedic asked Shelly.

"Yes, I'm her mother. Is she going to be OK?" Shelly asked.

"She is still very much alive, and we're doing everything we can for her, but right now, we need to make sure you're OK."

"But is she *OK*?" Shelly asked.

"Ma'am, yes, she's OK. Now, we are going to get you fixed up, as you need to go to the hospital as well." The medic began tending to the burns on her arms and upper chest. She felt around for any broken bones and found none, although Shelly's ankle was badly bruised.

"What is your name?" the medic asked.

"Shelly. I'm the girl's mother," she replied.

"Do you have pain anywhere else besides the burns, scrapes, and your ankle?" the medic asked.

"No, I don't think anything is broken, but my ankle hurts. The burns hurt, too."

"We're going to give you something for that. I don't see where you've broken anything, but I'm sure the doctor will order x-rays when you get to the hospital," the medic said.

"They're taking us to Saint Francis, aren't they? It's the closest." Saint Francis Hospital had a superior burn unit and a five-star reputation.

"Yeah, Shelly, that is where you and your daughter are going. We're almost ready to go," she said.

Shelly looked around and noticed the fireman who carried her daughter out. She looked at him as he was staring at Mikalya on the stretcher.

"Can you tell me who that fireman is?" she asked.

"Ma'am, I don't know, but I think he is with Water Witch 64," the paramedic said.

"Do you know his name?" she asked.

"Sorry, I don't."

As she was being readied to leave from inside the ambulance, Shelly continued to watch Abe out of the window. When they drove past him standing outside the ambulance that Mikalya was waiting to be lifted into, she sat up and yelled.

"STOP. PLEASE, STOP!"

The ambulance came to a stop right next to Abe, and the two of them locked eyes through the window. Shelly asked the paramedic in the back with her to release her for a moment. When she stood face to face with Abe, she could see the intense exhaustion in his eyes.

"You're the man who brought my daughter out," she said. He nodded.

"I don't know what to say to you right now. There are no words to thank you for what you did."

Abe gave her a faint smile. "It's OK."

"What is your name?" she asked.

"Abraham Gallagher," he replied.

"Ma'am, we have to get going now," the medic interjected, taking her by the arm and leading her back into the ambulance. Her eyes didn't leave Abe's until they shut the ambulance doors.

****

Abe turned his attention back to Mikalya, trying to get a good feel of what they were doing to her. Her injuries appeared to be extensive but not life-threatening.

"You're the guy who got her out of there, aren't you?" one of the paramedics asked.

"With assistance, yes," Abe replied. He pondered that he was being asked this question again.

"If she'd been in there much longer, she'd be dead now. Way to go!" the medic said with a smile.

"Thank you."

Abe looked on as they gently lifted Mikalya's stretcher and slowly wheeled her through the back doors of the waiting ambulance. She was still unconscious. He wasn't sure how much she would remember or even if there would be brain damage. But it wouldn't matter to him, anyway.

He stood and watched as the ambulance sped away. He was exhausted and utterly oblivious to the carnage still going on around him. *I'll find her. I'll see her again if it's the last thing I do,* he said to himself.

The station captain, Randy, and his lieutenant, Adam, heard the run on their radios and rushed right to the scene.

"Hey, man, way to go! You saved that girl's life. Good job!" Randy said.

Abe slowly lifted his eyes and looked over at him with only a blank stare. "Luis led the way in, and Lamar was with me. I couldn't have done it without them."

"I know. Don't worry. You'll all get your commendations. But you decided to go in. That took some balls. You all risked your asses in there. The house is a total loss, but the girl is alive. Bottom line, that's all that matters."

"Thanks, Randy."

"I'm going to get this mess closed out and head home. We'll talk later at the station, but you all did fantastic," Randy said.

Abe walked over to where Lamar was sitting on the ground.

Lamar looked up. "I'm fucking sorry, man. I got a little clumsy in there."

Abe shook his head, squeezing his friend's shoulder.

"That's bullshit, Lamar. You went in there with me with no fear. There was slippery shit and crap all over the place. The smoke and heat were getting worse by the second, but you were still there. It could have happened to men better than you, but I know of no other men better than you," Abe said.

"Same here, man," Lamar said, laying his hand atop his friend's, still resting on his shoulder.

"I think they're getting ready to take you in and get that knee looked at."

"I don't think anything is broken, but who knows? I just might be on crutches for a little while," Lamar said with a smile.

"Anything to get out of work, right?" Abe laughed.

"Yeah, anything. This might get me a few weeks off. Maybe next time I'll jump from a second-story window and get a couple of months," Lamar joked.

A chuckle escaped Abe's lips. It was the first time he'd smiled since the nightmare began.

"OK, man, let me look around and help get all this shit packed back up. I'll call you later. I can give you a ride home from the hospital, too. We'll get your car back to the house. When that knee is all right, we'll grab a cold one," Abe said.

"You're damn right we will," Lamar replied.

Along with Mikalya and her mom, Lamar was the third to be whisked off to Saint Francis.

Abe turned and looked back at the house. The fire was out, but it left a huge mess behind.

"Hey, man, are you alright? Luis told me what you guys did in there. Way to go!" Dennis said, walking over to pat his friend on the back with Luis in tow.

"Joint effort, my friend. No one gets left out of this one, but thanks, Dennis. It was too intense," Abe replied, glancing over at an exhausted Luis.

"Luis, you did a hell of a job in there. You're a natural with a fire hose," Abe said, smiling.

Luis looked puzzled by Abe's remark.

"That is kind of a weird thing to be a natural at," he said. "I could understand guitar, cooking, singing, baseball, or even a Gigolo. But a damn fire hose? Really, man?"

Abe looked at Dennis, then at Luis, before returning his gaze back to Dennis.

"I'm not sure I'd compare Luis's dick to a 300-psi fire engine hose. Sorry, Luis, I hope I didn't piss you off," Abe said.

"That's OK, Capt'n. You guys don't need to know how big my dick is, anyway, now, do you?" Luis retorted.

"Hell, no?" they replied in unison. Luis shook his head and grinned.

"Listen, guys, can you all head back to the station without me? I'm going to hang around here a bit and get a couple of things straight in my head. But I can't thank the two of you enough for what you did today. I could not have brought the woman out without you both," Abe said.

They clenched each other's fists before Luis and Dennis walked back toward the engine.

Abe took off his fire suit and laid it on the ground. Retracing the steps he'd taken barely an hour ago, he walked through the rubble to the spot where he'd found and picked up Mikalya. Now, a huge dresser that had fallen from a second-story window lay in the exact area. He blinked back at the thought that had he not gotten to her when he did, it could have fallen right on top of her. If the fire and smoke inhalation didn't kill her, the dresser would have.

After contemplating all that could have happened, he walked back outside and picked up his suit before making the long trudge back to the station. When he got there, Luis and Dennis were wrapping up the takedown of the engine. With no more calls coming in, they finally headed home, thankful for the next few days off.

****

Abe couldn't get through the door and into his room fast enough before he started peeling off his clothes for a long, hot shower, after which he crawled into bed and turned off the light. On a normal day, he would have read before going to sleep, but today had been anything but normal. He lay there in the dark, staring up at the ceiling, his mind wandering. He wondered what she was doing at that very moment and started to plan when and how he would approach her in the hospital. He had no clue what kind of woman she was. He just knew, without knowing why it was so intense, that he was already falling for her. But would she reciprocate those feelings? Could she reciprocate? He didn't know, but he intended to find out.

# Chapter Five:
# Mikalya's Awakening

After a couple of days' rest, Abe decided it was time to go back and really sort out what had happened to him at 1411 Crestbaum Street just two days earlier. Every detail of the fire was etched in his memory.

He jumped in the car and headed over, parking in front of all that was left of the house. Unable to move, he sat and stared. It was his first serious fire run.

He remembered exactly where his engine parked and what Luis, Dennis, and Lamar did once they were all mobilized. He remembered the mom's frantic behavior, but he certainly understood why.

Nothing had been cleaned up yet. The mess was exactly as it was when he walked away.

Bracing himself, Abe got out and walked up to the back door where they had been holding Mikalya's mom back from going inside. He looked down at the ground and could still hear her screams. The look of utter despair on her face and her frantic pleadings for help were the deciding factors for him to go in. There was something else, though, something, or someone he could not get out of his mind.

He carefully entered the house and slowly followed the path that Luis led him and Lamar on. The debris was extensive, so he moved carefully. When he looked up, part of the second story was gone but most of the damage was on the first floor and around the stairs.

As he continued the path through the kitchen, on into the dining area, he evaluated what, if anything, he could have, or would have, done differently. There was really nothing that he could think of. Time had been of the essence; it was not about trying to save the structure but about saving a life. That was it. The entire rescue took about fifteen minutes, although it felt like a lifetime, but the mission had been accomplished, and that's all that mattered. Captain Randy was satisfied with the entire operation. A life had been saved. *Her* life. Mikalya's life.

Abe was now at the edge of the stairs. He pushed away another huge item of furniture… so charred he couldn't make out what it was. It was the spot where she had lain. He remembered the alarm that came across their radio saying a woman was trapped on the second-story floor of a house. He looked up the stairway toward the hallway, piecing together what possibly happened.

*When Mikalya tried to get out of the house, she panicked, as most people would have. She probably ran down the stairs a little too fast and, in the process, lost her footing. That's when she must have fallen and hit her head on the bottom stair banister post, possibly breaking her leg.*

*As she lay there passed out, hot embers fell on her from the second floor, causing burn marks on her back. Quite surely, she breathed in a little too much smoke, but being on the floor might have helped her as being down low possibly eliminated too much smoke damage to her lungs.*

That was how he summed it up. If she had laid there even for a few more minutes, she would have burned alive while her mom was outside, having to witness the hideous event.

Abe reached down and picked up a smaller piece of the stair step. Oddly enough, it was still in good condition, with minimal burn marks. It was the only one that was.

This girl, Mikalya, who he knew nothing about, was dominating his every waking thought. He couldn't pinpoint if the intense feeling for this stranger was just some illusion of sympathy or if it was something more. But what he was sure of was that he could not get her out of his head. And now that he was standing in the middle of her house, those feelings intensified. *That* was the reason he had come. Even with the house in the state it was in, he could feel her. He could see that she and her mother had lost a lot and smoke would have damaged goods upstairs.

He turned around and pretended that Mikalya was still in his arms. He knew what he had to do. He had come back to the house to sort it all out and to be sure of what he was feeling. Now he was. His next stop would be Saint Francis Hospital.

He walked back to his car, driving away to find the closest florist.

****

"Yes, sir, can I help you?" the clerk asked.

"Uh, yeah, I need a get-well bouquet of some sort," Abe replied.

"You have a sick wife or girlfriend?" the clerk asked.

"Well, not exactly. It's for a woman I don't even know, whose life I saved in a house fire a few days ago."

The clerk looked at him with an expression of shock and surprise.

"My God, are you serious? Did you really? Are you a policeman or a fireman?" she asked.

"Fireman."

The clerk nodded with an expression of appreciation. "Wait a minute. Was it that house fire on Crestbaum Street? I know the people that live there… Shelly Arabella, and her daughter, Mikalya."

Abe's demeanor sharpened. "So how do you know them?" he asked.

"I grew up with Shelly. We went to school together and hung out a bit. I used to babysit Mikalya. She's a darling. Are *you* the one that pulled Mikalya out of the house?"

Abe had a thousand questions running around his head, but he didn't want to appear too eager. "Yeah, I'm the one, but I had a lot of help. Can I ask you a question?"

"Sure, fire away, no pun intended. By the way, are the flowers for Mikalya? Sorry, I had to ask," the clerk said, grinning.

"Well, yeah, they are."

"That's so sweet of you. That Mikalya is a doll. She's a little clumsy at times, so Shelly acts like some sort of divine protector. I guess that's what good mothers are anyway. She's a self-appointed gatekeeper for any guy Mikalya goes out with. I guess that's the reason Mikalya hasn't had a lot of boyfriends."

"Does she have one now?" Abe asked.

"Not that I know of," the clerk replied quickly. *And even if she does, not anymore,* she thought.

A faint smile crept across her face.

"Have you spoken to her mother since the fire?" Abe asked.

"Yeah, I called yesterday morning to see how she was doing. She suffered some minor burns and a few scrapes and bruises. She's been discharged, but Mikalya has a broken leg, some burns, and a concussion. She'll be there a little while longer. Shelly is just relieved Mikalya is still alive. She was going to check the fire station to see how to get a hold of the fireman who had gotten Mikalya out of the house. All she knew was it was some guy named Abe. I guess that's you, huh? And here you come, strolling up in here. She was damn lucky to have you," the clerk said.

"Could you do me a huge favor? Would you please not tell Shelly that I was here? Please?" Abe pleaded.

"Sure, no problem," she said.

"Great. I really appreciate that. Now, I need a dozen red roses and a dozen yellow roses in a nice vase. I'm going to take them to Saint Francis. I want you to put this note with it, too," Abe said, pulling a notecard from the rack and writing on it before sealing the envelope.

"No problem. We can get this delivered today."

"No, that's OK. I want to take it myself."

"OK, give me a few minutes to put it together. I'll be right back."

Abe walked over and looked out the window. He had learned a little more about Shelly and Mikalya just by stumbling into a flower shop. *Was it coincidence, or was it fate?* he wondered. He settled on fate.

The clerk returned with a beautiful arrangement of red and yellow roses. "How do you like it?" she asked.

Pleased, he replied, "It's perfect."

"Just be careful. I'll put the vase in this box, so it'll be OK in the car," she said.

"Ma'am, I really appreciate this. And I can't believe, of all the flower shops in the city, I walk into the one where the person knows Mikalya!"

"Fate, I suppose. I just want to say, too, what an incredibly courageous thing you did by going into that burning house and saving her life. She would have died if it weren't for you, and Shelly knows that big time. She thinks you're a god."

Abe smiled. "Ma'am, I'm far from that. I can't even win at a round of poker," he joked. He paid up and picked up the large box from the counter.

"Again, I can't thank you enough. By the way, do you know where they're going to be living?" he asked.

"I think with Shelly's aunt in the Lakewood area on the north side of town. I don't think Shelly had much insurance on their furniture and clothes, so they'll have a rough time for a while. The little insurance they had will cover some of their things, but not all, by any means," the clerk said.

Abe was taking it all in. "Well, things have a way of working themselves out, and I am sure it all will. Thanks for everything," Abe said, waving as he headed out the door.

Abe placed the box with the vase in the passenger seat of his car. It would take him thirty minutes to get to Saint Francis Hospital. He was glad of that, as it would give him time to think.

As he drove, his mind was filled with contradictory thoughts about whether he was doing the right thing. He was following his heart. It had only been a couple of days since the fire. He knew her name. He knew her mother's name. And now he knew more about her actual injuries. He had seen her at her worst, and still, he was drawn to her. Two major twists of fate now drove him even more.

*If she had a concussion, she could still be unconscious when I get there. But what if she isn't? If she is awake, will she remember anything? Does she have a boyfriend? Or worse, a fiancé? What kind of woman is she? Will she be attracted to me? The lady at the flower shop made no mention of her father. Am I attracted to her out of sympathy? Whatever happens in that hospital room, I'll accept it. And I will leave like nothing ever happened.*

He was now pulling into the hospital parking lot. Abe felt more fear now than when he rushed into the burning house. No other woman had ever had this kind of effect on him before.

"Sir, are you going to take the ticket?" the woman at the parking booth asked. He was so lost in thought he didn't even realize he had pulled up to it.

"Oh, yes, ma'am, I'm sorry," he replied. Abe took the ticket and slowly navigated the parking area. He found an open spot right next to the sidewalk that led to the main door. *Damn, when I don't want a fucking close spot, there it is!*

He turned the engine off and sat for a couple of minutes. Now, his mind was completely blank. He stepped out of the car, walked around to the passenger side to grab the vase, and went inside the hospital. The elevator doors were opening just as he was about to press the button. *Perfect timing,* he thought. The clerk at the flower shop had already given him the room number. When he got to the floor, he headed for the nurse's station.

"Hi, can you tell me where Room 206 is?" he asked.

"Sir, it's down the left hallway here and then on your right," the nurse replied.

Abe turned and peered down in that direction. The moment of truth had arrived. This moment was all that he had been thinking about since the fire.

"Ma'am, can I set this vase here while I use the restroom real quick?" he asked.

The nurse looked the flowers over carefully and smiled.

"Sure, the men's room is just over there," she said, pointing.

Abe walked in and checked his hair and clothes. He was looking as good as he could. He popped a breath mint, took a deep breath, and walked out. Grabbing the vase, he cautiously walked toward the room, stopping right outside of it to listen. He heard nothing and noticed that the room was dark. He slowly pushed the door open.

As he walked forward, he noticed a cot on the far side of the room with her mom sleeping on it. As he walked in further, he saw her, Mikalya. Lying on her back in the bed. All he could do was stop and stare. *My God, there she is.*

He sat the vase down on the table by the window. He could hear her mom snoring lightly from the corner. Walking back to Mikalya's bedside, he stared down at her, knowing that he was in love. If there had been any doubt before, it had vanished.

Looking up, he saw the IV connected to her arm and read the vital signs on her monitor. They were promising. Her injuries were as he expected. All that he cared about was that she was alive.

Looking down at her and her mother sleeping, Abe decided it would be best for him to leave before they awoke. He didn't want to be a bother to them or to cause any confusion. He'd gotten what he came for to see Mikalya and deliver flowers to her room, along with his personal message. She would know. He leaned into her and noticed her faint breathing. After standing and blowing a kiss at her, he quietly tiptoed back out the door. The same nurse who had given him directions was still at the nurses' station.

"My name is Abraham Gallagher. Can I ask you a few questions about Mikalya Arabella in Room 206?" he asked.

"Sir, are you a relative? We aren't supposed to give out information to anyone outside of the family," she replied.

"Well, no, but I'm the fireman who saved her life in that house fire a few days ago," he said.

The nurse's tone went from firm to accommodating. "Oh, my God! You're the one who saved her! Her mother is so grateful to you; you're all she talks about! Did you meet her?"

"No. She's in there sleeping. I really don't want to wake her. I'll be back later, but for now, can I get a little information on Mikalya's injuries? She appears to have a broken leg, some burns at her mid-section, and what seems to be a concussion. Her vitals look OK on the monitor," Abe said.

The nurse nodded. "You pretty much nailed it. There is still a little heat and smoke damage to her lungs, but that is healing nicely. The doctors expect that she will make a full recovery, but not for a while. The concussion is the biggest concern right now, although there doesn't appear to be any permanent brain damage. But we just don't know when she's going to wake up. If you have another minute, can I get my friend? She'll want to meet you," the nurse said.

Abe nodded reluctantly, but he really wasn't in the mood. Grandstanding was not his thing.

The nurse called what seemed like every medical personnel on that floor to come and meet him and congratulate him. He just stood there, embarrassed.

In a matter of minutes, they flooded him with questions. He felt like he was at a press conference. The only thing missing were cameras and microphones.

"How did you find her once you got inside the house?" one nurse asked.

"How did you get her out so fast?" asked another.

"Have you saved a lot of other people, too?"

"How long have you been a firefighter?"

Abe gave brief, polite answers, wanting it all to end.

"What made you decide to become a fireman?" the IT guy asked. That question struck a nerve with Abe.

"Well, I usually don't like to talk about that, but I will, since this is a rather unusual gathering. Several years ago, when I'd finished my junior year in high school, my parents and I were traveling to a relative's wedding when we saw a horrible car accident happen right in front of us. To make this story short, although we tried, we couldn't save two of the people from one of the cars that was on fire. All we could do was stand there, watching it happen and listening to their screams."

Abe looked down at the floor with nothing more to say, leaving a somber tone hanging in the air. When he looked up, he had a weird smile on his face.

"And that's why I became a fireman," he ended. "Well, you all are busy, and I need to get going. I really appreciate the care you are giving to Mikalya. If you would, could you not tell her who I am or that I was here? And it was really nice meeting all of you."

"No problem, sir," one of the nurses spoke up.

Walking back toward the elevator, Abe felt he had made a huge step in his move toward Mikalya. His sole focus now was on the next time he'd get to visit her.

****

The next day, at Saint Francis Hospital, the attending care nurse, Cynthia, went in to check Mikalya's IV. All her vitals looked good, and her IV drip was stable. Mikalya had not regained consciousness. Cynthia brushed Mikalya's hair over as it had gotten in her face and covered her nose.

While she was still smoothing Mikalya's hair away from her face, she noticed a faint movement in her eyelids. It appeared that Mikalya was trying to open her eyes. Cynthia stood back and waited, smiling.

Mikalya's eyelids fluttered again, and the slits appeared, displaying a portion of the whites of her eyes. Suddenly, Cynthia remembered that when Shelly left that morning to go back to her aunt's house, that she had reminded Cynthia should anything happen, to call her immediately. She was so caught up in the *awakening* that she almost forgot. She ran to the computer, grabbed the number and began dialing, hitting the alert button for a doctor at the same time.

"Ms. Arabella, it's Cynthia Gladden, Mikalya's nurse! Listen, I think she is trying to open her eyes! Her eyelids are fluttering, so she is trying! She's also moaning a little!"

There was a bout of silence on the other end of the line.

"Oh, my baby's come back! I'm leaving right now!" Shelly replied.

"OK, I'm going to wait with her until you get here!" Cynthia promised.

"God, I can't thank…." Shelly's voice trailed off. As she stood up, grabbing her purse, the phone flew out of her hand. She left it on the floor and ran out.

"Ms. Arabella, are you there? Are you there?" Cynthia asked, with no response, so she hung up.

Returning to Mikalya's room, Cynthia noticed that her eyelids were fluttering even more. She pulled a chair closer and sat down to hold her hand.

"Mikalya, honey, are you in there?" she whispered.

Cynthia felt the light squeeze of her hand.

"Yes! Squeeze my hand again! I'm right here!" Cynthia said.

Mikalya lightly squeezed her hand again.

Cynthia's eyes welled with tears. "Mikalya, do you want to say something, honey?"

Mikalya's eyes opened slowly. "Am I dead?"

After a few days of uncertainty, Cynthia was boiling over with joy to see that her patient was starting to recover. She laughed a nervous laugh. She had taken a keen interest in Mikalya ever since she was assigned to her unit.

"No, you're not dead, but from what I hear, you came close, honey. You're in the hospital. My name is Cynthia, and I'm your nurse."

Mikalya's eyes rolled back and forward as she struggled to make out her surroundings. "Is my… Is my…?" Mikalya struggled to complete her sentence as she coughed.

"Honey, you don't have to say much right now. Rest. I called your mom, and she's on the way here. Can you take a drink of this?" Cynthia asked, guiding a glass of water to Mikalya's mouth.

Surprisingly, Mikalya took several big gulps from the straw and then turned her head to have it taken away.

"Is my mom OK? Where is she?" she asked.

"Yes, honey, she's OK. She had some burns and bruises, but she is all right, and very excited to see you. I just called her, and she's on her way here right now. Tell me how you're feeling," Cynthia said.

"I feel heavy, like I'm glued down," Mikalya replied.

"You have a cast on your leg. When your mom gets here, she will come in to speak with you. Don't worry, sweetie, you're going to be OK."

Mikalya's lips turned up into a tiny smile while she asked for more water. "So, you are Cynthia?"

"Yes, I have been in charge of your care since you got here."

"How long have I been here?" Mikalya asked.

"Well, just a few days. Try not to talk. You'll need your strength later. Your mom should be here soon. She's been here every day since you were brought in. By the way, I love your names, Mikalya and Shelly."

"God, my leg hurts, and it hurts to breathe. Are my injuries serious?"

"Well, your leg is fractured. The doctor will come in to talk to you about your injuries. They say you took a spill down the stairs trying to escape the fire. I'll get your pain medication adjusted to make you comfortable."

While Cynthia stepped away to get her medicine, Mikalya stared up at the ceiling. She had just come out of a coma and was trying to process what happened to her in the fire, becoming more alert by the minute.

Suddenly, the door flew open, and Shelly blew into the room like a hurricane. She stopped just short of Mikalya's bed and stared at her.

Mikalya was startled by her mom's abrupt burst through the door, but the joy of seeing her caused her heart to race.

They stared at each other for a few seconds. This was the first time Mikalya had seen her mom since the day of the fire. It was also the first time Shelly had seen her daughter awake since the fire. They had survived a horrific event, and their gratitude for making it out alive was evident in their facial expressions. Shelly knew that her only daughter had almost lost her life, and if it was possible, in that moment, she loved her even more.

Shelly looked at Mikalya with her leg cast on, her head still bandaged, bruises on her face, burns on her back, and the IV sticking out of her arm. Her eyes filled with tears.

Mikalya gave her a teary-eyed smile.

"God, I wish I could hold you in my arms right now, sweetie!" Shelly said with tears streaming down her cheeks.

"Mom, get over here and give it a try," Mikalya said meekly, holding up one arm. The other she could barely move.

Shelly leaned in and put her arms lightly around Mikalya's shoulders. Mikalya returned the hug as best she could with her one arm. Holding each other, mother and daughter couldn't stop the cries of joy overwhelming them both.

Cynthia walked into the room and, noticing their exchange, backed right out. Shelly released Mikalya and stood up, pulling the bedside chair closer.

"Mom, are you alright? I see they bandaged your arms and shoulder. You're limping a bit, too. Did you try to come into the house when you got there? You did, didn't you?" Mikalya said, without needing an answer.

"Yes, honey. I was trying to save you," Shelly replied.

"I know I didn't get out of that house by myself. I know I didn't. The last thing I remember was falling down the stairs. So, I want to know *who* got me out of the house. Was it you? I need to know," she said.

"No, sweetie. It wasn't me," Shelly replied, taking Mikalya's hands and looking into her eyes. *What kind of mother am I? I couldn't even rescue my own child,* she thought. Her eyes welled with tears. She had Mikalya's full attention.

"Honey, listen. After you called me, I immediately called 9-1-1, too. I wasn't far from the house, and I got there before the fire trucks showed up. The last thing you told me was that you were upstairs. By the time I pulled up, I could see the flames and smoke coming from everywhere.

"Some of the neighbors were standing around, but they didn't know you were inside. Some of them called 9-1-1, as well. When I got to the back door, I tried to go in, but the smoke was getting stronger, and the fire was moving quickly. There was a lot of burning grease in the kitchen, and it was catching everywhere.

"I tried to get to the stairs but just couldn't, baby. Somehow, I made it through the kitchen, but then I realized the sleeve of my blouse was on fire. Then, a hard blast of smoke hit me, and I had to run back out. My eyes were burning so badly, and I couldn't see anymore.

"As I was running back out, I twisted my ankle, so I hobbled to a safe spot on the ground to try to put the fire out that was growing up my arm. When I tried to go back in, the flames and smoke had gotten much worse in just those couple of minutes, but I was still determined to go back in to save you, but the neighbors held me back—they wouldn't let me go back in. They said if I went back in, there's no way I'd come back out."

Mikalya had never felt so much love for her mom as she did in that moment.

Shelly started sobbing uncontrollably, wiping away the blinding tears that kept her from seeing her baby's face.

"I am so sorry, baby! I am so sorry for that! Oh, God, I am!" Shelly cried. Shaking uncontrollably, she laid her head in Mikalya's lap.

Mikalya stroked her mom's hair.

"I kept telling them to let me go, that my baby was in there, but they kept holding me back! God, please, don't hate me, honey. If you would have died in there, I would have never forgiven myself. I prayed so hard for God to send down a Guardian Angel."

"Mom, look at me," Mikalya said, grabbing her mom's face upward.

Shelly continued crying on Mikalya's lap.

"Mom, please, look at me!"

Shelly lifted her head slowly, her eyes locking with Mikalya's.

"Mom, it's OK. You tried. God knows you tried. It's OK. I would have never wanted you to kill yourself just to get to me. And it sounds like, if you did go back in, you wouldn't have made it out. Then, we *both* might have died. But we didn't. We're still here, holding each other. We're still together," Mikalya said with a reassuring smile.

"I hope you don't think less of me for that," Shelly said.

Mikalya smiled and lovingly pulled her mother's head against her chest. "Mom, how could I ever think less of you? You've always taken care of me and been there for me. No one else has done that… just you, Mom."

They held each other in silence. When Mikalya was sure that her mother had calmed down, she asked more questions.

"So, when are your bandages coming off?" she asked.

"In a few days. The doctor will look at them and will either put a fresh set on or he'll say I don't need them anymore. I couldn't drive for a couple of days, but I'm better now. But forget about me. My only concern is you and how you're feeling."

"I'm sure the house is a disaster. Did we lose everything, Mom?"

Shelly wiped her eyes and gave a so-so gesture.

"We'll be staying with Aunt Loretta up in Lakewood for a while. She's been so good and says that we can stay as long as we need to. She's been out shopping for us—for clothes and things. You know, we did have some insurance, but right now, all we have is literally the clothes on our backs until I can get back in there and see what is salvageable. Everyone is pitching in on my job for us, too. Ron has been so good; he told me to take as much time as I needed. I'm using vacation and comp time to keep the money coming in. And sick time, of course, too," Shelly said.

Mikalya smiled, then just as quickly, her lips turned into a frown.

Shelly could see that the conversation was about to go in another direction.

"Mom, I want to ask you again. You told me you prayed hard for a Guardian Angel to come down and save me. Apparently, one did, and whoever it was saved my life. We both know I didn't get out of that house by myself. What happened after they held you back? I knew how bad the fire was getting before I fell. I would have died there if no one had come inside the house. I wouldn't be here now, so tell me, who really saved me?"

"Yes, there was a Guardian Angel, baby. One did come," Shelly said.

"Well, who was it? Who saved my life?" Mikalya pressed for answers.

Shelly gazed lovingly at her daughter, then turned and slowly pointed toward the table next to the window, which held a beautiful vase with red and yellow roses.

"Honey… he did," Shelly answered. "I noticed them there when I left and asked the nurses where they came from."

Mikalya looked over and stared at the roses for a few moments. The colors glistened like stained glass from the sunlight that was streaming in.

As Mikalya stared out the window, an emotional jolt went through her body. The jolt didn't frighten her, but it calmed her in a way she had never experienced. After coughing a bit, several minutes passed before she spoke again.

"Mom, can you bring them over here?" she asked.

Shelly got up and walked over to the table, carefully lifting the vase and slowly walking it over to Mikalya. As she went to sit them on her bedside table, Mikalya stopped her.

"No, bring them to me. I want to touch them," she said.

Shelly moved the roses close to Mikalya's face so she could smell them.

Lifting her back off her pillow, Mikalya noticed the note tied to one of the roses.

*Wishing You a Very Speedy Recovery ~Abraham*

Mikalya lifted her arm and touched the flowers, counting them. There were twenty-four, all with their thorns clipped. She brought a few of them up to her nose again, closed her eyes, and took a long, deep breath.

Seeing the look on her daughter's face, Shelly knew that Mikalya was experiencing more than gratitude for the stranger who had saved her life. Sight unseen, she was falling in love.

Mikalya took another long, deep breath and closed her eyes again. When she opened them, she noticed that deeper down in the vase was a note card hidden between the flower stems.

"Oh, my God, Mom… can you pull that out for me?" she asked.

Shelly looked down and pulled out the card, damp from its proximity to the water.

With her one functional arm, Mikalya attempted to open the card, but with no success. Shelly knew how independent her daughter was and how she often refused her mother's help, but this time, she knew that her assistance would be appreciated, so she opened the envelope and placed it in her hand.

Mikalya's mind raced back and forth. The stranger who saved her… her stranger… had sent her flowers. *Or had he delivered them himself?* she wondered.

*Hello,*

*My name is Abraham, or Abe, as my friends and family call me. In case you are wondering, I am the one who pulled you from your burning house. I hope these roses will bring you a bit of sunshine when you awake from your coma. They say that roses have healing powers, so I hope these will work for you.*

Confused, Mikalya read and re-read the note again, silently repeating his name. *Abraham.*

"Mom, who is Abraham?" she asked, laying the note beside her on the bed. "Did you see him? Did you talk to him?" Mikalya continued.

"Yes, honey, I did," Shelly replied.

"What was he like, Mom?"

"Well, the medics were prepping you just outside the back of the ambulance, and I noticed him standing there, just looking at you. I had the opportunity to thank him and ask his name before they put me into the other ambulance."

"What did he say to you?" Mikalya asked.

"I can't remember his exact words. It was chaotic, and there wasn't a lot of time for pleasantries. I was in pain, and he was filthy and, I'm sure, exhausted, as well."

"Did he introduce himself as Abraham or Abe, Mom?" Mikalya asked.

"Mikalya, I think he said Abraham and this conversation has come to an end because you're exhausting me."

Mikalya smiled. "I'm sorry. Come over here and give me a hug."

Any impatience that she felt with Mikalya's line of questioning quickly departed with the invitation of a hug. Shelly stood up and leaned over Mikalya's bed, squeezing her tightly but carefully.

"OK, now you can put the flowers on my bedside table. If I fall asleep, please don't let anyone take them away. Can you tell Cynthia to let the other nurses know as well?"

"Of course," Shelly nodded.

"God, I can't wait to get out of here. If it wasn't for Cynthia and the morphine, I'd be miserable."

As they were laughing, the door swung open and in walked the doctor, with Cynthia in tow.

"Hello, Mikalya! I'm Doctor Hart, the doctor who treated you when they brought you into the ER a few days ago. Do you feel up for a little chat so we can talk about what happened to you?"

"Sure," Mikalya replied, settling back into her pillow, instantly at ease with the doctor's bedside manner.

"First of all, you're one lucky patient. As I understand it, if you had been in that house much longer, it would have been a different story, but we all thank God you're here. Let's go over your injuries.

"You have second-degree burns on your leg and stomach as well as on your back where it was exposed. Luckily, there are no burns on the leg with the cast on. We're treating these burns with Silver Sulfadiazine, a new-generation burn cream, which should cut down on the healing time.

"Now, of course, your right leg is broken, hence the cast. You'll have to keep that on for the next six weeks or so. And finally, you have a mild concussion. We didn't find any serious bleeding or brain damage from it, but we do want to keep you here for a little while longer until we are completely sure none will develop," Doctor Hart concluded.

"How much longer, Doctor?" Mikalya asked.

"Well, let's just say another week to ten days. It could be sooner, but I just don't know yet. We need to keep a close eye on that noggin of yours," he said, smiling.

"Don't worry! I'm not going to let anything happen to you!" Cynthia chimed in.

"And I'll be camped out here, too," Shelly added.

Mikalya smiled.

"Well, I'm just glad to be alive and that my injuries weren't worse than they are."

"You definitely had a Guardian Angel watching over you. Oh, and speaking of guardian angels, I heard the fireman who pulled you out of that house was here asking about you. I think he was the one who brought those beautiful flowers on the table over there," Doctor Hart said.

Mikalya's demeanor changed as she looked over at Cynthia.

"Honey, I was off and only saw them this morning," Cynthia said, without Mikalya saying a word.

"Who did he talk to? Who was on duty?" Mikalya asked.

Shelly looked up at the ceiling, wishing away the topic of the mysterious fireman.

"Let me find out for you… hang on," Cynthia said, scurrying out the door.

"Well, I have to continue my rounds," Doctor Hart said, interrupting the silence. "Any other questions for me right now?"

"No, Doctor, we're fine. I'm sure we'll see you soon," Shelly said, standing to shake the doctor's hand.

When Doctor Hart walked out of the room, the door swung back open as Cynthia came back in.

"Connie was on duty when he stopped by. She remembers talking to him, and she says he seemed like a nice fella. She also said he was cute, and he insisted on delivering the flowers to your room personally. You both must have been asleep when he came in and came right back out. He wouldn't have been allowed in here if he hadn't been the one who saved your life."

A frown creased Mikalya's brow. "My God, you mean to tell me *he* was in this room? Mom, you didn't see him?" she asked nervously.

"Honey, I was out like a light for only a couple of hours. He had to have slipped in then," Shelly replied.

"Damn, I missed him," Mikalya said.

Cynthia pulled out her cell phone and called Connie.

"Hey, it's me. Can you fill Mikalya in on that handsome stranger who came by and brought the flowers?" Cynthia asked. "Here's Connie. I'm going to finish my rounds, and I'll be back," she said.

"Hi, Connie, it's Mikalya."

"Hey, how are you doing? I'm so glad you are back with us!"

"Well, I finally came to. I'm sore and a little fuzzy, but hopefully, I'll be back on my feet soon."

"You'll get there faster than you think. We'll take good care of you. Now, Cynthia said you want to know more about that guy who delivered the flowers."

"Yeah, Connie, can you tell me what he was like?" Mikalya asked.

"Well, I don't know that I could tell you any more than Cynthia has already. He came by when you were still out of it, and he left the flowers. He asked that we not tell you that he was here."

Connie continued, "He was soft-spoken and seemed a little shy. He was about six feet tall and well-built… nice-looking guy. Oh, and he was polite. That stood out to me. I think he said he'd check back in on you in a few days."

"Did he say when exactly?" Mikalya asked.

"No, he didn't. We told him you'd be here at least until the end of the week. I'm sure he'll be back before you get out of here," Connie finished.

"Connie, would you do me a favor? If he comes back and you're on duty, unless I'm dead, please wake me, no matter what anyone says." Mikalya frowned, looking over at her mom.

"Not to worry, Mikalya. I'll alert some of the other nurses, and I'll also place a note in your chart. How about that? Don't worry. We're on it."

“Thanks, Connie. I really appreciate this,” Mikalya said, ending the call and then looking over at her mom.

“Well, I did find out which firehouse he works at. It’s not far from here. I could…” Shelly began.

“Mom! You let me go through all that… chasing down information, and all along, you knew where he worked? Geez, Mom! No, just let it ride for now. Hopefully, he’ll come back like he said he would.”

“Well, whatever happens, we need to personally thank him and the rest of the firemen who were there,” Shelly said.

“You want to take them some brownies, Mom?” Mikalya asked, laughing.

Shelly smiled at Mikalya’s snide remark.

“Maybe we will when we’ve both fully recovered,” she replied.

Cynthia walked back through the door, and Mikalya handed her the phone with thanks.

“Well, what did Connie say?” Cynthia asked.

“Not much, but he did tell her that he would come back by again. I just wish I knew when that would be,” Mikalya said.

“Well, Mikalya, if, or should I say… when he comes back, trust me, I’ll wake you both if you’re sleeping. This feels like a fairy tale,” Cynthia said with a wink and a smile.

"If he comes back, that will be the fairy tale," Mikalya replied.

"I'm sure he will. Listen, why don't you get some rest? I have more rounds to make, and then I'll come back and check on you. If you need anything, the button is there to your right. Shelly, are you going to stay a while?"

"I'll be here for a few hours and then head home for a shower before I return for the evening."

Shelly handed Mikalya a couple of magazines that she had brought for her, then settled back in the chair next to Mikalya's bed to work on her crossword puzzle.

"Geez, Mom, how do you figure those things out? All the words they ask for are weird words that I'm sure no one's ever heard of before. Then, they ask these stupid questions, like *What is a four-letter word for a rock that rolls?*" Mikalya said, rolling her eyes.

Shelly glanced at Mikalya with a serious expression. "I'll bet it's lava," she said with a straight face before bursting into laughter. Mikalya started laughing, too, holding her head to try to calm the pain.

"You seem to be getting better quicker than I expected but just as I hoped. This morning, I wasn't sure that you would even open your eyes, and now, here you are making fun of my crossword puzzle, young lady."

Mikalya's shoulders drooped, and her expression softened. "Mom, I'm sorry. You know I'm only teasing you. I love you more than you know." As quickly as the tears welled up in her eyes, Shelly saw the lone tear making its way down her right cheek.

Pushing the chair back as she stood, she leaned over Mikalya and gave her a big squeeze. "Sweetie, you don't have to apologize. I know you're only teasing me, and I love you more than you know, too!" she said.

Shelly could tell that Mikalya was getting tired.

"Listen, it was only a few hours ago that you came to. You've had a lot of activity in and out of that door, so I think it's time for you to rest. I'll stay here until you doze off again. Then I'll run home, grab a shower, and be back in time to have dinner with you. How does that sound?"

"Sounds like a plan, Mom. What time do you think you'll get back here?"

"Let's say around six, and I'll be staying the night, of course. We'll order your evening meal together when I get back. I'll get me something from the cafeteria."

"I love you, Mom," Mikalya said again. "Oh, and do you think you can pick me up a few makeup essentials, please? Just the basics and some moisturizer."

"Ditto," Shelly said with a tear in her eye. Ten minutes later, she could hear Mikalya breathing softly. Shelly quietly gathered her things. She stared at Mikalya lying on the bed. Outside of the day she gave birth to her, this was the only other time she had seen her daughter in such a helpless state.

Her eyes welled up again. She kissed Mikalya gently on the forehead and headed out the door. Walking down to her car, she made a mental note not to forget the makeup on the way back.

***

Awake from her nap, Mikalya lay in the bed, thinking about what the doctor and Connie had said about the mysterious stranger who saved her life. Although she couldn't get him out of her head, she needed to focus all her energy on recovering and getting out of the hospital. She had just awakened from a coma that day.

Alone in her room after all the in-and-out traffic from earlier, her thoughts trailed back to her injuries. What bothered her the most was her broken leg.

Something as small as going to the bathroom and all the other thousands of minor things she took for granted would now require a major effort. She shuddered when she closed her eyes and imagined how much worse it could have been. She stared out the window, unable to clear her mind.

*What if Abraham hadn't come in when he did? How much worse could it have gotten? The fire would have surely reached me, and I could have had severe burns all over my body, including my face. I could have been disfigured.*

She began to shudder. She told herself to stop thinking about all the "what if" scenarios. What happened happened, and the bottom line was that it could have been much worse. In the grand scheme of it all, she was lucky. Mikalya knew it, and she thanked God. She made a tiny sign of the cross across her chest and vowed this would not be the last time she would do it.

As her thoughts of gratitude to the Creator diminished, thoughts of gratitude to Abraham moved into her head. She stared at the vase of roses once again, wondering when he'd come back. *If* he came back. She was hoping that when he did, she would be awake, alert, and wouldn't *look* sick.

Mikalya felt herself getting drowsy again, so she adjusted her bed downward to try to get a nap in before her mom returned. She knew that with the IV in her arm and a broken leg, it would be difficult to sleep on her side the way she was accustomed to. With the morphine helping with the pain, this would be the first night she would try to sleep lightly. Initially, she welcomed deep sleep as it took her mind off the pain. She had never had morphine before, but she liked the way it relaxed her while also easing her pain. It made her hospital stay more bearable. As she shifted this way and that in bed, she knew there would be no way she would be able to turn on her side. She pushed the call button beside her bed.

"Yeah, honey, what is it?" Cynthia asked, walking into the room.

"Cynthia, I'm used to sleeping on my side, but with the cast on, that's proving to be a hard thing to do. Is there *any* way I can sleep on my side tonight?"

"Unfortunately, no, at least not right now."

Cynthia laughed when Mikalya made a sour face, showing her displeasure at her response.

"You won't be here much longer. Connie and I are going to make you as comfortable as possible. You're healing nicely, so you'll be out soon. Doctor Hart is going to do another scan on your brain the day after tomorrow, and if that looks good, you may be out of here by the end of the week. But that cast will have to stay on for several more weeks. I think the doctor said about six," Cynthia said.

"Yes, he did say six, didn't he?" Mikalya retorted.

"Hey, your mom will be back soon for dinner. Do you want me to turn the TV on and get you the remote?"

"Sure. Thanks."

Cynthia finished up and left the room. Mikalya lay there with the TV on, gazing out the window and occasionally coughing. Her throat was still a little tender from the smoke inhalation. At 6 p.m. on the nose, Shelly walked through the door with a sack from White Castle and a bag containing some toiletries and makeup.

Mikalya sniffed the air and gave her mother a dirty look. "You know better than that!" she said. For the time being, she was on a strict hospital diet.

"I know, but a little won't hurt." Shelly winked, covertly angling the bag toward Mikalya, who reached in and grabbed a double hamburger. A guilty grin lit up her face before she put the burger up to her mouth and took a big bite. A sensation of tasteful ecstasy pervaded her senses.

"God, I swear, sometimes, this is better than sex." Mikalya sighed as Shelly's expression turned to one of shock.

The door opened, and Cynthia walked in. She immediately noticed the White Castle bag and, of course, the smell.

"I overheard you two talking about sex, and you really need to watch your diet for now," she said, pointing at Mikalya. "Dinner is on the way. Um… I couldn't steal one of those from you, could I?" she asked Shelly.

Shelly held out the bag like someone was bumming a cigarette from her. "Go for it. I always buy more than I can eat," she said.

Cynthia grabbed one, and it was gone in three bites.

"I wouldn't let anyone else on the floor know that you have this. They'll either quarantine you, or there will be a riot," Cynthia said.

Cynthia stayed until the White Castle bag was empty, then disposed of it in the waiting area.

****

Shelly spent the next day and night with Mikalya. As Cynthia had mentioned, Doctor Hart ordered more tests to determine the state of Mikalya's concussion. He concluded that she needed a few more days in the hospital, and it would probably be another week or so before she got out. Though not pleased to learn that she would not be released right away, Mikalya was happy when her head bandage was removed.

"Honey, listen. Beginning tomorrow, I need to go to work during the day for a few days until the weekend, but I will be here at night. Are you going to be OK?" Shelly asked.

"Not to worry, Mom, I think I'll be fine. Cynthia and Connie are great, and I'm feeling a bit stronger."

Just then, there was a knock at the door.

Mikalya frowned at Shelly, then made a desperate attempt to arrange her hair as Shelly got up to open the door.

"WAIT!" Mikalya said, brushing her hair repeatedly.

*Dammit, where's a mirror and a brush? Crap!*

"OK, go ahead and open it," she whispered to her mom.

Shelly looked back at Mikalya and then slowly opened the door. It was Sandy, the clerk from the flower shop.

"Hey, Sandy, how are ya?" Shelly said.

"Oh, I'm OK. I came to see how you guys were doing. Honey, are you OK?" she asked Mikalya.

"Yeah, I have some burns, a concussion, and a broken leg, but outside of that, I'm fine." Mikalya laughed.

"I know it's not pleasant, but you hang in there. I do have something to tell you that might make you feel a little better," Sandy said.

Shelly's ears perked up.

"That little vase of flowers over there on the table, I put those together," Sandy said.

"You're the second person that has seen him. He got those from *your* shop?" Mikalya asked.

"Yeah, he came in the other day and ordered the vase. He's damn cute, and he really seemed to want to meet you and your progress. Did you see him when he brought them over?"

"Unfortunately, Mikalya and I were both asleep when he came into the room. We missed him, although Connie, the night nurse here, talked to him a bit when he came by. She said almost the same thing you did," Shelly responded.

"Well, Sandy, in your opinion, is he a keeper?" Mikalya asked, raising an eyebrow with a sly smile.

"He's a no-brainer," she replied.

Sandy stayed a little longer before getting up to leave. "I have to get back to the shop. I just wanted to stop in. If you need anything, please let me know. Oh, and these homemade brownies are for you. I'm not sure if they're doctor-approved, but they sure taste good."

Sandy gave Mikalya a hug before turning toward the door.

"Thanks, honey. We'll catch up a little later," Shelly said as Sandy blew a kiss and left the room.

"Well, we now have a second opinion," Shelly said, giving Mikalya a thumbs up.

Mikalya held out her hand, and they high-fived each other.

They stayed up half the night just talking about this and that and Abe. Any questions Mikalya had about Abe would be answered sooner than she thought.

Shelly then drifted off to sleep, but Mikalya stayed awake, listening to the radio. A song came on she'd never heard before. "There's Something About Your Touch" by Francesca Beghe caused her ears to perk up. It reminded her of a man named Abe, whom she had never met.

# Chapter Six:
# Abraham Returns

By the time Mikalya awoke the next morning, Shelly was already up and brushing her teeth in front of the mirror in the bathroom.

"Are you leaving already?" Mikalya asked.

Shelly walked out of the bathroom. "Yeah, honey. I need to go and grab a quick shower, then get to work by eight. I have to get on the road earlier because Loretta lives farther out I'll be at work for a half day just to get things caught up a bit, and then Loretta and I are going to go out and pick up some clothes and other things we need. We don't even have enough underwear right now."

Mikalya shook her head.

"Has anyone been by the house? Aunt Loretta, maybe? She's been by here, right?" she asked.

"Loretta came by the very first day. She also went by the house and said it was a mess. I'm going to drive by it on the way, but I'm sure it will be depressing. Thank God we have some home insurance. Loretta got the ball rolling with them. By the way, that's another stop I need to make today.

"We're lucky to have a family like Loretta. She offered us her house and everything. I didn't even have to ask. Well, I have a lot to do, but I'll be back by dinnertime." Shelly leaned down to hug Mikalya and then left. Mikalya lowered her bed and then closed her eyes.

****

Shelly drove up to her aunt's and found the key, just where Loretta said it would be. Loretta would be at work now.

She walked upstairs and looked at the bedroom she and Mikalya would share. After her shower, she felt so much better and was surprised at how fast she was moving, considering her injuries from the fire. She hurried back down the stairs and rushed out to work. She pulled into the parking lot and went straight to her boss's office.

"Hey, Shelly, are you OK? How is Mikalya? I heard she was out of the coma," her supervisor asked.

"She's doing better, Kelly. Thanks for asking. The doctor wants to keep her for observation for a few more days."

"Well, that's good news. She'll be out before you know it. I have most everything caught up for you. Do you see how neat your desk looks?" Kelly asked, smiling.

"I want you to take a couple of weeks off and get things straightened out. You have plenty of comp time to use and if you run out of sick time, etc., we will make another plan. I'll bring in a temp. After Mikalya gets home, we'll work out your return."

"My God, Kelly, I don't know what to say. You've been so good to me over the years. Thank you so much. But, while I'm here, I can—" Shelly began, but Kelly cut her off.

"No, you can't. You have a daughter over at Saint Francis that needs you. Remember, I didn't have that luxury when my Karen had that accident. You remember the bastard who was our supervisor before me?" Kelly asked.

Shelly gave her a sour look. "Damn, Kelly, don't remind me. The best day of my life was when that prick got fired and you took his place. I really lobbied for you to get that position."

"I know you did, and I'll never forget it. Now, I want you to scoot along. We'll be fine here. Yes, we will need you back at some point, but not before you take care of all that you need to. Now, out of here. Just call me in a couple of days and let me know how you and Mikalya are."

They had a little more "out the door" chit-chat about work and a few other personal things. Shelly tearfully hugged her boss and was on her way. Her next stop would be the insurance company, but she needed to go by the house first and take a look at it. When she got there, she parked beside it and just stared. It was still ribboned off by the police in some areas.

She got out of the car and walked up close to it. She remembered where she had been standing and where the neighbors were holding her back. She just stood there, taking in all the panicked feelings once again. Part of her was angry at them for not allowing her to go back in, but the sensible side of her understood. If she had gone back in that last time, she might not have survived, and Mikalya wouldn't have a mother.

Shelly had managed to buy the house. Mikalya was only ten years old when they moved in. While nothing fancy, it was perfect for them. It was close to her job and close to the schools that Mikalya would attend.

She had watched her daughter grow up in that house and go through all the confusion of her teenage years all the way to a young lady of twenty.

Shelly carefully screened any boy who went out with her. She was never quite satisfied with any of them and remembered that there was one in particular who had hurt her badly. *That's part of the reason she's single now*, Shelly thought.

She saved money for Mikalya to go to vocational school for secretarial and computer study. Mikalya did well in her studies and then got an office job at First National Bank. She had the job for only a year when she got laid off due to a merger. The bank president and most of the upper executives received handsome buyout packages, but Mikalya and the other employees retained their health care coverage for six months, which would cover her hospital bills now.

She learned a hard lesson in how life works. That incident, and the boyfriend from a couple of years earlier, had made her somewhat cynical in general. Shelly had tried to counteract that as best she could, but it was difficult. Mikalya was as headstrong as they get.

Shelly walked a little farther into the house and peeked in. She still wasn't quite sure exactly where Abraham had found Mikalya. The inside of the house in its current state frightened her but it wasn't anything that couldn't eventually be rebuilt. She had seen all she needed to see. She was glad that the neighbors who had been there that day were not around, as she wasn't in the mood for conversation.

Shelly had reminisced long enough. There was no more time for anger. It had all worked out. Mikalya was safe, and that's all that mattered. She had to move on and rebuild. As she had a hundred things to do today, slowly walking back down the drive, she briefly glanced back toward the house before getting back into her car and driving away.

Pulling into her next parking lot of the day, she nervously entered the front door of Union Insurance Company. Although she had been a loyal customer for ten years, this would be the first claim she had ever filed a claim with them. Shelly didn't even have a copy of her homeowner's policy with her, as it burned in the fire. Loretta had called the insurance company to get things rolling for her.

Shelly walked up to the front desk.

"Hi, may I help you?" the receptionist asked.

"I'm here to see Sally Thompson," Shelly replied just as the agent entered the room.

"Hello, Ms. Arabella! Come right in. Have a seat. How is your daughter?" she asked, gesturing toward a chair.

"All things considered, she's fine. She has a broken leg and a mild concussion. They want to monitor her for a few more days before they release her."

"Good, that's the main thing…that she's OK. Now, I've looked up your account and pulled a copy of your policy. Your aunt said you didn't have a copy, which is perfectly understandable. Let me explain how this will work. First, to put your mind at ease, you are covered for the rebuild and ten thousand dollars for contents replacement," Sally said.

Shelly didn't show it, but she felt like the weight of the world had been lifted from her shoulders.

"That's great news!" Shelly replied.

"Well, you've been with us for quite a while, and I've been in your shoes, and it ain't fun, is it?" Sally joked.

"No, it's not fun, but we're lucky to be alive," Shelly said.

"So true. Now, you'll have about $50,000 to rebuild your house and $10,000 to replace furniture, clothing, and anything else you need. What you need to do now is contact a reputable builder and get that ball rolling.

"Tell the builder this is an insurance claim and to contact me through the rebuild process so we don't exceed the maximum amount. Here are a couple of my business cards. Once your claim is fully processed, we'll cut you a check for the contents."

"That's great, Sally. You've been really helpful and have taken a huge load off my mind."

"Well, that's what we're here for. Now, let's get this paperwork filled out so we can get you on your way."

As the two of them continued to go over the details of the claim process, something else was brewing that would change the course of their entire existence.

****

Abraham couldn't wait for this day to arrive. He had requested a few days off from the firehouse for the sole purpose of visiting Mikalya in the hospital. The captain had granted his request for the time off.

It had been a couple of days since he delivered the flowers. Anonymously, he had called ahead and inquired about her status. She was now out of her coma and receiving visitors.

He was both nervous and hopeful as he headed toward the hospital, but there would be no hesitation on his part when he arrived. He was going to see her, and she was going to be awake. *What is meant to be will be,* he thought.

Mikalya was lying in her hospital bed, watching TV, when suddenly, she felt strong cramps in her abdomen. She hadn't gone to the bathroom since she had awakened from her coma, and from past experience, she knew what the pains were. She and her mom affectionately referred to them as "poop cramps."

Waves of anxiety and embarrassment hit her simultaneously as the thought of using a bedpan ran through her mind. With a broken leg, she couldn't actually sit on a toilet, so her options were limited.

Reluctantly, she hit the buzzer, hoping Cynthia would *not* be the nurse on duty to answer it or her mother would come through the door before anyone else did. She'd prefer a stranger to help her in this case.... someone she didn't know at all. Thankfully, a new CNA came through the door.

"Hi, Mikalya. What can I help you with?" she asked.

"I am so sorry, but there's no sexy way to say this. I have to take a dump," Mikalya replied.

The CNA could tell by the look on her face that Mikalya was embarrassed. She smiled, then headed over to the supply closet and pulled out a nice, shiny, clean bedpan.

Mikalya grimaced and finished as soon as she could.

"Don't worry. I've done this a million times. In fact, I cleaned you up once while you were in your coma. I am so used to this," she reassured Mikalya.

"What is your name?" Mikalya asked.

"I'm Sophie!"

"Thank you so much for taking care of me like this, Sophie. It is so admirable and sweet of you," Mikalya said.

"It's OK. I actually like what I do. I love helping people."

"I can tell. I'm lucky to have you."

"Hey, how about a sponge bath and I can do a little something with your hair? How does that sound?" Sophie asked.

Mikalya smiled. "That sounds wonderful."

Sophie spent the next hour getting Mikalya cleaned up. She fixed her hair and even put a tad bit of makeup on that she grabbed from what Shelly brought her. She held the mirror up for Mikalya.

"What do you think?" she asked.

"OMG! I'm sure this is a lot better than when I came in here!"

"You look great! Now, listen, I need to finish my rounds, but at least you're feeling a little better. I'll be back before my shift ends to look in on you," Sophie said.

"OK, Sophie, thanks again!" Mikalya watched the nurse quickly walk out the door. She was thankful that she was surrounded by such caring staff.

Mikalya looked at the clock on the wall hanging over the television. It was 5 p.m., and Shelly said she would be back by six. Mikalya began flipping through the TV channels when she heard someone outside her door.

*That can't be Mom yet. She said she'd be back at six.*

The door partially opened, followed by a knock.

"Knock, knock," a strong yet soothing male voice said. Mikalya assumed it was a member of the hospital staff. She was wrong.

"Yeah, come on in," she invited.

The door opened slowly, and in walked one of the most beautiful men she had ever seen.

When they locked eyes, Mikalya knew that it was *him*. Abraham stopped in his tracks.

While still staring, Mikalya unconsciously clicked the off button on the TV remote in her hand.

For a few moments, they simply stared at each other. Similar waves of emotions wash over them both.

*My God, he's here, there he is*, was Mikalya's first thought.

*There's my girl. That's her*, was the first thought that went through Abe's head.

Mikalya's expression exuded wonder, fear, joy, confusion, affection, and love all at the same time.

Abe picked up on all of it.

Both had an immediate feeling of certainty. Mikalya kept staring; Abe spoke first.

"Hi, I'm Abraham Gallagher. My friends and family call me Abe. And you're Mikalya."

"Yes, I am. Thanks for telling me… who I am, that is," Mikalya joked. A warm feeling swept over her like a soothing spirit. She felt safe, so she settled into a secure comfort zone, giving the butterflies permission to fly away.

"Yes, Abe, it's me. How are you?" she continued.

It was the first time Abraham had heard her voice. Its tone and resonance assured him that his visits to her were not in vain. "I'm fine, but the real question is… how are you?" he replied.

"Well, outside of a concussion, a broken leg, and some pesky burns, I'm really OK, thanks to you. And I'm alive! Also, thanks to you," she said, looking into his eyes as tears began to well up in hers.

"I'm sorry. I don't mean to be a downer, but it's been… well… a little difficult… and scary… and hard… and… it's good to see you!" she said with a big smile.

"It's good to see you, too, Mikalya. And I'm glad you're recovering nicely," he said with an air of confidence. Relieved that she was happy to see him, too.

Mikalya glanced over at the flowers.

"I know you brought those. They're gorgeous, and I love roses, by the way."

"They are my mom's favorite. I was always partial to them, and I love the way they smell. Plus, when they're dried, you can crumble them up and put them in like… a potpourri pot."

An awkward pause fell over the room as they both looked around, avoiding making eye contact. Mikalya was the first to resume the conversation.

"Abe, listen, I think it goes without saying, but I cannot even begin to thank you for what you did for me. I wouldn't be here if it wasn't for you. I just can't…" she began.

Abe put a finger up to his lips. "Shhhh. Let's not talk about that right now. How much longer do you think you'll be in here?"

"Well, they're really monitoring my head injury, and then there's this damn broken leg. The burns are healing well, the doctor says. I'm surprised and relieved that my burns weren't more extensive… again, all thanks to you."

"Your burns came from burning drywall material falling on you. You were passed out, so you couldn't have known all that was happening to you or around you. Right after I lifted you up, a large dresser fell through the top floor right above you and landed right where you had been lying, passed out."

Mikalya stared at him intently once again.

"So, you're saying the dresser would have—"

Abe cut her off. "Yes, that's right. And I thought we weren't going to talk about this right now."

"Yes, you're right. I'm sorry. Well, anyway, the doctor said they don't see any further damage from the concussion; I could be out of here in a week or so. I did just wake up from a coma, so they're being extra cautious and making sure there's no more bleeding."

"I know. That's pretty much standard procedure. It's called covering their butts, but that's a good thing. How's your primary care nurse?" Abe asked.

"She's great. Her name is Cynthia. She's here but leaves around seven. Then, my nightcare nurse, Connie, comes in. When she comes in, I'll introduce you. My mom, Shelly, is coming back to have dinner with me at six if you'd like to stay to meet her."

Abe opened his mouth to respond that he had already met Connie and that meeting Shelly might be too soon when the door swung open after a slight and brief knock. It was Shelly.

*She's not supposed to be here for another thirty minutes. She's never early,* Mikalya thought.

"Hey, honey, I…" Shelly said, stopping mid-sentence when she saw Abe. The last time she'd seen him, he was hovering over her daughter as Shelly was being driven away in an ambulance.

"You look familiar," she said. She made an embarrassed facial expression and then immediately felt like an idiot.

Mikalya rolled her eyes and covered her mouth to keep from laughing at the silly expression on her mom's face.

Abe held out his hand. "I'm Abe. I remember you. You're Mikalya's mom, right?"

Shelly stared. Mikalya kept her hand over her mouth in anticipation of her mom, some goofy comment coming out of her mom's mouth.

"Yeah, it's me, or, I mean, I am. Yes, I'm Mikalya's mother," Shelly sputtered.

Mikalya couldn't hold it in any longer. She burst into laughter. "MOM!"

Shelly looked over at her. "What?" Shelly asked.

"Ms. Arabella, I'm glad I finally got to formally meet you and your daughter," Abe said, loosening up the conversation.

"It's good to meet you under better circumstances, too. Now, do you make hospital visits and bring roses for all the people whose lives you save?" Shelly asked, surprising herself at the frankness of her question but curious to see how Abe would answer.

Abe looked over at Mikalya with his response. "No."

Mikalya looked away so that he wouldn't see the smile spreading across her face.

"So then—" Shelly began before Mikalya interrupted her.

"So, Abe, on behalf of my mother and I, we thank you so much for the lovely flowers and for taking the time to come and check up on me. Oh, and for saving my life!" she added, glancing over at Shelly.

Abe nodded. He found Mikalya's behavior and personality charming. She had a cool but lazy, intelligent air about her, combined with a sprinkle of smart-ass.

"No problem. It was my pleasure. Will there be anything else?" he asked, attempting to mimic a hospital orderly.

Mikalya didn't want him to leave.

"Well, will you be joining us for dinner?" she asked.

Shelly glanced over at her daughter, whom she knew all too well. This was only the beginning. She could feel it.

Inside, Abe was elated but tried not to show it. The roses, combined with his visit, were the perfect strategy. She wanted him to stay, but he wanted to play it cool for as long as he could.

"Well, actually, I need to get going. I just wanted to stop in for a bit. Anyway, you need to spend time with your mom. But if you're up to it, how about we make it a date tomorrow?"

Mikalya smiled. She knew that he really didn't have to go; that was just his way of dangling a carrot in front of her. *Typical macho man,* she thought. Also, until he really got to know her better, she might think it weird if he came on way too strong. What he didn't realize was that Mikalya didn't care how strong he came on as long as he came on. She would take it from there.

"You got yourself a date...*uuhhh*, I mean a hospital visitation date. And you had better be here at 5 p.m. sharp because, after that, the doors are locked," Mikalya said.

Shelly stood silent at the exchange.

Mikalya waited for a response. She didn't care how forward she might have been, only that he had gotten the message loud and clear. She would be expecting him, and he had better show up.

"Well, five it is! Aside from dinner, would you like me to bring anything else? White Castle? Long's doughnuts?"

Mikalya's smile grew wider.

"You like White Castle?" she asked.

"Ever since I was a little kid. Do you really like them?" he said.

"Oh, God, yes! You see, I knew there was another reason I liked you besides you pulling me out of a burning house. I grew up on White Castle, too!"

Shelly instantly took on an embarrassed expression and shyly looked down at the floor.

"So, you like me more now that you know I like White Castle?" Abe asked.

"Well, I'm not sure yet, but we'll talk about that more tomorrow, so don't be late. OK?"

"You got it," he replied.

"By the way, what's that in your hand?" Mikalya asked.

"Oh, it's nothing special… just a little get-well card for you. I wrote a little verse in it. Most of the cards on store racks are a little sad or too cheesy. I hope you like this one," he said, handing her the card.

Mikalya looked over at Shelly and then opened the card.

*I heard you were getting a little burned out on life; I, too, can relate to all the pressure and strife.*

*You looked so incredible in your cozy hospital bed; With your beautiful hair all shiny and red.*

*Now and forever, you'll be in my prayers; I am so thankful I was the one who found you lying at the edge of the stairs.*

Mikalya read and then re-read the card again before looking up at Abe, tears waiting in the corner of her eyes. She put the card down and motioned with both arms for him to come closer to the bed. "Get over here and give me a big hug, dammit," she said.

Abe quickly obliged.

"So am I. See ya tomorrow," she whispered in his ear, kissing his cheek before releasing him.

"See you then," he replied.

There was one final stare into each other's eyes.

He then looked over at Shelly. "It was nice seeing you again, Ms. Arabella," he said, reaching for Shelly's hand.

"Same here," she replied.

They both watched as he exited the room.

Once the door shut, Shelly plopped in the chair, armed with questions for her daughter.

"How long was he here before I showed up?" she asked.

Mikalya didn't even look at her.

"I don't know, twenty minutes or so. Not long enough. But one thing is for sure. If he'd come forty-five minutes earlier, he'd have caught me on a bedpan," she replied.

Shelly laughed hysterically.

"Oh, my God, that's a good one. We'll have a drink over that line when you get out of here. You know I could blackmail you with that one if I wanted to, right?" Shelly asked, holding her stomach and still laughing.

“Yeah, but you won’t. Hey, can you hand me the menu? I have to get my dinner ordered. What are you going to eat?” Mikalya asked.

“Who was that guy that just walked out of your room? He walked right past me on the way in,” Cynthia said, walking through the door.

“He came in to give Mikalya a sponge bath,” Shelly said jokingly.

“What?!” Cynthia asked excitedly.

“Well, it was more of a mental sponge bath,” Shelly said.

Mikalya looked at her mom and rolled her eyes.

“His name is Abraham Gallagher, and he’s the firefighter who saved my life…the one who carried me out of the house. He’s also the one who brought the flowers the other day,” Mikalya shared.

“You’re kidding!” Cynthia said. “My God, he *did* come back. Tell me about him!”

“He’s really cool, a nice guy, a gentleman, and I think he really likes me.”

“And it’s obvious you really like him,” Shelly chimed in. She could see that this guy was different and that Mikalya was different around him. As she had done in the past, she vowed to not interfere. Mikalya was old enough to make her own decisions and choices.

Her protective maternal instincts were starting to surface once she had seen what was transpiring. However, something inside told her this Abraham *thing* was different. The whole relationship was starting out differently. It wasn't like he picked her up in a bar or met her on some sleazy dating service. This was different, very different. It's rare that any relationship started out this way. She could sense, too, that Abe exuded sincerity and caring for Mikalya. She picked up on it right away.

He obviously had his act together, big time. No one else she ever knew in her life could do what Abe did for her daughter that day. She owed it to Mikalya to see just how this was going to play out. She saw how her daughter interacted with him and the expressions on her face. If nothing else, he'd certainly make her healing process here faster and much more bearable. She decided, right then and there, to not interfere this time, like she'd done in the past. Her intuition had not let her down before and wouldn't this time.

"Mom, yeah, I admit I like him. Wouldn't you like the guy who saved you from a burning house?"

"Yes, I get it. He does seem like a really nice guy. You know, I only want the best for you. In all things."

"I know. But, this time, just take a step back and let this… whatever this is, play out. I think you'll be pleased in the end."

"Not to worry. I've already decided not to interfere in your relationships anymore. You're old enough to make your own decisions. Just don't forget about your old mom, OK?"

"Listen, go on and order your dinner so that we can eat," Shelly continued.

Cynthia checked Mikalya's vitals.

"Mikalya, my shift is over, but Connie will be in soon. I'll see you in the morning. By the way, you're starting to look a lot better," she said with a wink. "Is there anything you need before I leave?"

"No, not right now, Cynthia. Thanks, though."

"Hey, when you get out of here, the three of us should go out for a drink. How does that sound?" Cynthia asked.

Shelly smiled. "That sounds like a great idea. I'd love that," she said.

Cynthia popped back to the nurse's station and then stuck her head in and waved goodbye as Mikalya's dinner was being pushed through the door on a cart.

She and Shelly chatted for the next couple of hours, with Shelly sharing the events of her day, ending with the assurance that their lives would be back on track soon.

Mikalya could hardly sleep that night; she was anticipating Abraham's visit the next evening. It would be a weird date of sorts, but she didn't care. All she cared about was seeing him again.

****

Mikalya opened her eyes the next morning and heard her mom moving about in the bathroom… again. "Where are you off to today?" she asked.

"Good morning to you, too, sleepyhead," Shelly replied. "I'm off to meet with the builder, and then I'm going to run to the mall."

"When are you coming back?" she asked.

"Sometime around three. I have a lot to go over with the builder. We have to get that house done ASAP. Listen, is there anything you want from the store? I'm going to pick up some groceries and drop thcm by Lorctta's."

"No, Mom, just get what you think we need. Shall I trust your judgment on underwear? Just nothing granny style," Mikalya said.

Shelly leaned down and kissed Mikalya's forehead. "See you this afternoon," she said.

"Sounds good," Mikalya replied.

"Oh, and listen. Abraham said he was coming back today around five. I am going to be out of here before that time, so you two can have some time alone."

Mikalya looked at her mom lovingly, with a pout on her bottom lip. Shelly knew exactly what that look meant; her daughter needed her space but still loved her deeply.

"Thanks, Mom."

Shelly smiled as she walked out the door.

Against her supervisor's wishes, she went to work for a couple of hours. Then, she met with the building contractor at his office to get the ball rolling on the rebuilding of their home.

The contractor informed her they could begin clearing the debris left behind by the fire in ten days or so.

After she met with the contractor and ran by a couple of department stores, she noticed that it was already close to four, well past the time she promised Mikalya she would return. She hurried back to the hospital to spend a few minutes with Mikalya before Abraham arrived. She didn't want to interfere with their time together, so she'd stay until his arrival.

"Hey, honey, I'm back," Shelly said, entering the room. When she got closer to Mikalya's bed, she noticed a copy of *Time* magazine in her hands. "What are you doing with that? You've never read that before."

"Cynthia brought it in. She said the guy a couple of rooms down didn't want it anymore, so she dropped it off here. God, all the crap going on in the world!" Mikalya said.

Shelly took the magazine from her and threw it in the trash. "You don't need to be reading that right now. I want you to think positively. Now, listen, I'm not going to staying long. I assume Abraham is still coming. He seems like the kind of guy who pretty much does what he says he's gonna do. You don't need me hanging around while you two get better acquainted."

"Mom, you know you can stay. No matter what happens or doesn't happen, you're my mother, and I love you."

"Honey, I know that, and right back at ya. But I can tell that you really like this guy, outside of him saving your life. And to be honest, I'm getting some good vibes from him. Whatever this might be, I want it to at least get off to a good start. When a guy comes to spend time with a woman he really likes for the first time, the last thing he wants is for her mother to be hanging around *supervising* the situation. I mean, you're not twelve years old anymore. Besides, Aunt Loretta is insisting that we go out for drinks tonight. These burns on my arm are still a little annoying, and I think I'm due for a couple of glasses of wine. I'm sure you'll be fine."

"Would you at least stay until he gets here, then you can politely excuse yourself?"

"Sweetie, of course, but then, I'm leaving. I don't want him to feel uncomfortable. Are you nervous?"

"Actually, I'm not. That's the weird thing about it. I feel more comfortable than I've ever felt around someone new in a long time," Mikalya said when a quiet knock came at the door.

Shelly looked at her watch. It was five on the dot.

"Come in," Mikalya said, glancing over at Shelly with a smile.

"Room service," the cleaning lady said, pushing through the door.

The smile on Mikalya's face dropped.

"Ma'am, can you come back a little later? Maybe get a couple more rooms first, then come back here? I'm sorry, but I'm expecting someone," she said.

"Sure! I'll come back later," the housekeeper replied.

When the housekeeper opened the door to leave, Abraham's hand was positioned to knock. She stepped aside to let him in as she waved and left the room.

Mikalya's smile returned. *I knew he'd be here,* she thought.

"Hey!" she said.

"Hey. How are you?" Abe replied.

"I'm just a wee bit better than when you were here yesterday. But just a wee bit," Mikalya said, her smile growing wider.

"How are you, Ms. Arabella?" Abe asked.

"I'm fine. I'm just leaving. I still have a lot of things to do in preparation for us rebuilding," she answered. "Thank God we have homeowner's insurance."

"Thank God that you do. You'd be surprised how many people don't. If you don't have money, rebuilding is just about impossible," Abe said.

"Well, you two have a good time, or at least as best you can in here. Honey, I'll see you in the morning. Nice seeing you again, Abraham. Oh, and please call me Shelly. Ms. Arabella is so formal. Bye, you two," she said, kissing Mikalya on the forehead and walking out the door.

Mikalya and Abe followed her out of the room with their eyes before turning and locking eyes with each other. An awkward silence ensued, as this was the first time they were really alone together long enough to talk. Mikalya decided to speak first.

"Abe, there's a chair there on the other side of the bed. Can you bring it over here to this side?" Mikalya asked.

"Sure." He squeezed over and pulled a large chair out with one hand, lifting it over her bed and then placing it close to the other side of the bed. She was amazed at the ease with which he moved the chair. Those strong, deliberate moves had excited her.

"So, is there anything I can get you: a glass of water or maybe even a magazine from the gift shop?" he asked.

"Oh, thanks, but I still have some water, and I haven't been reading much at all. I've been either sleeping or up talking with my nurses. Mom has been here every day, too. I don't know what I'd do without her. We're extremely close, but I think you already sensed that," Mikalya went on.

"Yeah, I did, and that's a good thing. I had that closeness with my parents, and I was lucky they stayed together. I think when a divorce goes down, especially a nasty one, it screws up the kids' heads. Unless one of the parents is a real jerk, and the family just wants them gone," Abe said.

"I agree," Mikalya replied as the door to her room swung open after a brief knock.

Abe jumped up to take the food tray from the orderly. "Here, let me get that," he said as the orderly rolled Mikalya's overbed table across her lap. Then, Abe gently set the tray down in front of her.

Thanking Abe for his assistance, the aide left the room.

"OK, young lady, is that table high enough for you? Do you need it adjusted? Would you like me to change the angle somewhat?" Abe asked jokingly. While he waited for an answer, he put the straw in her drink, took the lid off her main course, and unwrapped her silverware. Finally, he sat down, noticing Mikalya staring at him again.

He was starting to love the way she just stared at things, especially him.

Mikalya looked down at her food tray. "God, this is just like being at the Waffle House," she said, smiling.

"Well, the food's a little better there," Abe said. "You like the Waffle House?"

"I love it. I'm kind of a breakfast food girl. Give me some greasy sausage, a cheese omelet, a pile of hash browns with sourdough toast, and I'm in heaven."

"You know, the first minute I met you, I had a feeling that we would have things in common," he said.

"OK, funny man, let me see what culinary delights lie in front of me here. Ah… I see green beans, little red potatoes, a roll with butter, vanilla pudding, and a wonderful-looking piece of meatloaf. Care for a taste?" Mikalya offered.

Abe had heard too many horror stories about hospital food but didn't want to share them with Mikalya just as she was about to eat.

"You know, that looks delicious, but I already grabbed a bite before I came over. You just enjoy," Abe said.

"OK," she replied before digging in.

"Is there anything in particular you'd like to watch?" he asked, picking up the remote from her bed.

"Can you put it on Animal Planet for now and leave the volume down so we can keep talking? Thank you, sir," she said. She didn't want to get wrapped up in what was on TV since Abe was there. This was a good time for the two of them to get to really know one another better, and she didn't want to blow it. If he was kind enough to come by and visit her in the hospital, the least she could do was give him her undivided attention.

"How long can you stay? Do you have other plans after you leave here?" Mikalya asked.

"Well, I am off for the next several days, so I can stay for as long as you want. How long would you *like* me to stay?" he asked. He knew it was a loaded question but went with it.

Mikalya was not shy to come right back after, of course, she finished chewing her food. After she got over the slight nervousness of Abe being there, her hunger finally set in. One good vibe she got from Abe was the fact that she really didn't have to play games with him. She felt comfortable shooting straight from the heart. She went for it.

"Well, to tell you the damn truth, I'd love it if you would keep me company the entire night. In all honesty, I don't want you to leave at all. I'll talk to Connie, my night nurse, and ask if we can get a cot in here for you. But I don't want to impose. If this is too much too fast, please just tell me," Mikalya said.

Abe looked at her. The expression on her face exuded hope and fear at the same time. She had allowed herself to be vulnerable with him. How could he say no? If Abe was not fully aware of Mikalya's true feelings toward him, he was now. Mikalya had temporarily stopped eating and was looking directly into his eyes. Abe also realized just how intense Mikalya could be and how she didn't hide her feelings and emotions.

"I'm not too busy for *you*. I'd love to stay with you tonight," he said softly as Mikalya reached out her hand to him. He squeezed her hand lightly, rubbing his thumb across the softness of her palm. Their relationship had begun. A very unorthodox situation had brought them together. There would be no flirting or pretending. From here on out, their efforts toward each other would be of protection on a physical and spiritual basis.

They held each other for several minutes, then withdrew.

“Listen, why don’t you finish eating, and I’ll run down to the cafeteria and grab a little something to bring back up. Do you want anything?” Abe asked.

“I would love a Diet Coke.”

“You know, those things are bad for you, but I’ll bring you one anyway. Is it OK with your doctor?”

“I really don’t have a lot of diet restrictions right now. I don’t drink Coke that often, but one sounds really good.”

Connie watched Abe walk out of Mikalya’s room and head toward the elevator, so she decided to pay her a visit.

“Hi, how are you doing tonight?” Connie asked, peeking her head into Mikalya’s room before walking in.

Mikalya could tell by the look on her face that she had seen Abe.

“I get the impression you’re not asking about my health,” Mikalya responded.

Connie smiled without even looking at her.

“I just saw a certain male leave your room, and I do believe it was the same one who brought you the flowers a few days ago. Am I correct?” she asked.

“Yes, that was Abraham, Connie. I was wondering if… well… it would be OK if he stayed in the room with me overnight? He’s really polite and would be a big help to your staff and—”

Connie cut her off. “Yes, of course, he can. If your mom is not going to be back, then he can use hers.”

Mikalya smiled at her. “Thanks, Connie!”

“Mikalya, the way he looks, I’d be requesting a cot, too… a queen-sized one so we could sleep together!” Connie said, laughing.

Mikalya blushed through her laughter. “You’re a bad girl, Connie,” she giggled. Connie gave her a wide-eyed look of surprise.

“Now, just what is that supposed to mean?” Connie asked.

“Stop making me laugh! You know what I’m talking about!” Mikalya replied.

“Well, let me clarify. A queen-sized cot holds two people,” Connie said.

“I’ve never heard of a queen-sized cot before,” Mikalya replied.

“But you can imagine?” Connie said.

“Connie, did you come in here to check my vitals or to make me laugh so hard I’m almost about to wet the bed?” With a look of mischief on her face, Connie checked Mikalya’s monitor.

“Everything looks good. All your numbers are where they should be right now. How do you feel physically?”

“I feel OK. No dizziness, and the pain from my burns has gotten much better. Whatever you gave me is working great. I mean, it’s still here, but I can deal with it. It's just my damn leg. I can't wait to get out of this cast. It throbs so bad! It's hard to even pee."

"Just hang in there. That leg pain will dissipate soon enough, but you'll have that cast on for a while longer. The concussion is the big thing. Your neurologist, Doctor Hart, will be by tomorrow to check in on you. Let him know how you're feeling. He's one of the best neurologists in this area. He'll get you fixed right up. Listen, when you get fully healed, let's all go out for a well-deserved drink. It's on me. How does that sound? I assume Abe *would* join us. Right?" Connie asked.

"Connie, I'd love it. And I noticed you threw Abe's name in there. How do you know it just might not be someone else?" Mikalya asked.

"You're not that dumb," she said. Mikalya just looked at her.

"Thanks for everything, Connie," Mikalya said.

"I'll be back around in a couple of hours. Just hit the buzzer if you need anything. Or better yet, just send Abe to the nurse's station," she said with a wink.

"Oh, sure, then I'll never see him again," Mikalya replied.

"You might be right. We'd keep him! Would you like for me to take your tray?"

"No, thanks, I want to finish everything. I'm surprised that I even have an appetite for this hospital food," Mikalya said.

Connie smiled and headed off to her next patient.

Mikalya flipped through the channels a little too anxiously. Abe had been gone for well over thirty minutes, and she had no idea what was keeping him. Their first real encounter had gone well, she thought. A blind man could see that they liked each other. She didn't know where those feelings had come from, and she didn't care. She reasoned that not a lot of other men could not, or would not, have done what he did. Certainly not the yahoos she had encountered over the past few years. Mikalya wondered what he saw in her. What man would be attracted to a girl laid up in a hospital bed with body burns and a broken leg? And what other man would be attracted to her now with a mild concussion, and still with body burns, and a broken leg? Although the burns seemed to be rapidly healing, Doctor Hart said there would be some scarring. Abe could be out with any woman he wanted, yet he was hanging out in a hospital with her. The thought brought a smile to Mikalya's lips.

Abe had decided to make a quick trip around the corner from the hospital to a little mom-and-pop shop he was familiar with. Instead of a snack from the hospital cafeteria, his mind settled on a good hamburger. Their sundaes were famous, so he decided to pick one up for Mikalya instead of the bad soda she had requested. If she didn't like sundaes, this one would blow her mind. He'd been gone longer than expected, so when his food was ready, he practically snatched the bag from the server's hand and ran back to his car.

"Hey, you were gone for a while. I thought you were just going to the cafeteria," Mikalya said as Abe rushed through the door with a bag in one hand, a cup in another, and another box under his arm.

"Well, I did head toward the cafeteria but made a detour out to my car and around the corner to The Frosty Mug for one of their incredible hamburgers and a special treat for you," he said, handing her one of the milkshakes. "You've heard of The Frosty Mug, I assume," Abe said.

"Yeah! I used to eat there a lot in high school. Mom and I would go over there every now and then, but I haven't been there in a while. It's really good. I just finished my scrumptious meal here. So, what is that little surprise you have in there for me?" Mikalya asked.

Abe carefully and very slowly pulled out his tenderloin and put it on the food table still in front of Mikalya's bed. Then he pulled out a mysterious-looking container.

Mikalya deduced that it was a sundae, but she acted like she was still in suspense. However, the way Abe brought it over would surprise her.

“I hope I don’t need another shot of morphine after this,” she said, smiling.

Abe slowly pulled out a beautiful, old-fashioned glass sundae and laid the container he had paid extra for right in front of her. He had them pack it in a way that the whipped cream topping with the nuts and cherry wasn’t mashed down. He carefully unwrapped his masterpiece until it was fully exposed in all its glory. The whipped cream sat on top of it all in divine symmetry. The cherry was impeccably balanced and centered on top, with all the nuts in perfect order. Abe ordered a large, so the size alone was enough to get Mikalya’s attention. It looked like some sort of chocolate whipped cream fountain. Also, there would be plenty for the two of them if Mikalya was unable to eat it all. That was in the back of Abe’s mind as well.

“My God, Abraham, that’s incredible,” she said after one sip of the concoction made its way off a spoon into her mouth. “This is really good! Thank you! How in the hell did you get that back in one perfect piece like that?”

“Do you really like it?” he asked.

“Absolutely not!” she said.

Abe’s face dropped, along with his heart. He had wanted to share with her something he loved, and she didn’t even like it.

"I love it! And it feels so good on my throat!" she continued, smiling at his expression changes.

"You got me with that one, Mikalya. You're such a jokester. I'm glad you like it. It's one of my favorites."

"Let's see, so far, you've saved my life, given me the most beautiful damn roses I've ever seen… actually the only roses anyone's ever given me, and the best sundae I've ever had in my life. You're shooting three and O. It's going to be hard to top all this. So, are you going to try?" she asked boldly.

She gave him an ever so slightly mischievous look.

Abe looked back at her with a serious expression on his face.

"Do you want me to?" he asked.

When he looked at her that way, all of Mikalya's pain disappeared into thin air. A very different kind of feeling took its place. Like a child, she slowly tugged at his shirt, motioning him closer to her face and putting her mouth right next to his ear.

"Well, hell yes," she whispered in seductive softness.

# Chapter Seven: The Shining

Abe slowly pulled back and looked into Mikalya's eyes. She had made yet another serious move on him. Her eyes begged the question: *What are you going to do next?*

Leaning forward, he put his hand on the side of her face, the first time he'd touched her like *that*. Leaning closer, he put his lips gently on hers.

Mikalya's eyes closed in ecstasy, and for several seconds, she completely lost track of time and where she was. She could feel every cell in her skin gently ripple, like small waves in a sea of liquid turquoise. Ecstasy enveloped her entire body. She put her arm around Abe's shoulders and stroked his hair.

They remained locked in their passionate kiss, Abe enjoying the sound of Mikalya moaning as the kiss intensified.

Suddenly, their beautiful moment was shattered when the door swung open. It was the CNA, Sophie.

Abe and Mikalya tried to gather themselves, but it was too late. Sophie had seen them and stopped dead in her tracks.

"I am so sorry. Oh, God, I am so sorry. I didn't mean to just barge in here," she said.

Embarrassed, Abe and Mikalya could do nothing but smile at her.

"I just came in to see how you were doing and get your tray if you're done eating and it looks like you are." She blushed. "Sorry, I didn't mean it like that. Are you done? I mean, are you done eating? That's what I meant," she said.

Still flushed with the embarrassment of being caught like a teenager, Abe moved away from Mikalya and allowed Sophie full access to the bed area, looking around the room uncomfortably.

"No, it's OK, and yes, I am done," Mikalya said, her hair mussed and out of place.

"Oh, look, your sundae has spilled," Sophie said.

"Oh, crap, honey… I mean… Abraham, can you get that?" Mikalya asked.

"I can get it; he doesn't have to," Sophie offered before Abe could move.

"Trust me, he's accustomed to little crises and big ones, too," Mikalya went on as Sophie scooted in quickly to collect the food tray.

Abe hadn't said a word since Sophie had burst into the room. He exited the bathroom with a wet towel, but before he could move toward the table, Sophie moved closer to him.

"I can take that for you, sir," she offered.

Mikalya noticed the way that Sophie looked at Abe and how her voice lowered when she spoke to him. She didn't like it.

Abe handed her the wet towel, and Sophie quickly cleaned the spill from the tray.

"Is there anything else you need?" she asked Mikalya.

"No, we can take it from here. Just take the tray for now," Mikalya replied curtly.

"Would you like for me to close the door after I leave, or would you like it open? I mean, it's up to you."

"It's OK. Leave it open," Mikalya replied dismissively, her eyes following Sophie as she quickly exited the room with the tray and towel in hand.

Mikalya and Abe watched the doorway until Sophie was out of the room. Then, they looked at each other with surprised expressions and chuckled softly.

"*Uhm…* should we close the door?" he asked.

"Well, I didn't see that coming," Mikalya said, ignoring his question.

"That's because your eyes were closed," Abe replied.

Mikalya burst into laughter.

"You didn't answer my question, silly. Should I shut the door?" he asked again.

"Well, let's wait a few minutes. I don't want them to think that when the door is closed, *something's* going on in here, if you know what I mean."

Abe snickered. "Oh, so we're going to be coy about it. We both know that she saw us making out. But I've got an idea. After we've gotten all our laughs out, I'll close the door just a few inches every five minutes. Then, once it's finally closed all the way, they won't even realize that it was ever open to begin with. How does that sound?"

Mikalya's eyebrows creased. "That might make more sense after I've had another shot of morphine."

"I'll bet you a dollar that she's already told everyone at the nursing station we were in here making out," Abe said.

"Connie's the charge nurse tonight, and she's cool. Besides, she already knows about you. You know what? Just go ahead and shut the door."

Abe obliged, then looked down at his watch.

"Now, is your mom coming back tonight? I notice her cot's still here."

"I don't think so. She said she was going out for drinks with her aunt later. Anyway, I'd rather have her doing that, and you stay here instead."

Mikalya wasn't shy about expressing her feelings, and Abe loved how direct she was. It was one of the many refreshing qualities about her that he admired. His past held memories of too many women who played games, too afraid to say what they really wanted, and too insecure to mean any of it. As young as she was, Mikalya was far from playing games. She knew exactly what she wanted, and she'd made it known that she wanted him. He walked over to the cot and pressed down on it with his hand, as if testing its stability.

"Actually, I prefer extra firm. This appears to be extra, extra, extra, extra firm. And extra lumpy," he teased.

Mikalya smiled. "It's the best I can offer right now. Maybe you'll get that extra firm mattress someday." The cot was too small for his tall frame, but she sensed that he didn't mind at all.

He took a seat on the cot, then lay back, his left leg dangling to the side. "Hell, it's not that bad. I've slept on much worse."

Their conversation was interrupted by the phone's ring. It was Shelly.

"Hello, Mom," Mikalya answered.

"Hey, how are you? Is he still there?" Shelly asked.

"Well, what do you want to know first? How I'm doing, or if he's still here?" Mikalya shot back with a mischievous wink at Abe.

"He's right there, isn't he?"

"Yeah, and I'm doing well, Mom. Thanks for asking."

"Well, that's good. Aunt Loretta and I are still out having a drink. We're going to order dinner soon, then head back to her house."

"That's more than fine, Mom. Just take a break. Enjoy yourself a little. You've done a lot."

"Do you think he'll stay the night with you?"

"Yes," Mikalya whispered into the phone, turning her head away from Abe so that he wouldn't hear her mom quizzing her as if she was a child.

"OK, that's fine, but don't do anything—" Shelly began.

"*Uuhhh*, yes, Mom, I'm glad that you're enjoying your time with Aunt Loretta. You both have a wonderful night," Mikalya said, interrupting her.

Shelly got the message loud and clear. "Ha, ha, OK. You two have a good night as well. I'll call you in the morning."

"Night, Mom, and thanks for calling. Love you. Bye."

Mikalya quickly pressed the END button on her cell phone before Shelly could say more.

"Love you too, honey," Shelly managed to squeeze in before the line went silent.

"How is your mom?" Abe asked, sitting up on the cot.

"She's fine. She's out right now with Aunt Loretta enjoying some drinks and about to get dinner."

"With all that you two have been through, she more than deserves it."

"You're right. And, besides, when I get out of here, I'll be celebrating, too. Maybe, just maybe, we can celebrate together. What do you think?" Mikalya asked.

Abe couldn't quite identify the look she was giving him, but he knew that he liked it. "I already know where we're going," he replied.

"Where?" she asked.

"It's this quaint little spot, nice atmosphere, a really cool place."

"I'll bet it's some watering hole where your fireman buddies hang out. Right?"

"Well, I can't say for sure. It would spoil the surprise. I'll keep you in suspense. We'll make your wanting to go there a primary impetus for wanting to get out of here."

"Impetus… I like that word. It means, like, driving force."

"You are indeed correct, Miss Mikalya. I'm impressed."

"Abe?"

"Yeah," he answered, noticing the change in her tone. He got up from the cot and moved closer to her bed.

"Can I ask you a question?"

"Sure, what is it?" he asked.

"Are we on a first date?"

Abe couldn't tell if she was being facetious or if she was serious. At any rate, he sensed he should answer quickly. "Well, let's see… I'd say our first date was the day of the fire, except I didn't officially ask you out."

"No, I'm serious. I'm not the kind of woman who hides her feelings. I like being with you and feel extremely comfortable around you. I don't know what it is. I sense that you feel the same. That's the strange thing about it. I think I feel what you feel. I hope you don't think I'm weird."

Abe took her hand and squeezed it.

"You're not weird at all. I felt something for you the first time I picked you up from the edge of those stairs in your house. I'm not sure what it was, but just that it was. The only purpose in my life at that moment was to get you out alive; then I'd figure the rest out later. Does that make sense to you?"

"It does make sense, but I have another question."

"Fire away," he replied.

"Are you still trying to figure things out?"

"No, I'm not. It's getting clearer, much clearer," he said, leaning forward and kissing her lips. As he pulled away gently, he began stroking her hair.

"I'll let that speak for itself for now. But, in the meantime, I am going to play nurse. Let me get you some fresh water, and then we'll find a good movie on TV. It's nine o'clock. There should be something good on."

He adjusted her pillows and straightened her covers. Mikalya was blown away, once again, by his gentleness. As they began flipping through the guide, there was a knock at the door.

"Sorry to bother you, but I need to get your vitals. Hey, mister, how are you doing?" Connie asked, walking over to Mikalya's bed. "We chatted a few days ago when you brought the flowers. Do you remember?"

"Yes, I do. I'm doing well, and thanks for asking. But it's our patient here who we should be concerned about, and I think she's doing better. What do you think?" he asked.

"From where I'm standing, she appears to be progressing nicely. We'll see what the doctor says in the morning. Here, let me take a look at those burns."

Connie pulled the bandage off Mikalya's arm and cleaned the area that had been burned. Then she reapplied the medicated cream and put on a fresh bandage.

"There, is that better?" she asked.

Mikalya flexed her arm like she was going to take a basketball shot. "Why, yes, it is!"

"Good, I can't get over how well you're healing. I've never seen burns heal that fast, but I'm pleased about it. As I said, the doctor will be making his rounds around 9 a.m., and he'll check everything himself then. How does your head feel?"

"Well, I can think straight if that's what you're asking. Do you think the doctor will allow me to try to walk in the cast for a bit in the morning?"

Connie stared at her and laughed. Abe looked up at the ceiling and rolled his eyes.

"I'll tell you what. Save that question for the doctor. How does that sound?" she replied.

"That's fine."

"Do you need anything for pain right now?" Connie asked.

"How about another squirt of morphine around eleven or so before I go to sleep?"

"You got it. I'll be back later. Do you want anything else?"

"No, I think I'm good for now."

"Abe, do you need anything?" Connie asked.

"No, thanks, Connie. I'm fine."

"Thanks for hanging out with Mikalya. I'm sure your presence is helping the healing process."

Abe smiled. "Thank you for those kind words."

"I'll be back later," Connie said, disappearing out the door.

"So, you want another shot of morphine, huh?" Abe teased.

"You're talking about me being goofy… did you see yourself when Connie came in? You looked like a frightened school kid, being called on to sing in front of the class," Mikalya teased.

"What are you talking about… my singing voice is just fine!" he shot back. "But let's get back to the movie. Do you remember *The Shining?* It starts at nine. How about it?"

"Yeah, the one with Jack Nicholson. It's pretty good," she said, pleased that Abe had a sense of humor to match hers.

"No, this is the one that was on TV a while back. It's like a three-part mini-series. It has Steven Weber and Rebecca DeMornay in it. It's every bit as good as the Jack Nicholson version, and maybe even better. They say that it closely depicts Stephen King's actual book. It's on for the next three nights, starting tonight. Have you seen that one before?"

"No, I've never even heard of it," she replied.

"You have to see it. It runs from nine until eleven tonight, tomorrow, and the night after that," Abe said, flipping through the channels.

"Hey, that's great. Let's go for it. Good job, Mr. Gallagher!"

Abe found the channel and adjusted the sound.

"Is that loud enough for you?" he asked.

"Turn it up just a tad. Can you put the cot closer to the bed in case I get scared?" she asked.

Abe moved the cot over as far as it would go. Unfortunately, the cot lay lower than Mikalya's bed, and he couldn't get a good view of the TV.

"How about I go over to the other side and sit in the chair? That's going to give me a better view of the TV… and you." He winked.

Mikalya smiled as her eyes followed Abe as he moved across the room, turning the light off before taking a seat.

"Well, that's so sweet that you want to see me *and* the TV! And lights out, too!" she said.

Abe gently took her hand. Mikalya instantly felt safe. She knew that she could never be frightened when he was around.

Abe wasn't ready for Mikalya's reactions to the horror film. It was cute and unnerving at the same time. As she *oohed*, *aahed*, and cursed her way through, he couldn't tell if she was joking or serious. She must have grabbed his hand a hundred times.

Suddenly, the door flew open, and Connie came rushing into the room.

"Mikalya, are you OK? I was just walking by and…" she began.

"Oh, I'm sorry, Connie. We're watching a scary movie, and I freaked out. But everything's OK," she answered in a hushed tone.

"Do you want that shot of morphine now?" Connie asked, relief settling across her face.

"Let's go for it. My leg is throbbing again, and I really want to concentrate on this movie."

"OK, be right back."

Mikalya and Abe returned to the movie.

Connie quietly scooted back in and gave Mikalya her nighttime squirt of pain-relieving bliss.

"Thanks, Connie," she whispered.

Connie winked and quietly closed the door behind her.

As the movie was nearing its end, all Mikalya could think about was whether or not Abe was going to come back the next night and watch part two with her. She didn't want him to leave at all. She was also starting to get tired as the morphine began to set in.

"Well, what did you think? Did you like it?" Abe asked.

"I loved it. You're right. It is a little better than the Jack Nicholson version. Now, I want to read the book," she replied. "Listen, I have a huge favor to ask. Can you help me up and into the bathroom? I hate to ask, but it would be a huge help if you could. If that's too big of an ask, I can ring for a nurse."

"Of course I can help. There's no way I'm going to just sit here while you need help. But we're talking about the bathroom, not a bedpan, right?" he teased.

Mikalya frowned at him.

"Well, isn't that a romantic gesture? I've done the bedpan thing a few times, and I really want to try to use a regular toilet. I hate getting on bedpans. It's so degrading," she said.

Abe nodded in agreement, inwardly thankful that he didn't have to go down that road with her. He got up, moved his chair away from the bed, and maneuvered his way toward Mikalya.

"I understand. Now, is there any way you can try to at least sit on the edge of the bed? I know it will be clumsy with the cast, but can you give it a try? I can help you."

Mikalya made a face and pushed herself up with both her hands until she was sitting upright. Her burns hurt a little, but not enough that she couldn't use her arms.

"Hey, that was great! You moved faster than I thought you would. Now, can you swing your legs toward me and then put your feet on the floor?"

Mikalya took a small breath, forcefully swung her legs around, and placed her feet right on the floor in front of Abe. She was sitting upright at the edge of the bed facing him.

"That was fantastic, Mikalya! Now, do you want to lean on me, or would you prefer to use crutches?" he asked, impressed by her determination.

"Can I just lean on you? I really have to pee, and I'm afraid it's going to take longer with the crutches."

Abe laughed and sat down next to her, placing his right arm around her waist.

"What I want you to do is put this arm around my shoulder. Then we're both going to slowly get up and head toward the bathroom. Once I get you in there, I'm going to sit your butt down on the toilet, then let you do your thing with the door closed while I wait outside. When you're done, just yell. It will be easier than you think," he said.

"OK, Dr. Abe."

"Now, on the count of three. Are you ready? One, two, three!" Abe said, hoisting her up alongside him.

Mikalya wobbled as they headed steadily to the bathroom. Abe got her through the door and carefully plopped her down on the toilet, just as he'd said. Mikalya smiled at his gentle strength.

"See, it wasn't that bad. Can you take it from here without me?"

"Yes, I can, believe it or not. Abe, thank you!"

He winked as he shut the door behind him. While he waited, he began tidying her bed just as Connie walked back through the door.

"Hey, did my patient manage to escape with a bum leg?" she asked.

"You didn't see her running down the hallway?" he asked with a grin. "No, I helped her to the bathroom. She leaned against me to get there, but we made it there safely and in one piece."

"Hey, thanks for doing that. That's the first time she's been out of bed since she's been here. How bad was she struggling?" Connie asked, impressed by his efforts.

"It took a bit of effort, I could tell, but she didn't hesitate to do it, and she held her balance pretty well, considering that leg cast."

Connie's response was interrupted by the flush of the toilet.

She and Abe looked at each other with amusement.

"ABE, ARE YOU THERE?" Mikalya yelled.

Abe headed toward the bathroom as Connie finished tidying the bed where he'd left off. He opened the door just a tad.

"Are you decent?" he asked.

"Who's out there?" Mikalya whispered.

"It's Connie. Is it OK to come in?"

"Yeah, I'm finished. Come on in. HI, CONNIE!" Mikalya yelled out again.

"Hey, I'm here. But I guess you have a personal assistant now?" she replied.

"Well, kind of. He's well-trained, too. Watch this," Mikalya said.

Connie walked over to stand in front of the bathroom.

"OK, you can do this again. We'll take it slow, just like we did last time. Ready?" Abe asked.

Mikalya got her arm around Abe as he lifted her gently off her feet. She hobbled out of the bathroom with him by her side, and in clumsy slow motion, she plopped down on the bed.

"TA-DA!" she said, looking over at Connie with a grin on her face, pleased with her accomplishment.

Connie clapped and gave her a broad smile of approval.

"Wow, little girl, well, big girl now, you did a great job. I don't think you're ready for a prime-time trip to the toilet on your own, but you did well. And Mr. Gallagher, bravo to you, too. Were you a physical therapist in another life?"

"No, but I've always wanted to play one on TV, like in one of those hospital shows."

"I imagine you'd want to play a fireman," Connie said.

"No. There are too many scenes they wouldn't be able to show if I was a TV fireman."

Connie and Mikalya looked at him, confused. Mikalya wondered what he meant, but she wasn't going to pursue it.

"Well, I have to get back on my rounds, but I always like paying a visit to Room 206," Connie said, breaking the awkward silence.

"OK, Connie, we'll see you a bit later," Mikalya replied.

Once Connie left the room, Mikalya's attention immediately turned back to Abe, who was pulling his chair back over to her bed.

"*The Shining* is one scary flick. Could you stay in a huge hotel like that for months all by yourself, or even if there were other people with you?" Mikalya asked.

He thought for a few seconds. "That's a very good question. In an exceptionally huge hotel like that one, out in the middle of nowhere, it would be tough. It would depend, too, on how much they were paying me. For a small amount of money… forget it, but if it were substantial, I just might do it."

"What do you consider substantial?" Mikalya asked.

"Well, for five or so months, I'd consider doing it for five thousand dollars a month," he said.

"Wow! That's a lot. So, assuming they would pay that, would you do it alone, or would you want to bring someone with you?"

"Assuming someone would want to even come with me, yes, I would want at least one more person there."

"Then who would you choose to go with you?" she asked.

Abe looked at her for a moment, unsure where her line of questioning was going.

"Well, it would have to be someone I trusted… someone whose company I would enjoy for that length of time. I would prefer it to be someone who…" Abe's voice trailed off a bit.

"Someone who…?" Mikalya pushed, gesturing with her hand for him to keep going.

Abe remained silent. He wanted to answer the question just right without going too far, not that Mikalya would have cared.

"Someone who… well, who I really cared for and loved. I wouldn't want to do it with one of my fireman friends or drinking buddies. That would get old after a while. But, if it were a wife or a girlfriend, that would make it more pleasant," he answered.

"That makes sense, Abe, and I agree with you. I don't think I would want to do that with my mom or a friend, either." She reached over and put her hand in his.

He squeezed it gently and smiled. Mikalya started to doze.

"Hey, your meds are kicking in because you're nodding off. Do you need to make one last trip to the bathroom?"

"If you wouldn't mind. I'm sorry for nodding off," Mikalya apologized.

Abe stood up from his chair again. "OK, just remember what we did last time," he instructed.

He lifted her gently, and they made their way back to the bathroom.

Same as before, he sat her down and then patiently waited outside the door. The ringing of the phone took him away from his thoughts. He debated whether to answer it or not.

"Abe, can you get that?" Mikalya called from the bathroom.

"Mikalya Arabella's room," he answered.

There was silence on the other end until the delayed response came through the phone.

"Hi, this is Mikalya's mom. Is she there? I mean, I know she's there, but why isn't she answering the phone herself?" Shelly asked.

"She's in the bathroom right now. Hang on, let me see if she's ready to come back to her bed," Abe said, walking over to the bathroom door.

"Mikalya, it's your mom on the phone. Do you want me to tell her to wait or have her call back?"

"Can you ask her to just hold on a second?"

Abe walked back to the phone. "Shelly, she'll be here in just a moment."

"Thanks, Abe," Shelly replied, pleased that he remembered her name.

"OK, I'm ready now," Mikalya called out from the bathroom.

"On my way!"

Settling back into her bed, she held the phone up between her chin and her shoulder. "Hi, Mom. How's it going?" she asked.

"The question is, how are things going with you? You apparently made it to the john, but you couldn't have done it alone. I assume Abe or one of the nurses helped you?"

"It was Abe, and he was great. He made it so easy."

"I'm sure he did," Shelly teased.

"Mom! Anyway, we just finished watching part one of *The Shining*. It was so good."

"Honey, I'm glad you enjoyed the movie. Listen, I know it's late, and it's also nice of Abe to be there helping you, but is there anything you need?"

"No, thanks. I'm fine. Are you coming tomorrow?"

"Of course I'm coming to see you tomorrow. I got a lot done today. And before I forget, Aunt Loretta says, 'Hi' and to tell you she loves you."

"I love her, too. Thank God we have her, Mom."

"Believe me, I know. I'll let you go now. I can hear the tiredness in your voice. Try to get a good night's sleep, and don't do anything silly. I'll see you in the morning."

Mikalya pulled the phone away from her ear and frowned at it as if her mom could see her. "Silly? I hope you don't mean what I think you mean. But I'm a little flattered you think I have that much agility right now," she replied.

"I'm only teasing you, Mikalya. Goodnight, hon."

"I know you are. I still love you. See ya in the morning. Night."

Mikalya placed the phone's receiver back on its base. "I loved the movie and really want to see the next part," she said, turning back to face Abe.

"So, are you busy tomorrow evening?" he asked.

Mikalya's face lit up like a bonfire. *He really is interested*, she thought. "I'll try to squeeze you in. It will be fun," she said.

"Yeah, it will be a good time. But it's pushing midnight right now. Before I get situated on this cot, let me get you some water and tuck you in, just as any good nurse would."

Abe finished tucking her in, turned out the light, then settled back on the cot. He knew it wouldn't be comfortable, but under the circumstances, he'd manage. As he lay there in the dark, he could hear Mikalya's gentle snoring, so he knew that she had drifted off quickly. Staring up at the ceiling, he thought back over the past several days since the fire. His mind drifted back to the card game they were playing at the fire station right before the alarms sounded. He remembered that he had come into work hungover that morning. In his mind, he couldn't believe all that he'd done that day.

Abe was just as exhausted as Mikalya and fell off to sleep shortly after she did. Not long after, a short yet lucid dream took over his mind. In the dream, he and Mikalya were shopping together in some sort of department store. Something caught her eye, and she ran ahead of him. Suddenly, she stopped and turned back to him.

*'Abe, come here and look at this! It's on sale, too. Abe! Abe!'* she said in his dream.

Abe quickly started in her direction, but then the dream ended abruptly, and he was jarred out of his sleep.

"Abe! Abe!" Mikalya called.

Abe was awake now, and Mikalya *was* calling his name. He jumped up quickly, looking around for the clock. It was three in the morning.

"Hey, I'm right here. What's wrong?" he asked nervously.

"You're going to kill me, but I have to go to the bathroom again, and it's not to pee. It hurts so bad," she said.

"OK, let's get you in there quickly."

Abe propped her up against him and got her back to the bathroom.

"I don't know how to thank you for this. I am so embarrassed," she said. Abe could see tears in her eyes, so he kneeled in front of her and stroked her hair.

"Hey, listen, don't worry about it. We all do it. Miss Universe does it. Tom Cruise does it. The President of the United States does it. And you may not believe this, but even I do it. You have nothing to apologize for or be embarrassed about," he soothed.

Mikalya took his hand and rubbed it across her face. The tears stopped.

"I'll be right outside. Whatever you need, let me know," Abe said, walking to the door and closing it behind him. He went over to Mikalya's bed and plopped down. He had never been laid up in a hospital before, but he could feel her pain and the difficulty in having to ask for assistance, even to do something as simple as use the bathroom.

When a nurse came in to check on Mikalya, she asked Abe if there was anything she needed. He could have said, "Yes, she needs help off the toilet," but he didn't. When he heard Mikalya stirring, he got up and walked over to the bathroom door.

"Are you OK in there?" he asked.

"Yeah, Abe. You can come in now. I'm decent, but the atmosphere isn't. You may need a hazmat suit. We forgot to turn the fan on," she said, laughing. She was disgusted with herself, but all she could do was laugh her way through it.

Abe opened the door carefully and pinched his nose shut as he walked in, immediately flipping the fan on. It was his attempt at being funny and lightening the mood. If they were going to move forward in a relationship, he knew that he had to handle this situation with a strong dose of sensitivity and humor. The last thing he wanted to do, and the last thing Mikalya needed, was for him to come across in a ridiculing manner. He walked over to her and gently pulled her hands away from her face.

"Wow, this is what the fire station smells like after we've eaten some of Lamar's signature firehouse chili. I'm quite used to this," he said jokingly.

Mikalya looked at him, not knowing how to respond but realizing that laughing her way through it would make it easier. "You might be quite used to this, but not from *me*," she said.

"Look, I figure if this is the worst you can throw at me, I'm sure I can pass the test. Is this a test? You're doing this on purpose, right? Were you ever a schoolteacher?" he asked.

"Why, of course! Last year, I taught gastroenterology science at Harvard Medical School. You didn't know that about me, did you?"

Her quick wit endeared her to him even more. "OK, OK, I get it. Let's continue this conversation in a more dignified setting. I'm sure your butt's getting sore."

Once Mikalya was tucked back into bed, Abe sat down next to her. "OK, it's after 3:30 now. Do you think you can get back to sleep?" he asked.

"Yes, if you turn the bathroom fan off. It's still on. Unless, of course, you think we need to leave it on for the next several hours, just as a precaution," she joked.

"I think we'll be OK. I'll turn it off now," he said, getting up and heading for the bathroom. "How's that?"

"Much betta! Thanks," Mikalya said in an English accent.

"OK, get some rest, and we'll pick this up later in the morning, after we've both had some sleep."

"Can't wait," Mikalya purred, slowly drifting off.

****

Mikalya opened her eyes to Cynthia's smiling face standing over her bed.

"Hey, how'd you sleep last night?" Cynthia asked.

Blinking the sleep away, Mikalya opened her eyes wider and looked over to see if Abe was still on the cot. He was—stirring in his sleep.

"I slept well, except in the wee hours of this morning when I had to go to the bathroom," Mikalya replied.

Connie heard Mikalya's comment as she was passing by the room and popped her head in the door. "She had some personal help with that," she said teasingly.

Overhearing their gabfest, Abe decided it was better to keep his eyes closed.

"I can see that," Cynthia chortled, nodding over at Abe.

After Connie had gotten Cynthia up to speed on Mikalya's chart, Connie held Mikalya's hand. "Well, it's time for me to head home. I'm off the next couple of days, but you need to keep working on getting better. You hear me?"

"You got it! Have fun on your days off!" Mikalya said, hugging Connie before she exited the room.

"I've been in here five days now, right?" Mikalya asked.

"Yeah, but you're progressing well. Doctor Hart will be coming around soon to take a look at you. In the meantime, here are your pills for the morning. How is the pain?" Cynthia asked.

"The burns don't hurt as much as they did, but my leg still throbs. I'm still getting those headaches, but not as bad as before."

"Well, that's a good sign. We're going to take you off the morphine drip and replace it with a pain medication in pill form. It will help. That's one of the things Doctor Hart will be discussing with you today. Breakfast will be on the way soon. How is your friend doing over there?" Cynthia quizzed.

Abe remained still and kept his eyes closed.

"He's been great… helping me get to and from the bathroom and doing a lot of other little things. We watched *The Shining* on TV last night. He's going to hang out with me again today, so we can watch the second episode tonight. We both like horror movies," Mikalya rambled on.

"I do, too. I read the book, and it was really good," Cynthia shared. "You know, I'm glad he's here for you. But I must finish my rounds. If you need anything, just holler."

***

As Cynthia headed back to the nurse's station, she noticed that Connie was still there, so she jogged a little to catch up to her before she left. "Can I ask you a question?" she said, rounding the counter.

Connie looked up. "Sure, but I think I know what it's about."

"Apparently, he spent the night last night. Was that the first time?" Cynthia asked.

"I'm not sure, but I'll bet you it won't be the last. He's been good for Mikalya, and last night, we hardly did anything for her because he did it all. Even took her to the bathroom and put her on the pot. He seems to be a really nice guy. I'm about ready to give him a nurse's uniform and a stethoscope."

"Is it true that they only met a few days ago, after he saved her from that fire?"

"Yes," Connie replied. With a quizzical expression, she anticipated Cynthia's next question.

"So, it kind of looks like… well, it seems like… I mean, it appears to me they're dating," she said hesitantly.

Connie nodded. "Yep, that's what it appears to be. What a way to meet someone—in a hospital, of all places. Not a lot of guys would do what he's doing. I got to hand it to him… I think it's so romantic."

"I agree. It's different but in a cool sort of way. Anyway, enjoy your time off, and we'll catch up later."

"Thanks, and good luck today," Connie yelled back as she headed toward the elevator.

****

Mikalya looked over at Abe once Cynthia left the room.

"You can open your eyes now," she said.

Abe rolled over. "How did you know I was awake?" he asked.

"I just did. Connie and Cynthia were too much for you, I know. I can sense you're a tad shy about being here with me."

"No, not really. I just don't want to be in anyone's way," he replied.

"You're not, so don't worry about that."

"That's good to know. So, my plan for today is to go back and check my apartment and then check in at the firehouse to let them know how you are… but that's after you've had breakfast. When I finish with those two stops, I'll head back here."

"I was hoping you had some vacation days," Mikalya said.

"Oh, I do, and I'm in here until you get out," Abe said.

Mikalya's heart skipped a beat. She was so happy to hear that Abe would be spending another day with her.

"Abe, that makes me feel good. It really does. You're so much better than morphine," she swooned.

"Well, I'm not sure how to respond to that, but I'll take it," he said just as the door swung open again. It was a CNA with her food tray. She placed it on the table in front of Mikalya and turned and left. Mikalya didn't even have time to thank her.

When Mikalya lifted the lid on the plate of food, her face turned pale.

Abe looked down at the plate and made the same face.

"I cannot eat this. It looks disgusting," she pouted.

"OK, how about I run over to that diner around the corner? I've eaten there a few times, and their food is delicious. I can bring you back some real food."

Mikalya motioned him closer, to which Abe obliged.

"That would be wonderful," she whispered in his ear, "and make sure the whites of my eggs are cooked, not runny."

"Will there be anything else, Marie?" he asked. A puzzled expression crept up her face.

"Marie Antoinette. You know who that is, don't you?" he asked.

Mikalya shook her head from side to side. "Wasn't she the one that said, 'Let 'em eat pasta,' or something like that? Oh, no, wait, it was 'Let 'em eat pie,' or wait, it was cake. Right? It was cake!" she exclaimed.

"You are sick. Hang tight, and I'll be right back," he said, scurrying out the door.

Mikalya put the lid back on the breakfast plate and pushed the entire table away from her bed. She stared out the window, allowing her mind to drift. Things had been such a rush for her since the fire, and she still could not comprehend the severity of what had happened. But, oddly enough, she did understand what *could* have happened, and Abe was the most valuable player in that scenario.

Mikalya wasn't a religious person, but she considered herself spiritual, with a strong belief in karma.

She was still deep in thought when Doctor Hart and his nursing assistant pushed through the door without warning. Cynthia was right behind them. Mikalya wished her mom and Abe were there for the conversation with the doctor, but Cynthia was there, so she was OK.

"Well, hello, Mikalya. How are you?" Doctor Hart asked. "Let's take a look at you."

The doctor asked her to lift her gown so that he could assess the burns. "Let's remove this bandage and clean it up so that I can get a better look at what's going on," he directed the assistant.

The nurse removed the bandage and cleaned the wound as she had been instructed to do.

"I must say, your burns are healing nicely. You mentioned that the pain with the burns was not as bad, but that could be morphine. Let's take you off that and see how the pain is then.

"If you find it's intensified, there is something else we can give you that will help. I'm going to order a couple of scans for this afternoon, an MRI and CT to check your lungs and head. Those will give me a good idea of any lingering swelling and how your lungs are doing.

"Mikalya, as far as that leg goes, healing will just take some time. Get used to that cast for a while. I heard you were able to get up and use the bathroom with some help. That's good. Just keep working on that. Do you have any questions?" Doctor Hart asked.

"No, not really, Doctor. I appreciate everything you all have done for me."

"Thank you. We are doing our best to get you healed and out of here quickly. I see you haven't touched your food. It's important that you keep your appetite up and eat as much as you can. It helps with your healing," he continued.

Although Mikalya smiled and nodded her agreement, inside… her stomach was turning at the thought of eating the hospital food they had just served.

"OK, we'll talk later," Doctor Hart said as he and his assistant moved to leave.

Cynthia stayed behind. "Not bad! You're doing good. The burns do look better, and you're not coughing as much as before. All good signs," she said, giving a thumbs up.

"Why does he want to do those scans?" Mikalya asked.

"It's just routine. The scans will give him a much better idea of how much your head and lungs have healed. I am hoping it will reflect that the brain swelling has gone down even more. His main concern is that nothing's going haywire in your head. If he sees progress there, you'll be closer to getting out of here."

Mikalya took Cynthia by the hand. "I'm glad I got to know you. You've been so good to me," she said.

"You're easy to love. Here, give me a hug," Cynthia replied, leaning down to squeeze Mikalya. "But I have a question for you."

"Sure, you can ask about Abe," she replied with a chuckle.

"Wow, you can read minds, too. So, I know it's none of my business, but he spent the night last night. And I know he was the one who saved your life. And I've seen the way you look at him. He seems like a nice guy, and God knows he's good-looking. So, I have to ask… are you guys dating?"

"Well, I have strong feelings for him, and not just because he saved my life. I've felt strong emotional ties to him ever since I saw those roses he brought me.

"Then, when I actually got to see him and talk with him, the feelings intensified. Cynthia, what man would come to a hospital to visit someone he didn't even know, then stay with them and help them the way he has helped me—especially in the condition I'm in? I am at my worst right now, and he doesn't care. I'll probably have burn scars, and he doesn't care about that, either. It's not like he saw me sitting across a bar, all sexy and cute. When he first saw me, I was a heap of mess and passed out. I had burns on my back and broken bones. That's not exactly desirable date material.

"And you're right, he is an attractive man. I've been on dates where I thought I had dolled myself up to the max and put on the charm, but the guy never even called me back. But this one has seen me at my worst, and he's still here, so I feel confident saying that we are dating."

She opened her mouth again to say more but then decided to wait for Cynthia to speak instead.

"Well, that's that. You seem happy, and that's all that matters," Cynthia said with a smile.

"Thanks, Cynthia. I appreciate that."

"OK, I'm done here. Do you want me to take your breakfast tray?"

"No, just leave it for now. I'll try to eat a little more first."

"Did Abe leave for the day?" Cynthia asked.

"No, he'll be back in a bit. He ran off to a nearby diner."

"Be careful about what you eat. Your throat is probably still a little sensitive due to the smoke you took in."

Mikalya gave her a blank stare as she now sensed Cynthia knew that Abe had run out for better food.

"I will, ma'am," Mikalya replied.

"OK, we'll be back around two for those scans. They won't take too long, and getting out of this room for a bit will do you some good. See ya later!"

Once alone, Mikalya turned on the TV and quickly flipped through the channels. Nothing looked interesting, but her focus wasn't on watching TV anyway.

The clock on the wall said 8 a.m. Her mom would be coming by soon, and Mikalya wondered if she'd be there by the time Abe returned.

Mikalya was sure that her mom knew one day she'd be in a serious relationship, although she probably hadn't anticipated it happening so soon and so quickly.

She loved her mother, and with each day's passing, she valued her opinion on all things… even the guys she dated. She sensed that Abe was smart enough to be respectful of their closeness, and hopefully, one day, the two of them would share a close bond as well. Only time would tell.

# Chapter Eight: Crystallization

Shelly was still hurt by her last relationship, which had killed her self-esteem. She wasn't proud of it and had lectured Mikalya on more than one occasion on the evils of getting involved with someone who did not love her, no matter how much she might love him.

A few years after she lost Clifton, Shelly dated around a little, but there was one man she liked more than the others, and she wanted Mikalya to like him, too. Mikalya could tell that her mom was into the guy, but from the start, she got nothing except bad vibes from him. He would make odd, inappropriate gestures toward her mother right in front of her, and some of the things he said were inappropriate as well.

Mikalya didn't like the way he looked at her, either. She swore that she would never be alone in the same room with him, and she always declined invitations to go out with the two of them when she was invited. Those times when he would stay overnight at their house, he would walk around the next morning in nothing but a robe. Mikalya hated that.

Then, there were just too many occasions when Shelly tried reaching him by phone but couldn't. Don had even stood Shelly up on one occasion, but she blew it off. But it was the day he showed up at their door drunk that Mikalya realized that he was bad news for her mom.

One day, she expressed her concerns to her mom, saying the day would come when he'd dump her. Shelly took offense to that, so from that moment on, Mikalya kept her mouth shut. Then, one night, a few weeks after that conversation, Shelly was excited that Don was taking her out on the town. She spent over an hour getting ready because it was some fancy new restaurant that he said he wanted to take her to. Shelly waited and waited, but Don never showed up; he didn't bother to call, either. When she called him, she got no answer.

"Don, this is Shelly, honey. I hope you're OK. I suppose you're on your way here," she said to his answering machine.

Thirty minutes passed—then another thirty—and another, with no return calls.

Mikalya sat quietly, pretending to watch TV, but what she was really doing was watching her mother slowly fall apart.

"Something must be wrong, or he would have called. Don't you think so? I mean, he would have called. God, I hope he's not been in an accident," Shelly rambled on.

Mikalya looked at her mother but did not respond.

After another agonizing hour had gone by, Shelly slowly sat down on the sofa in shocked silence.

Mikalya noticed the tears in her mom's eyes. She turned off the TV and moved closer to her mother on the sofa, putting her arms around her and squeezing her tightly. Shelly looked at her through swollen red eyes.

"Hey, you still have me," Mikalya said.

Shelly's sobs were barely audible as she sat blankly, staring into Mikalya's eyes. "You were right, honey. I knew you were right the whole time, but I wanted to believe him. Deep down, I knew this was coming. I should have listened to you from the beginning," she said, stroking Mikalya's face.

Mikalya remembered that moment as if it were yesterday. A strong knock at the door snapped her out of her daydream; then, her mom walked into the room with a huge smile on her face. Mikalya was glad that the sad moment was behind them.

"Good God, I was just thinking about you," she said, happy to see a smile on her mom's face.

"I hope they were good thoughts," Shelly replied.

Mikalya decided to keep her thoughts to herself.

Shelly's attention quickly turned to the cot next to Mikalya's bed.

Mikalya saw her glance at it as she motioned Shelly over to give her a hug.

"Mom, listen, as you might have guessed, Abe spent the night last night. A half-hour ago, he ran out to get me breakfast. He'll be back soon."

Shelly smiled. "I know. I know. It's OK. Is it alright if I stay? I have some good things to tell you."

Mikalya's daydream about Shelly passed through her head once more before she flashed her mom a loving smile. "Mom, you don't have to ask that. I don't care where you are, or what you're doing, or how bad a mood you might be in, or how bad a day you had. You're always welcome any place and any time in my life."

Shelly looked at her daughter quizzically. "I thought they took you off the morphine drip," she teased.

Mikalya smiled and shook her head just as a knock came at the door.

Shelly ran over to open it. Abe walked in with two large, greasy to-go sacks.

"Room service," he said.

"Abe, I can smell the aroma and the grease! Wow, you did it. I knew it! And I'm starving!" Mikalya said.

"That smell has made me hungry, too! Abe, is there enough in one of those white bags for me?" Shelly asked.

"Sure! I've got plenty. When I heard you and Mikalya talking on the phone last night, it sounded like you might be swinging by this morning. So, instead of two greasy plate specials, I got three," he said, holding out the bags. He glanced over at the cot and then back at Shelly, who was staring at him. He was sure that she knew he'd spent the night.

"It's OK," she said, following his gaze. "To tell you the truth, I'm glad you're here with my daughter."

"Hey, I want to eat. How are we going to do this?" Mikalya asked, interrupting the awkward moment.

"Let me get this cot out of the way, and then I'll serve both of you ladies."

Shelly sat down and watched Abe in action.

Abe sat the breakfast sacks down and quickly folded up the cot. Then he left the room and quickly returned with a chair and two plastic food trays.

"OK, Miss Arabella, let's get you served first."

Mikalya loved it when he called her Miss Arabella.

Shelly noticed the hypnotic look that had taken over Mikalya's face as she watched Abe move about the room.

Abe took Mikalya's tray of hospital food and dumped it all into one plastic bag. Then he rolled the serving cart over to her bed and positioned it in front of her. After he'd removed all the contents of the bag, he stood back and gestured as if he were a waiter.

"Well, ma'am, there you go. I know it's not quite as hot as it was, but I guarantee that it will still be delicious."

"Right now, I don't care how hot it is or isn't. You did a wonderful job, Abe!" Mikalya said, clapping her hands gleefully.

"Now, Miss Arabella, number two, you're next," Abe said, turning to Shelly.

Shelly was taken aback at how attentive Abe was to her daughter. He had made a great impression on her… again.

Pulling out a ham and cheese omelet, hash browns, and an order of bacon, he carefully arranged it on one of the trays and handed it to Shelly. She was stunned at how much of a gentleman he was.

"How did you know that I love ham and cheese omelets?" Shelly asked, looking up at him.

"I didn't," he replied.

"I thought Mikalya might have said something to you."

"No, she didn't say a word. I winged it all."

“Abe, come on and sit so that you can eat as well,” Mikalya said.

“This is great. Where did you get this?” Shelly asked.

“A little diner a few blocks from here. It’s the best mom-and-pop place around, and I’d put it up against any of the best chain restaurants,” Abe said.

“Well, it’s delicious, that’s for sure. Thanks so much for feeding us this morning, Abe,” Shelly said, through fingers covering her mouth.

“By the way, what part of town do you live in?” she continued.

“I’m about thirty minutes from here. Down on Ransom Avenue,” he replied.

“I’ve got a good idea where that’s at. That’s a nice area.”

“It’s just a nice working-class neighborhood. The crime rate is low, and the neighbors are friendly.”

“Tell me, have you ever been married? Do you have any kids?”

Shelly’s line of questioning caused Mikalya’s left eyebrow to rise. She glared at her mom.

Shelly knew that look. Her daughter had used it on her before. “I’m sorry, Abraham, I didn’t mean to pry.”

"It's OK, Ms. Arabella. I'm only twenty-five and have never been married. I don't even have a girlfriend… but I wish I did," he said, winking at Mikalya.

He continued. "And no, there are no little Abrahams in my life. I graduated from Howard Sanders high school seven years ago. I played football and ran track there. I had a B/C grade average.

"After high school, I worked in construction for a few years. The money was good, but I really wasn't satisfied with that. I knew there was something more out there for me. I guess you could say it was my life's calling. So, about a year ago, I was talking with one of the guys I worked with. He'd seen an ad in the paper where the city was looking to hire new firemen. If you met the preliminary requirements, they'd put you through the eighteen-week training program. So, he and I decided to go for it. We knew the program was going to be tough, and not every applicant would make it through. We also knew it would be a crapshoot, and we'd have to quit our jobs. But we did, and here I am."

Since Abe had shared so much, Shelly felt comfortable pressing for a bit more. "What about your family… and your friends?" she asked.

"Well, my parents are still together, and they live here in the city. I've got a younger sister, Julie, who lives here, as well, with her husband and little boy.

"In my spare time, I just hang out with friends, work out, and, well, that's my life story. Oh, and I like horror movies, too." He laughed.

By the time he had finished speaking, almost all his food was gone. Mikalya looked at his tray.

Abe followed her gaze. "When you're a fireman, you learn to eat fast. It's just habit now."

"How refreshing… a nice guy with his head screwed on straight. A major leap from most of the jerks *I've* dated," Shelly said.

Shelly approved of Abe.

"Ms. Arabella…" Abe began.

Shelly cut him off. "Once again, please call me Shelly. Anyone who saved my baby girl's life can call me by my first name for sure," she said.

Abe nodded with his hands cupped in a prayer pose.

Mikalya was shoveling down her last few bites of food when a girl from the cafeteria came in to pick up the trays.

"All done now?" she asked.

"Yes, you can take it all away now. Can you also take those to-go containers?" Mikalya asked. "My dear darling friend brought outside food in."

Abe jumped up and began helping the girl collect all the breakfast debris.

"It's OK, dear darling friend." She smiled. "I'll get it. You just relax."

Mikalya looked at the girl with a frown as she left.

"Mr. Gallagher, that was certainly one of the most outstanding breakfast meals I've ever had. Once Mikalya gets out of here, we have to—" Shelly started, but Mikalya cut her off.

"It's OK, Mom. You don't have to cover up for that witch. That was rude, and I'm—"

Shelly interrupted before Mikalya could go any further. "Hey, first of all, lower your voice. Second, I agree she was a little out of line, but I don't think she *really* meant anything by it. And thirdly, I'm one hundred and one percent sure she got the message just from the scowl on your face."

Abe walked over and sat down next to Mikalya.

"You know you don't have anything to worry about," he said.

"I know. I know. I'm sorry, I just…" Mikalya apologized.

Abe had a way of calming Mikalya down, and Shelly loved their dynamic. She needed someone with a calming presence like his around her. Any other disposition would have proved an extremely volatile relationship.

"Abe, I'll be having a couple of scans around two this afternoon. I haven't had the chance to tell you that," she said, changing the atmosphere in the room.

"Would you like for me to be here for that?" Abe asked.

"Well, yes, of course. I expected that you would be. Mom, Abe, and I are watching part two of *The Shining* tonight. Would you like to join us? Maybe we can have a pizza delivered here."

Shelly thought for a second. "Let's see what comes back from your scans. Who knows, with any luck, you might get discharged today."

"Listen, ladies. I'm going to head home for a bit and check on things. I need to grab a shower, too. Mikalya, I'll be back later, in time for your scans. Shelly, I'm sure you'll be here, too."

"Of course, you need to go check on things. When are you coming back?" Mikalya asked.

Abe looked up at the clock. He knew that Mikalya would probably keep her eyes on it until his return.

"It's ten o'clock now. I want to get out of here so you and your mom can catch up as well. I'll be back here around one thirty for your scan. Is that OK?"

"That's fine! Now, go on and take care of what you need to so you can get back here!" she said.

Abe reached over and kissed her forehead. She took his hand and pulled him closer to her, whispering in his ear.

"Thank you for being here. You don't know what it means to me that you're here."

"I'm here for you. No matter how long it takes you to heal. You can always count on me. OK?"

His words mesmerized her.

Shelly sat on the other side of the room, witnessing the intensity of their private conversation.

"Now, I have one more question," Abe said to the room.

"Yes?" Mikalya was the first to speak.

"Do you have to pee again before I leave?" he asked as a light smirk formed on his face.

Shelly burst into laughter.

Mikalya was caught off guard by the question but quickly rebounded. She looked back and forth between her mom and Abe with a comeback that didn't disappoint.

"No, but I have to take a dump. Can you get a bedpan and wait until I'm finished? Then I'll need help cleaning up."

"Well, Shelly, you get her cast leg, and I'll get her arms. Let's drag her in carefully, pull her gown up, and prop her up on the toilet. We'll shut the door to give her some privacy, and when she's done making noises, we'll go in and get her," Abe said with a straight face.

"OK, you two clowns, listen," Mikalya capitulated. "I'm glad you're having fun at my expense, but I really do have to pee."

When Mikalya was finished and tucked back into her bed, Abe bent down to give her a hug and another kiss on her forehead.

"Well, ladies, I'll see you both this afternoon."

Alone at last, Shelly looked over at her daughter and smiled. She had seen her daughter in a new light, all grown up and falling in love. "You know, honey, I'm glad Abe has come into your life… our lives. If not for him, I'm sure the staff would find you an intolerable witch," she said.

Mikalya didn't bat an eye at her mom's comment and slowly shook her head in agreement. "Mom, he's better than morphine."

"But, all jokes aside, how are you feeling?" Shelly asked.

"Not bad. I'll feel better after we get those scans out of the way."

"You and me both. But let me fill you in on what's going on with the house and everything else."

Mikalya sat quietly as her mom spoke, and although she nodded at the appropriate moments, her mind was on Abraham.

"We're going to be fine, so no need for you to worry about anything. I've already contacted a builder who can get started soon. You and I will be picking out new home décor before you know it! It will be fun! By the way, Aunt Loretta is going to be here soon. She really wants to see you."

Mikalya's face lit up.

"That's great! I can't wait to see her!"

"I think she's even more excited that we'll be living with her for a while. Once this is all settled, I want to help her out, too. She's got a bit of credit card debt hanging over her head. Though she's been paying on it, the interest is keeping her from paying it off, so when we settle everything with the house, I want to take care of that for her."

"That's a great idea, Mom. I love Aunt Loretta. And wasn't Abraham's breakfast great?" Mikalya asked distractedly.

Shelly looked up, confused by the question that had come out of the blue. "Mikalya, did you hear anything I just said?" she asked.

"Oh, I'm sorry, Mom. My mind was still on that delicious breakfast he brought us. Anyway, you ought to stay for a while and watch part two of *The Shining* with us."

"Honey, when Loretta gets here, and you're back from having the scans, we're leaving. I want you and Abe to continue getting to know one another—even if you have to do it in a hospital room. Once you're out of here, there will be plenty of time for the four of us to get together."

"Thanks, Mom," Mikalya said.

"You're welcome. Aunt Loretta and I are here when you need us, and Abe will be here after we leave."

"That's great. I really appreciate you all staying until after I've had the scans."

The soft knock at the door and the sweet "hello" that followed put a smile on Mikalya's face. It was her Aunt Loretta. "Come in," Shelly invited.

"Hey, baby girl, how are you doing?" Loretta asked, rushing through the door wearing a huge smile on her face.

Mikalya beamed. She held out her arms as her eyes filled with tears.

"Hey, Aunt Loretta! I was already feeling good, but so much better now that you're here!"

Witnessing the love between her daughter and her aunt almost brought tears to Shelly's eyes.

After giving her a big squeeze, Loretta stood back and took a good look at her great-niece.

"Well, all things considered, you look fantastic! You've still got a bit of raccoon eye, but you look great!"

"Thanks, Aunt Loretta. That's probably because Abe… I mean this guy… I mean, a friend of mine is coming by to watch some TV with me tonight."

Loretta gave Shelly a wink.

"*Hmmmm*, I believe your mother already mentioned something to me about this fireman named Abraham… but you call him Abe, right? I want to meet this young man! Now, when can we make that happen?"

"He's coming back this afternoon, so if you hang around, you can meet him then. You'll like him, trust me," Mikalya said.

"I'm sure I will," Loretta replied.

"Aunt Loretta, thanks for staying," Mikalya said.

Loretta walked up to the bed and kissed Mikalya on the cheek.

"Of course, but I'm going to run down to the cafeteria for a cup of coffee. Shelly, do you want to come?" she asked.

"Sure," Shelly replied, grabbing her purse and blowing Mikalya a kiss from the doorway. "We won't be long, I promise."

****

Shelly and Loretta made their way down to the cafeteria, snagged their coffee, and then grabbed a table as their conversation continued.

"Shelly, I was thinking. I'd love to help with Mikalya. You mentioned that you were going to take a few days off to care for her, but how about if we alternate days? I can be with her for a few days, and then you can be with her for a few days. I know you have a lot on your plate, so I'd like to help where I can."

"Oh, my God, Loretta, that would be a tremendous help. You would do that for us?" Shelly asked, wiping away the tears forming in the corners of her eyes.

"Heck yes! Why wouldn't I? You've bailed me out before. Don't you remember that time I was stuck down in Acapulco after that bastard stole my purse?"

Shelly threw her head back, laughing.

"Oh, God, I'd all but forgotten about that. The thought of you being stuck down there in that mess horrified me. Do you remember the turtle story?"

It was Loretta's turn to burst into laughter. "Oh, yes, how could I forget? That was in that one weird restaurant off the beaten path. I think it was called El Guapo's or El Groucho's or El Grumpy's… or something like that. You still remember that?" Loretta asked.

Shelly nodded. "I sure do!" she said, holding her stomach as she laughed harder.

"I was just sitting there, eating some of the best enchiladas I'd ever had in my life, which quickly turned into the worst enchiladas I'd ever had in my life. Then, out of nowhere, this turtle waltzes through the front door and then stands there in the middle of the floor, just looking around at everyone like it was a normal day on the job.

"After that, it slowly lumbered off. What was so funny was that all the patrons were looking around, wondering what the manager was going to do about this stray turtle that had just wandered in."

Shelly was in tears, laughing at Loretta telling the same story that she had told four or five times before, each time a slightly different version.

Loretta finally regained her composure enough to speak. Shelly's laughter had sent her into fits of laughter, too. "Well, anyway, the point I was trying to make was that it was one of the *shittiest* vacations I'd ever had in my life," she said.

"It was the next morning that my purse was stolen, and I called you from the hotel in tears. Do you remember that? You wired me money right away and helped put a stop to my credit cards. Then you helped me get the plane tickets squared away. And to top it all off, you even gave me enough money to finish out my vacation. I will never forget that. So, you see, it is I who owes you," Loretta said.

Shelly smiled and took her hand. "Auntie, you would have done no less for me had the tables been turned. You're already extending us the same love and kindness… right now," she said.

Loretta looked at her with a loving smile. "Whatever you need from me… you got it. No questions asked. But there is another thing we have to consider once she gets out of here, and quite frankly, while she's still in."

"Abe will be back before they take her down for the scans. I am convinced those two are getting serious about one another. I can see it in Mikalya's eyes, and I see it in him, too. But I do like him a lot. He seems as solid as they come. Yes, the way they met was unusual, but I thank God every day for what he did for my daughter."

"If he's good enough for you, that's all that matters. I can't wait to meet him. It does sound, though, like whatever plans we have regarding Mikalya's care will need to include him. Am I wrong?" Loretta asked.

"No, you are not, not at all. Let's finish up this coffee and head back up. Did I tell you that Mikalya has Abe bringing her all sorts of food from the outside?"

Loretta shook her head. "Are you kidding me? How did she get so lucky?" she asked with a chuckle.

****

As they walked in, Mikalya looked up. "What happened to you guys? Where did you go?" Mikalya asked when her mom and aunt walked back through the door.

"Aunt Loretta and I were down in that cafeteria reliving our memories, that's all. Did you order your lunch yet?"

Mikalya rolled her eyes. "It's on the way," she said, looking out the window, wondering when Abe would reappear.

When the cafeteria brought Mikalya's food up, she picked at it for several minutes, not eating much at all.

"Aren't you going to eat more than that?" Shelly asked.

Mikalya shook her head and pushed the food cart with the tray on it away from her bed.

"Well, it's almost time for your scans anyway," Shelly said. "I know those results are going to be good news. Every sign of improvement moves you one step closer out the door of this hospital."

Loretta noticed the sadness in Mikalya's eyes, and walked over and stroked her hair. "Everything will be just fine. You're a strong girl," she said.

Mikalya took Loretta's hand and put it up to her face. "Thanks, Aunt Loretta. I'm glad you and Mom are here."

Anxiously awaiting Abe's return, Mikalya dropped Loretta's hand and sat up when she heard a knock at the door.

"Hey, Mikalya! We're going to get you ready before too long. Doctor Hart will be in soon to go over the procedure. There's really not a lot to it," Cynthia said reassuringly.

"Thanks, Cynthia. Can they go down with me?"

Cynthia, along with some of the other nurses, had grown attached to Mikalya and hated denying her anything, but some things were out of their control. "No, I'm sorry, but you won't be gone long at all. They can wait right here in your room until you come back."

Mikalya took the opportunity to take some short walks on the crutches while she had people around her. She'd tried a few times with the nurses and was proud of her progress but was going to continue to let Abe help her until she could manage by herself. But she was distracted and couldn't keep her eyes off the clock on the wall. Its hands inching closer and closer to 2 p.m., but still, there was no sign of Abe. She began to worry, but before she could verbalize her worries, there was a knock at the door. Her demeanor quickly changed, and she lit up like a Fourth of July sparkler when Abe walked in.

When he walked across the floor to give Mikalya a hug, Loretta couldn't help but think she was seeing one of the guys from a Chippendale calendar walk right by her, but she kept that thought to herself.

"Hey, you," he said.

"Hey, yourself," Mikalya replied.

Abe gave her a peck on the cheek, then turned to face the other ladies in the room.

"Hi, Shelly."

Shelly smiled, waving. "Hi, Abe! Glad you made it back. I want you to meet my Aunt Loretta. Loretta, this is Abe… the man who saved Mikalya's life."

"Thanks, Shelly, but I was only doing my job." Abe blushed, winking at Mikalya.

Mikalya jokingly batted her eyelashes in his direction. But what he didn't know was that every time he winked at her, chills raced up and down her spine.

"Abe, the nurse just left and said they would be taking Mikalya down soon. We'll have to stay put until she's done and back here in her room," Shelly said. "She won't be away from us for long."

Another brief knock on the door, and Doctor Hart strolled in.

*This is a revolving door for sure,* Mikalya thought.

"Hi, Doctor, come on in," Shelly said, waving him in.

He looked around the room, nodding his collective hello to everyone present.

"Mikalya, this first test is just a scan of your brain to let us know where the swelling is. Although we won't be releasing you today, your neurological signs are improving, though you're not one hundred percent yet. Worst-case scenario is that you may be here a couple more days, but we'll see. After we get the results back, I'll swing by again so we can talk. How does that sound? Do you have any questions? Does anyone have any questions?" he asked.

"Sounds good, Doctor… no questions," Mikalya replied.

Doctor Hart waved goodbye with his clipboard and disappeared out the door just as quickly as he had come in.

A few minutes later, Mikalya was being wheeled out on a gurney down to radiology.

As Shelly, Loretta, and Abe waited, they chatted. Loretta was absolutely infatuated with Abe but in a respectful way. Just as Shelly did, she found him extremely polite, intelligent, and humble.

After a while, there was a bit of commotion outside the door, and then in walked Cynthia with hands outstretched as if she were a product model on *The Price Is Right* show. "Voilà! I return to you, Miss Mikalya!" she announced gleefully.

As Mikalya's gurney slowly entered the room, she smiled at her mom, her aunt, and Abe—happy that they were all together, waiting for her. The nurse wheeled her next to the bed and carefully helped her back into it.

"We're going to wait here until Doctor Hart comes back with the results. Then, Aunt Loretta and I are going to do some shopping. Is there anything I can bring back for you?"

"No, thanks, Mom, I don't need anything. We're just going to hang out and watch the movie."

"Hey, are you sure you guys don't want to stay? There's a great pizza parlor called Giancana's that's not far from here. They don't deliver, but it's worth the drive to go pick it up. We eat it all the time at the firehouse," Abe said.

"I've passed it a few times but never stopped in. Is it that good?" Shelly asked.

"It is, and the more I think about it, the more I want it," he said, rubbing his hands together.

"Sounds good to me, Mr. Abraham. Whatever you want," Mikalya chimed in.

"Thanks for the offer, Abe. That's sweet of you, but as I said, Aunt Loretta and I are going to head out for some shopping. But once Mikalya's out of here, we're going to have one hell of a party, trust me, with pizza and all!"

"Mom, that's a great idea! Make sure that Cynthia and Connie are on the guest list!"

Shelly walked over and squeezed Mikalya's hand. "When you get out of here, you can have anything you want. You deserve it after all you've been through."

Mikalya looked up at her mom and smiled. "I'm holding you to that, Mom."

Cynthia breezed through the door. "I was outside the room next door charting. Did I hear my name?"

"You did. Mom is taking all of us to Vegas for a Chippendale show!" Mikalya blurted out with a sly grin.

Shelly's mouth dropped, surprised by Mikalya's outburst. "Cool! I'll check to see when they're going to be there so we can make our flight reservations! I have some vacation time that I need to use anyway!" Cynthia said.

Mikalya looked over at her mom and her aunt with a sneaky grin still on her face.

"Guys?" she said, her eyes going around the room, looking at the three, who were all staring back at her.

Silence pervaded the room.

When Abe noticed that everyone else seemed to be tongue-tied, he decided to speak.

"Ladies, I think it's a great idea for you all to take a trip. I'll even drive you to the airport if you need me to!" he offered.

"If we're just going to see sexy men without their clothes on, maybe Abe and his firehouse buddies could give us a show instead. It sure would save us a lot of money," Mikalya joked.

Abe blushed. The chuckles coming from the ladies ceased with Doctor Hart's brief knock and entrance into the room.

"Well, it looks like we have a party going on in here. I hope I'm not interrupting anything," he said.

"Oh, no, Doctor, of course not. We were just discussing some future travel plans," Shelly said.

Abe stood there, thankful for the incredible timing of Doctor Hart's appearance. However, the air in the room had completely changed, and all attention was now on the doctor.

"Well, I have your results, and both are pretty encouraging. There's still a bit of brain swelling, but it's going down faster than we expected. I see no evidence of any bleeding. Now, Miss Arabella, you're still not completely out of the woods yet, so I'd like to keep you here… one, possibly two more nights, just to be safe, but I don't see you staying here beyond that window," he said.

Shelly folded her hands in a prayer pose and looked up at the ceiling, relieved.

Loretta and Cynthia smiled at Mikalya, and Abe gave her a thumbs up.

"Doctor Hart, that's great news! Isn't it?" Shelly asked excitedly.

"Yes, that's fantastic. So, Doctor Hart, what you're saying is, I'm not going home tonight, but maybe tomorrow? Or the day after?"

"That's pretty much it. But I'll be back to see you tomorrow, and we'll go from there. Any more questions?" he asked.

"No, Doctor, we appreciate everything you've done," Shelly answered.

"In that case, I'll see you tomorrow," he said.

Once the doctor was out the door, they all started high-fiving each other. Cynthia gave an excited yelp and a thumbs up, then left, too.

"Oh, my God, honey, I am soooo happy for you!" Shelly said, pulling Mikalya into a big bear hug.

Abe stood next to her, holding her hand, while Loretta stood at the foot of her bed.

"Mom, you were so funny! One minute, we're talking about flying to Vegas to see a bunch of guys take their clothes off, and the next minute, you've got your hands folded and looking up to heaven."

"Honey, I think she was praying for you and the Vegas trip," Loretta said.

"You all are so funny. Loretta and I are going to take off now. Abe, you're staying, right?"

"I am, Shelly. You ladies have a good time and be safe. I'll be here taking care of our girl."

"Mom, you guys aren't leaving already, are you?" Mikalya asked.

Shelly smiled and gave Mikalya another kiss. "It's OK. I'll be back tomorrow. Besides, you've got Abe here. I love you."

Loretta walked up closer to Mikalya. "You're almost out of here. I thank God for the good news we got today. So, just enjoy your movie time, and we'll see you later."

They waved goodbye and headed out the door.

Alone again, Mikalya looked over at Abe. He walked over to the bed and gently pulled her forward. When he touched her, she felt no pain.

"I'm so happy for you, Mikalya. So happy," he said.

Mikalya's eyes welled with tears. "I wouldn't be here if it weren't for you," she said.

"*Shhhh.* I don't want to hear that again. What was meant to be was meant to be. I never really knew, or cared, what that meant until I met you," he said, gently laying her back on her pillow and looking into her eyes.

"I am convinced now that the only reason I was drawn to being a fireman was to find you. If I'd gone in another direction, that probably wouldn't have happened."

Mikalya's teary eyes looked into his. She nodded in agreement. "So, you're saying I almost had to die for us to meet?"

Abe could tell that she was trying to make the situation lighter.

"Abe, I know what you're saying. I guess what *I'm* saying is that, of all the firemen who could have arrived first on that scene, it was you who did. You got there at just the right moment. I would have been dead minutes later. And it was you who decided to go in after me. My mom said that you didn't think twice about it. That's fate."

"Or maybe it was something else. Something drove me into that house toward you. Do you know what I'm talking about?" he asked.

Mikalya put her arm around Abe's neck and gently drew him closer. "You have to know that I've fallen in love with you. Tell me you know. Tell me," she coaxed.

Abe was mesmerized by the intensity in her eyes. "Baby, I know. I can feel it. I'm in love with you, too. I'll say it again. I have fallen in love with you. Can you feel my love?"

"Yes, I can. Of course, I can," Mikalya replied, pulling him even closer and pressing her lips against his.

Their tongues touched in a level of comfort, sensation, and ecstasy that neither of them had experienced before.

Their kiss lasted only a minute before they were interrupted by a knock at the door. With clear frustration, they separated and composed themselves.

*Why now?* Mikalya wondered.

"Come in," Mikalya called out across the room.

"Hello. I am Pastor Gerald Sims from Mount Zion Christian Church, and I do visitations here at the hospital. I hear your recovery is going well, and we thank the Lord for that. I'd like to say a prayer to you for your further recovery. Would that be OK with you?" he asked.

Given what they were engaged in only seconds before the pastor walked in, Abe and Mikalya tried hard to suppress their laughter.

Not daring to refuse an offer of prayer by a pastor, Mikalya and Abe looked at each other quickly, then nodded their heads simultaneously.

"That's fine, Pastor. Please, go ahead," Abe said.

"Sister, what would you like prayer for?" the pastor asked.

"Um, well…" Mikalya stuttered, looking at Abe. He shrugged his shoulders at her silent plea for help. "Um… Pastor, how about just praying for my healing and speedy recovery?"

The pastor smiled, nodded, and bowed his head. Abe and Mikalya followed suit.

"Dear Father…" he began.

Like two little kids, they smirked at each other while he was praying. After only a couple of minutes, he was done.

"Amen. Is there anything else I can do for you?" he asked.

"No, Pastor, you've done great, and we thank you," Abe said.

"OK. If you're ever in the area on Sundays, please feel free to visit our church, Saint Michaels. It's right there on Highway 46, next to the Walmart," he said.

It was all Mikalya could do to keep from laughing.

"We certainly will," Abe said.

The pastor smiled and waved as he left the room.

"A church next to Walmart? What?" Mikalya giggled.

"Hey, quiet! He could be in the next room," Abe whispered, trying to contain his laughter, too.

As she was adjusting the pillows behind her back, Mikalya looked up and noticed the clock on the wall. "We have about six hours before part two of *The Shining* starts. I'll make you a deal. I'll trade you my hospital meal for whatever you run out and bring back," she said, her eyelashes fluttering.

Abe rolled his eyes and threw his head back. "Ha! Nice try, kiddo. You call that a deal? Sounds more like a shaft to me."

Mikalya made a pouty face and then folded her arms.

"OK, it's a deal, sort of. I'll make a food run here soon, but I get to choose off the menu. That's the deal. Maybe I'll compromise and give you a little input. How about Chinese?" he asked.

Mikalya looked at him and grinned.

"I'm always in the mood for Chinese," she said.

“Well, you’re in luck! I can always eat Chinese, too. How about I run out for food around five? That’ll put me back just in time for the start of the movie.”

“Sounds good,” Mikalya replied.

Abe pulled his chair up to Mikalya’s bed and grabbed the hand lotion sitting on the table. When he took her hand, a smile spread across her face. When he began massaging it, she closed her eyes and let her head fall back against her pillow.

After he had massaged her left hand for several minutes, he gently laid it down by her side.

Mikalya’s eyes never opened.

He pulled his chair around to the opposite side of the bed and took her other hand. But this time, he began massaging her arm above her elbow, then working his way down to her fingertips and back again.

Abe watched Mikalya’s face every second. When he stopped, one eyelid flew open and looked directly at him for a few seconds.

Abe sat there, smiling.

Mikalya could see by the expression on his face that he was teasing her. “Is that it?” she asked.

Abe chuckled. "It's going to be if you want that Chinese food before the movie starts. How about a rain check? I promise you a rain check," he said.

Mikalya opened both her eyes. "Aside from being a good fireman and great kisser, now I find that you're a hell of a masseuse! I better copyright you before someone else does," she said.

"Works for me!" Abe affirmed.

# Chapter Nine: Goodbye Saint Francis

Abe got up out of the chair and wiped the excess lotion off of Mikalya's hands and arms. He went into the bathroom, checked himself, and walked back out to Mikalya.

"OK, I'm getting ready to head out. Outside of the spring rolls, what else do you want?" He knew a good way to get to know someone more was to see what kind of food they liked.

"Anything garlicky with chicken. The hotter, the better. Make sure you bring a lot of that sauce back with you, too. I like stir-fried rice, not white. On the stir-fried veggies, I want anything with broccoli and onions," Mikalya said.

Abe made a strong face when she said that.

"Sorry, but broccoli and onions are actually very good for you. You didn't know that, little guy?" Mikalya asked.

"They make you fart, too. You didn't know that, little girl?" Abe retorted.

"Well, they don't make me fart. Maybe you. And, even if they did, you seem like the kind of strong guy that could handle it. I just know it in my heart, Abraham," Mikalya said. She put her hands over her heart and looked up at the ceiling when she said that.

That was the bizarre part of Mikalya's humor coming out now that he loved. He had never met a girl that made him smile quite as she did. Abe had to mentally strain a bit for a comeback.

"Yeah, I suppose, but I… *uh*… do better with farts… *um*… if I have a fire hose and an oxygen mask on. At least, that's how I was trained," he said.

Mikalya broke out laughing. "Are you telling me that in fireman school, you were trained to put out fart fires?" Mikalya said while laughing hysterically.

Abe barely cracked a smile.

Cynthia just happened to be passing by Mikalya's door and could hear her giggling. She quietly stepped closer. She could see that Abe was in some sort of theatrical pose, describing some sort of fart story. She wasn't about to miss this one.

"Yeah, kind of. Water doesn't cut it. We must use a special hose and certain chemicals," he said.

Mikalya lay there, still giggling. "God, what kind of chemicals?" she asked.

Abe looked at her, and he wasn't sure if he could keep coming back to this conversation, but he tried.

"Well, let's see. So, if we get called on a fart fire, it's usually a three- or four-alarm. We don't have a lot of time to get ready. The hose we have to pack is called a… well… a cork hose," he said.

Mikalya rolled her eyes and indicated to him to go on.

Mikalya then noticed Cynthia at the door.

She would come in but decided to stay in the shadow, so Abe wouldn't see her. She made a gesture for Mikalya to stay quiet and just stood there, listening to what Abe thought was a private joke.

"The special chemicals, well, they're very special. Once we get to the scene of the fart fire and have properly assessed the situation, we put our masks on and get out the cork hose. Then we go looking for the source of the fart fire. We stick the cork hose into the source, then spray the special chemicals into the affected area," Abe said.

Now, Cynthia was quietly giggling from just outside the door, and Mikalya was loudly giggling from the bed. Abe maintained his theatrical pose.

"But you never told me what the special chemical was, Abe?" Mikalya said. She was now goading him to keep it going. He had a small audience, only half of which he was unaware of.

"Lysol Early Morning Breeze," he said.

Mikalya broke up laughing hysterically, and now Cynthia's laughing behind the door was obvious.

Abe turned around in embarrassment and saw Cynthia in tears.

Mikalya was looking back at her and tried to stop but couldn't. This whole conversation was her fault, and she had to back Abe out of it.

"Oh, God, it's OK now. You can stop. God, I'm sorry I made you do that!" Mikalya said.

Cynthia walked into the room and stood next to Mikalya.

Both had tears in their eyes and applauded his Shakespearean performance.

Abe was speechless. He looked back and forth between Cynthia and Mikalya in utter shock.

They kept giggling.

Abe took hands out of the air and looked over at Cynthia.

"How long were you there?" he asked.

Cynthia shook her head like she didn't know. "Oh, God, Abraham, I don't know, just a few minutes."

"Hey, watch it. Only I can call him Abraham," Mikalya said.

They started laughing again.

Abe looked around and scratched his head. "OK, Mikalya, I'm going to run out for the Chinese. Oh, and I'll bring back a can of Lysol Early Morning Breeze, as it appears we have a fart fire in here with you girls. At least, that's what I smell," he said.

The girls continued to giggle.

Abe leaned over and kissed Mikalya. "Do you need to pee, or more, again?" he whispered into her ear.

"No, not now, but thanks anyway," Mikalya whispered back.

"Give me about ninety minutes to get back here," Abe said. He then exited the room.

"Heavens to Betsy! I've never seen that part of him. How in the hell did that conversation get started?" Cynthia said.

Mikalya shook her head. "Hell, I haven't either. I feel so bad. It started with a silly couple of lines while he was on his way out the door. He's running out to pick up some food, and I told him I wanted broccoli and onions in the stir fry," Mikalya said. She started giggling at the tail end of that statement, and Cynthia broke out laughing again.

"OK, now I know. We have to stop. I've got to tell Connie this story when she gets back from days off for night shift. She loves that kind of stuff." Cynthia said.

"You mean impromptu fart orations?" Mikalya asked.

Cynthia shook her head. "Yeah, impromptu fart orations. Are you guys going to watch part two of *The Shining* tonight?" Cynthia said.

Mikalya nodded. "It starts at nine tonight."

"The cafeteria will be here soon to get your dinner order. I know Abe's coming back with the Chinese food, but just get a little something, like some fruit or applesauce," Cynthia said.

"I promise I will," Mikalya said.

"I think I said before when you get out of here and are ready to party, you're going out with Connie and me. We may see if a couple of the other nurses want to go. I really want to get you out for some real girl fun," Cynthia said.

"Sounds interesting. I didn't know nurses let their hair down that much," Mikalya said.

"Oh, honey, you have no idea what we have planned for you," Cynthia said.

"Now, I'm scared. I know Mom will want to bring Aunt Loretta and her friends, Jenny and Latisha," Mikalya said. Then, that classic fallen angel look spread across her face.

"The more, the merrier. We'd love to meet them. Just be ready! Listen, I'm going to finish my rounds. Do you need anything right now? Any pain?" Cynthia said.

"Well, maybe a pain pill here soon. My leg is throbbing a little bit, and I want to enjoy the movie. Is that OK?" Mikalya said.

"Sure, one pain pill coming up. Be right back," Cynthia said.

In the meantime, one of the cafeteria girls came in to take her dinner order.

Mikalya took Cynthia's advice and ordered some fruit and a dessert and even managed to get an extra one for Abe. She lay there in her bed, just wondering about everything, and it occurred to her just how far she and Abe had come. She had been just going with a natural flow that she had absolutely no desire to stop.

The fire was just over a week ago, and she was already planning her life with him. He was on her mind during every waking moment and even during some of her sleeping moments. She knew that he was here for her now but, as women do, just wondered if he thought as much about her as she did him. *He had to,* she thought. *Surely, he must!*

Her thoughts were interrupted once again as Cynthia reappeared with her pain pill. "Enjoy!" she said.

Mikalya gulped it down with some water and patiently waited for Abe to return. It wasn't long before he did, and she heard Abe's familiar knock on the door. She could tell his knock from all the other ones.

"Room service once again," he said, entering the room. He walked in with one large white sack surrounded by a heavenly aroma of garlic, Szechuan pepper, sesame oil, and chili spice. Abe set the sack down next to Mikalya's bed.

She looked over and stared at it. Then she started to reach into the bag.

Abe slapped her hand. "Not yet," Abe said.

She gave him a sour look and pulled her hand back. "You're too damn cruel sometimes," she said.

Abe looked back at her, puzzled. "Really? How is that?" he said.

Mikalya gave him one of her famous smiles to fit the occasion. "Well, hell, it's obvious. Do I have to explain?" she asked.

"Yeah, you do, but not right now. Let me finish setting this up. I'm starving," he said. Abe sat everything up, once again, like a pro.

As he finished, the cafeteria brought Mikalya's fruit and two desserts.

Abe had brought in silverware and plates.

Mikalya loved watching Abe set dinner up for her. He pulled her dinner table up to her bed and then laid the food out in front of her, out of the boxes and onto the plates.

"My God, you went down to the cafeteria and got them to give you plates and everything!" Abe nodded and then served the food.

Mikalya inhaled. She closed her eyes for a second, then reopened them. "Dammit, Abraham!" Mikalya said with a sigh.

Abe looked at her with a slight expression of accomplishment. "Yes?" he said.

"Thank you," she said.

Abe smiled and stroked her hair. "It's OK. Let's eat!" he said.

Mikalya dug in. "God, this is good. What did you say the name of that place is?" Mikalya asked.

Abe had a load of food in his mouth and had to finish chewing before he could answer.

"The Chinese Pavilion. We'll go there someday after you get out," he said.

"I'd love it," she said. Cynthia waltzed back in with Connie as the shifts were changing at 7 p.m.

"My God, it smells good in here. What in the hell are you eating?" Connie said.

"Hey, it's good to see you," Mikalya said. "But what are you doing here? I thought you were off?"

Connie walked over, and they both gave each other a very tight hug. "I got called in to cover a sick shift. Hi, Abe. I'd hug you too, but if I did, Mikalya would give me a stir fry shampoo. So, I'll just wave," she said.

"Connie, you can hug him, for God's sake," Mikalya said. Connie settled for a wave, and so did Abe.

"OK, my shift is ending, and I'll say *ciao*," Cynthia said.

"*Ciao*? I thought that's what we are doing now, eating?" Mikalya said.

Abe looked up as if agreeing with her. Connie and Cynthia started to laugh.

"No, *ciao* is Italian for, goodbye. I'm saying goodbye," Cynthia said.

Mikalya's face got red. "Well, I guess I'm just an idiot hillbilly," she said.

"I think I am, too. I didn't know that. Hell, the only other language I know is Pig Latin," Abe said.

"Wait a minute. I *do* know some Italian words: spaghetti, ravioli, linguine, and let's see, Roma tomato and Caesar salad," Mikalya said.

"It's no big deal. Hell, that's one of five words I know in Italian. But now, you've taught me some more," Connie said, laughing.

"Mikalya, you're a trip! OK, I'm out of here for now. Goodbye!" Cynthia said. They all waved her out.

"I assume it's another night of *The Shining*. Mikalya, try to eat that fruit there. I think Cynthia gave you a pain pill, so you should be comfortable," Connie said.

Mikalya gave her a wink.

"Let me get started on rounds, and I'll check in on you again when the movie starts at nine. Sound good?" Connie asked.

Mikalya and Abe were still shoveling down their food. Mikalya smiled and nodded.

They finally finished, and Mikalya gently pushed the tray away from her bed. "Damn, that was good, but I can't eat another bite," she said.

Abe nodded in agreement. He got up, cleaned it all up, and straightened out Mikalya's covers.

"Abe, honey," Mikalya said.

Abe knew that tone of voice now. It meant she wanted or, more importantly, needed something. He had a hunch about what it was. "Yeah, I know. Which one is it?" he asked.

Mikalya held up her hand in a peace symbol sign. She was still not fully confident of using the crutches by herself in front of him.

"My little hippie girl. OK, you know what to do," he said.

Mikalya lifted herself, and Abe came over and helped her into the bathroom.

On the way, she lost her footing, and both swayed sideways back onto the bed.

In doing so, Mikalya's leg cast hit her bedside table and knocked over her glass of water. They both broke out laughing.

Sophie, the CNA, came running in. "Is everything OK? Are you alright?" she asked. Mikalya and Abe looked up, red-faced.

"We're OK, Sophie. We're OK, aren't we, Abraham?" Mikalya said, smirking.

"Yeah, we're just fine. But if you want to lend us a hand, that would be great," Abe said.

Sophie figured out they were clowning around too much to be really serious now and helped Abe get Mikalya to the bathroom and back.

Nine o'clock came around, and Abe got Mikalya all positioned on the bed to watch the movie.

"So tonight should be good. I think this is where Jack Torrance really starts to get freaky," Abe said.

"Wait, in the book, isn't this where Danny finally goes into Room 217, and that horrible, evil lady is in the bathtub?" Mikalya asked.

Abe made a frightened face. "You know, I think it is in the original movie that scared the hell out of me. It's supposed to be even scarier in this version," Abe said.

Mikalya pulled the covers over her head. She spoke from underneath.

"Want to come in here with me?" she asked.

Abe reached over slowly and pulled the cover away.

"Boo!!" she said.

Abe didn't blink an eye or barely even flinch. His stare at her remained solid and constant.

Mikalya was both shocked and impressed. She pulled the covers all the way off her and looked at Abe, who now raised his eyebrows.

"Were you trying to scare me?" he asked.

"Well, yeah, I was," Mikalya said.

"I'll let you do it the next time. How's that?" Abe said.

Mikalya thought that was an incredibly strong comment. But, then again, she thought about what his profession was.

"OK. OK," she replied.

Abe smiled. He flipped the TV on just as the movie was starting.

She and Abe *ooh'd* and *aah'd* their way through it. The part about the lady in the bathtub was indeed part two and just coming up.

"Oh, shit, here's the part. It looks like he's heading toward the room now," Abe said.

Mikalya reached over and grabbed Abe's hand, pulling it toward her. In the movie now, Danny Torrance was heading up the stairs toward Room 217 with the key in hand. He now stood in front of it.

Carefully putting the key in the door lock, he twisted the doorknob open and entered the large suite.

Walking into the bathroom, he thought that he heard a noise, like a drip from a water faucet from behind the curtain in the bathtub. He now had the distinct feeling that he wasn't alone in the room.

Abe and Mikalya's eyes remained transfixed on the TV set.

As Danny Torrance inched toward the bathtub, he got the distinct impression that there was someone in there. He was now right up against it, and he carefully started to part the shower curtain. He yanked it back and peered in. Sitting inside the tub was the most evil, ugly, and frightening human being he'd ever seen in his life.

Danny sprang back in utter horror. The woman looked right into Danny's eyes and sang the creepy song about the little boy.

"*Ahhhh*, crap!" Mikalya cried. She squeezed Abe's hand as tight as she could. Even Abe made a slightly disgusted face.

The woman stepped out of the bathtub and headed straight for Danny, who, by this time, had managed to make it out to the hallway. However, he made the mistake of just standing there in shock instead of bolting further away. As he stood outside of Room 217 in horror, the woman pulled him back in.

At that moment, the girl from the cafeteria entered the room to get the food tray and looked up at the television.

"Shit, WHAT was that?" she said. She grabbed the tray and ran out as fast as she could.

"God, did you see all that?" Mikalya shrieked.

"I've seen people that actually looked like that after a fire when we were in training," Abe said.

"What? You're kidding! Tell me you're kidding," she said.

Abe shook his head.

Mikalya decided not to pursue that conversation any further.

"Hey, that was a roller coaster ride," Mikalya said.

Abe shut the TV off and looked up like he heard something. Mikalya trusted his instincts completely and looked at him.

"What?" she asked.

He looked off toward the bathroom.

"What?" she asked again.

"*Shh.* Wait a minute," he said. Mikalya was now a little scared. "Do you hear that?" he asked.

"Honey, you're scaring me. Hear what?" she asked.

"That dripping sound coming from the bathroom. Oh, my God!" Abe said.

Mikalya's eyes opened wide. She picked up one of her pillows and threw it at him.

Abe managed to duck in time, and the pillow hit the wall. Abe picked up the pillow and threw it back at her. It skimmed off her leg cast like a frisbee, then shot up and hit her smack in the face.

Mikalya put her hands over her nose like it was broken.

Abe came back over to the bed and hugged her. "Poor baby. I didn't mean to throw that hard," Abe said.

As he was hugging her, Mikalya slowly reached her other hand around and grabbed her water glass, which still had a bit of water in it. She very carefully poured it over his head. Abe reared up so fast it shocked her.

"Damn, that wasn't fair! Be careful!" Abe said.

Mikalya sobered up quickly, as she could tell Abe didn't like that. He wasn't angry, but she realized she went over the line.

Abe caught himself quickly. "I'm sorry, hang on. I'll be right back." Abe then turned the TV back on. He hit the restroom while there was still a commercial break. He wiped himself off and looked into the mirror. He knew he caught Mikalya off guard with his reaction. He needed to go out and make it right.

Exiting the bathroom, he saw the slightly unnerved expression on her face. He walked right over and sat back down next to her.

"Listen, I'm sorry. Whenever I get an unexpected splash of water, it reminds me of the fire in your house. As Luis was blasting away once we got inside, water was coming down all over me. I'm so sorry," he said.

Mikalya's demeanor immediately changed to compassion. She pulled him closer and stroked his hair. "I'm sorry, it was stupid. Kids do that," she said.

"No, don't apologize. I kind of had it coming after throwing the pillow," Abe said.

"Well, maybe you kind of did, just maybe," Mikalya said. She got the customary smirk on her face.

"Maybe? Really?" Abe said.

Mikalya grabbed the pillow again and threw it at Abe, who caught it and gently bopped Mikalya over the head. She grabbed the pillow while Abe still had it and pulled it toward her, with Abe still attached to it. She got him right where she wanted him and pulled the pillow from his hands.

As they wrestled, the movie started again.

They both looked at each other with sexual frustration.

"You know, we can't really do anything in here," Mikalya said.

"I know. I know," Abe said.

They both settled back to watch the scene in the kitchen, where Danny tells Wendy and Jack that the hotel they're all staying in is, indeed, haunted, and they have to get out and fast. Jack goes up to check out the crazy woman who attacked Danny in Room 217.

"What's really creepy in this movie is the music. I know I'll hear this in my dreams," Mikalya said.

"It is a little off the wall," Abe agreed.

They continued to watch the movie until it ended. Mikalya had to go to the bathroom one more time.

He got her back in bed just at the time Connie came in for her rounds. "I didn't want to interrupt the movie with you guys. How was it?" she asked.

"Well, part two was really good. That scene where that creepy lady comes out of the bathtub is out there," Mikalya said.

Abe nodded in agreement.

"I've been out with women like that before," Abe said. Connie's eyebrows raised.

Mikalya grabbed her pillow and pointed at him like she was going to throw it.

Abe ducked. "Well, the guys at the firehouse tried to set me up with a couple of women that looked like her. That's all I was trying to say," he said.

"I assume you turned them down," Connie said.

Mikalya looked over, waiting for an answer.

"Well, I did meet them initially. I didn't want to be rude. When I finally managed to get a few stiff drinks down, they looked pretty good. I especially liked the one with the snakes in her hair and the vertical eye pupils," Abe said.

"YUCK!" Connie said.

"Well, now you have a woman with burn marks on her back, a mild concussion, and a broken leg. I'm hoping that's sexy enough for you," Mikalya said.

"More than enough," Abe said.

"OK, Mikalya, how is the pain?" Connie asked.

"Not too bad. I'd love another pain pill to help me sleep," she said. What was really getting to her was that she couldn't change positions well while sleeping throughout the night.

"No problem. Listen, Doctor Hart will be in tomorrow to check things out again. I know things went well today, so I have a good feeling about everything. Do you feel OK?" Connie asked.

"Yeah, as good as I can. I can't wait to get home soon," she said.

"You will. You will. Be right back."

"Hey, I kind of liked the sound of that," Mikalya said.

"Me, too. I think maybe she knows something. Let's keep our fingers crossed," Abe said.

"Mom will be over in the morning. I'll tell her what Connie said," Mikalya said.

Connie returned with her pain pill.

Mikalya swallowed it immediately. Within thirty minutes, she would be yawning.

"Hey, sleepyhead, you're getting tired. I think it's about that time," Abe said. "At least you made it through the movie."

"I am sleepy, and of course, I made it through the movie. What am I… a child? Care to tuck me in?" Mikalya asked, laying her head back against her pillow.

Abe gave her a kiss and rubbed her temples. In no time, she was snoring. He turned off the light and headed out the door, down the hall to the elevator. Unlike Mikalya, he was still wired, so he decided to go outside for some fresh air.

Walking out of the main lobby and into the parking lot, he found an open gazebo off to the side of the building and sat down. He looked up at the sky, appreciating the beauty of the bright, full moon. For a moment, he wondered who had sat in that same spot many years prior, looking up into the same beauty that was now staring down at him.

He looked off to his right and could see the wing Mikalya was on. Ever since the fire, things had moved at a quick pace. He hadn't spoken to anyone from the firehouse for several days. He missed hanging out with the gang.

They had no idea what was going on between him and Mikalya. They didn't even know her name.

Still looking up at the moon, he smiled at the thought of her sleeping in her room, and he couldn't wait to get back to her.

Out of the corner of his eye, he noticed someone walking toward the gazebo. He was strong, but he had to be careful, as the hospital wasn't in the best part of town. As the figure got closer, he saw what appeared to be a young woman. She was so engrossed in the conversation she was having on her cell phone that she didn't even notice him.

Abe could hear that she was crying and talking at the same time. As she got even closer, she was startled as she looked up to find she wasn't alone.

"Oh, God, I didn't see you!" she said, sniffling and wiping her eyes.

Although there was plenty of room for her to sit, Abe stood to get a better view of her.

"Miss, I'm sorry. I didn't mean to startle you. My name's Abe," he said, extending his hand.

She took a step back and stared at him for a moment, then looked around, embarrassed.

"It's OK. I'm a fireman, and I am as safe as they come."

The girl looked down, then back at him. "My name's Linda. I need to sit down," she said.

"Yeah, no problem," Abe said, stepping out of her way. "I don't mean to pry, but are you OK? I assume you came from the hospital?" he asked.

The girl looked at him, wiping her eyes again with a large wad of tissue. "No, I'm not OK. My dad just died. I watched him take his last breath thirty minutes ago," she said before breaking down again.

Abe sat down next to her. "Linda, I am so sorry."

"No, I'm sorry. I didn't expect anyone to be out here. This is just so hard!"

The moonlight hit her face, illuminating a look of despair. She wore the look of a sixty-year-old woman but in a sixteen-year-old body. All he could do was stare. "Do you want to tell me what happened?"

"You know, it's really weird. Ever since I left the room and walked out here, a sense of peace and relief has come over me. Do you think that's strange?" she asked, looking up at the moon.

"Linda, I've never had anyone close to me die, so I can't say that I know what you're feeling right now."

She didn't respond but listened as he continued.

"All I can say is, he's in a much better place now. If you don't mind my asking, what happened to him?"

"He had acute leukemia. There's no cure for it, and once you get it, there isn't much time. He only had a year once they diagnosed him. God, what he went through, it was terrible," she said.

"Well, his suffering is over now. I didn't know him, but I think he'd want you to go on with your life. He'll always be with you. I don't think we really die anyway. We just move into a spiritual form in another dimension. Why we're here in this life, I'm not sure, maybe to be tested. Who knows? I think if you abide by the laws of karma, you're OK, and you seem like a nice enough person, so I'm sure your dad was a good man."

"He was, and he was the best father a girl could hope for. I'm not sure that I buy into the heaven and hell theory, though. My dad made some mistakes that shouldn't be held against him for eternity."

"God made us human. He or she knows that we won't be perfect all the time. Is the rest of your family up there?"

"My two sisters and mom are still up there in the room, distraught. My mom wouldn't let them take his body—she's hysterical, and I can't handle that right now. I just left. Was that cruel?"

"No, everybody grieves differently. Under the circumstances, they may not even know that you're gone."

Linda smiled faintly. "Maybe you're right. They'll have to pry my mom away from that bed. I'm sure she's still there. A few minutes before he died, he looked at all of us and…" she stopped and grabbed her arm. "Oh, did you feel that?" she asked, looking around.

"Did you?" she asked again when a cool breeze swept across her body. The temperature was different from the surrounding air, and it soothed her.

Abe nodded, rubbing his arm.

"Yeah, I did. I'm not sure what that was, though," he said.

Linda stood, looking around in the darkness.

"Oh, my God, I can feel him! I can feel him!" she said. "Do you think it was really him? Do you think it was my dad?"

"Linda, if that is what you felt in your heart and soul, then it was him. He's telling you he's OK and not to worry. He found you down here."

Tears began streaming down her cheeks. She fell into Abe's chest and hugged him. He recoiled initially in shock but allowed her to mourn.

"You're right! You're right! It was him. Oh, God, thank you!" she sobbed.

Abe held her like a big brother would and let her cry. After a couple of minutes, she abruptly pulled away and looked at him.

"I have to get back up to the room! I gotta go now!" she said, straightening her hair and wiping her eyes. She slung her purse over her shoulder and gave Abe a big hug.

"Thank you so much for being here when I came down. God made sure of that." She hesitated. "My father made sure of that. That was him in the breeze. He knew that because I wasn't alone down here, I wouldn't be frightened. He knew I'd figure out that it was him if I felt safe. He knew it!"

Abe could see her bloodshot eyes in the moonlight. Linda released him from her embrace, took a step back, and touched his face.

"Thank you, Abe," she said, before turning and running back toward the hospital. Abe watched her until she disappeared into the darkness. Confused, he sat back down, wondering what had just happened. He hoped he'd never experience anything like it again.

****

Mikalya was asleep on her back when she was awakened by a sharp cramp in her calf. It was a painful charley horse. “Abe! Abe!” she called out.

Looking over toward the cot in the corner, she noticed that it was empty. It didn’t appear that he was in the bathroom as the door was wide open and the light was off.

“Abraham!” she yelled loudly. “Where are you?”

Mikalya’s screams made their way to the nurse’s station, and Connie rushed down the hall. When she entered the room, she could see that Mikalya was in distress. “What’s wrong, honey?”

Mikalya was holding her leg, looking around the room.

“Where did Abe go? He’s not here,” she said frantically.

Connie took Mikalya’s hand off her leg. “I’m sure he’s around here somewhere. What’s wrong with your leg?” she asked.

“It’s hurting so badly,” Mikalya replied.

Connie left the room and quickly returned with muscle relaxant cream, a compress, and a pain pill. “Here you go. Swallow. With all of this, you’re going to feel a lot better… soon. I need you to finish this entire glass of water, too. It will help with the cramping.”

"Thanks, Connie. I don't know what I'd do without you," she said, drinking all the water down and handing Connie the cup back. "But have you seen Abe?"

"I think he slipped out about an hour ago. He didn't say anything. I just saw him walking by as I was leaving another patient's room. He went to the elevator, and that was the last I saw of him. I'm sure he probably went down to get a snack or get some fresh air. He'll be back soon. You lie back and relax if you need anything, just buzz. OK?"

Mikalya sighed. "Thanks, Connie. I'll just wait until he gets back. Leave the door open, would you?"

"Sure! See ya later," she said.

Mikalya's pain subsided, and she could relax again, but a new pain soon took its place. Now she lay in her bed, staring up at the ceiling. She missed Abe and wouldn't be able to get back to sleep until he was there beside her.

****

Abe stood in the gazebo for a few more minutes, still staring at the moon. After his encounter with Linda, his mind was blank. Suddenly, a shock went through him, and he knew that it was Mikalya. "See you around," he muttered softly, looking up at the moon as he headed back inside.

Walking as fast as he could, he made it back up to the floor she was on. As he got closer, he could see that the door to her room was open, and the light was on.

"Hey, babe, you're awake. You were snoring when I left. If I'd known that your nap was going to be so short, I wouldn't have left," he said.

"It's OK. I got a charley horse, and it hurt like the dickens. I called out for you, but Connie came instead. She took care of everything, and now I'm better. Where were you?" Mikalya asked.

He decided against sharing his encounter with Linda. "After you fell asleep, I couldn't sleep. So, I went outside to get some fresh air over by the gazebo on the west side of the hospital. It's nice out right now with a full moon."

"Please don't leave me again unless you tell me first," she said.

Abe sat down on the bed and began gently massaging her temples. Mikalya's eyes rolled back slowly.

"Does this feel good?" he asked. "And don't worry, I won't leave you again… promise."

"Thank you," Mikalya replied, her eyes still closed. "That does feel good. Don't stop."

Abe continued to massage until Mikalya was snoring again. He gently rose from the bed, turned off the light, then quietly laid down on the cot. This time, he fell off to sleep as well.

****

During the time that Mikalya and Abe were watching *The Shining*, Shelly and Loretta were in the process of polishing off a full bottle of Chopin Polish potato vodka. They were drinking chilled shots and loving every minute of it.

Loretta rotated chilled shot glasses in and out of the freezer.

"Where in the hell did you get this? You don't need to even mix it with anything," Shelly said.

"It's a little pricey, but it's worth it. I like how the buttery texture just rolls around on your tongue. Isn't it great?" Loretta said.

"That it is," Shelly responded. She looked over at Loretta with a bit of sadness.

"I know Abe is going to take my baby away from me someday. I need to get ready for it," Shelly said, sitting around the coffee table with Loretta. "I knew it when he sent those flowers. That should have been my first clue."

"You mean that vase of roses in her room is from him?" Loretta asked.

"Yep. He came by one night when Mikalya and I were sleeping and left them. I didn't see them until the next morning."

"Wow, how romantic. Was there a card?" Loretta asked.

"Yeah, there was, but Mikalya didn't share with me what was in it. Maybe one day she will… or maybe she won't," Shelly said solemnly.

"In the short time that I was there, I could see that she was falling in love with him—just from their interaction with each other. He wouldn't be sleeping on that tiny cot in her hospital room if his feelings weren't as equally strong, too. Under the circumstances, I doubt that he's trying to get in her pants. But wouldn't you be in love with him, too? I mean, he's hot and smart, and he saved her life! Hello!" Loretta joked.

Shelly stared into her drink.

"Yeah, I know, but it still hurts to know that my days with her are numbered. She's had her moments, and I've had my episodes with her, but I love her so much, Loretta." Shelly wiped away the tears starting to form in the corners of her eyes.

"What was that line out of *The Godfather*? 'Instead of losing a daughter, you'll be gaining a son,' or something like that. That's close enough, anyway. But do you get what I'm saying? I mean, Abe's a strong guy on every level. He's not your run-of-the-mill, off-the-street dumb jock. It took balls of steel to do what he did to save Mikalya's life. That alone is good enough for me. Good God, what man would come back to her hospital room and hang out with her in the condition she's in unless he cared about her? I mean, he even carries her to the toilet to poop, Shelly."

Shelly smiled.

"But he doesn't stop there! Oh, no! Then, he bravely goes back and carries her out! Now that's love!"

The mood lightened as the ladies roared with laughter.

"Well, my sweet niece, it's going on midnight, and I've got to be at work in the morning," Loretta said, noticing the time. "I was so happy with the results of Mikalya's tests today. She'll be out of that hospital before you know it. Call me from the hospital tomorrow. Love you," she said, rolling on her knees to get off the floor.

"I will. See ya tomorrow," Shelly replied, heading off to the kitchen to empty what was left of her drink.

****

The next morning, Mikalya lay in bed, staring up at the ceiling. When she heard movement, she looked down at Abe, lying on his side. She could see that he was awake.

"Well, good morning, sir. How long have you been awake?" she asked.

Abe rolled over and looked up at her. "Well, to tell you the truth, only for a few minutes. I didn't want to disturb you if you were still sleeping, so I just lay here."

"That was mighty thoughtful of you."

"I know it was, wasn't it?" he teased. "Would you like some breakfast from your new favorite place?"

"Abe, you don't have to do that. I don't want you to feel as if I'm using you or anything like that, and getting me breakfast daily could become costly…"

Abe put two fingers to her lips.

"Shush," he commanded. "Money's not an issue, and it never will be. I don't mind going out for you. I have to eat, too, you know. Really, I don't mind at all. If that's what you want, that's what you shall have."

Mikalya nodded, his fingers still covering her lips.

"Will it make you happy?" he asked.

Mikalya nodded again.

"Well, then, it's worth it," he said, removing his fingers and leaning down to kiss her lips. "What time is it, by the way?"

"Seven-thirty. They'll be around for the breakfast order soon. I was just going to request some coffee and a yogurt cup with some fruit in it. Do you want one? I can probably sneak an extra one in."

"Coffee sounds good, especially since I feel like I'm still half asleep. What time is your mom coming?"

"She should be here around eight. She called earlier."

With only a bump at the door, Connie breezed into the room with a cup of coffee in each hand.

"It's nursing station coffee, but it does the job. I even brought a little 2% milk and some sugar packets. I'll set it all right here. Help yourselves because I gotta run," she said, rushing back out the door.

"Connie, you're a godsend. You read my mind," Abe said.

Abe prepared their coffees and handed a cup to Mikalya.

"She's either got a sixth sense or the hearing of a hunting dog." He laughed.

"Both, I think. Hey, this coffee's not too bad," Mikalya said. They sat in silence for a few minutes, sipping their coffee.

Abe was thinking about his conversation with the young girl the night before. She was too young to lose her dad, and he felt bad for her.

"What are you thinking about?" Mikalya asked.

Abe looked up, a little startled. "I heard that someone died last night on the third floor. That's too bad, huh?"

"That is too bad. Wow," Mikalya said.

Abe chose not to share anymore. There was no need to. He didn't want to open what could turn into an ugly can of worms.

The phone rang, breaking the silence of the room. It was the cafeteria calling to get Mikalya's breakfast order.

Abe checked the time again. "Listen, why don't I head out to pick up breakfast? I'll get a little extra for your mom. Is Loretta coming, too?"

"I don't think so," Mikalya answered.

As Abe prepared to leave, the phone rang again. This time it was Shelly.

"Hey, honey!"

"Hi, Mom. Where are you?" Mikalya asked, looking over at Abe, gesturing that he was heading out the door. Mikalya waved.

"Well, I am slowly but surely making my way to you."

"Abe's gone out to get breakfast for us. He's getting some for you, too."

"That's nice of him. I want to give him some money," Shelly said.

"He won't take it. He's too much of a gentleman. We'll take him out for beer and pizza when I'm out of here."

"For what he's done for us, he deserves a lot more than beer and pizza. But I love your innocent simplicity. That's a compliment, by the way," Shelly said.

"Mom, I know he deserves a lot more. Trust me. I know. How far away are you now?"

"Not too far—I may be about thirty minutes out," Shelly replied.

"OK, drive safely. Abe should be back with food by the time you get here."

"I hope so. I'm starving. Thanks, honey. I hope we get more good news today. Are you excited?"

The door to the room swung open before Mikalya could answer. It was Doctor Hart and Connie, wearing a huge smile.

"Mom, I'll see you when you get here. The doctor just came in," she said, hanging up without awaiting her mom's reply.

"Well, Miss Arabella, how do you feel this morning?" Doctor Hart asked.

"To tell you the truth, Doctor Hart, outside of the leg, I feel pretty good. And I got a good night's sleep, too!"

"Any headaches?" he asked.

"No, I watched a movie with no problem."

He looked at her burns briefly, then at her chart, making notes.

"Well, all your vitals look good, and the blood work looks good, too. Unless you want to hang out here for the rest of the week, I think you can go home today. How does that sound?" he asked.

Mikalya's face lit up in a huge grin. "Are you serious? Connie, is he serious? I can go home today. Really?" Mikalya asked.

"Yep. This is it!" Connie confirmed, walking over and giving Mikalya a squeeze.

"I'll get the paperwork going. One of the nurses will be in with some forms for you to sign, and they'll go over medications and post-hospital care with you. You'll have to come back here to rehab that leg," Doctor Hart said, ticking off his to-do list for her. "Any questions for me?"

Mikalya was still in shock. "No, not right now, Doctor. Thanks for everything!" she said, shaking his hand enthusiastically.

After he left, Connie took Mikalya's hand.

"When are your mom and Abraham coming? You have good news for them, don't you?"

"Well, Abe just ran out to get food, and Mom should be here soon. I can't wait to tell them! It's really happening! I mean, I should have been dead, but now I'm going home!" Mikalya exclaimed.

Connie hugged her. “And I’m so happy for you, but I’m gonna miss seeing you in this room.” She kissed Mikalya on the forehead and headed out the door.

She hadn’t been gone five minutes when Shelly walked in. “Hey! Sorry I’m late, but traffic was—”

“Mom! Listen, Doctor Hart was just here and… well, guess what?” she asked excitedly.

Shelly could tell by the look on her face and the excitement in her voice what her news was.

“Today? Really? You’re being discharged today?” Shelly’s purse slid from her shoulder and dropped to the floor.

Mikalya nodded. “My discharge papers are being prepared; then, I’m out of here! Are you sure you’re ready to take care of me until my leg heals?”

Shelly’s eyes filled with tears. She leaned down and squeezed Mikalya as tight as she could without hurting her. “I can’t wait to take care of you. Aunt Loretta and I have prepared a space for you at her house so that you’re comfortable. Remember that ratty storage room of hers? You wouldn’t believe it now. You’ll love it. And it’s the closest one to the bathroom. She can’t wait to have us. I’m so happy for you! For us! Where’s Abe?”

"He should be back any moment with food. Now I'm starving," Mikalya said, rubbing her stomach.

"OK, let me start packing you up. You'll want to get a shower before you leave."

Shelly was rushing about the room, packing up Mikalya's things, when Abe knocked on the door and then walked on in.

"Room service again," he announced as he carried the food to the table. He sat the food down and looked at them, noticing the smiles on their faces.

"OK, what's going on? I take it we're not watching part three of *The Shining* tonight," he joked.

Mikalya's smile grew wider as she motioned him over to her and held out her arms.

"Well, we are… just not here. We're out of here in a couple of hours!"

Abe squeezed her hand. "Yes!" he said.

Mikalya beckoned him to lean down and put her mouth to his ear. "Are you sure you're ready for me?" she whispered.

"I feel like I've been ready for you all my life. It's hard to believe we didn't even know each other, and now, this," he said.

Mikalya pulled him in closer for a kiss.

Abe loved the way she flashed her eyes at him. He was under her spell but offered no resistance. "Hey, I have a little something for you," he said, remembering the small, wrapped box he had.

"Baby, you didn't have to do this, but I'm glad you did," she said. Mikalya opened the box and laid eyes on a stunning pair of turquoise earrings.

"Abe, I love these! You know turquoise is my favorite color! Where did you get them?" she asked.

"I saw them at an Indian fair. They're handmade with sterling silver posts. I knew you'd like them."

"I'll wear them on our first official date." Mikalya couldn't stop smiling.

"OK, you two, let's eat our breakfast, and then we'll finish getting her packed. There's a lot to do here. Mikalya, would you like to have your shower after you eat?" Shelly asked.

"Can Abe give it to me?"

"Mikalya, c'mon. That wouldn't be appropriate."

Mikalya folded her arms and pouted.

"You need to behave until you're fully healed. Got it, missy?" Shelly said.

"Yeah, yeah, yeah," Mikalya mocked.

After they finished eating and Shelly returned to packing Mikalya's things, Connie walked in.

"Hi, Connie. Mikalya would like to have a shower before she leaves. Would you mind helping with that?" Shelly asked.

"Sure," Connie said, taking a seat on the bed next to Mikalya. Placing her arm behind her back, she put her cheek against Mikalya's. "I can't stop telling you how much we're going to miss you."

"I'm going to miss all of you, too. But just because I'm not here in the hospital doesn't mean that we can't keep in touch. You guys have my number, and I have yours, so we'll see each other," Mikalya replied, turning to kiss Connie's cheek.

"Well, I have to put some time in up on the third floor, so I probably won't see you again before you leave, but you know the plan… as soon as you're well enough," she said, blowing a kiss.

Shelly stopped packing and looked around the room. Everything had happened so fast, and their lives had changed so dramatically, all in an instant. She hadn't even had time to catch her breath.

After the CNA had come and gone and Mikalya was safely back on her bed after her shower, she insisted on putting on her makeup.

A few minutes later, a nurse came in with her discharge papers. Before the nurse left, Shelly asked for a wheelchair escort.

"I feel like Dorothy leaving the land of Oz," Mikalya said, surveying the room.

Shelly laughed. "Honey, this was not Oz or Munchkin land, not even close."

Standing in the corner with his hands in his pockets, Abe chuckled.

Shelly stood back and held the door open for the nurse to come through with the wheelchair. "OK, are you ready? Your ride's here," Shelly teased.

"Yes, I'm ready, but I want Abe to wheel me out."

"I think it's hospital policy that medical personnel handles that," Shelly replied.

"Mikalya, she's right. Don't worry. I'll be right beside you," Abe chimed in.

"OK, but stay right beside me."

They headed down the elevator to Shelly's car.

Once Mikalya was seated comfortably inside, Abe went to his car so that he could follow them to Loretta's. When they arrived, he picked her up and carried her into the house where Loretta was anxiously waiting. She almost didn't wait for Abe to move out of the way after he lowered Mikalya to the sofa before she rushed in to give her a big hug.

"Honey, I am so glad you're here! We have your room all ready, and it's close to the bathroom. While you're working on healing, those contractors will be building you a new home!" she said excitedly and all at once.

"Aunt Loretta, thank you. I will be working hard to get back on my feet as fast as I can."

"I know you will," Loretta said. "Now, Abe, can you help us get her to her room?"

****

A couple of weeks went by; then, it was time for Mikalya to begin her rehab. She went in and met her physical therapist, Elyssa Donovan, with the beautiful accent that Mikalya loved. She had come over from Galway, Ireland, the year before, and the two hit it off immediately.

Elyssa was a classic beauty. She had bright blue eyes, long, beautiful red hair, and a witty, sassy personality. Although some may have found her tough exterior intimidating, Mikalya could sense that deep down, she was a sensitive, caring person. She was also a lot of fun to be around.

Mikalya often wondered what had happened in Elyssa's past that caused her to put up the wall that she did when she first met someone. She was confident and professional, with a great sense of humor, and she was a good therapist. The fact that she was also a friend of Connie's was enough for Mikalya to like her and want to get to know her better.

"I'll have you walking on this leg in no time," she said. "Just stick with me for the whole process. It won't be easy, but I'll be with you every step of the way."

****

The weeks of Mikalya's recovery and therapy flew by. She talked on the phone with her friends from the hospital frequently. They would even drop in on her from time to time to see how things were going.

Shelly watched as Mikalya and Abe grew closer by the day. She and Loretta liked him and felt that he fit right into their family.

After several weeks, Mikalya's cast came off, and she was walking on her own. Shelly and Loretta both resumed their regular work schedules as Mikalya no longer needed much assistance.

One day, her friends from the hospital showed up out of the blue. Loretta and Shelly were there as well.

"What brings all of you here at the same time? Mom, what's going on?" she asked.

"I'm just here," Shelly said, throwing her hands up and walking over to sit next to Mikalya. "Connie, the floor is all yours."

Connie stood in front of Mikalya. "Mikalya, as healthcare professionals, it's our duty to make sure our patients have a full recovery. Although you're walking again, and you look great, we're not fully convinced that your recovery is as thorough as it should be. So, we've arranged a trip for all of us to go to Las Vegas and see that Chippendale show we talked about!" Cynthia announced gleefully.

"After we get back, we'll re-evaluate your progress. But we feel confident this will push your recovery along quite well. Does everyone agree?" Connie added.

Mikalya was shocked and looked from Shelly to Loretta, then back at the girls, then back at Shelly again.

"Mom…" she began.

Shelly nodded. "Honey, we all fly out Friday night of Labor Day weekend!"

For a moment, Mikalya was silent. "Did you tell Abraham?" she asked, hands clasped.

"He's all for it! But go ahead, call him now if you want," Shelly encouraged.

The girls waited patiently as Mikalya carefully touched each number on her phone's keypad. She smiled when she heard his voice.

"Abe, I assume you know all about the Vegas trip and the Chippendale show," she said when he answered.

"I do… and I think it's a great idea! I want you to go. But first, I get to have you," he said. "Now that you're walking again and on the road to a full recovery, I'd like to take you to my favorite bar, The Fat Angel. It's where all my buddies hang out. Luis, Lamar, and Dennis… they'll all be there when we go. And feel free to invite whoever you want. The more the merrier! Does that sound like a fair trade? I get to have fun with you before you run off to have fun with your friends?"

"Yes, it does, Abe! Can we dance, too?"

"You can dance all you want, babe. Now, I know your girls are still there, so enjoy your company, and we'll talk later."

"Yes, we will. Can't wait. Talk later," Mikalya said, ending the call. She looked around the room at her friends and family.

"Well, what did he say?" Shelly asked.

"He thinks it's a great idea, but he's got me first, next Saturday. He's taking me to a bar called The Fat Angel to party with his fire buddies. I'm sure some of the guys who helped save me will be there, so I'll get to thank them. He invited all you guys, too, if you want to come," she said.

"Well, I'm going. I want to meet those other guys," Connie chimed in.

"The Fat Angel, I've heard of that place. Shelly, why don't we go, too?" Loretta said.

"Oh, I wouldn't miss it for the world!"

"Who knows… there just might be some cute firemen there," Loretta said, winking at Shelly.

"It's a date, Auntie!"

# Chapter Ten:
# Twenty Minutes after Midnight

The day had finally arrived. It would be Mikalya and Abe's first date. Even though Abe wouldn't arrive to pick her up until five, Mikalya began getting ready at three. Their newly rebuilt house would tie in with her new relationship.

While Shelly sat on her bed and watched, Mikalya tried on outfit after outfit. Even after all she'd been through with the fire, she was still an attractive girl with a great figure.

"I'm not fat, am I?" Mikalya asked her mom.

"No, of course not."

"How do I look in this one?"

Shelly shook her head. "Listen, this place sounds a bit informal. If I were you, I'd just put on that nice pair of cutoff jeans, the red top you had on earlier, and the shoes with the small heel. That's a great ensemble. And you can even dance in those shoes."

Mikalya took her mom's advice. "OK, how about now?" she asked.

Shelly gave a toothy grin with a facetious thumbs up.

"With that outfit, you could start a stampede in a monastery."

"Huh? What?" Mikalya asked, puzzled.

"Listen, that's your outfit. You look great. Trust me, Abe will love it! Loretta is going to pick up Karen first since she's already out, then swing by to get me. We'll probably leave before you guys do."

"OK. Thanks for helping me select an outfit, Mom. Love you!"

Shelly scurried off to get ready. She finished just as she heard the honk of Loretta's horn.

Mikalya fussed over her makeup, then splashed Chanel No. 5, remembering it was his favorite. She wanted to be perfect for Abe.

When she heard the crunch of the tires pulling into the driveway, she peeked out the window. It was him. She did one final mirror check and gave herself a thumbs up.

She waited for the doorbell to ring, then opened it nervously.

"Hello, Mr. Abraham," she greeted.

"Hi," he replied.

Mikalya welcomed him in and gave him a huge hug.

"God, let me look at you. You look fantastic!" he said.

"Do I look better than when you carried me out of the house a couple of months ago?" she asked, twirling in front of him.

"Well, I'd say so. This is the first time I've seen you dolled up, and I love it. I'll carry you into the toilet any day of the week!" he said with a wink.

"You saw me at my absolute worst, and you still fell in love with me. Now, you're seeing me at my absolute best. Never thought I could look like this, did you?"

With no response, Abe stood staring at her.

She loved the way he looked at her—as if he could see right through to her heart.

"I never doubted that you could," he said. "We should get moving. It looks like it's about to rain, and I want to get you inside before it starts."

Mikalya grabbed her purse, and they headed to the car. The Fat Angel was only twenty minutes away.

"Mom, Aunt Loretta, and my friend, Karen, will meet us there. I think Mom's friends, Latisha and Jenny, may swing by, too."

"That's fine. We'll try to get everyone at the same table. That's one reason I wanted to get there early."

"I can't wait to meet your friends. Let's see, there's Luis, Dennis, and Lamar, right?" Mikalya asked.

"That's the crew. Luis will have his wife, Carla, there, and Lamar will bring his girlfriend. Dennis will probably be without a date." He paused. "I want to dance with you tonight. Would that be OK?"

"You pick the songs, and we'll go for it. How do you like it, slow or fast?" Mikalya asked.

Abe looked at her and noticed the sly grin on her face. "We are talking about dancing, right?"

"Well, uh, yeah, I mean, what else would I be referring to, you with the dirty mind?"

"You're the dirty one in this car, not me," Abe teased.

A loud crack of thunder boomed.

"Crap, here it comes. Thank God we don't have much farther to go. When we pull up, I'll drop you off at the door," he said.

Mikalya shook her head. "No, go on and park. We'll walk in together."

Abe found a spot not far from the front door and pulled in.

"Well, are you ready for our first date?" he asked.

"I'm more than ready."

He reached into the backseat and got his umbrella, then jumped out and hurried around to open Mikalya's door, shielding her from the rain as they made their way toward the door of the bar. A strong gust of wind blew the umbrella up and out of Abe's hand, leaving them to rush inside.

Mikalya stood in the doorway, drenched and disheveled.

"Stay right here. I'll be right back," Abe said, running to grab paper towels.

As he walked back toward Mikalya, he noticed how beautiful she was despite her drenched appearance and makeup running down her face. He took the paper towels and gently began wiping the black wetness from her cheeks and under her eyes. Mikalya offered no resistance. When he began wiping her hair, she stopped him and took the paper towels from his hand.

With one lean paper towel, she dried his face, shirt, and neck, then rubbed the paper towel slowly over his hair until it was almost dry.

"There, that's better. Now, I'm going into the little girl's room to see what I can salvage, sir. I shall return shortly," she said.

"I'll do the same. See you back out here," Abe replied.

The ladies' and men's rooms were back-to-back, sharing a common wall.

As Abe stood in front of the mirror, getting himself together, he could hear Mikalya speaking, but he couldn't make out what she was saying. When he finished, he waited outside the ladies' room.

"Who were you talking to?" he asked when she walked out.

"Oh, my God, Abe, why didn't you tell me that the rain had wiped away all my makeup?" she asked.

"Shit, it came off when I was wiping your face. I'm so sorry. I really am."

"Oh, don't apologize. I just don't want to embarrass you in front of your friends, looking as if I've stepped out of a horror movie, that's all. It's OK. I had my little emergency kit in my purse, so problem solved before anyone could see me."

Abe wrapped his arm around her shoulder. "Mikalya, you would look good if you put relish and mustard on for makeup. And this crowd? Hell, they don't care. All they care about is that I'm happy. That's it."

Mikalya gave him a peck on the lips just as the door swung open, and Shelly and Loretta walked in, laughing.

"Well, well, well, what is going on in here?" Shelly asked.

"Long story, Mom. Abe, I'll see you out there, OK?"

With a brief nod at Shelly and Loretta, Abe winked at Mikalya and exited into the main bar area.

Luis and Carla were waiting at the bar.

"How are you, man?" Luis asked.

"Hey, guys, I'm good. We had a little rain mishap on our way in, so Mikalya's freshening up in the bathroom."

"We can't wait to meet her, Abe. I'm hoping we will become fast friends," Carla said.

"I'm sure you will, Carla. And thank you," Abe replied.

As they headed off to their table, Dennis walked in alone.

"How goes it, buddies? Where's the girl of the hour?" he asked.

"In the bathroom, wiping off rainwater," Abe replied.

Dennis sat down next to Abe. "That storm's a bitch. It's supposed to go on all night, too."

"No date tonight?" Luis asked, grinning at Dennis.

"No, not tonight. The pickings have been slim lately."

"Hey, everyone, we're here," Lamar announced, walking up to the table with his girlfriend, Sonja. "Where's your lady, Abe?"

"Since everyone's asking for her, I suppose I better get her out here. Can you guys push these two tables together? There will be twelve of us. I'll be right back."

Before he could knock, the restroom door opened, and Mikalya appeared with Shelly and Loretta right behind her.

"Oh, there you are," he said. "Everyone's asking about you."

"OK, let's go meet your friends, then," Shelly said.

Abe led the way to the table, now crowded with friends. Holding Mikalya's hand, he pulled her in front of him as if she were the main float in the Macy's Thanksgiving Day Parade.

The gang looked up at her in awe.

"Well, everyone, finally… here is my Mikalya, in the flesh."

Mikalya blushed and waved. "Hello, everybody."

Everyone greeted her enthusiastically by getting up to hug her, one by one. Abe continued the introductions of Shelly and Loretta, and soon, they were joined by Mikalya's friend, Karen, and Abe's boss, Captain Randy, and his wife.

"So, this is Miss Mikalya. The woman I've heard so much about lately," Captain Randy said as Mikalya stood to greet them.

"Thank you, Captain Randy," she said, patting his hand, then turning to face everyone at the table. "I am so, so glad to meet every one of you. It's hard to believe it was only a few months ago this terrible thing happened to me and my mom. We all know that I wouldn't be alive today if it hadn't been for Abe and the rest of you and all that you did to save my life.

"Captain Randy, these are your well-trained men," she continued, looking around the table. "I owe all of them, and you, a huge amount of gratitude. Abe, you didn't give up on me, even as the house was crashing down around us, I'm told."

Tears streaming down her face, Mikalya brushed Abe's attempt away to try and pull her back down to her seat, but she wasn't done yet.

"There aren't any words strong enough to express what you did for us. All I can say is… thank you so much from the bottom of my heart. Thank you! I pray to God someday that I can…"

Mikalya's voice trailed away as she was overtaken by her tears, so she decided to take her seat without completing her sentence. She was grateful that Abe was there, holding her hand. He leaned over to kiss her cheek, then whispered something in her ear.

By the time he finished, Mikalya was smiling and kissing his forehead. She cleared her throat and began to speak again.

"Well, as I was saying… thank you all again. I'm sorry I got so choked up a minute ago, but now it's time for us to party!"

Captain Randy walked to the bar and ordered a half dozen pitchers of beer. Dennis, Luis, and Lamar focused their attention on Abe.

"Man, she's a doll," Dennis said.

"I second that. And she seems nice," Lamar added.

"Abe, we like her. Just remember, it was I who led you to her," Luis chimed in.

Abe nodded.

"Luis, my friend, indeed you were, so *thank you!*"

Abe noticed Mikalya across the room with her mom and motioned her over. Once everyone was seated, he rose from his seat.

"OK, everyone, I'd like to make a toast." He looked down at Mikalya.

"It's amazing how a person's life can change so quickly, and under the circumstances, mine did. Fortunately, this time, it was for the better. I didn't meet this beautiful woman under normal circumstances, but, as a fireman, my life wasn't exactly normal, to begin with, right?" he chuckled, looking in the direction of his friends.

"If I never accomplish anything else in my career or in life, I will always, always consider it a success because I found this beautiful girl, who is now a huge part of my life. So, here's to you, my darling Mikalya. I love you!"

Everyone raised their glasses in a toast.

Mikalya's eyes teared up as she stood to give Abe a hug and a kiss. Again, she was lost for words.

Just as Abe finished his toast, his parents found their way over to the group, heading straight for Mikalya.

"Mom, Dad, I want you to meet Mikalya," Abe said. Mikalya put her hand out.

"Hey, you don't have to be so formal," Abe's mother said. She then gave Mikalya a big hug, as did his father.

"So, this is Mikalya. Welcome, is all I can say. I'm sure we'll get to know you well. It's so hard to talk around all this noise right now," his father said.

"I know it is. Yes, you'll definitely get to know me well," Mikalya responded. Abe could immediately sense his parents' first impression approval.

With the jukebox blaring and the beer flowing, the party was in full gear.

"So, Mikalya, are you a good dancer?" Lamar asked.

"I don't know. It's been a while since I've been on the dance floor. Let me get a couple more beers in me, and we'll see if I still have it," Mikalya replied.

Abe looked at Mikalya. "If I played a slow song, would you dance with me?" he asked.

"I'd like that," she said.

"Something About Your Touch" by Francesca Beghe flowed from the jukebox. Abe led Mikalya to the dance floor, his arms already wrapped around her waist. Her arms found their way around his neck as they began moving slowly to the rhythm of the song.

"I hope you like this song. Isn't it beautiful?"

"It is. I want this to be our song," she whispered.

Mikalya was in heaven—loving the feel of his arms around her waist. *He always knows just how to touch me.*

****

Across the room, Loretta and Shelly were taking note of the men there.

"I'll have to come here more often," Loretta said.

"They're a wild bunch, Auntie. They'd eat you alive. But we can certainly scoot back in here for a drink sometime," Shelly replied.

****

When Abe and Mikalya returned from the dance floor, Lamar leaned over to Mikalya.

"Well, you've had a few more drinks," he said.

"You really want to see me dance again, don't you? Any particular song?" she asked him.

Abe chimed in. "What about 'Soul Kitchen' by The Doors? You told me in the hospital you really liked them."

"That works for me! Grab your change, and let's go for it," she said.

Abraham, Mikalya, Lamar, and Sonja all got up and went over to the jukebox.

Abe put the money in, and the music began.

With the music in full swing, Mikalya and Abraham moved in rhythmic coordination while Lamar and Sonja danced a few feet away, watching them.

As the song progressed, Mikalya fell into a rhythm all her own, forgetting that she had a partner… Abe. Strong and sensual, her moves mesmerized him as he stopped to watch her belly dancer moves. Commingled with mystery and sexuality, it was all pure Mikalya.

Lamar and Sonja, along with Abe's parents and everyone else in the bar who could see the dance floor, took notice of Mikalya's twirling hips and raised hands as she danced around Abe.

The seduction in her eyes let him know that she was no longer dancing with him. This show was exclusively *for* him. By this time, even the bar staff was watching.

When the music ended, Mikalya bowed to the thunderous applause from the crowded bar.

"Good Christ, I didn't know she could dance like that," James said. Beth looked over at James.

"Well, that's your future daughter-in-law, honey," she said.

"You think so?" James asked.

"I know so. Have you seen the way he looks at her and how she looks at him? There's no damn question in my mind."

"If he likes her, I like her," James said.

"Agreed, one hundred percent. Can you pour me another beer?" she said.

Loretta looked at Shelly, completely stupefied. "Did you know she could do shit like that?"

"Hell no! I've never seen her dance, period, let alone dance like that. She didn't get that from me, and her father hardly danced at all when we went out! I just don't know."

Back from the dance floor, Mikalya took a sip of beer, then looked over at Lamar and winked.

"Well"—Lamar grinned—"I must say, you're an excellent dancer! I'm glad I didn't bet any money against you."

"Mikalya, you were amazing! You don't give lessons, do you?" Sonja asked jokingly.

"Thanks, guys. That was nice of you to say," Mikalya replied, leaning over to kiss Abe on the cheek.

"What did you think?" she whispered. "That's the only opinion that matters to me."

Abraham was still in shock. He looked at her intently and then leaned over in her ear. "That was the most sensual and sexy thing I have ever seen. I can't put it into words. It was beautiful. It was another dimension of you to see and love," he said.

Mikalya whispered back.

"You know I'm fully healed now, right?" she asked. "Could you tell by the way I moved on the dance floor? You know what this means, don't you?"

Abe knew exactly what she meant. Up until now, they still had not been intimate. He wanted to be sure she was physically ready.

"Mikalya, I cannot wait to have you. I need to know that you're ready, though. Are you?" he asked.

Mikalya smiled. "I am, my love."

"Well, that means you're coming home with me tonight," he said, pulling her in for a kiss.

As the waitress was handing the bill to them, Captain Randy came over. "Hey, what is the damage report? I know it's going to be ugly," he said.

Shelly clung on to it.

"Randy, that's OK. It's the least we can do for what your crew did for us," Loretta said.

"Have you looked at that thing yet?" he said.

A lump formed in Shelly's throat as she opened the tab.

She and Loretta both peered into the folder.

"Oh, shit, am I reading that right? Surely, to God, there's a mistake. Did we drink that much?" Loretta said.

Shelly made the sign of the cross. "No, it's probably right. Anyway, we're in no condition to contest it. Hell, I can't add right now. Shit, we'll have to use our credit cards," Shelly said.

Randy continued to stare.

Dennis, Lamar, and Luis all offered to help pay, but Shelly refused them. "Thanks, everyone, but this is something I have to do. It's OK."

Loretta and Shelly got their credit cards out and instructed the waitress to split the bill fifty-fifty.

Abraham and Mikalya walked over. "Shelly, is there a problem?" he asked.

She shook her head. "No, Abe, we're OK, but thanks," she said.

Mikalya could tell it wasn't and snuck around to the waitress's station to check the bill for herself. She secretly motioned for Abe to come over. Randy followed close behind.

"Damn, did you see this? We can't let her and Loretta pay for all this by themselves. Hell, this is over $600!" Mikalya said.

Abraham agreed. He and Mikalya both pulled over one hundred dollars out of their wallets.

Abraham immediately gave the waitress her tip in cash. "Let me quietly go around to the guys and see what I can do. Go ahead and let her run the charge and pay on their cards like they want," he said.

Randy then went around to Luis, Dennis, and Lamar. They ponied up immediately, as did Sonja and Carla. All in all, they managed to pull together over $550 without Shelly or Loretta finding out. They handed the cash to Mikalya, who split it in two. The tip had already been paid.

As the waitress came back with the credit card slip, Abraham spoke up. "I already tipped her in cash. You don't have to add anything," Abraham said.

Mikalya stepped forward with the cash. "Mom and Aunt Loretta, this is for you. We all pitched in. This will come in handy when that credit card bill comes in," Mikalya said.

Shelly could not refuse her own daughter.

They all hugged, and then Shelly, Loretta, and Karen went home, as did most of the rest of them. Abraham and Mikalya remained at the table.

"Hey, I want one last dance to *our song* before we go. Can you play it again for me?" Mikalya asked.

"Of course," he said, leading her back to the dance floor.

With the bar now empty and the song at its end, Mikalya and Abe continued slow dancing as if there was no one in the room but them.

After the song ended, they continued to dance, even though the bar had cleared out. Abraham ordered one last drink for him and Mikalya.

"Hey, I want to get something special for you. Have you ever tried a Black Russian?" he asked. Mikalya shook her head.

"Well, they are a mix of Kahlua and vodka. But I have them made with Chopin Polish vodka, which is smooth as hell and makes the drink smooth as hell," he said.

"Oh, bring it on!" Mikalya said.

The two drinks came with the last call, and Mikalya loved it.

It would become one of her favorite beverages.

"I'll never forget this moment, Abe, never. I hope you won't, either. I want you to remember something for me."

"What's that?"

"I want you to remember this exact date and time," she said.

Abe looked at the clock on the wall. It was 1:33 a.m.

"I want you to remember exactly what I'm wearing right now. I have on jeans and a pinkish-red button-down top with black medium-heeled, open-toe shoes, a gold necklace, turquoise earrings, and a thin black belt. I'm wearing Chanel No. 5. perfume, too. Do you remember what the bar tab was?" she asked.

"Yeah, it was $617.25," he said.

"Yes, it was."

"Mikalya, I won't forget any of this, anyway, but why are you telling me to remember all this? Will there be a quiz later?" he chuckled.

"I just want you to remember. Now, can you take me home?" she asked.

"You mean 'home' as home to your mother's place or to my place?"

"Your place, silly boy."

They thanked the waitress and the bartender. It was pouring outside. Abraham could feel that Mikalya was drunk to the point where she needed assistance to the car. She did well up to and through that last dance, but apparently, that was all she had the stamina for.

Abe got her into the car and put her seat belt on. As he got in and sat down, he saw Mikalya's head drop back against the headrest, and her eyes closed.

She started to mumble. "Abe, honey, thank you for everything. I love you so much, so, so much. I wonder if my dad's OK. Do you think he's all right? Have you seen a lot of burned-up people? I almost burned up, didn't I? You know, I think my mom loves you, too, but she can't have you. I'll never fucking speak to her again if..." Mikalya said.

Now she had fully passed out as Abe was starting the car.

He leaned over, brushed her hair, and kissed her.

After a short ride, they pulled into Abe's drive. He got out and walked to the passenger side to help Mikalya.

"Honey, come on, let's get inside the house," he said, slowly helping her to her feet.

"Abe, I need to use the bathroom," she said.

When he led her to it and shut the door behind her, he could hear her throwing up. He opened the door, and there she was, face down in the toilet. He grabbed a towel and rushed over to help her clean up.

She knelt there for a few minutes, trying to compose herself. "That's what I get for drinking too much on an empty stomach. I hope you're not grossed out."

"No, don't worry about it. I've seen much worse, believe me. Let's get your mouth rinsed out with some mouthwash then I'll help you into the bed in our guestroom... just until you feel better."

Once she was all tucked in, he leaned over, rubbed her hair back from her face, and kissed her forehead.

"Thanks, honey," she said. "You'll be duly rewarded in the morning. I love you."

"I love you, too. You get some rest and get up when you're ready. I'll be in my room."

Before he could finish his sentence, she had closed her eyes and fallen asleep.

****

The morning came quickly. Abe rolled over to beautiful rays of sunlight streaming through his window, and his first thought went to Mikalya. He wondered how she was.

He got up, brushed his teeth and washed his face, then walked into the hallway. The door to the bedroom where Mikalya was remained closed. He decided not to wake her but instead headed to the kitchen and started the coffeepot. A strong cup would wake him up fully.

As he sat there reflecting on the events of the night before, he thought he heard a noise in the hallway. Before he could react, hands covered his eyes.

"Guess who?" came the female voice.

Abe smiled, then slowly reached around Mikalya's entire body, lifted her, and then pulled her over the back of the sofa. With perfect precision, he positioned her on his lap. Her hair was messy, and all her makeup was gone, but she was still beautiful in his eyes.

She wrapped her arms around his neck. "I want to kiss you… but yucky morning breath," she said, covering her mouth. "No toothbrush."

Noticing that she was wearing only her panties and the top she had on the night before, Abe winked and smiled.

"That's exactly the way I want you right now," he said.

"And how's that again?" she asked.

"Just the way you are at this very moment."

Mikalya smiled as Abe gently pulled her face closer. She closed her eyes as his lips slowly met hers in a passionate kiss. She could feel his erection under her, making her hot and forcing her to pull back for a moment, but the intensity in his eyes drew her back to his mouth once again.

Abe rubbed her back up and down and in circular motions, allowing the escape of her quiet moans as the kiss intensified.

Mikalya pulled back once again and looked at Abe. Ever so slowly, she lifted her body from his lap and stood in front of him, reaching down to the bottom of her top and pulling it straight up, then off, exposing her breasts. It was the first time Abe had seen them; he couldn't help but notice how wonderfully shaped and full they were.

Abe could sense her pride in her body, exposing it the way she did as she stood over him, teasing him as her knee parted his, making room for her to move in closer.

"Do you want to pull my panties down, or do you want me to do it?" she asked.

Abe knelt in front of her and put his hands around her waist, grabbing hold of the elastic top of her underwear. As he pulled the tiny piece of cloth down over her knees, her breath hitched in anticipation and she carefully stepped out of them. Their eyes remained locked as Abe swiftly pulled his own shorts down, and Mikalya knew how ready he was.

Wrapping his arms around her naked body, Abe looked into her eyes. He had never felt such beautiful suppleness in his life. All tension and pressure vanished from his mind as ecstasy took over his spirit.

"Baby, this is heaven to me. I feel so much for you right now. I love you," he said.

"You have no idea what I'm feeling right now… but maybe you do. I love you more than you'll ever know," she whispered, looking up at him with that expression of lazy passion in her eyes that he adored.

Both naked, he picked her up and carried her into the bedroom, laying her gently on the bed, where they held each other lovingly.

Their lovemaking went on until they were both totally spent.

Afterward, they went into the kitchen and started to prepare their breakfast.

"Well, was I worth risking your life for?" she asked.

Abe smiled. "If I had died in there with you, we simply would have made love in the afterlife."

"Someday, we will. Someday," Mikalya said.

****

About a week later, Shelly got a call from Cynthia. Their Las Vegas trip was drawing near, and it was time to finalize all the travel details. With nine of them going, there was a lot to iron out.

Cynthia, Elyssa, and Connie had pitched in for Mikalya's airfare and the show tickets. They reserved two side-by-side double queen bedrooms at Caesars Palace, where the Chippendales would be performing on Friday.

It was Wednesday before Shelly, Loretta, and Mikalya began packing. Abe was over and would drive some of the girls to the airport, along with the help of Karen's mom and her SUV.

“This trip is going to be so boring. Heck, I have no idea who the Chippendales are?” Mikalya whined.

“Go and have a good time,” he replied. “Connie and Cynthia went through all this trouble just for you. You don’t want to disappoint them.”

“You’re right. We’ll be back Sunday night. Thankfully, it’s not a long trip.”

****

Thursday afternoon, the girls arrived in Las Vegas. As they got out of the airport van and walked toward the casino, Mikalya looked around in wonder. She was awestruck at the elegance and magnificence of Caesars Palace. Shelly and Loretta had heard her complaining to Abe the night before, so they were tickled by her reaction to the opulence before her. She had to be prodded through the main front doors.

As they walked through the hotel lobby, the attractive group of women turned heads as they made their way to the check-in counter. Loretta loved the attention but kept her excitement in check.

When they finally reached their rooms and finished unpacking, they freshened up and headed down to the casino for drinks and slot machines.

"Let's tie a good one on tonight," Connie said. "I'm feeling lucky."

After a fun night of gambling and drinking, they had dinner and a long walk down the strip. Mikalya had fallen in love with Vegas and hoped to return one day with Abe.

****

The next day, they slept in, then rented a large van and went sightseeing. When they finished touring, they returned to get ready for the Chippendales show.

"If everyone's ready, let's go down for drinks," Elyssa suggested. "We've got a couple of hours to kill before the show starts."

Their drinks arrived in record time, and the bartenders were attentive to their every request. Shelly remained standing after the others had sat down.

"I'm going to make this short and sweet," she said, raising her glass. "This is to my wild, crazy, but extremely beautiful daughter. Honey, I'm so glad you're here with us!"

Mikalya smiled and stood to give her mom a hug. The rest of the girls raised their glasses to toast and gave a round of applause.

They ran through a couple of rounds of drinks when Elyssa started talking about a story about a bat that seemed to attack her in the library where she was studying one evening.

"I was in my last year of physical therapy school at the University of Limerick, in all places Limerick, Ireland. I was studying alone one night in a room off the main library. It was a little creepy, but it didn't bother me until I noticed this thing flying around the room. It was weird because it started flying away from me like it was scared. But then, every time it circled around, it would fly a bit closer and a bit closer. I couldn't figure out what the hell it was at first, but then I realized it was a damn bat," Elyssa said.

"How the hell did it get in there?" Loretta said.

"There was an open window in the hallway, so it had to have flown in through there. I tried ignorin' it so I could study, but the little shit kept on circlin' around. I looked around for something to throw at, and believe it or not, I found an empty eyeglass case someone left lying around. I threw it at him and missed.

"I thought, *Oh, shit, now he's really coming after me*. It circled one more time, then came straight at me. I went 'AAHHH' and ducked down. God, I thought I heard it *whoosh* right past my ear. Then I ran over and pulled a book off the shelf. I saw it fly toward the other end of the room then; it must have known I was grabbing those books to throw at it, and it came at me again. I screamed and threw the first book at it, which missed," Elyssa said, laughing.

"What was the title of the book?" Cynthia said.

"Hell, I don't remember, Cynthia. I think it was *Proper Pet Care* or something. Will you shush up? Then, after I missed, I got sooo freaked out that I ran down one of the other aisles. I stayed there for a minute, then slowly peeked out, but I couldn't see it. I thought: *This is bullshit. I'm not getting anything done. I'm outta here!*

"So, I ventured out of the aisle and started to get my stuff together. Then, out of nowhere, that little shit came at me again. I went 'SSHHIIIIITT' and threw the next book at it, and, I'll be damned, I almost got it. But then it flew in some weird pattern and came at me again! I had to run down two aisles over," Elyssa said.

"Well, they fly so crazy they're so hard as hell to hit with anything," Shelly said.

"No shit, so I grabbed a third book off the shelf," Elyssa said.

"And what was the title of that one?" Connie asked.

"Uh, it was *How to Excel at Corn Hole*, I imagine. Dammit to hell, why are ya askin'?" Elyssa asked.

The girls were now laughing hysterically. Cynthia and Connie had both heard this story. Each time she told it, there was always some new little nutty detail they'd never heard before. Her thick

Irish accent added to the flare of the story. It came across as prim and proper, but then, when she threw in a swear word or two, the girls thought it was even funnier.

Elyssa took another sip of beer and continued. "Anyway, Miss Librarian, I had one more shit, I'm sorry, I mean shot. See what you're makin' me do? It then landed on another ceiling tile and just clung there, staring at me, or, I guess, laughing at me. If I'd been in a better mood, I would have just packed up and left, but that little monster soured me big time, so now I wanted it dead.

"So, I snuck over a little bit closer to it and just lobbed my last book at it as hard as I could, and I hit the tile right next to it. Then, I thought, *Shit, I'm out of books, and my luck's run out as well. I can't hold it off anymore*. So, I crawled on the floor to where my purse and book were. As I got up and grabbed everything, that little peckerhead came at me again. I screamed and ran out the door. I was runnin' down the hallway screamin': 'Get away from me, get away from me!' I was running so fast I hit the custodian head-on and knocked her back on her ass. The floor had a lot of shiny wax on it, so she slid on her butt right into the wall. I had to stop and help her up. She looked at me like I was fuckin' crazy," Elyssa said.

"'I'm sorry, ma'am, I didn't mean to knock ya down,'" I said.

"'Miss, if you don't mind me askin', what are you runnin' from?' she asked. I looked around and saw that little shit was gone. I must have flown out that open window I ran past.

"'Well, ma'am, a bat was chasin' me out of where I was studyin', and that's what made me run into ya. I am so sorry. Let me help you up,' I told her.

"So, I helped her up and brushed her butt off and sent her on her way. And that's the end of my bat story," Elyssa said.

The girls were wiping the tears out of their eyes when Shelly had to ask the last question.

"Elyssa, if you don't mind me asking, what was the title of that last book you threw?" she asked.

Elyssa looked at her, flashing her beautiful green eyes.

"Well, you would have to ask, wouldn't ya?" she said.

All the girls were intently listening for her answer.

Elyssa took a big sip of her beer. She then answered. "Well, I'll tell ya. I believe it was *How to Effectively Piss Off a Bat.*"

They sat around sipping their drinks and getting mentally prepared for the 9 p.m. show.

****

It was almost 20:30 when they arrived at the Rio Suite Hotel, where the show was to be, and got seated at their table.

Mikalya noticed the theater filling up quickly with women of all ages, backgrounds, and styles. She also noticed a change in her mom and aunt and the other girls as well. Aunt Loretta and her mom were laughing a bit loudly. Connie, Elyssa, and Cynthia had let their hair down and were clearly having fun. The anticipation of what was about to go down at Caesars Palace was contagious. Once their drinks arrived, Mikalya sat back in nervous anticipation.

"Look at these crazy women," Shelly said, surveying the room. "They're like a pack of wild animals. The Chippendales better be ready and careful."

"The look in their eyes. My God, I've never seen anything like this," Loretta said.

Mikalya noticed it all, but her thoughts were on Abe.

Karen looked over at her. "Do they really take their clothes off?" she asked. Mikalya rolled her eyes.

"Well, I guess they do. I've never seen the Chippendales before." Shelly overheard the conversation.

"Karen, let's put it this way… For what we paid to get in here, they'd damn well better take their clothes off."

"Karen dear, we didn't come here to watch them change into their PJs," Elyssa said with a wink. The girls ordered another round of drinks.

As the lights dimmed, the announcer's voice covered the room loud and clear, just as the dancers burst through the curtains in a cloud of glitter and glory, minus the same in clothing. Silence bounced off every wall. The women could cut the high voltage electricity in the air with a knife.

Karen stared expressionless through peek-a-boo fingers. Shelly looked over at Mikalya, trying to gauge the expression on her face.

Suddenly, the room went wild, with women screaming at the top of their lungs. Cynthia, Elyssa, and Connie started to hoot and holler, along with the hundreds of women in the audience. They went wild. Mikalya stared and was completely overwhelmed.

Shocked, she watched the two normally subdued professionals who had cared for her in the hospital bounce up to the stage and stuff money into the shorts of one of the dancers.

Her aunt was close behind, motioning for Shelly to come along.

Shelly kept staring at the stage, torn between her image as a mother to her daughter sitting next to her and her female desires.

Loretta turned around and motioned for Shelly to come up to where one of the dancers was next to her. She even held out a couple of dollars.

"Shelly, come on! Come on over, now!" she screamed.

Shelly smiled and shook her head. Elyssa leaned over to Mikalya.

"Nudge your mom to get up there. I think she's holding back because of you," she shouted above the noise.

Mikalya tapped her mom on the back. "Go ahead, Mom. It's OK. Give him a couple of dollars for Karen and me."

Shelly slowly got up and headed toward Loretta. Grabbing a few dollars from her purse, Karen jumped from her seat.

"Wait a minute, Shelly, I'm coming, too!" she yelled.

Elyssa sprang up and helped Karen to the stage.

Mikalya looked around and noticed that she was the only one still at the table. All the other girls and half the audience were tucking money into the G-strings of the male dancers and getting kisses.

The show, along with all the women's over-the-top behavior, went on for almost ninety minutes. But even with all the madness going on around her, Mikalya could only think about Abe, wondering what he was doing at that very moment.

When the girls finally made their way back to the table, Mikalya had begun a slow fall into a full bout of withdrawal. This was the first time she and Abe had been away from each other since he'd come into her life, and she was missing him terribly. She knew he was on duty at the fire station but still wondered if he was simply sitting around shooting the breeze with the guys or if he was inside a burning building with a roof about to fall on his head.

Shelly looked over at Mikalya and noticed her pre-occupied expression. "Honey, what's wrong?" Shelly asked. "Are you OK?"

Shelly could tell that she was a little drunk. "Mom, I'm going to call Abe. I'll be right back," Mikalya replied.

Shelly stroked her hair.

"Go ahead. Be careful. We'll be right here."

Mikalya got up and quickly walked out of the showroom and into a quiet place where she could think and talk. She dialed Abe's cell phone number, praying he would answer.

"Mikalya, is that you?" he said into the phone.

Mikalya breathed a sigh of relief.

"Oh, my God, Abe, it's soooo good to hear your voice. Damn, I miss you. What are you doing? You're not on a call, are you? Are you at the firehouse safe? How are the other guys?" she rambled on without taking a breath.

Hearing the slur of her words, he could immediately tell she'd been drinking.

"Are you OK?" he asked. "How's Vegas? Isn't tonight the Chippendale show?"

"It's nice, but I want to be here with you. I miss you. Abe, do you think of me when I'm not around? Have you been thinking of me tonight? I've been thinking of you. I really have. I mean, I miss you. Do you know what I mean? Do you know?" Mikalya asked as tears rolled down her cheeks.

"Mikalya, take it easy now. You know I've been thinking of you ever since you left the other day. You're all I've thought about."

Once Mikalya heard Abraham's voice, she calmed down, and the crying subsided. Abe knew exactly how to lovingly subdue her.

"I'm sorry, honey. I'm sorry. I just needed to hear your voice," she said, wiping away her tears. "I feel like an idiot, but I can't help it. I don't want to help it."

"You're not an idiot. We miss each other, and I'm glad you called. Now I know you're OK. Aren't you at the Chippendale show?"

Mikalya softly laughed. "Yeah, it's going on for a bit longer. The women in there are nuts. You'd think none of them had ever seen a nude man before."

"Are they as sexy as I hear they are?" he asked.

"They're all right, but nothing compared to you. I'll bet you a hamburger, a side of fries, and a beer that your dick's bigger than any of theirs!" she said, laughing.

Abe smiled and shook his head. "How are your mom and Aunt Loretta doing?" he asked.

"They're having a good time. Aunt Loretta must have tucked half her paycheck into the shorts of every male dancer in that room. She won't be able to pay for food tomorrow… I'm sure of it."

Abe laughed.

Mikalya turned around and saw her mom coming toward her. "The show's over. We thought we'd go out and grab a bite to eat before heading back to the room."

"Hey, go ahead. I'm OK here. I'll see you guys back at the airport on Sunday. You can call me tomorrow if you want. But be safe. Tell everyone I said, 'Hi.' And don't forget, I love you."

"I love you too, baby, so much! I will call you tomorrow. I promise."

They hung up, and Shelly escorted Mikalya back to the group, now disbanding for dinner.

Everyone had a great time in Vegas except the guest of honor. Through a forced smile, Mikalya thanked them for their generous weekend. She had faked it well, all the while missing Abe. She was anxious to get back home and move on with her life with him.

****

It had been almost a year since Mikalya first laid eyes on Abraham. In that time, the relationship between the two had strengthened dramatically. Now, she could not imagine life without him. She could almost read his thoughts and feel his soul.

Every time they went out together, it was a new adventure. Each date felt like the first. She had never felt such an intense degree of love, strength, and protection. Every time Abraham was in their newly rebuilt home, he could, and did, pinpoint the exact spot where he found Mikalya.

Instead of the edge of the stairs, that point was now in the middle of the downstairs living room. Whenever Abe came over to pick her up, she would lead him over to the spot where he'd found her lying and make him close his eyes. Then, she would tiptoe to plant a kiss on his lips. She'd hug him tight like a little girl and tell him how much he was loved. This period was, by far, the happiest of her life. She had never laughed or smiled as much as she had since Abe entered her world.

One weekend, he surprised her with a five-day trip to The Walter Raleigh Hotel in Youghal, Ireland. The day they touched down in Dublin was the first anniversary of the fire. Mikalya had no idea if the trip was meant to coincide with that day, but she felt certain that she would soon find out.

The Raleigh Hotel was a beautiful resort along the ocean. Mikalya had never been out of the country, so she found Ireland mesmerizing.

One night, after dinner, they walked along the beach and sat down in a secluded spot overlooking the Irish Sea.

"Honey, I can't begin to tell you how incredible this is. Are you having as good a time as I am?" she asked.

"You don't have to ask that. I've been planning this since the moment I carried you out of that house," he said.

She laid her head on his shoulders.

"So, let me get this straight. You thought of all this while you were in the middle of a huge fire with a house falling all around you?" she asked, smiling.

"Yeah, pretty much as I recall," he replied.

"Why Ireland? I mean, don't get me wrong, I love it here. So much so that I don't want us to leave."

"I don't know. I have some Irish in me from my dad's side, and I've always felt connected to it. I wanted to come here but with someone special. Maybe that's the reason… I wanted to bring you here to strengthen our connection. It helps me to bring it full circle. Now, we'll always have an excuse to come back and visit, won't we?"

Mikalya tightened her hold on him. “We don’t need an excuse to go anywhere together. I feel at home and at peace here.”

“You know, they say Ireland is one of the most haunted places in the world. Have you ever heard about Carmun, the Celtic witch?” Abe asked.

“No, I haven’t. Tell me about her.”

“She’s some sort of goddess of evil magic who supposedly roams around the Irish countryside at night. And she’s someone you don’t want to run into.”

“Really? What did, or does, she look like?” Mikalya asked curiously.

“I read tales about her when I was a boy. I never had many nightmares when I was young, but for some reason, I had a few about her. One night, I dreamed that she came through my bedroom wall from the outside and walked right up to my bed, staring at me as I slept. Her eyes were a deep green at first, but then, the irises slowly went from round to vertical, like a snake. They say she’s beautiful but has this evil intensity about her you don’t sense at first. If you run across her, she seems like a shy, pretty girl, but the more you talk to her, the more you start to feel uncomfortable and frightened. She senses your fear but does nothing to quell it. Then, finally, she—”

"Honey, that's enough," Mikalya quickly interrupted. "I don't want to hear anymore. You never told me a witch haunted your dreams. That bitch doesn't scare me, and if she ever harms you, I'll take her witch hat and stick it in her rear, pointy side first. When it comes to protecting you, I can be a witch, too!"

Abe looked at her and laughed.

"Yes, that's another reason I brought you here. You're an angel, and you have the power to counteract her evil. I know you can destroy it. I felt that from the beginning with you, and I feel it now. I haven't feared her ever since you came into my life. I don't fear her now, even here."

"Oh, Abe, that's the sweetest thing I ever heard, and I'm glad I make you feel safe from that witch. But is that the only reason you brought me to Ireland… to tell me about her?"

Abe looked into her eyes and stroked her hair. "No, I brought you to Ireland to ask you to marry me," he replied.

Mouth wide open, Mikalya stared at him.

He pulled a little box out of his pocket and slowly opened it.

It was a beautiful, clear, and shiny, one-carat diamond ring.

"My beautiful Mikalya Arabella, will you marry me?" he asked, gazing into her deep crystal blue eyes.

Mikalya looked at him, and he could see her eyes glisten in the moonlight.

Her red hair blew in the ocean breeze. She was the most sensual creature he had ever seen in his life.

She touched the ring and looked at Abe. He took it out of the box and placed it on her finger.

Her eyes welled with tears. "Yes, Abe, I'll marry you! Hell Yes! I promise I'll save you from that nasty witch, Carmun. She'll never frighten you ever again," she said, throwing her arms around his neck.

"Thank you, baby girl," he whispered, pulling her closer into a passionate kiss.

From the very beginning, they knew this moment would come.

Abe walked Mikalya closer to the shore and slowly undressed her. Then he removed his own clothing. They made love in the open moonlight to the sound of the gentle waves rolling in from the Irish Sea.

The days she and Abe spent in Ireland were the happiest of her life. She hadn't even left, but could not wait to return to Ireland someday.

Mikalya and Abraham had decided not to tell anyone of their plans until after they got back.

****

Upon arriving back home, Mikalya and Abe went to her house first to drop off her luggage. Shelly met them at the door.

"Hey! The travelers are finally back! Did you have a good time? Abe, did you take good care of my little girl?" Shelly said, giving Mikalya a tight squeeze.

"Of course," Abe replied, before turning to get the rest of Mikalya's luggage.

"Ouch! What was that?" Shelly asked, stepping back from Mikalya, who still had her arms around her.

Mikalya had just accidentally scratched her mom's arm with her diamond engagement ring. "Oh, Mom. I'm sorry; that was my fault," she said, quickly pulling her hand back.

"Wait a minute! What was that? Do you have a hangnail?" Shelly asked.

Mikalya looked over at Abe, who was standing by with a sly grin on his face.

"Well, Mom, not exactly," Mikalya said, holding out her hand.

Shelly lowered her eyes slowly to take a good look at Mikalya's hand. "I'll be damned. My baby is gonna get married! Abe, you proposed to her in Ireland, didn't you?"

"Yeah, Shelly, I did!" he replied. "Pretty soon, I'll be calling you Mama. What do you think of that?"

"That's great news! We have to start planning. Can I call Aunt Loretta and tell her? You know she'll want to be in on all this. You and Abe can wear what you want, and we'll take care of everything else! You won't have to worry about a thing! Abe, do your parents know yet? Have you two set a date yet?" Shelly fired off.

"No, not yet," Abe answered. "You're the first person we told. We thought we'd just drop off the luggage and then run over and tell them, too. We wanted to tell you first and in person. As far as the date goes, we've selected Memorial Day weekend. That's ten months from now and will give us plenty of time to plan."

"Well, I'll tell you what. Go on over and tell them now. Mikalya, I'll unpack for you. I'm sure you're tired from the flight. When you get home, you can go straight to bed," Shelly said.

****

They headed over to Abe's parents to give them the news.

When they were done, they went to Abe's house.

"Well, we did it. The most important people now know that we're getting hitched!" Mikalya said. "Listen, I know Mom will try to dominate the planning on this, but I'll tell her to chill and—"

"Honey, it's OK," Abe interrupted. "If Shelly wants to spearhead the planning, I'm sure it will be fine with my parents. They're more laid back. I know they'll want to help financially, though. But, whatever happens, I want you to be happy. OK?"

Mikalya hugged him so tightly that Abe almost lost his breath.

Exhausted, they lay back on the sofa and fell asleep.

****

Over the next few months, Shelly and Beth were busy planning their children's wedding. Shelly had a good feel for the kind of wedding Mikalya wanted. The wedding would be outdoors, and the reception would be at a country club that James and Beth belonged to. Mikalya wanted to return to Ireland for their honeymoon at the same place they'd stayed before. Abe wanted whatever would make Mikalya happy.

****

With the wedding day only a few weeks away, Abe decided to take Mikalya out for a late-night dinner to talk over the wedding plans. They decided on a little jazz place over in Chesterton they'd never been to before called The Jazz Kitchen that they both wanted to try. The reservations were for 9 p.m., and they arrived a little early.

Mikalya was wearing a colorful, loose-fitting hippie-style dress Beth had given her, along with turquoise sandals and beautiful gold bracelets.

Abe could not stop staring at her.

"Do you have any idea how amazing you look tonight? You look incredible!" he said as they were being seated.

"Thanks! You look like you belong on a Chippendale calendar, yourself!"

"What do you think of this place?" Abe asked, looking around.

"It's nice. I really like the piano bar and the jazz band. There's nothing like listening to good music while you're having dinner and a drink."

"Well, how do you feel about the wedding plans so far? Are you happy with the way everything is going?" he asked.

"Yeah, I am. One nice thing coming out of all this is my mom and aunt have become really good friends with your mom. Do you know they've been out partying three times that I know of? Do you also know that, after the wedding, they're talking about going to Vegas for another Chippendales show? Your mom really wants to go."

Abe's eyebrows shot up.

"Uh, listen, let's pretend you didn't tell me that. I mean, I really don't think my dad would mind. I really don't, but you know, I just can't picture my mom doing something like that."

"Well, I think it would be a riot. Hell, I'd like to be in on that one so that I can send you pics of your mom tucking money into a male dancer's briefs with his dick six inches from her face," Mikalya said, laughing.

Abe frowned and rolled his eyes, making a funny face that made Mikalya laugh even harder, so hard that tears streamed down her face. Abe looked around to see if the other patrons were looking at them.

"Will you stop? Quit!" Mikalya said forcefully in a hushed tone.

"Hey, chill out a bit. Everyone is looking at us," he said.

"Me, chill out? Well, don't make those goofy shit faces in public. OK?"

When they finished dinner, they hung around for more of the music.

"Hey, I like this song. Do you want to dance?" Abe asked.

Mikalya nodded, and they headed for the dance floor.

Abe held her close, and she clung to him as the music played.

"Abe, I'll never ask much of you at all, but can you promise me one thing?"

"Yeah, honey, whatever you want," he replied.

She hesitated before she spoke again. "Promise me that if something ever happens to me, you will never give up looking for me. I want you to wait for me. OK?"

Abe looked at her, confused by what she'd said, wondering what she meant. The aura of the evening took on an ominous tone that Abe couldn't put his finger on. "Of course, but are you planning a trip I don't know about?" he joked.

Mikalya looked at him with a serious expression. Then she looked up at the ceiling in a slight daze.

This left Abe even more unsettled.

"No, but…" she began.

"No, but what?" Abe asked, stopping the dance.

"No, but you never know. My God, I made a rhyme," she said.

"Seriously, what do you mean?"

"Shush, and let's finish our dance," Mikalya said.

They danced in silence for a few more songs, while Abe was left perplexed.

After the dance, they strolled to Abe's car. As he was about to open the passenger door for her, Mikalya took his hand and looked at him. Then, they took a walk further in the car park and the path beyond to settle their food. Mikalya was feeling good that all was going well with the planning of their wedding. She loved Abe dearly, and she intended this to be her only marriage. As they continued walking toward Abe's car, it was about twenty minutes before midnight. Mikalya stopped Abe and looked at him once again.

"Abe, please hold me for a couple of minutes before we get in."

Abe put his arms around her and hugged her tightly.

She put her mouth up to his ear. "Baby, don't forget what I said, OK?" she whispered.

Abe began to worry even more, but he tried not to show it. He attempted to blow it off and chalked it up to Mikalya being overly dramatic. But nonetheless, the ominous feeling persisted.

"I won't. I promise," he said.

The night was cool and breezy, with millions of tiny little stars and a beautiful three-quarter bright moon lighting up the night.

Abe couldn't keep himself from staring at Mikalya, looking surrealistically beautiful in the streaming moonlight.

Helping Mikalya into her seat and shutting the door, Abe walked around to his side, got in, and started the car, glancing at the car's clock. It was late, and although the night had been enjoyable, all he wanted to do was get home… safely. It was about ten minutes until midnight. He pulled out of the parking lot and made a left turn onto the highway, back toward his house. Thankfully, there wasn't a lot of traffic out this late.

Mikalya kept looking over at Abe as he drove.

"Honey, are you OK?" he asked, noticing her glances. "Were you going to say something?"

"Just that I'll always love you. Please, don't ever forget that," she replied.

Abe was bewildered again. "Same here, same here. Oh, and get your seatbelt on." He had his left hand on the steering wheel and his right hand on his right leg. Mikalya didn't move. She sat, staring straight ahead.

Mikalya took his right hand and started to gently caress it while she stared straight ahead. Suddenly, a large deer ran into the road, not twenty feet in front of them. Abe saw the deer but didn't have time to react safely.

As the car sped directly into the two-hundred-pound buck, it fishtailed sideways at a high rate of speed, and the passenger side of the car slammed into a large oak tree on the side of the road.

The impact of the crash was so tremendous that Mikalya's body was thrown against her passenger door with great force before it bounced back into the seat. It all happened in a matter of seconds.

As the car came to a stop against the tree, Abe was violently shaken, and it took him a few seconds to come around. He was in shock but started to slowly assess all that had happened. He began to move around as best he could, immediately looking over at Mikalya's seat.

Her window was completely blown out, the door was smashed in, and her seat was all the way back. She was lying on it, facing him, with her eyes open.

Abe was sore but could move his arms and legs without much pain. He undid his seatbelt, leaned over, and looked closer at Mikalya. She was motionless.

"Honey, are you OK?" he asked nervously.

Mikalya was able to move her eyes and looked up at him. Her lips began to move, communicating in a hoarse whisper. "Hey, what happened? Are you OK?" she asked, with no panic, shock, or fear in her voice or her facial expression.

Abe looked at her as a lightning bolt seared through him. It was an extremely odd answer. He started to try to assess the condition she was in.

"We slammed into a tree when that deer crossed in front of us. Do you remember? Are you in any pain? Can you tell me how you feel?" he asked, realizing that her dress was blood-soaked from her waist down.

"I feel OK, I think. I think I'm OK. It's alright, just help me up," she said.

Abe put his hand on her back and started to rub it. "Can you feel this?" he asked.

"Feel what?" she replied.

"Mikalya, just stay right here for a moment. I'll be right back," he said, turning around and slowly exiting the car.

As he was doing so, a car with two men in it had already stopped. One was on their cell phone, calling 9-1-1. The other man rushed up to Abe.

"Hey, I saw what happened with that damn deer. Are you OK? We've called for help," he said.

"My fiancé is still in the car. I think she's paralyzed, and there's a lot of blood on the lower half of her body. Do you have a flashlight?" Abe asked.

The man ran back to the car and quickly returned with a flashlight in hand.

Abe grabbed it and ran back toward Mikalya. The deer he had struck was in the middle of the road, injured and kicking about wildly.

Abe stopped as one of the men ran from the car with a knife in his hand, dropped to his knees in front of the deer, and put it out of its misery. He flinched as he watched, and when the animal stopped moving, he continued his trek back to his car.

"Mikalya, honey, I'm back. Hang in there; you'll be OK," he said, flashing the light over her body to see where the blood was coming from. Her dress was soaked from her thighs on down. There was also a massive pool of blood on the floorboard. He slowly lifted her dress and gasped. Both her legs were severed from the knees down, and she was losing blood rapidly.

He determined her spine was broken, and that's why she wasn't feeling anything. He assumed there had been damage to her spine, which was why she couldn't feel him rubbing her back. He turned the flashlight off. Looking at her, he began praying as he tenderly stroked her hair. Tears welled up in his eyes, but he could not let Mikalya see them, and no way would he tell her the serious condition of her body. He pulled his shirt off and ripped it up, trying to make tourniquets out of it. He wanted to stop as much of the bleeding as he could.

"Mikalya, an ambulance is on the way, OK? Listen, I want to put something on your legs to help you."

As Abe applied the tourniquets, he noticed a large gash in her upper thigh, as well. A sense of foreboding washed over him, and he hoped that he had done enough until the paramedics arrived with more lifesaving measures. But he knew that she was dying right in front of him.

"There's no pain. I'll be fine. Really, honey. Why aren't you helping me up?" Mikalya asked.

His eyes never left hers as he held her and rocked her back and forth. It was all he could do to keep the tears from streaming down his face, but he could feel them now. He wanted to be strong for her, but the feeling of losing her overwhelmed him.

"Just rest for a bit. It's better if the paramedics help you up. I think you have some bruises, and I don't want to do anything to hurt you more," he said.

Even with her current circumstance, Mikalya could still sense that something was seriously wrong.

"Abe, am I OK? Am I?"

He hesitated in his response, and she picked up on it.

"I'm not OK, am I? Honey, please tell me what happened, please. Will the ambulance get here before I fall asleep? I'm getting so tired," she said as the two men who had stopped to help ran up to the car.

"Hopefully, an ambulance will get here soon. Hang in there, man," one of them said.

They could tell that Mikalya was not in good shape by the way Abe was acting. It was clear that he knew he was going to lose her. They were too far out in the middle of nowhere for an ambulance to get there in time.

Mikalya's eyes looked tired. She kept mustering the strength to look up at Abe, and then her eyes would go blank as if she were looking right through him.

He continued to hold her with a feeling of hopelessness. She was dying, and he couldn't save her. He leaned down and hugged her as he motioned the two men away.

"I love you, baby. You don't know how much I love you," he whispered into her ear.

"I love you more, honey. I need to tell you something before I fall asleep. I'm getting so tired. If you wait for me, I'll come back to you. I know you'll wait. Won't you? Do you remember the clothes I had on the night of our first party with everyone? Don't forget," she managed to utter.

"Don't talk like that, please. God, don't say that!" he screamed, the flood of tears racing down his cheeks.

"I don't know exactly when, but I'll be back. I'll be watching you, so you'll be good. Is the ambulance here yet?" she asked.

Abe knew that she was rambling, and he held her as tight as he could. "Soon. It will be here soon," he said, attempting to make her comfortable.

Mikalya looked up at Abraham one last time. "Do you remember our song?" she asked.

Abraham looked down at her with a numbed expression. "Yes, honey, it's 'Something About Your Touch.' I will never forget it, I promise you."

"When you hear that song again, you'll know it's me. I'll love you forever. Do you know that…?" Her words drifted off—her sentence was left unfinished.

Abe took her pulse. Nothing. As she was slipping away, they never took their eyes off each other.

"Oh, God, no! Fuck no, no, no! Oh, God! Why her? Please, don't take her! Oh, no, please! God, please!" He sat in the car, rocking her body gently back and forth.

The two strangers could hear his cries. They knew. Far off in the distance, they also heard the faint sound of a siren, but it was too late. There was nothing they could do to ease his broken heart.

# Chapter Eleven:
# The Dark Side of the Mirror

At approximately 1 a.m., Shelly rolled over and glanced at the clock. A strange sensation awakened her from a pleasurable sleep. It had been deep and now she couldn't sense if she was asleep or awake. She rolled over again and stared up at the ceiling, wide-eyed and trying to figure out exactly what it was that woke her up. She had been dreaming but couldn't remember what the dream was about. Something was bothering her.

A second, much stronger sensation went through her soul like a spear, and she felt a distinct presence in the room. This wasn't her imagination, and it was unlike anything she had ever felt before, except when Clifton died. She had experienced a few graphic dreams about Clifton over the years, which she believed was him comforting her. There was just something about those dreams that had a certain "feeling" to them, but this one deeply concerned her. This was something different and unsettling.

A bit restless, she got up and slowly walked out of the bedroom and into the hallway, feeling an intensely strong cool breeze brush against her entire body, then go right through it. It was an incredibly strong feeling of warmth and love, as if someone was reaching out to her.

Shelly stopped dead in her tracks, closed her eyes, and clutched her chest. The hair on her arms stood at attention.

Thoughts of Mikalya quickly entered her mind, like someone had flipped a switch. *Oh, my God, is Mikalya OK? Is my baby OK?* The aura of the room wasn't normal. It was different now.

"Mikalya, honey, are you OK?" Shelly called out, looking down the dark hallway.

Suddenly, she heard a distinct whisper resonating graphically in her mind. It was a young female voice. "Love You," it said. It was Mikalya. Shelly's eyes opened wide.

Her cell phone rang, jerking her from the daze she was in. She looked at the caller ID. It was Abe. She couldn't bring herself to pick it up, and it continued to ring.

"Hello, Abe?" she finally answered, her body going limp before he even replied.

There was quiet on the other end for a few seconds. Finally, Abe spoke in a deliberate, low, hushed tone. "Shelly, I have horrible news."

Shelly just stared forward, expressionless. "Is she alive?"

Again, hesitation.

"We were in a bad car crash tonight. A large deer ran out in front of us on Highway 60. I had to swerve sharply, and we slid off the road. Mikalya's side of the car hit a large tree. She was fatally injured, Shelly. I am so sorry," Abe said.

Shelly could hear his cries through the phone.

Holding the phone up to her ear in silence, she stared at the wall in front of her. She knew that it was Mikalya, letting her know everything was OK. That thought was the only thing keeping her from collapsing at that moment.

"Where did it happen again?" she asked hesitantly.

"We were leaving The Jazz Kitchen in Chesterton and heading back on Highway 60 when the damn deer ran out in front of us. There was no time to stop. When I hit it, we spun around, and Mikalya's side of the car hit a tree hard. She didn't suffer, Shelly. I stayed with her, holding her the entire time. I am so sorry.

"The ambulance is going to take her to Coleman's funeral home, closer to home. I'm headed there now," he continued.

"I'll meet you there," Shelly said calmly. She hung up the phone and called Loretta, then she got dressed and slowly drove over to the funeral home.

Abe was already there, standing outside, waiting for her.

She walked up to him, and they hugged in tears. Loretta pulled in soon after.

"They've already taken her in. They said to give them a few minutes to clean her up," he said.

"Clean her up? How damn bad was it? Clean her up from what?" Shelly asked.

Loretta stroked Shelly's hair and looked to Abe for his response.

He hesitated before replying.

"I told you when I swerved to keep from hitting the deer, the car spun around, and her side slammed into the tree. The force of the impact caved into her. In the process, her back was broken, and the metal door imploded inward… cutting both her legs off below the knees and leaving a large gash in her right upper thigh. She had lost too much blood before I could save her," he said, pausing to wipe away the tears running down his face. "The saving grace was because her back sustained injury too, I don't think she felt a thing. She just went to sleep."

Shelly sank to her knees and emitted a guttural cry. All Loretta and Abe could do was hold her.

After a few minutes, Shelly pulled herself from the floor, wiped her eyes with the back of her hand, and headed inside. Loretta and Abe followed close behind.

Mikalya was laid out on a steel slab covered from the neck down. She looked like she was simply asleep.

Abe and Loretta assisted Shelly toward the table.

****

Shelly bent over and hugged her daughter. *Baby, I remember the day you were born like it was yesterday. You're with your daddy in heaven now. I know that he'll take good care of you. Thank you, honey, for letting me know you are OK. It meant a lot. I will be praying for you every day. Please, please come back and visit me.*

****

As Shelly rose from embracing Mikalya's body, Abe walked over and began stroking Mikalya's hair, laying his head on her chest.

*I'll never forget what you told me. I know you said it for a reason. I hope that someday, I'll learn what that reason was. I love you, baby. You'll always be the only one for me. I'll wait for you, OK?*

A few short hours ago, they were in a restaurant, enjoying a drink and a dance. Little did he know, however, that was not to be the last dance with his beloved Mikalya. She would be closer than he ever thought.

With one final kiss on Mikalya's cheek, Abe slowly backed away. Her body was still a bit warm.

Loretta was the last to say goodbye. Ever so gently, she hugged Mikalya's lifeless body and traced the outline of her face.

Loretta turned to pull Shelly back from the table, but Shelly resisted. Abe walked up behind to assist, and when he touched Shelly's shoulder, she looked up at him, her face stained with tears and pain.

Abraham and Shelly were both mentally and spiritually exhausted.

****

The funeral took place a week later. She'd be buried up at Mount Olive, next to her father.

****

After the viewing and the funeral, he and Shelly were the last ones standing over Mikalya's grave; both cried out and were emotionally paralyzed. All the immediate mourning had finally been done.

"My baby's gone. She's all I had. What am I going to do without her?" Shelly asked, never looking up from the ground.

Abe looked at her, then up at the sky and back at Shelly. "I don't know, Shelly," Abe answered. "I don't know."

Realizing that he was in pain as well, Shelly put her hand on Abe's shoulder. "Please, don't be a stranger. My daughter thought the Earth revolved around you. However, do me one favor," she said.

Abe waited for her to continue.

"If another woman comes into your life, I don't want to know about it."

"Shelly, that's something you'll never have to worry about. I promise you that."

Shelly smiled. She walked over, and they hugged tightly.

"Thank you. Again, don't be a stranger."

"We'll stay close, Shelly. I'll make sure of it."

One final embrace, and they went their separate ways.

While Shelly drove away, Abe just sat in his car with the engine running. As he turned to look back in the direction of Mikalya's grave, he decided to pay her one final visit that day. *This time, we'll be alone,* he thought as he killed the engine and pulled his key from the ignition.

He decided to walk back up to Mikalya's grave. "I love you, baby," he said, kneeling on one knee and rubbing his hand back and forth in the dirt. "I'll be back soon."

When he got to his feet again, a strong breeze swept across the area. It caught him by surprise and was unsettling, but he felt it was Mikalya. He blew a kiss up to the sky and then walked away.

As he drove back home, he turned on the radio. *The Flame* by Cheap Trick wafted through the car speakers. The timing couldn't have been more appropriate.

****

For the next couple of years, all Abe could think about was Mikalya. He cried for her. He ached for her. He missed her so much it was a physical pain.

One night, while sitting at the bar, he went over and over in his head her strange conversation that last night they were together. Even as she lay dying in his arms, her last words were an extension of that conversation. He couldn't put the pieces together as to why she talked about coming back if something ever happened to her and insisted that he wait for her. *What could she have meant?*

Then he remembered her party after she'd gotten out of the hospital. During their last dance, she asked him to remember what she was wearing. He could never forget. Tight jeans, pinkish-red button-down top, black medium-heeled, open-toe shoes, a gold necklace, turquoise earrings, and a thin black belt. She wore Chanel

No. 5 perfume. That memory would haunt him for years to come. Not a day would pass that he didn't try to make it all make sense.

****

The next couple of months were uneventful. Abe kept himself busy, taking any overtime at work he could get. Because he dove into his work so much, that part of his life was going well. When he wasn't working, he was either sleeping or drinking.

His friends at the firehouse occasionally tried to set him up on blind dates. He joked to everyone that he'd gone gay and was only interested in dating Johnny Walker, Budweiser, and Jim Beam.

Some people found that funny, but others thought it was sad. Abe didn't care either way. He was still mourning the love of his life, and if they couldn't understand that, *"then screw 'em all."*

He hung out at The Fat Angel more than he should have. He justified his time there as an extension of his work duties, as so many firefighters hung out there. He would drink and hit the jukebox to play, "Something About Your Touch" over and over again. Out of respect for Abraham, Rod, the bartender, kept that one song in the jukebox after many new ones hit the airwaves.

****

One night, Abe was lying in bed after a rough shift when he reflected on a recent fire run where two children and their mother had died. Sadly, they couldn't get there in time to save any of them. Their bodies were found as Abe and Luis waded through the rubble after the fire was out.

When he looked down at the little boy, he thought it was odd that over 90 percent of his body was burned, but the tiny little red shoes on his feet had not been touched by the fire.

As he reached to turn the lamp on, he heard a noise out in the hallway, so he stopped. It sounded like someone had opened and closed the basement door. *Is someone in my house? How would they have gotten in?* he wondered, despite knowing that he always kept the house extremely secure.

He reached over and pulled his loaded pistol from the nightstand, pointing it toward the door as he swung his legs over the side of the bed.

Slowly, he crouched down and inched his way out into the hallway, hiding behind his large TV. There, he had a master switch that, when turned on, lit up the house, including the basement and the outside.

He flipped that switch, and the entire inside lit up like an amusement park. He stayed hidden behind the TV, waiting for someone to make a move. There was no sound or movement as he carefully stood up with the gun pointed forward. He looked around as he walked to the front door. It was still double-locked, as was the back door. However, the basement door stood ajar. He swore that he'd closed it before he went to bed.

*So, it was the basement door I heard opening.*

The basement was not very big, and all that was down there were the laundry machines, water heater, and a sink. More importantly, there were no windows, so no one could have broken in from the outside.

As freakish as the situation was, Abe wasn't scared for some odd reason. He slowly descended the steps, looking left to right when he reached the bottom. As he stood there, he realized that there was no one else in the house.

Standing on the last step, a feeling of peace and contentment washed over him. He lowered his gun with full certainty that any perceived threat, real or psychological, was gone. He still hadn't figured out how the basement door had come open, but he had known doors to do that before.

He was tired. He made his way back up the stairs and into his bedroom. He shut the lights off and eventually fell back asleep.

****

About a week later, he was having a beer at the bar with Lamar. It was after a shift, and Lamar needed to get out and wanted to make sure that Abraham was with him. He wanted Abe alone for a little post-Mikalya talk. Their first round had arrived.

"So, man, I know it's been hard, but have you thought about bringing a new woman into your life yet?" Lamar asked as he sat with his old friend at a bar—their first real hang-out since Mikalya's death.

Abe took a large sip of beer, staring straight ahead.

"No, not really. A few people have tried to set me up, but I just don't have the spark for it. Lamar, I can't get her out of my head, man."

"Well, listen, I wish I could say that I understand what you're going through, but I don't. But you can't go on the way you are," he said.

"Why can't I? I'm doing damn good at work. Hell, I got that promotion to lieutenant, didn't I? I've kept the four of us together, haven't I?" he replied.

"I know. I know. But I'm talking about your personal life, your head. We all care about you, and we'd follow you into the hottest fire on the planet. But honestly, we miss the old Abe. Now, listen, Sonja knows this chick that—" Lamar began.

Abe cut him off. “Lamar, I love you to death, but I’m just not ready yet. Tell Sonja I’m sorry, but maybe a little later. I know you both mean well; I do. But I don’t know if I’ll ever be.”

Lamar looked at him and then raised his glass. They talked for a couple more hours before Lamar stood to leave.

“Listen, man, it’s been real, but I gotta get going. See ya Thursday,” he said, nudging Abe’s shoulder.

Abe ordered another beer, appreciating the time to be alone with his thoughts.

The basement door issue popped into his head. He thought he’d put that to rest that night, but here it was again, front and center.

*Why in the hell am I thinking about this again?*

A frightening shock wave went through him as he remembered the feeling he had at the bottom of the stairs that night.

*It didn’t fit into the rest of the scenario, or did it? The bottom of the stairs. Oh, shit! Oh, shit! Good God! At the bottom of the stairs, at the edge of the stairs, that feeling! It was Mikalya! Oh my God, it was Mikalya!*

Abe looked up and all around him. Luckily, there weren’t too many people in the bar. His whole demeanor changed. He was no longer in mourning.

*Now it all makes sense! It was Mikalya! She was leading me downstairs to the bottom step!*

Once there, she let her presence be known as best she could, he deduced.

His eyes welled with tears. *Mikalya, honey, I know it was you.* He picked up his cell phone and called Shelly.

"Hello, Abe," she answered.

"Shelly, I need to talk to you soon. It's about Mikalya," he said, panic in his voice.

"Abe, is everything OK? Have you been drinking? Do you want to have lunch, say, Thursday? Mikalya's been on my mind a lot, too."

"Does Thursday at noon work for you? We can meet right there at Iaria's," he said.

"Yeah, I'll see you then. And don't worry, Abe… it will all be OK."

Abe hung the phone up and got a six-pack to go. He needed to get back home to sort out everything in his head.

****

Walking through the door, knowing what he suspected, the house felt different. There was something else hanging in the air now. He popped open a can of beer and looked all around and up at the ceiling.

"Mikalya, honey, was that you? Please, tell me, was it you? Please!" He waited for some sort of answer or vibe… something. There was nothing. He walked to the bottom of the stairs, where that feeling had hit him.

Again, he called out to Mikalya. "I'm here at the bottom of the stairs where you were last week. Can you come back? I miss you so much, baby!" he cried. He closed his eyes and waited for any kind of sign. But again, there was nothing.

Abe waited for several more minutes, then trudged back up the stairs. He went for the fridge… and another beer. He was drinking faster now.

"I've been good. I really have. You know? I still love you. I hope you know that. I hope you do. I mean, I can't talk to you the way I used to, but I want you to know I always think of you. OH, GOD, WHERE ARE YOU, MIKALYA, HONEY?" he shouted, dropping to his knees in tears. He cried out her name again and again. Finally, he pulled himself up on the sofa and passed out.

****

Shelly arrived at Iaria's and waited at a table for Abe. She didn't have to wait for long.

"Hey, Shelly, how are you?" Abe asked, reaching out to give her a hug.

"I'm good, Abe; how are you? It's so good to see you! What have you been up to? You look great," she said.

"Thanks. Just working. Got a promotion, so that keeps me busy. Outside of that, nothing. No women, just so you know," he said.

Shelly smiled. "So, tell me, what's going on." She could tell by his demeanor that he was shaken. She had a feeling that this meeting was going to be intense.

Abe couldn't wait to speak. "It was early last week. I had just gotten home and was in bed getting ready to turn the light off; suddenly, I heard what sounded like the basement door creaking open."

The hair on Shelly's arms stood up.

"I went through the whole house to see if someone had broken in, and I found nothing. But then, I went downstairs, and when I got to the last step, I had a really weird feeling. It was calm and so peaceful."

That she got the night Mikalya died.

"I couldn't put my finger on it at the time, but a couple of nights ago, the night I called you, it dawned on me that this feeling hit me when I was standing on the last step. I was at the edge of the stairs,

Shelly. I was standing at the edge of the damn stairs, which is the exact spot I found Mikalya in your home! That's when the feeling hit. Coincidence? No way!"

Shelly was numb. "It was her, Abe. You know it, and I know it. It was her. I haven't said this out loud because I didn't want anyone to think I was nuts, but I've heard noises in her room. She used to get these coughing fits at night, and I've heard coughing. It just started a few weeks ago. It's her! I know it is!" Shelly said, brushing her hand across her tear-stained cheek.

Abe reached across the table and took Shelly's hand. In silence, they sat, trying to make sense of the events they'd experienced.

"I don't know what to do. I've tried calling out to her, and I got nothing," he said.

"Abe, I think she'll communicate with us in her own time. At least we know she's, well, not really gone, and that's something, right? I've never believed we just go out of existence when we die. We just simply enter another realm of existence. Call it the spiritual world, or the next dimension, or whatever, but I believe that we go on. Isn't it a law of physics that says energy or matter cannot be destroyed but only inter-converted, or something like that? I believe that. She's slowly coming back to us. She is. But I'll bet you the next time it's going to be more vivid and pronounced. You wait."

They finished lunch, essentially trying to figure out Mikalya's next move. They agreed to stay in touch more and contact each other as incidents occurred.

****

Driving to work, Abe began to doubt himself. Had he only imagined it all? Was he missing her so much that he'd forced himself to believe that it could be possible? Was his mind playing tricks on him? He so much wanted to believe it was her but was in doubt. Would something similar happen again? If it were Mikalya, would her presence be stronger the next time? His questions would be definitively answered in the middle of the 32nd Street fire.

****

There hadn't been any more incidents, such as the one at the bottom of the stairs, and as time went on, Abe began to focus more on his life. And although he still missed her deeply, he was no longer moping around, mourning her passing.

With his promotion, he had been able to keep him and his friends together, blocking all possibility of transfers of any kind. Work kept his mind busy, and he appreciated that. More time had drifted by. Abraham, Lamar, Dennis, and Luis developed into strong, experienced firefighters. Abe was still in the same basic mindset regarding Mikalya as well. It had been seven years since she died. He had not forgotten about her by any means. However, he was able to focus more on his life. There were no other episodes like the one he experienced on the stairway that night. He hadn't thought about it as much, and it concerned him. He did not want to stop grieving and missing Mikalya.

One afternoon, as they were sitting around discussing Luis's wife, who was about to give birth to their first child, the station alarm went off. Abe and his crew did the usual scramble. As the alarms came, it was determined that this fire was in a large commercial building in town. Abe's firehouse was the closest, and they would most likely be the first crew on the scene.

The fire had started in the basement level, spreading from an electrical room, based on the position of the smoke detectors. As Abe's engine roared onto the scene, they all knew the routine; Luis and Abe would enter the lower level, and Captain Randy would radio the layout of the area to Abe as they entered.

As the two descended the stairwell from a back entrance to the building, they could see the intensity of the fire.

"Randy, we're at the bottom of the stairwell now. Which way are we turning?" Abe yelled into his radio as Luis stood next to him, awaiting his directions.

"OK, from where you're at, move forward about thirty feet, then turn left, and that room is the first door on the right," Randy said.

Abe and Luis moved forward per Randy's directive. The closer they moved to the area, the hotter it got.

Luis aimed the hose and shot the appropriate chemical into the flames. As he was, Abe noticed scores and scores of stacked boxes in the main walkway that they were in, and some of the boxes were on fire.

Suddenly, one of them exploded, blowing off a dramatic number of sparks and smoke. Abe quickly opened one of the boxes and found flammable packing material inside.

"Randy, we're hitting the fire in the electrical room, but it's managed to spread to the hallway where we're at. There must be a hundred large boxes of packing material here, and these fuckers are catching fire and spitting out a lot of spark and smoke," Abe yelled into the radio again.

"Two more engines are just about here. Just try to keep it contained as best you can. I'll let you know when the others have entered," Randy replied.

Before Abe could respond, there was an explosion at the bottom of the stairs where they had entered. The fire had caught onto the boxes they had passed, but what made the situation worse were the flammable chemicals inside of the boxes. The situation was now beyond the scope of what Abe and Luis could handle.

Things deteriorated quickly when both Abe and Luis's helmet radios went out. That could have been caused by the shock of the explosion. Abe was now unable to respond to Randy or get direction intel from him on how to navigate out of the building.

Abraham and Luis were now trapped in an extremely dangerous situation, and their mission was now one of survival and escape.

Captain Randy could not get a response from Abe on the radio. The explosion must have blown their signal.

"Captain, what the hell happened down there?" Dennis asked.

"Something went off, and now I don't know where the hell they're at. That explosion just changed everything. This is turning into a goddamn rescue mission," he said.

More trucks had arrived, and the ground was aflutter with firefighters setting up and getting into position, but the fire below would have to be fought back before anyone could enter.

Abe and Luis were frantically looking around for an exit. There was no way they'd be able to put out the fire now, as it was spreading faster, and the area was filling with smoke. Their only focus was on how to get out alive and in one piece.

Abe motioned to Luis to get his attention, then pointed at his mask amplifier.

"Luis, we've lost radio contact with the captain, and we can't go back the way we came. We can try to make it down that hallway," he said, pointing, "but shit, I don't know where it leads. I have no clue where another exit is," Abe said frantically.

"We have to make it through there before those next stacks of boxes go up, or we're toast," Luis replied.

Abe nodded his agreement.

Luis blasted ahead with the hose, but it was only going to go so far. After that, they'd have to try and crawl their way out without knowing where they were going.

Suddenly, the hose stopped, and it wouldn't pull any farther. They were at the end of the line as the smoke and flames increased in intensity. They could barely see in front of them.

Luis could just stand there and keep blasting, but they had to get out of that area, or they were going to die. Luis kept blasting, keeping the flames away from them as best he could. They looked at each other with expressions of relative hopelessness. Unless help arrived soon with significant equipment, their chances were slim. Their situation was in a desperate stage, and they knew that their oxygen tanks wouldn't last much longer.

Abe began praying.

Without warning, a strong force entered his mind, urging him to look to his right. About six feet in front of them appeared a human-like form, but they couldn't completely make it out through all the smoke and fire.

Abe motioned for Luis to look in the direction he was pointing.

"Who in the fuck is that? No one could survive this shit!" Luis shouted.

All Abe could do was stare and shake his head.

The figure, though vague, seemed to be female. It moved in rapid and deliberate motions. It was facing them but started to move backward. Its outstretched arms motioned them to follow.

Abe turned to Luis. "I have no clue who the fuck that is, but what do we have to lose? It's our only chance. Let's go!"

The figure motioned them to get lower on their hands and knees. It easily came down to their level, and they moved forward.

Abe and Luis followed it about fifteen feet farther down the hallway until they were directed to make a right turn, landing them in another hallway. They continued crawling for what seemed like hours. The smoke was less severe where they were now, but another explosion occurred in the area they had just been led from. When they turned around, they could see a massive amount of flame behind them. It wouldn't be long before it would spread in their direction.

After leading them another fifty feet or so, the figure stopped abruptly and motioned them forward and up the stairway. As they did so, it approached Abe and embraced him.

Before he could react, he felt an incredible warmth and love that he had forgotten. The figure manifested itself to him for just a few seconds. It was Mikalya, smiling.

In Abe's mind, he heard her say, *Guess who?* Then, he could feel her spiritually, mentally, and emotionally kiss him. It was a kiss he had never experienced physically.

Suddenly, she disappeared, along with the beautiful feeling, leaving behind a shell-shocked Abe.

Luis looked over at him. "Hey, man, it's gone. I think it led us here. Let's get out now!"

Abe snapped out of it and followed Luis upstairs.

As they neared the top, three firefighters were bursting through the door.

"Goddamn, you're alive! How in the hell did you get as far as you did and find this exit with your radios out?" one of them asked, letting Captain Randy know they were safe.

"We don't know. We're not sure," Luis replied.

Abe did not say one word.

When they got outside, they were approached by several paramedics.

"Are you guys OK? Let's get your uniforms off and get you checked out," one of them said.

Abe and Luis sat down, exhausted and confused. Captain Randy came running up.

"Oh, thank God you two crazies are OK! How in God's name did you get out of there? How did you get to an exit clear on the other damn side of the building? The explosions down there were incredible. Fire and smoke belched out of the entrance you both walked into. Then we lost radio contact. With that level of smoke and fire, you should have both been dead!" he said, looking from one man to the other.

They looked at each other, then up at him.

"We just got lucky, I guess," Abe said. Luis looked at him but didn't speak.

"Well, anyway, you're alive and not really hurt. You both owe the big guy upstairs a cold one. I gotta run. You guys get checked out," he said.

A news crew came over to talk to them about the fire, but mainly to find out how they made it out alive. Still in shock, Abe and Luis tried answering their questions without sounding crazy.

The crew could tell that they were exhausted and didn't spend much time with them. Luis then looked over at Abraham. "What in the fuck went on down there, Abraham? Who was that?" Luis asked when the interview was over. "They should have been dead. There's no way! There's just no fucking way!" He then made the sign of the cross.

"Luis, I don't know. We just got lucky," Abe replied, shrugging.

****

Abe went home and took a shower, but instead of heading to bed to recover from the day's events, he got dressed and went out to a bar he'd never been to before. He didn't want to go to any place where he was known. He figured he'd be talking to himself more than he should be and wound up at some dive bar he'd never heard of.

After he ordered a beer, he replayed the events of the day over and over in his mind. The incident today only solidified what he already knew… it had been Mikalya at the bottom of the stairs in his basement.

Today, in the burning building, it was at the bottom of a stairwell that Mikalya had manifested herself to him. When he saved

Mikalya's life, it was at the bottom of a stairway. Tears welled up in his eyes. This was how she was making her presence known to him. He had also figured out why she said, "Guess who." The first time she was over at his house, she snuck up behind him, put her hands over his eyes, and said, "Guess who?"

He left the bar, and as he drove, he began to cry. A full moon illuminated the countryside around him. He turned on the radio, and a song came on he'd never heard before. It was a song called "The Conversation" by Karunesh. It was strangely haunting, but it fit the moment. He missed Mikalya terribly. He knew, without a shadow of a doubt, that she'd be with him all the time. He would never marry. He thought back on her dying words to him. She told him she would be coming back. She had been true to her promise.

Abraham pulled over onto the side of the road at a remote picnic area rest stop. He ran off farther into the wooded area beside it. Dropping to his knees, he cried out, "Mikalya, was that you? Was that you? Please tell me. Oh, God, don't leave me! When are you coming back to me? When?"

Abraham sat there for over an hour, depressed and confused. He was out in the middle of nowhere, but he wasn't frightened at all. When he looked up at the now full moon, he noticed how beautiful it was. He longed for Mikalya to be right there with him watching it, too. She was.

****

The next night, Shelly called Abe. She'd caught the story on the evening news about the fire and the interview with him and his friend. She was disappointed that Abe had not called her and that she had to learn about his near-death experience from the television.

"Abe, I saw the news. Why didn't you call me? Are you OK?" Shelly blurted out.

Abe paused before he spoke. "I'm sorry, Shelly. I was planning on calling you tonight and explaining it all. I'm just still a little freaked out."

Shelly's eyebrows raised. "Abe, what happened? The news story said you both should have been dead. No one, including your own captain, remotely guessed how you both managed to get to the other side of a large commercial building with all the fire and smoke. You had no radio contact, they said. Well?" she said.

"Shelly, we need a drink. What are you doing right now?" he replied.

"See you in fifteen minutes at Maggie's," she said.

****

"OK, tell me everything," Shelly said, even as she was walking across the room to meet with Abe.

Abe took a huge gulp of his beer. "It was her again," he said.

"I thought we were done, Shelly, but then, out of nowhere, something appeared… right in front of us! We couldn't make out who… or even what it was, but I know for sure that it was not a real person. Absolutely no one could have survived where we were!"

"I know where you're headed with this, but keep going," Shelly said.

"Anyway, this entity led us to this stairwell and just hung there, motionless, for a couple of seconds. Shelly, I know this is going to sound crazy, but then, it… she… showed herself to me! It was Mikalya! Smiling at me! Then, I could feel her arms… embracing me. I could actually *feel* her!" Abe began to tear up as he sat, staring at Shelly, hoping she'd believe him.

"My God!" Shelly said when Abe finished relaying the odd events of the fire.

Shelly took his hand. "Abe, you're sure it was her?"

"I'm one hundred percent sure it was her! It felt just like her! The feeling I got, it was her. Shelly, she saved my fucking life. And… and… remember the story I told you about my feeling her on the bottom steps in my basement? Same thing. It was her."

Shelly kept her hand on his while he cried it out. She motioned for a couple more beers.

"Abe, listen to me," Shelly began once he was calmer. "We don't need to cry now. We both miss her terribly. I've had a few dreams now where I thought it was her, too. She comes to me for a few seconds and asks how I'm doing. She takes my hand and tells me she loves me, and she always tells me not to ever forget her… as if I could. She's visiting both of us, but what happened to you the other day is incredible. You saved her life, and she returned the favor."

"I can't get some of her final words out of my mind. She told me to wait for her and that she'd come back to me.

"I don't know if I ever told you this, but after you all left the party at The Fat Angel, she said something strange to me then while we were dancing. She told me to remember everything about that night, down to the bar tab amount.

"I thought it was odd, but of course, I still have all that in my mind. I always believed she was a little psychic. We were waiting for a movie to start one night, and out of nowhere, she looked at me and said, 'I know what you're thinking.' I said, 'OK, what?' Then, she told me, and it blew my mind."

"What was it?" Shelly said.

"I was debating whether to run to the bathroom before the movie started. And, I'll be damned, she was right."

Shelly nodded. "Abe, it sounds to me like she had some sort of bizarre premonitions when she was alive, and she's working on coming back to us, just like she promised. I know that sounds far-fetched, but is it? There are all sorts of documented stories about people who have encountered loved ones again after they had passed on. This shit's not new. It's not."

"I know. I've read a few books on it since Mikalya died. It's been years, and I've had only a couple of these encounters with her. I've heard weird noises here and there and felt these feelings where I thought it was her. But how long will it be before she fully presents herself? I mean, I don't want her coming back when I'm in a nursing home," Abe joked.

They laughed.

"She won't. I think she's smart enough to know that wouldn't quite work for us," Shelly said.

"I hope these visits don't stop," Abe said.

"If I know my daughter, they won't."

"One of the last things she said to me was, 'When you hear that song, you'll know it's me,'" Abe said.

"What song is that?" Shelly asked.

"'Something About Your Touch' by Francesca Beghe. It was like our song."

"I'll be damned; you could be right. Any hints as to the time frame of all this?" Shelly asked with a chuckle.

"Not directly, but she died twenty minutes after midnight, if that means anything."

The crease in Shelly's forehead deepened. "Twenty years?" she asked.

"I'm not entirely sure, but I've listened to that song a lot over the years. Maybe it'll happen when we least expect it. We can only hope."

"You're right, Abe. This is out of our hands, but in the event she does return, will she come back to you or me?"

"I really don't know, Shelly. But, if it's me, I'll definitely be giving you a call!" he said.

****

As the years rolled on, sometimes slowly, and at other times much too quickly for Abe, he was thankful that he and his friends were still together at Water Witch 64. The one constant in his life was that they all had no desire to leave each other.

Lamar and Sonja got married.

The guys liked her a lot. She fit into the group beautifully. When they were all out, and Sonja got a few drinks in her, she would insist that she wanted to be a firefighter like Lamar and the rest of them. But the boys would always talk her out of it.

Luis and Carla now had two kids.

Dennis finally settled down with a girl named Tamera. She seemed good to him and was exactly like him in every way. They'd been together about two years now, which was a record for him, but the long term looked promising.

Randy Bowman was still captain, which no one complained about.

The synchronicity of the firehouse was in perfect celestial order.

The one thing that hadn't changed… Abe was still completely single. He went out for beers with the guys and attended all the poker games, but never with another woman. Eventually, the guys stopped trying to set him up on blind dates.

One night, when they were all out partying, Sonja decided to give it one more try. "You know, Mr. Gallagher, someday, you're going to have to move on with your life. You're one sad waste of male tail," she said.

"Sonja, I appreciate that, but I need time. I'm not over her by a long shot. I miss—"

Sonja cut him off. "I know, but there is going to come a time when you'll have to let her go. Lamar and I don't want to see you like this for the rest of your life. You've got to be fair to yourself."

"I told you guys already, my new boyfriend, Jack Daniels, is a great guy. Really, he is."

"You're incorrigible," she said, punching him lightly on the shoulder.

"Sonja, listen. I really, really appreciate all of you looking out for me and caring about me. I love the support and friendship. I'll tell you what. Let me think about it, and we'll pick up this conversation another time. Sound good?"

Sonja perked up and smiled. "I'll hold you to that, Abe."

"Trust me, I know," he replied.

While they were finishing up their drinks, Abe thought about his conversation with Sonja. He knew that he'd been fighting against meeting anyone new since Mikalya died. It had been quite some time since Mikalya's last contact with him. *Is Sonja right? Is it time for me to open myself up to love again? God, help me. What should I do?*

A few nights later, that question would be answered, but not by God.

****

It had been a particularly rough run on a highway with an accident involving a car fire. Abe and Dennis had to cut two teenage girls from a car that had exploded. There were no survivors. *No one should have to go through that*, Abe thought, reflecting back to the incident many years ago when he and his family happened upon a truck fire on the interstate.

He went home that night, troubled by what he'd seen in that car. He had worked on those types of accidents before, but for some reason, this one bothered him greatly. Exhausted, he peeled off his clothes and took a hot shower. He just wanted to pass out and forget the day.

As he lay in bed staring up at the ceiling, a strange drowsiness overcame him. It was more of a hypnotic, soothing opioid type of effect. Although he wondered why it had hit him so suddenly, he didn't try to fight it but gratefully succumbed without hesitation.

****

He awoke in unfamiliar but beautiful surroundings. In this strange place, he stood at the edge of a thick forest. It felt a little familiar, but it wasn't. Abe wasn't sure how he'd gotten there, yet he was completely comfortable and wandered in.

Moving through the thickly wooded world, he noticed how incredibly detailed it was. The environment was having such an intense effect on his senses that he was having trouble taking it all in, but he didn't want to stop.

He knelt and looked at the fallen leaves and blades of grass. He saw the minute detail in them as he rubbed his hand across. Standing, he looked up toward the tops of the trees and into the sky. For the very first time in his life, he saw the absolute beauty of the wind blowing through the leaves of the treetops. He saw the rays of sunlight streaming down in all the colors of the spectrum and gently bounced off whatever they hit. He felt the leaves, branches, and water giggle with delight as this incredibly powerful light touched them.

Abe put his hand out to try to catch some, but it only splashed off of his hand, shooting out in stunning multi-directional geometric patterns. He was in awe at the power of the sun. In the distance, he saw a flock of birds and could actually hear them.

He was urged to wander farther into the forest, and as he did, he came to an open field. This field was carpeted with the most gorgeous flowers of blue, red, yellow, orange, and lavender that took on incredible random patterns. He stood there and stared across the distance in total awe, then waded out into it.

He ran his hands through the flowers. Their softness and fragrance overwhelmed his senses. He closed his eyes as he took it in. Then he started to feel another presence. The presence grew stronger, and he looked around to try to locate it.

As he gazed across to the other side of the field, he noticed a figure wandering from the woods. He couldn't tell at first what it was, but then it crystallized quickly. Abe stood, unable to move as the figure walked toward him. It was a woman dressed in a traditional Irish peasant dress of turquoise. It was Mikalya.

She stopped to wave and smile and then continued walking.

As she got closer, he could feel a beautiful and radiant warmth emanating from her. It was so intense it brought tears to his eyes. He saw the purity of her crystal blue eyes, and the beautiful sunlight bounced off her skin and soft, long hair.

Mikalya slowed her walk as she got closer. When she was right up to him, she stood there, flashing her eyes. "Guess who?" she said with a sly smile.

Abe stared at her in a state of confusion.

"Oh, my God. Mikalya, is that you?" he asked.

She reached her hands up and stroked his face and hair. "Yes, baby, it is. I hope I didn't scare you, but it's the only way we can be together right now. You're not ready yet. Just spend some time with me here, and if you want, we can do it again. It is pretty, isn't it? Do you like it? Do you like my earrings? I wore them just for you," she said.

Abe put his arm around her waist and drew her closer. He put his other hand on her face. He felt her skin and her hair, and smelled her scent. He gazed lovingly into her face. Those were her eyes and certainly her smile.

When he opened his mouth to speak, Mikalya put her finger on his lips. "Shush. This is my thing. We don't have much time, so you have to do what I want, and I want to make love to you."

Mikalya pulled Abe's face and lips closer to hers and kissed him sensually. Then she took a few steps back and undid the back of her dress while, at the same time, waving her long hair in the wind. She turned around with her back to him and let her dress slowly fall to the ground.

As it lay there, Abe noticed the perfect curvature of Mikalya's body. He briefly thought back to the day he saved her life. He had fallen in love with her, even seeing her at her worst. In front of him now was Mikalya at her celestial goddess best.

Standing, looking out into the field, the divine sunlight illuminated her hair and body. As she ran her hands through her hair, Abe could see that her nail polish matched her dress. She was silently waiting for Abraham to walk up and touch her.

He pulled his clothes off and moved closer, standing right behind her, fully naked as well.

When his hands touched her skin, she spun around. "Do you want to touch me? It's OK," she said.

Abe slid his arms around her waist as Mikalya put her arms around his neck. He could feel her supple yet firm skin. Smiling, he rubbed his hands over the small of her back, up her rib cage, then back down to her perfectly curved backside, gently squeezing her buttocks with both hands. With each up-and-down stroke, he moved his finger farther and farther between her legs.

As he did, Mikalya smiled and closed her eyes.

Abe felt the goosebumps forming all over her skin.

Mikalya put her mouth up to his ear. "God, I miss that, sweetie. I can't describe how good that feels to me. Keep going, and do whatever you want," she whispered.

Abe closed his eyes, melting at the sweet sound of her voice.

Mikalya moved her hand down and softly squeezed him between his legs. Abe continued to press his fingers into Mikalya's body until he felt her fully inside. He slowly stroked all around until she moaned.

Laying her body on the soft bed of flowers, he looked into her eyes. "You're stunning. I didn't forget how beautiful you are," he said.

"You didn't know much about my face or my body when you picked me up from the bottom of the stairs. I looked horrible, but you still fell in love with me. I can *feel* that you've been a good boy."

He nodded while massaging her breasts, kissing each nipple back and forth. With each stroke of his hand between her thighs, her moans grew more intense.

Mikalya couldn't stand it any longer. She got up and prudently sat atop his face, then lay forward, gently guiding him into her mouth. She could feel the pleasurable flick of Abe's tongue. He felt so good that she couldn't concentrate on what she was doing. She wanted to feel him inside of her… now.

Mikalya lifted herself from Abe's face and lay on her back next to him, spreading her legs apart. He rolled over to accept her invitation and gently penetrated her.

They both eventually moaned aloud in pleasure and orgasmic ecstasy. In Abe's mind, their lovemaking went on for what seemed like a millennium.

Spent, they lay embracing each other, their eyes locked.

"That was the most beautiful experience of my life," Abe said, breaking their silence.

Mikalya's eyes remained staid on his mouth as he spoke.

"When will I see you again, baby? I pray it'll be soon. Please say it'll be soon. Please!"

Still gazing up into his face, Mikalya stroked his face and hair. Then she spoke in a soft and quiet tone. "It's not time yet. We must wait a little longer. Please, be patient with me. I love you more than you'll ever know. I'll never let you go. I want you to shush now and go back to sleep. Go back to sleep. Go back to sleep," she soothed.

Abe embraced Mikalya tightly but felt in his mind her time was growing short. He did not want to let her go.

"I miss you, Mikalya. I miss you so much! God, why did you leave? I miss you. Oh, God, I miss you!"

In the blink of an eye, it all changed. Abe woke up, clutching a pillow and crying out, "I miss you, Mikalya. I miss you so much. God, why did you leave?" He blinked and wiped his eyes, realizing he had awakened from a dream… a beautiful dream he'd been mercilessly cast out of. The odd aura he felt in the room left him confused and trying to piece it all together. He lay in bed, staring at the ceiling, completely unable to comprehend what he had just experienced.

# Chapter Twelve: Something About Your Touch

Abe pondered telling Shelly about his vivid dream. He wasn't sure how she'd handle the intimate parts, but he decided to go for it anyway, toning down the sensuality. They hadn't spoken in a while, so he figured it was time to catch up.

"Hey, Abe! Good to hear from you. So how have you been? Anything from Mikalya? Please tell me there is," Shelly said.

"This time, it was more vivid and longer. I was walking into a forest, and there was a clearing with a beautiful, colorful field of flowers…" he began and the blush crept up his cheeks. "It was so real, Shelly!"

A cheeky grin crept up Shelly's face. "Mr. Gallagher, did you have one of 'those' dreams?" she asked.

Taken aback by her forwardness, Abe replied, "Well, I'll be honest. Yes, we did. It was her idea. She said she didn't have a lot of time, but she promised she'd be back," he said.

"Abe, I had a dream, too. It happened just a month or so ago. But I just wasn't sure if it was real or my imagination. It didn't last very long.

"In my dream, she was in high school. During that time, I had been dating a guy named Don. Then, one day, out of the blue, he dumped me. I was hurt. One night, we got into a huge fight so bad I told him to take me home early, and I never wanted to see him again.

"I was in a chair in the living room, crying, when suddenly Mikalya came down the stairs, walked over to where I was sitting, and knelt in front of me. I remember being startled by her abrupt appearance.

"My emotional state quickly shifted from being hurt by this man to the joy of seeing her. I got such an incredible feeling of warmth and comfort from her. After kneeling, she wrapped her arms around my waist and laid her head on my lap. I started to stroke her cheeks and pulled her hair back behind her ears. It was odd, but this was a big deal in the dream because it stood out so much to me," Shelly said.

"What stood out?" Abe asked.

"When I pulled her hair back, I noticed she had the most beautiful earrings on, and I noticed they looked familiar."

Abe's antennae went up. "Shelly, can you remember what color they were?" he asked.

"That's easy. They were a rich, deep turquoise," she said.

Abe's breathing quickened.

"My God. Shelly, it was her! No doubt about it! It was her! In my dream, she had on these beautiful turquoise earrings! You may not know this, but when she was in the hospital, I bought her a pair of turquoise earrings. I got them at an Indian craft fair. They were handmade with these beautiful sterling silver posts.

"She went crazy over them and said she was going to wear them on our first date out of the hospital, and she did! She knew you'd be telling me about the dream!"

"I remember them! Abe, it was my Mikalya!" Shelly exclaimed.

"She's come to both of us around the same time. Shelly, she did say that she was coming back? This last time, she did say she's coming back," Abe said.

"Oh, I hope we have more dreams about her," Shelly said.

"No, Shelly, I mean *coming back* as in physically coming back."

Shelly looked at Abe with furrowed eyebrows. "She said that?" she asked.

"She said it to me the night she died and told me again in the dream I had. I think she's going to try to reincarnate herself if you believe in that sort of thing. But I think she's going to do it," he said.

Dazed, Shelly stared off into the distance.

"She told me I would know when but didn't give me any information past that. I keep remembering what she said to me at the party… that she wanted me to remember everything about that night. That all would have something to do with her return," Abe said.

"Tell me exactly what she said again, Abe," Shelly said, scrambling to find pen and paper. She pulled a paper and pen out of her purse to write it all down.

"On the dance floor that night of the party, these were her exact words. *'I want you to remember this exact date and time. I looked at the clock. It was 12:33 a.m. and a half-hour before closing time. She said I want you to remember exactly what I'm wearing right now. I am wearing jeans, a pinkish-red button-down top with black medium-heeled, open-toe shoes, a gold necklace, turquoise earrings, and a thin black belt. I'm wearing Chanel No. 5. perfume too. Do you remember what the bar tab was?' I said it was $617.25."*

"And that was everything," Abe finished as he relayed Mikalya's every word to Shelly. "I thought she was drunk when she said all that, but it's like… she knew that something would go down and that she didn't have much time left with me."

"She never talked that way to me. But, you know, Abe, I always had a premonition about her, like something was going to happen. Did she ever give you any idea of when she might attempt to come back?"

"No, she didn't except when I heard that song."

"That song you spoke of last time?" Shelly asked.

"Yes. 'There's Something About Your Touch' by Francesca Beghe. It's a beautiful song. We danced to it the night of that party. We both loved it." he said.

"Well, have you heard it?" Shelly asked.

"I played it a couple of times right after she died, but I just couldn't listen to it anymore. It's still on the jukebox at The Fat Angel. Even though it's almost twenty years old, they keep it on there because of me," Abe said.

"*If* she does manage to reincarnate herself, as you think she might, how in the hell will we know?"

That was an interesting question, and Abe had to think long and hard about it, but he came up with a logical answer.

"We'll know when the dreams stop. Because if she becomes physical again, she cannot come back that way. We'll know."

"You're right, Abe. How could we not know?"

Little could they deduce at the time that the dreams would, indeed, stop.

****

He decided one night to head over to The Fat Angel for a few drinks, which had become a frequent tradition before days off over the years. He sat down at the bar and started sipping a beer.

No sooner did he finish it than he heard *that* song, 'There's Something About Your Touch,' wafted through the air from the jukebox as Abe sat at the bar.

A sharp chill went through him as he turned abruptly in the direction of the music. He noticed a woman walking away from the jukebox and sitting at a table with a group of women. Abe stared at her from across the bar. *Could it be? No way!*

The woman did not look in his direction.

Abe quickly got up and walked over to her table.

"Uh, excuse me, miss, would you like to dance?" he asked.

The woman looked up, startled. However, Abe's good looks enticed her to accept.

He led her to the dance floor and lightly held her as he looked into her eyes for any kind of sign.

The woman looked back at him with a puzzled expression.

"Miss, can I ask you a question? Why did you play that particular song?" he asked.

"You know it? Not many people do. Well, it reminds me of when my husband and I first went out on a date. Sorry, but I'm married. Just out with the girls, kicking back with a few drinks. Does that song mean something to you?"

"Yeah, a bit. I mean, it's our favorite song... for me and my fiancé, that is. She died years ago, and I have never heard it played in public until tonight. I saw you walking away from the jukebox when it started playing, and I was just curious."

"I'm sorry to hear that. We're out for a concert and stopped here for a few drinks. You can join us if you want," she offered, waving her hand out into the air in invitation.

"No, but thanks, anyway. I need to go now," he said, releasing her and quickly walking away, leaving the stunned stranger on the dance floor.

He paid for the one beer and left the bar in a hurry, embarrassed at how he'd asked the woman to dance and then ran out, leaving her alone on the floor. The entire situation made him uneasy. It was the first time he'd heard that song in quite a while.

He stopped and picked up some beer and decided to just drive, with no particular destination in mind. Without any thought, he pulled into the parking lot at Saint Francis Hospital, where Mikalya had recovered after the fire. Stepping out of the car, he looked up at the window to the room she was in, remembering the room number as 206. Then he turned his gaze to an area across the parking lot.

*It's still there after all these years!* Off in the distance was the gazebo he'd sat under many years ago.

Abe walked over, took a seat, and cracked open a beer. He thought back to the night he was there while Mikalya was sleeping. He remembered the young girl who wandered up, distraught at having lost her father.

Abe remembered exactly what the weather was like that night. It was eerily the same and with the same full moon that shined down on the two of them so many years ago. Under the full moon, he drank until he had no more beer to drink, then laid his head back, taking in the sky. He couldn't get the woman at the bar out of his head and the fact that she had played their song. His and Mikalya's song.

Abe's eyelids began drooping from exhaustion and too much beer. When he felt his head rolling back, he snapped into an upright position as quickly as he could and looked around. *I cannot fall asleep here! If a security guard came along, it wouldn't be good.*

Walking back to his car, he pulled out the bottle of iced coffee that he kept in the glove compartment. He opened it, headed back to the gazebo, and took a swig. The soft breeze was calming, just as it had been when he and Mikalya had made love in the field in his dream.

Abe could hear the crunch of leaves from footsteps out in the field. Turning his head in the direction of the noise, he saw a woman walking toward the gazebo, just as it happened years ago when

Mikalya was in the hospital. *This is one hell of a coincidence,* he thought.

The woman strolled into the gazebo as if she knew that someone else was already there or knew who was there. She walked over to the same side that Abe was on, then leaned against the railing, looking out toward the hospital lawn. She was only a few feet from Abe.

There were a couple of minutes of silence, and then the woman spoke as she looked over at Abe.

"So, what brings you out here tonight? This is a strange place to be on a Saturday night at this hour. Are you visiting someone here at the hospital?" she asked.

Abe looked back over at her. He got an odd feeling from her but wasn't the least bit uneasy.

"No, not now, but I did visit someone here years ago, and somehow, I ended up here tonight while I was out taking a drive." The woman looked up at the moonlight.

"Interesting," she replied.

"Yeah, it's a pretty interesting story. I'm a fireman, and I pulled that young woman from a house fire. She had some injuries, and they brought her here. So, I came to visit her. That's how I found this gazebo."

"Did you know her? I ask because I'm sure firemen don't pay hospital visits to everyone they save. Do they?" she asked.

"Well, a few do, but this person was my first. It's a long story," Abe replied.

The woman smiled. "I have some time if you want to tell me about it. You never answered my question… did you know her?"

"No, not when I went into a burning house to rescue her, but I sure as hell did by the time I sat her on the ground outside."

"What do you mean?" she asked.

"Something hit me the moment I knelt down next to her at the edge of the stairs where I found her. The house was starting to come down, and I didn't have much time. By the time I picked her up and carried her out, it was just a few minutes. I have no damn clue how this happened or why. But, in that tiny amount of time, I somehow fell in love with her. When the ambulance carried her off, I watched it until it disappeared. Then, I found out what room she was in, and I started to visit her here. Luckily, she fell in love with me, too," Abe ended, recounting the story of his and Mikalya's meeting and their subsequent whirlwind love affair.

"Well, what woman wouldn't under those circumstances?" she asked.

"Well, I was lucky for a while, but life wasn't meant to be that good to me for long," he said.

"Why do you say that? Is there more? I'm a good listener," she said.

Sharing the details of his life with a stranger had not been on Abe's list of things to do when he decided to go for that drive, but for some strange reason, he felt compelled to continue. He now got the feeling that this woman already knew the answers to the questions she was asking.

"We had a great first year together. I asked her to marry me on a trip to Ireland, and we started to plan it right away. Then, shortly after we got back, she was killed in a car accident. I'd only known her barely a year," he said.

Abe really didn't want to continue the conversation, but then the woman said something that got his undivided attention. She looked at him and then glanced off in the distance with a slight smile on her face.

"How do you know she's gone?" the woman asked.

All of Abe's fatigue and drunkenness disappeared. The woman's words had gotten his attention. Now he felt uneasy. *Is this some weirdo messing with my head now? This is getting a little bizarre,* he thought.

Intrigued though by her response, he replied, "I don't, not really. Why did you ask that?"

The woman shrugged. "Well, are you still dreaming about her?"

"No, not now. I did for a while, though."

"I mean, the way I see it, if someone has passed away and plans on coming back, either through spiritual feelings or dreams, well, they are really on the other side. On the other hand, if that same deceased person has stopped communicating from the other side, well, maybe they're not on the other side anymore. Does that make sense?" she asked.

"Yeah, it does. I pray that's the case here," he said.

"Any other women in your life since then?"

"No, there haven't been, believe it or not. How weird is that?"

"It's not weird at all. It's possible if you really loved her."

Abe was getting a very ominous feeling of *déjà vu* coming over him. "Who the hell are you?" he asked.

The woman turned sharply and looked at him, then looked back out over the grassy lawn. "I have to go now. Maybe I'll see you at The Fat Angel sometime soon. Goodbye, Abraham," she said, disappearing into the moonlight.

Paralyzed to the point of not being able to speak, Abe ran out of the gazebo after the woman but was unable to find her anywhere. He stood there, recalling their interaction.

*How in the hell did she know my name, and how did she know I hung out at The Fat Angel? Has she been stalking me? It's the only damn way she could have known that information. I don't ever remember seeing someone like that there! How did she know I would be at this gazebo tonight? I didn't even know I'd be here!*

*Was it... No, there's no way. No way!* But again, he couldn't shake the feeling of *déjà vu.* She said that he might see her in The Fat Angel soon.

A chilling thought ran through his mind. *She asked if I still had dreams about her! If I still had dreams about Mikalya? How would she have known that? How would she have known that I had any dreams about her to begin with? How?*

****

The morning alarm cruelly went off for the millionth time since Mikalya had been taken from him. Not yet awake, Abe subconsciously reached over and pushed the snooze button.

It had now been twenty-plus years to the day since her death. Abe would try to block that out of his mind today. In the mornings past, as he lay in bed struggling to find any meaning to the day's tedious and repetitive activities, this morning felt different. He blankly stared at the ceiling, hoping that this day would not depress him.

Work proved to be uneventful, and when it was over, he headed over for a beer.

He pulled into The Fat Angel around 8 p.m. It was pouring with rain, but luckily, there was an empty parking space not far from the door. He got out of the car, slammed the door, and ran to the entrance.

As luck would have it, on a Friday night, there were still a couple of seats left at the bar despite the crowd that was forming.

*I'm just here for a few*, he thought, nodding at Rod, the bartender. Rod returned the nod, acknowledging he'd be right over. Abe turned his attention to the rain outside. *This weather is the same as it was the first time I brought Mikalya here.*

A painful flashback involuntarily intruded into his consciousness.

*"Hey, wild woman, hurry up, or we're going to get soaked!" Abe said.*

*"I can't run as fast as you, Abe. I don't think my damn leg will ever be the same. Here, take my hand and pull me along," Mikalya said.*

*Abe turned and grabbed Mikalya's outstretched hand. He gently led her on as they ran toward the front door.*

*They stood there, laughing.*

*Then Mikalya suddenly got a stern look on her face. "Listen, Mister, I just got out of the hospital a week ago and can't run as fast as you yet," she said.*

*Abe could tell that she was trying so hard to hold back her ever-so-sexy grin. "I know. I was there that afternoon, if you'll remember. I literally picked you up," Abe shot back. Then he stuck his finger in her ear.*

*This tickled her, and they started to laugh.*

*After a few seconds of laughter, they looked into each other's eyes, and Mikalya put her arm around Abe's neck, sensuously and slowly pulling his lips toward hers. It was the way she looked at him right at that precise moment that made him—*

Abraham was then inadvertently snapped out of his daydream by Rod. "Abe, my man, haven't seen you here in a while, it's been at least twenty-four hours," Rod joked.

Abe, still entranced by the rain, turned toward the window.

When Rod got no response, he gave him a few seconds to answer, knowing where his head was. Then he quietly laid a cold draft in front of him.

Abe had known Rod for many years, as The Fat Angel was a favorite hangout. Although he and the other guys from the station frequented the bar, it was his personal sanctuary when he needed to be alone after a tough shift. Wanting to include Mikalya in every part of his life, it had been a must that he bring her there.

Rod still remembered the first night Abe and Mikalya came barging through the front door together, half-drenched but laughing hysterically. He remembered the way they stood there, shaking their clothes off before Abe went into the restroom. Mikalya looked over at Rod and shook her head with a, "Where in the hell did he go?"

Abe came out with paper towels and started to gently wipe the rainwater off Mikalya's face, hands, and arms. In the process, however, he slowly wiped all her makeup off.

Mikalya could sense it coming off, and she put up a token resistance, but honestly, she didn't seem to care. She was laughing the entire time.

"Hey, what are you doing? Wait a minute. Oh, no. Abraham, dammit, wait…" Mikalya said. Rod knew that they were both madly in love with each other. He wouldn't say anything to Abe of the thought in his head now. Abe finally spoke.

"Rod, this is the first rain we've had in… I don't know how long. Why in the hell can't it rain when I'm out running?" Abe said, coming out of his daydream.

"Yeah, I know, but no rain is good for me because I don't have to mow the damn grass every time I turn around. That gets old," Rod said.

"I suppose. The crowd probably won't get any bigger than this because of the rain."

"You may be right. Although it's busy, the crowd's usually bigger by this time on a Friday. People don't like rainwater with their drinks. When they come here, they want to look cool. But there's no cool when you're all wet and soggy, right?" Rod chuckled.

"I used to feel that way, but I don't give a shit anymore, you know?" Abe said.

"Well, Abe, you still look good, even when your hair's drenched."

"Oh, Rod, you're not going gay on me, are you? I can't help you there, man," Abe said.

"Well, if I hadn't met Linda, who knows? I didn't have much luck with women until I met her," Rod said.

Abe thought about what Rod said about Linda. There had been times when his friends would mention their significant others, and he'd fall into a depression. But for some strange reason, it didn't affect him tonight. A year ago, it would have, but not tonight.

Sipping his beer, Abe's thoughts went to the strange woman he'd met under the hospital gazebo. He deduced that the only way she could have known anything about him was to snoop around here… the place he spent most of his time outside of work.

"Rod, I have a weird question. Over the past, say, couple of years, has there been a woman in here asking about me?"

Rod made a funny face. "Not that I'm aware of. I mean, this isn't a normal bar. You know for yourself that it's mostly firemen, their wives, girlfriends, family, and friends who come in here. It's not really a pickup type of place," Rod said.

"I know that, but I ran into this broad recently outside of the hospital. I was out for a drive to clear my head, ended up there under the gazebo, and she walked up. You know, they have that big gazebo in the back of it. I'd had a few beers and just decided to sit out there one night. Then, a bizarre woman walked into it and started talking to me like she knew me. Well, she did! We hadn't even introduced ourselves, but as she was leaving, she said she'd see me at The Fat Angel and said my name."

Rod was taken aback.

"That's weird. Have you ever seen her before? What did she look like?" Rod asked.

"I didn't get a good look at her because it was dark, but she had long hair that fell past her shoulders and this intense look in her eyes. That's all I remember. I'd never seen her before, but I got one hell of a vibe from her."

Rod thought for a minute. "How tall was she?" he asked.

"I don't know… maybe 5′4″ or 5′5″, right in there. She was hunched over the railing most of the time we were talking," Abe said.

The more Abe spoke, the more he could see the wheels spinning in Rod's head. Abe could tell that something clicked with him. "Rod, do you remember something?" Abe asked.

Rob's expression was of intense confusion. "Well, there is this woman who started coming in a couple of years ago. I hadn't seen her in a few months, but she'd come in, sit down at the bar, order a couple of drinks, then leave. She didn't really talk to anyone. She had the hair length and height you described, but that's all I remember. She did have gorgeous eyes, though."

"What did she drink?" Abe asked.

"Hell, I can't remember. The last time I saw her was a couple of months ago," he said.

"Can you remember if I was in here when she was?" Abe asked.

"Abe, I don't know, but when or if she ever comes in again, I'll call you."

"Rod, I'd appreciate that. Hell, we don't even know if that's the same person or not."

Abe started to think again about how the whole day was feeling strange to him as soon as he got up. As it wore on, especially since he came into The Fat Angel, the strangeness was morphing into an unfamiliar euphoria of sorts. It wasn't the beer, as he'd only had a couple at this point. He did notice it was starting to get dark out and still lightly raining, but it had turned into more of a mist.

After his conversation with Rod, Abe sat at the bar for several hours… thinking. Although he was pacing himself, he was starting to get tipsy. That was his intention, as tonight was another anniversary of Mikalya's death. He had not been back to The Jazz Kitchen. He needed to drink it all out of his mind. He always had a high capacity for alcohol and generally held it well, but tonight, he didn't care if he did or not. He ran into a couple of firefighters from across town he knew and shot the shit with them for a while.

They eventually went home. Outside of that, no one else he knew was in there.

He noticed that the jukebox had not played in a while for some strange reason. People were always feeding it change and dancing next to it. He thought now would be a good time to play "Something About Your Touch" but decided against it.

Around 12:10 a.m., a car pulled up to The Fat Angel and parked up front. Whoever was inside wanted to ensure that the people inside the club couldn't see them coming. Immediately, the car's headlights went off, but the person inside just sat there.

Finally, a young woman emerged, and through the mist, she walked toward the front door, unfazed by the wet weather.

Once inside, she went into the ladies' room and checked herself. Her clothes and makeup were now nicely intact. She looked one last time in the mirror, took a deep breath, then walked out of the ladies' room and into the bar.

With only a few people left inside, it was easy to spot the man at the far end of the bar. She knew exactly who he was and sat down at the opposite end, looking straight ahead.

Abe noticed her out of the corner of his eye, but he had no desire to strike up any more conversations with strangers. However, he thought, *That's odd, here some strange broad wanders in at thirty minutes 'till closing? Who the hell does that?*

As Rod walked toward her, he noticed Abe's curious expression.

"Hi, ma'am; just to let you know, we're ready to do the last call. What will it be?" Rod asked.

The woman looked around, then looked back at Rod. "Give me a Black Russian with Chopin vodka," she said. Rod looked a bit surprised as that was not a normal request for that drink.

Immediately, though, Rod recognized the woman. She was the one Abe had described earlier. He fixed her drink and sat it down in front of her. Still staring straight ahead, she took a sip.

Abraham was unable to hear that exchange.

The woman continued to stare straight ahead while she sipped her drink.

As Abe swilled his last beer, he started to notice her more but didn't look directly at her toward the opposite end of the bar. He was getting an odd feeling about her; he couldn't quite put his finger on it. He thought for a minute that it might be one of Mikalya's friends. *But, shit, wait a minute, why was he thinking of Mikalya at this moment?*

Rod strolled over to Abe's side of the bar and leaned across it. "Abe, that strange broad I said has come in here before? She just sat down at the other end of the bar. That's her!" he said, throwing his head back over his shoulder.

Abe looked and saw the woman sipping her drink. "What's she drinking?"

"A Black Russian with Chopin vodka. A bit unusual, but that's what jogged my memory. That's what she ordered the last time she was here. I'll back off, but I'm here if you need me," Rod said.

Abe started to feel her with an emotional intensity that he had long suppressed. He discreetly looked down at the end of the bar where she sat. He had to see what she was like. His plans to leave in the next few minutes took a dramatic turn as he felt drawn to her.

As he looked, the woman mirrored his moves and turned toward him.

They locked stares with each other at the same moment. Her strong gaze sent a spiritual warmth through him that made him gasp. Now, he couldn't take his eyes off her. As they continued to stare, the woman took her drink and rose from her seat.

She walked down to where he was sitting and sat down next to him. A lightning bolt shot through him as he looked into her crystal blue eyes. He recognized those eyes. Her sensuous stare sent a shock wave through him. Yes, he knew this woman. She had several physical features of a woman he was together with and loved long ago. She gently and sensually eyed him up and down, then started to speak.

"Hey, have you ever had this drink before?" she asked. Abe couldn't speak.

She knew he wouldn't be able to, so she continued. "It's called a Black Russian. A mix of vodka and Kahlua. I really like it."

Abe was frightened to the point of shaking, but he somehow found the nerve to speak. Cautiously, he opened his mouth.

"Are you the girl from the gazebo?"

The woman swished her drink around a bit and nodded. "What kind of vodka did you put in that drink?" he asked. The woman smiled and stirred the drink with her finger.

"Well, it's called Chopin. It's a smooth Polish potato vodka. It really makes the drink. Here… want a sip?"

She held the glass up to his mouth. Then she took another sip. Abe went numb as he continued staring at her. She smiled back at him.

The woman was clearly directing the conversation toward a purpose, and Abe knew it. He glanced up at the clock above the bar. It read 12:33 a.m. He started to believe what he agonizingly suspected.

"What are you looking at? The clock? Yeah, it's 12:33, isn't it? Do you like my earrings? Aren't they cool?" She held the earrings out in the palm of her hand to show him. They were turquoise. The woman was dressed in jeans and a pinkish-red button-down top, with black medium-heeled, open-toe shoes. She had on a thin black belt and a beautiful gold necklace. He smelled what he knew was Chanel No. 5 perfume.

Abe looked her up and down as tears welled up in his eyes. *My God, those are her eyes looking back at me.* The details of a beautiful evening years ago came rushing back to him. *I want you to remember this exact date and time. I want you to remember exactly what I'm wearing right now. I have on jeans and a pinkish-red button-down top with black medium-heeled, open-toe shoes, a gold necklace, turquoise earrings, and a thin black belt.*

*Oh my God, this is it!*

Abe recalled Mikalya's words from that night. He now had two questions for the stranger.

"What was the bar tab that night?" he asked.

"Now, that's an odd question. Hmm… let's see. You're talking about *that* night, right? OK, I believe it was $617.25. We thought it was just too much for my mom and Aunt Loretta to pay, so the rest of the gang pitched in and paid it. Or am I thinking of another night? Next question," she said.

Abe could barely get the next question out. "What was our favorite song?"

She looked up like she was really thinking. "If I can find it on the jukebox, would you dance with me?" she asked.

"Yes, of course I will."

She got up and walked over to the jukebox. She fed the change and hit the buttons. As she walked back, their song began to play, "There's Something About Your Touch" by Francesca Beghe. She walked right up to Abe and stroked his hair as he brushed the back of his hand across her cheek. She took his hand and led him to the dance floor.

Holding each other tightly, they stared into each other's eyes as they swayed to the music. They held each other tightly. It was an embrace that was very assuring and comforting to Abraham.

Her gestures were completely familiar to Abe. It was her smile and the way she talked that were recognizable, and it made him emotionally unstable as he realized what was happening. He remembered Mikalya's dying words. *"If you wait for me, I'll come back to you. I know you'll wait. Won't you? Do you remember the clothes I had on the night of our first party with everyone? Don't forget."*

But saying such a thing and actually happening were two completely different things. How much credence can you place on the words of a disoriented, dying woman? But this woman was different.

"Can I ask you one more question?" he asked.

"Sure."

"What is your name, and what is mine?" he asked.

She flashed the most beautiful smile he'd ever seen, and then, she spoke. "Abe, honey, it's me, Mikalya. You pulled me out of a burning house when I was knocked out at the edge of the stairs. We took a beautiful trip to Ireland, where you asked me to marry you. I've been watching you every moment since I left you.

"Then, I decided to return to you as I promised. I'm still twenties, and you're almost in your fifties," she said.

Tears streamed down Abe's face. He looked at her and then broke out sobbing as he held her close. Only Crystal Mikalya Arabella could have known the answers to those questions.

The song ended, and they returned to the bar. Mikalya led Abraham back to his seat at the bar. She sat down next to him. True to her word, she had come back to him.

"Abraham, do you recall all the things I told you about remembering what I was wearing the night of our first party? And do you remember what I said to you the night I died by your side in the car? I know you do. I don't know much of anything. But I've always had a sixth sense about everything, especially when it came to you.

"Abe, I don't know how, and I don't know why, but I had a feeling my first life with you would be short, and that's why I asked you to remember all those crazy things. When I knew I was going to die that night, a strange calm came over me.

"When I was on the other side, I was given the choice to come back here or stay there. I loved spending time with my father, but I knew I had to come back to you. We're all interconnected here in this dimension, and even more so where I came from. I was able to choose my destiny more than at any other point in my existence, and I chose you.

"Even on the other side, I discovered we have known each other beyond this life. We go back over a thousand years together. You'll find out someday."

Abraham sat, blown away by all he'd just heard. He gazed at her and then finally spoke. "I don't doubt one word of what you say, Mikalya. We have so much to talk about, so much. Are you going to tell Shelly all that you've shared with me? She's had a rough time of it, too."

"I haven't gotten that far yet. I'm just not sure how Mom will react. If you want, we can talk about that. She'll believe whatever you say, I know that."

"Mikalya, thanks for saving my life in that fire. I know it was you."

"Yes, it was, and it wasn't easy, let me tell you. You were so sweet in the dreams we had together. You know what I'm talking about," she said.

"That was really you, Mikalya. I didn't want those dreams to ever end," Abe said, pulling her into another embrace.

"I'm going to pay the tab and get us out of here," she said.

*Rod, the bartender, had been watching this whole episode unfold from behind the bar and was absolutely dumbfounded. He was confused watching a strange woman he'd infrequently seen in the place before waltzing in just before closing.*

*The strange woman zeroed in on Abe immediately. This was far from a casual pickup. He wondered just what the hell she said to Abe at the bar and on the dance floor that made him completely lose control of his emotions. Now, this woman pays his tab and is preparing to take him out of the bar. He had to say something. Should he call the police? Since Mikalya died, he had never known Abe to be involved with another woman, either casually or seriously.*

Abe was sitting on the bar stool with his hands over his face when Rod walked over.

"Ma'am, do you know this man?" he asked Mikalya, afraid that Abe was being taken advantage of due to his inebriated state.

"Rod, you don't remember me, but I know Abraham Gallagher better than you do. I know him better than his mother does," she said.

Rod was blown away by her response. There was a frightening familiarity about this woman that he couldn't put his finger on.

*You don't remember me*, he thought. *What in the hell is she talking about?*

"It's OK. I'm going to drive him home now. He's in no condition to get behind the wheel," she said.

Rod looked at Abe, then back at Mikalya.

"Rod, it's fine. I know her. I'll try to explain someday," Abe said.

Mikalya helped Abe off the barstool and led him out to the car.

Rod watched as they left. He knew that something well beyond logic and reason had happened, but he couldn't figure out what. The rainy mist had subsided and turned into a beautiful, balmy, and breezy night. As they approached his car, Abraham started to speak.

"Why didn't you say anything in the gazebo?" Abe asked as they walked to the car, his arm around her waist.

"I was just checking you out one last time before I came back to you. I had to make sure it was you. It took me a lot of years to figure everything out, but I did. It's a weird journey, you know. You must go by intuition and feelings of *déjà vu*. I thought about it, and you, constantly. I was pretty sure the first time I laid eyes on you that you were the one I was looking for.

"Then, there were the dreams after I was born and growing up. I had several dreams about some fireman who was a good friend of mine. I dreamed I was with him in Ireland, and I dreamed about our first date. I had dreams about how you saved me and when we were in the hospital together. I even had a dream about how I died. Thank God for them. I was being guided back toward you.

"The gazebo wasn't the only time, either, Abraham. I've been in The Fat Angel several times. You just didn't notice me, which was the way I wanted it. I also started to talk around to people too.

"If I'd come to you sooner, you wouldn't have been certain it was really me. I needed to wait for the right time and the right place. I think I found it, didn't I?

"I'm so happy you waited for me. You did! I learned some incredible things on the other side. There are only three things that matter in this life. That's love, knowledge, and how we treat each other in this life. That's it. That's all we can take with us. One of the best ways to defeat evil is to just be simply honest with yourself. Evil cannot get through that. It can't. It's a powerful protection," she said.

Abe looked at her for a few seconds in complete wonder. He was barely able to fathom the advanced degree of knowledge Mikalya had just shared with him. He then spoke.

"Yeah, honey, you most certainly found the right time, and yes, I did wait. You knew that I would," he said as the clouds cleared, exposing a bright full moon.

As Mikalya and Abraham approached his car, they stopped, and Mikalya looked up.

"My God, isn't that beautiful? Look up at the sky, Abe."

Abe was afraid to look up. He thought if he did, when he looked back down, Mikalya would be gone. It would have all been a cruel, drunken illusion. He could still see the crystal blue of her eyes, even in the darkness.

"It's OK, you can look up," she said.

Abe slowly lifted his eyes off Mikalya and reluctantly looked up at the moon. He stared at it for a few seconds, then looked back down at her.

"See, I told ya," she said.

"Yeah, you sure told me, didn't you?" Abe replied, leaning down to kiss her.

"You're taking me back to our place in Ireland, aren't you?" she asked.

"I sure am," he said.

"Oh, and one more thing. The next time we go for a late night out, let's just stay in town where there's no deer running around," Mikalya said, trying not to laugh.

Abe burst into laughter. "Trust me. We will. We sure as hell will."

They got into Mikalya's car and drove as the bright full moon illuminated their way back home.

# The End

www.ingramcontent.com/pod-product-compliance
Lightning Source LLC
LaVergne TN
LVHW051922300525
812591LV00007B/58
*9798869371515*